On the street

Lubin slithered from the basket and crossed the road at Stick's heels. She was a cross between a polecat and a ferret, larger than either, with sharp pointed features and the lean build of the weasel family. When Stick paused in the doorway of the building from which the sounds of the scuffle were coming, she flowed over the toes of his boots and into its foyer, off to one side. Her hiss was the assailants' first hint that they were no longer alone.

They were three Bloods, beating up on a small unrecognizable figure that was curled up into a ball of tattered clothes at their feet. Their silver hair was dyed with streaks of orange and black; their elfin faces, when they looked up from their victim to see Stick standing in the doorway, were pale, skin stretched over high-boned features, silver eyes gleaming with malicious humor.

They were dressed all of a kind—three assembly-line Bloods in black leather jackets, frayed jeans, T-shirts, and motorcycle boots.

"Take a walk, hero," one of them said.

Stick reached up over his left shoulder and pulled out a sectional staff from its sheath on his back. With a sharp flick of his wrist, the three two-foot sections snapped into a solid staff, six feet long.

"I don't think so," he said.

—from "Stick"

FIREBIRD
WHERE FANTASY TAKES FLIGHT™

Waifs *and* Strays

CHARLES DE LINT

Preface by Terri Windling

FIREBIRD

AN IMPRINT OF PENGUIN GROUP (USA) INC.

Grateful acknowledgement is made to Happy Rhodes for the use of the lines from "Words Weren't Made for Cowards" from her album *Warpaint*. Copyright © 1991 by Happy Rhodes. Lyrics reprinted by permission. For more information about Happy's music, contact Auntie Social, P.O. Box 162, Rifton, NY 12471, or go to www.auntiesocialmusic.com

FIREBIRD
Published by Penguin Group
Penguin Group (USA) Inc., 345 Hudson Street, New York, New York 10014, U.S.A.
Penguin Books Ltd, 80 Strand, London WC2R ORL, England
Penguin Books Australia Ltd, 250 Camberwell Road, Camberwell, Victoria 3124, Australia
Penguin Books Canada Ltd, 10 Alcorn Avenue, Toronto, Ontario, Canada M4V 3B2
Penguin Books (N.Z.) Ltd, 182-190 Wairau Road, Auckland 10, New Zealand

First published in the United States of America by Viking,
a division of Penguin Putnam Books for Young Readers, 2002
Published by Firebird, an imprint of Penguin Group (USA) Inc., 2004

1 3 5 7 9 10 8 6 4 2

Preface copyright © Terri Windling, 2002
Additional copyright information is to be found on pp. 393.
All rights reserved

ISBN 0-14-240158-7

Printed in the United States of America

this is for Sharyn November

(no, I'm not sucking up)

and for Nina Hoffman

lovely and talented

and occasional roommates

with one another

CONTENTS

The Mythic World of Charles de Lint

by *Terri Windling*

STEP INTO THE WORLD OF CHARLES DE LINT, "THE concrete forest" of an urban landscape, and soon you'll hear a drumbeat and a fiddle drawing you into shadowed streets where an ancient magic can be found and Old Man Coyote awaits. Coyote, the Trickster, is the one-who-crosses-boundaries in Native American legends. He is the guide who leads us from the world we know into the twilight mythic realm—a dualistic figure, creator and destroyer. A storyteller. Like Charles himself.

The Tricksters of world mythology go by many names. In traditional tales, Trickster is clever, unpredictable, and thoroughly outrageous. Sometimes he's the god who brings the gifts of fire, storytelling, or music to humankind; in other tales, he's a sly and wily god of chaos and destruction. But even in his darker role, Trickster is generally a positive force, breaking through outmoded rules and ideas with the tricks he plays.

Charles, like the Trickster, is an author who seems to have two sides to his nature. As a creator and storyteller, he has brought whole worlds to life in almost fifty books for children and adults—while, in a more contrary guise, he brings a sly, wily humor to his life and work, bent on overturning outmoded ideas about myth, life, and fantasy writing. Like Trickster, he's a boundary crosser—regularly jumping the wall that separates fantasy fiction from mainstream literature, cleverly dismantling another brick on each and every journey.

Charles was born in the Netherlands, of Dutch, Spanish, and

Japanese ancestry. His family emigrated to Canada when he was young, moving through various towns in western Canada, Quebec, and Ontario (as well as Turkey and Lebanon) due to his father's work for a surveying company. One result of this nomadic upbringing was that Charles turned to books for companionship—particularly those filled with magical tales by the likes of Sir Thomas Malory, T.H. White, and Katherine Briggs. He discovered Tolkien, and went on to read the myths that were J.R.R. Tolkien's source material, and then the fantasy classics published in Lin Carter's Sign of the Unicorn series. In addition he was (and is) a voracious reader in a variety of fields, including mainstream fiction, mystery, horror, science fiction, nonfiction, and poetry.

After he finished school, he intended to become a Celtic folk musician, not a writer, taking jobs in music stores in Ottawa while playing gigs on the weekends. Although music was the focus of his life, he always wrote magical stories as well—but only (he thought) for his own amusement, until another young writer encouraged him to send his tales out for publication. Soon, to his surprise, he began to sell his work to various small presses, and eventually to larger publishers in New York City. His first big publication was *The Riddle of the Wren* (Ace Books, 1984)—a traditional "imaginary world" novel that received encouraging reviews. With his second novel, however, Charles's wife (and muse) MaryAnn Harris encouraged him to develop the kind of fiction that has since become his trademark: tales that infuse modern urban settings with myth, music, and magic.

This novel, *Moonheart*, received an overwhelmingly enthusiastic reception by fantasy readers, carving out new urban territory in a genre full of books that were then largely pastoral and quasi-medieval. Though others among his fantasy-writing peers also published books with urban settings, Charles is generally considered the primary pioneer of "urban fantasy"—for he went on to explore the magic of city streets in story after story, winning the World Fantasy Award for his short-story collection *Moonlight and Vines* in 2000.

And yet, Charles says: "I didn't set out to create a genre. The term 'urban fantasy' is connected to my description of the *Jack of Kinrowan* books, which I called 'Novels of Urban Faerie,' and [the term] has followed me ever since. However, what I usually see being described as urban fantasy is high fantasy transposed onto a contemporary scene, you know, grand quests and the like. I think I've moved on to different things; my novels are more character driven now." Charles uses the term "mythic fiction" to describe his more recent body of work.

In the pages that follow, you'll find a wealth of stories drawn from different stages of Charles's career—from early "urban fantasy" tales set in the author's home city of Ottawa to more recent stories set in Newford, an imaginary city somewhere in North America, where ancient mythic themes are reenacted in a modern context. Some of the tales come from the good green hills that lie beyond the Newford city limits. Others come from enchanted lands beyond any hills we know. Two stories come from Borderland, a series of "punk elf" anthologies (as one reviewer dubbed them!) that Charles and I and several other fantasy-writing friends created back in our wayward youth. What all these stories have in common is a love of language, music, and myth—and of the potent real-world magic that is born from friendship and compassion.

A Charles de Lint story usually concerns the "outsiders" of modern society: punks, street people, runaway children, mystics, misfits, and eccentrics of all sorts, whose lives are touched, illuminated, and changed by a glimpse of Mystery. If there is an overall theme linking his work (in addition to that of mythic tales re-told), it is one that runs contrary to the hip nihilism in vogue today: a celebration of the creative process—in particular, the creation of family, community, and a purposeful life in the face of such obstacles as poverty, homelessness, illness (of the body or soul), violence, fear, and despair. The legends he brings into a modern context are from both the Old World and the New: Celtic, Rom, and other European tales carried here by various immigrant groups, braided with tribal tales from the Native peoples of our continent.

"Our lives are stories," Charles says, "and the stories we have to give each other are the most important. None of us have a story too small and all are of equal stature. We each tell them in different ways, through different mediums—and if we care about each other, we'll take the time to listen."

Some of the above quotes come from interviews with Charles de Lint conducted by Lawrence Schimel and Mike Timoni.

Author's Note

THIS COLLECTION CAME TOGETHER IN MUCH THE SAME WAY that *Dreams Underfoot*, an earlier collection of mine, did: I got a call from an editor.

In the case of *Dreams Underfoot* (which has now grown into a series of four books collecting my various stories set in Newford), I was going to contract for a novel with Tor Books when my editor, Terri Windling, told me she was interested in adding a collection of my Newford stories to the contract. At the time I hadn't even realized that there were enough stories for a collection, but I counted them up and, sure enough, Terri was right. Needless to say, I was pleased with the idea of having all those stories published together in one volume. And I'm also pleased that, eight years later, the book is still in print.

Because the thing about stories is, they don't always have a long shelf life. They get published in magazines that might be on the stands for a month or less, or in anthologies that usually remain available for only a little longer than that. Then they're gone. So writers always like it when someone's interested in collecting these waifs and strays and putting them together between the covers of a single book.

You can't really make a living writing short stories—novels are where the bread and butter is in this field. But writers still return to them, again and again. I can't answer for others, but I know one of the reasons I love them so much is that they're the perfect length to take chances, to stretch as a writer. If you mess up, you've only lost a couple of weeks' work. Do that with a novel and you've lost a year or more of your time.

But I digress.

For the book in hand, I got a call from Sharyn November, my editor at this very publishing house, asking if I'd be interested in doing a collection of young adult stories for her. Again I was surprised. Not only was I unaware that I had enough stories (in fact, I had more than enough and a few had to be left out), but I'd never considered that I was writing what might be considered YA stories.

But it turns out Sharyn didn't want a book *for* teenagers, so much as one *about* them, and this I could most certainly deliver. The truth is, even if I'd been writing stories for teenagers, I would have approached them in the same way as I'd already written these: being true to the characters and their lives as they unfold, and telling their stories in the same way I write any story, rather than searching for a special "teen" voice. The one rule of thumb in writing YA fiction is don't write down to a younger reader. Teenagers know when they're being written down to. I remember that I did.

I was a voracious reader when I was younger. I think I read an average of two books a day from about the age of eleven or twelve into my early twenties. I still have the reading appetite of that younger self, but unfortunately, I don't seem to have nearly so much time to read anymore.

I say unfortunately because I still love meeting fictional characters and getting lost in their stories. Even though I write books now, and so understand a little more about how the magic works on the page, and have a regular monthly book review column (in

The Magazine of Fantasy and Science Fiction) which gives me a more critical eye than I had when I was younger, when a story does its job right, I'm gone. I'm *in* that story, hanging with the characters, happily lost in the pages.

And now that I think of it, that may well be the reason I don't read as much as I used to. Because when I write a story now, I'm writing something I'd like to read but that no one has written, so I have to write it myself. When I sit down every day to work on my first drafts, I'm eager to get to the task because I want to spend time with these characters. And I want to find out What Happens Next.

The hard work, the *real* work, comes in the subsequent drafts when I have to make sure everything is in the story that should be, when I take out what doesn't fit; when I polish the flow of the words, tighten the plot, worry over descriptions, dialogue, and the hundred and one other things that are necessary to make a story work.

* * *

To choose the stories for this book, I went through all my short fiction, setting aside those pieces that had teenage protagonists, and I sent them off to Sharyn.

The singer Tori Amos, when discussing her songs, calls them her girls. I know just what she means. Left to my own devices, I'd have been unable to decide which of my boys and girls would be excluded from the party, so I was pleased to leave it to Sharyn's judicious and discerning eye to decide which would work the best.

I hope, when you read these stories, that you'll be as engaged with them as I was when I was writing them. I also hope that they might spark an interest in you to tell your own stories—not only because I'd like others to have the same pleasure I get out of the actual process of writing, but for the selfish reason of there then being more stories out there for me to read.

* * *

If any of you are on the Internet, come visit my home page at www.charlesdelint.com.

Charles de Lint
Ottawa, Spring 2002

Waifs *and* Strays

TAMSON HOUSE

TAMSON HOUSE

One of the best things about being a writer is that, no matter what your personal circumstances might be, in your stories you can vicariously be anyone and live anywhere.

Tamson House is a huge rambling affair of a building that I daydreamed about for years, but wasn't actually able to visit until I began writing my novel Moonheart (1984). I didn't know the characters, only meeting Sara and Kieran, Taliesin, Blue, and all the rest while I was writing that book and the stories that were later collected in Spiritwalk (1992). But oh, I knew that house with its tower and mysterious gardens hidden inside so well. . . .

Merlin Dreams in the Mondream Wood

mondream: an Anglo-Saxon word which
means the dream of life among men
I am Merlin
Who follow the Gleam
—Tennyson,
from "Merlin and the Gleam"

IN THE HEART OF THE HOUSE LAY A GARDEN.

In the heart of the garden stood a tree.

In the heart of the tree lived an old man who wore the shape of a red-haired boy with crackernut eyes that seemed as bright as salmon tails glinting up the water.

His was a riddling wisdom, older by far than the ancient oak that housed his body. The green sap was his blood, and leaves grew in his hair. In the winter, he slept. In the spring, the moon harped a windsong against his antler tines as the oak's boughs stretched its green buds awake. In the summer, the air was thick with the droning of bees and the scent of the wildflowers that grew in stormy profusion where the fat brown bole became root.

And in the autumn, when the tree loosed its bounty to the ground below, there were hazelnuts lying among the acorns.

The secrets of a Green Man.

* * *

"When I was a kid, I thought it was a forest," Sara said.

She was sitting on the end of her bed, looking out the window over the garden, her guitar on her lap, the quilt bunched up under her knees. Up by the headboard, Julie Simms leaned forward from its carved wood to look over Sara's shoulder at what could be seen of the garden from their vantage point.

"It sure looks big enough," she said.

Sara nodded. Her eyes had taken on a dreamy look.

It was 1969 and they had decided to form a folk band—Sara on guitar, Julie playing recorder, both of them singing. They wanted to change the world with music because that was what was happening. In San Francisco. In London. In Vancouver. So why not in Ottawa?

With their faded bell bottom jeans and tie-dyed shirts, they looked just like any of the other seventeen-year-olds who hung around the War Memorial downtown, or could be found crowded into coffeehouses like Le Hibou and Le Monde on the weekends. Their hair was long—Sara's a cascade of brown ringlets, Julie's a waterfall spill the color of a raven's wing; they wore beads and feather earrings, and both eschewed makeup.

"I used to think it spoke to me," Sara said.

"What? The garden?"

"Um-hmm."

"What did it say?"

The dreaminess in Sara's eyes became wistful, and she gave Julie a rueful smile.

"I can't remember," she said.

* * *

It was three years after her parents had died—when she was nine years old—that Sara Kendell came to live with her uncle Jamie in his strange rambling house. From an adult perspective, Tamson House was huge, an enormous, sprawling affair of corridors and rooms and towers that took up the whole of a city block; to a child of nine, it simply went on forever.

She could wander down corridor after corridor, poking about in the clutter of rooms that lay spread like a maze from the northwest tower near Bank Street—where her bedroom was located—all the way over to her uncle's study overlooking O'Conner Street on the far side of the house, but mostly she spent her time in the library and in the garden. She liked the library because it was like a museum. There were walls of books, rising two floors high up to a domed ceiling, but there were also dozens of glass display cases scattered about the main floor area, each of which held any number of fascinating objects.

There were insects pinned to velvet, and stone artifacts; animal skulls and clay flutes in the shapes of birds; old manuscripts and hand-drawn maps, the parchment yellowing, the ink a faded sepia; Kabuki masks and a miniature Shinto shrine made of ivory and ebony; corn-husk dolls; Japanese *netsuke* and porcelain miniatures; antique jewelry and African beadwork; Kachina dolls and a brass fiddle half the size of a normal instrument. . . .

The cases were so cluttered with interesting things that she could spend a whole day just going through one case and still have something to look at when she went back to it the next day. What interested her most, however, was that her uncle had a story to go with each and every item in the cases. No matter what she brought up to his study—a tiny ivory *netsuke* carved in the shape of a badger crawling out of a teapot, a flat stone with curious scratches on it that looked like Ogham script—he could spin out a tale of its origin that might take them right through the afternoon to suppertime.

That he dreamed up half the stories only made it more entertaining, for then she could try to trip him up in his rambling explanations, or even just try to top his tall tales.

But if she was intellectually precocious, emotionally she still carried scars from her parents' death and the time she'd spent living with her other uncle—her father's brother. For three years Sara had been left in the care of a nanny during the day—amusing herself while the woman smoked cigarettes and watched the soaps—while at night she was put to bed promptly after dinner. It wasn't a normal family life; she could only find that vicariously in the books she devoured with a voracious appetite.

Coming to live with her uncle Jamie, then, was like constantly being on holiday. He doted on her, and on those few occasions when he *was* too busy, she could always find one of the many houseguests to spend some time with her.

All that marred her new life in Tamson House were her night fears.

She wasn't frightened of the house itself. Nor of bogies or monsters living in her closet. She knew that shadows were shadows, creaks and groans were only the house settling when the temperature changed. What haunted her nights was waking up from a deep sleep, shuddering uncontrollably, her pajamas stuck to her like a second skin, her heartbeat thundering at twice its normal tempo.

There was no logical explanation for the terror that gripped her once, sometimes twice a week. It just came, an awful, indescribable panic that left her shivering and unable to sleep for the rest of the night.

It was on the days following such nights that she went into

the garden. The greenery and flower beds and statuary all combined to soothe her. Invariably, she found herself in the very center of the garden, where an ancient oak tree stood on a knoll and overhung a fountain. Lying on the grass sheltered by its boughs, with the soft lullaby of the fountain's water murmuring close at hand, she would find what the night fears had stolen from her the night before.

She would sleep.

And she would dream the most curious dreams.

"The garden has a name, too," she told her uncle when she came in from sleeping under the oak one day.

The house was so big that many of the rooms had been given names just so that they could all be kept straight in their minds.

"It's called the Mondream Wood," she told him.

She took his look of surprise to mean that he didn't know the word.

"It means that the trees in it dream that they're people," she explained.

Her uncle nodded. " 'The dream of life among men.' It's a good name. Did you think it up yourself?"

"No. Merlin told me."

"The Merlin?" her uncle asked with a smile.

Now it was her turn to look surprised.

"What do you mean, *the* Merlin?" she asked.

Her uncle started to explain, astonished that in all her reading she hadn't come across a reference to Britain's most famous wizard, but then just gave her a copy of Malory's *Le Mort d'Arthur* and, after a moment's consideration, T. H. White's *The Sword in the Stone* as well.

* * *

"Did you ever have an imaginary friend when you were a kid?" Sara asked as she finally turned away from the window.

Julie shrugged. "My mom says I did, but I can't remember. Apparently he was a hedgehog the size of a toddler, named Whatzit."

"I never did. But I can remember that for a long time I used to wake up in the middle of the night just terrified, and then I wouldn't be able to sleep again for the rest of the night. I used to go into the middle of the garden the next day and sleep under that big oak that grows by the fountain."

"How pastoral," Julie said.

Sara grinned. "But the thing is, I used to dream that there was a boy living in that tree and his name was Merlin."

"Go on," Julie scoffed.

"No, really. I mean, I really had these dreams. The boy would just step out of the tree and we'd sit there and talk away the afternoon."

"What did you talk about?"

"I don't remember," Sara said. "Not the details—just the feeling. It was all very magical and . . . healing, I suppose. Jamie said that my having those night fears was just my unconscious mind's way of dealing with the trauma of losing my parents and then having to live with my dad's brother who only wanted my inheritance, not me. I was too young then to know anything about that kind of thing; all I knew was that when I talked to Merlin, I felt better. The night fears started coming less and less often and then finally they went away altogether.

"I think Merlin took them away for me."

"What happened to him?"

"Who?"

"The boy in the tree," Julie said. "Your Merlin. When did you stop dreaming about him?"

"I don't really know. I guess when I stopped waking up terrified, I just stopped sleeping under the tree so I didn't see him anymore. And then I just forgot that he'd ever been there. . . . "

Julie shook her head. "You know, you can be a bit of flake sometimes."

"Thanks a lot. At least I didn't hang around with a giant hedgehog named Whatzit when I was a kid."

"No. You hung out with tree-boy."

Julie started to giggle and then they both broke up. It was a few moments before either of them could catch their breath.

"So what made you think of your tree-boy?" Julie asked.

Another giggle welled up in Julie's throat, but Sara's gaze had drifted back out the window and become all dreamy again.

"I don't know," she said. "I was just looking out at the garden and I suddenly found myself remembering. I wonder what ever happened to him?"

* * *

"Jamie gave me some books about a man with the same name as you," she told the red-haired boy the next time she saw him. "And after I read them, I went into the library and found some more. He was quite famous, you know."

"So I'm told," the boy said with a smile.

"But it's all so confusing," Sara went on. "There's all these different stories, supposedly about the same man. . . . How are you supposed to know which of them is true?"

"That's what happens when legend and myth meet," the boy said. "Everything gets tangled."

"Was there even a *real* Merlin, do you think? I mean, besides you."

"A great magician who was eventually trapped in a tree?"

Sara nodded.

"I don't think so," the boy said.

"Oh."

Sara didn't even try to hide her disappointment.

"But that's not to say there was never a man named Merlin," the boy added. "He might have been a bard, or a follower of old wisdoms. His enchantments might have been more subtle than the great acts of wizardry ascribed to him in the stories."

"And did he end up in a tree?" Sara asked eagerly. "That would make him like you. I've also read that he got trapped in a cave, but I think a tree's much more interesting, don't you?"

Because her Merlin lived in a tree.

"Perhaps it was in the idea of a tree," the boy said.

Sara blinked in confusion. "What do you mean?"

"The stories seem to be saying that one shouldn't teach, or else the student becomes too knowledgeable and then turns on the teacher. I don't believe that. It's not the passing on of knowledge that would root someone like Merlin."

"Well, then what would?"

"Getting too tangled up in his own quest for understanding. Delving so deeply into the calendaring trees that he lost track of where he left his body, until one day he looked around to find that he'd become what he was studying."

"I don't understand."

The red-haired boy smiled. "I know. But I can't speak any more clearly."

"Why not?" Sara asked, her mind still bubbling with the tales of quests and wizards and knights that she'd been reading. "Were you enchanted? Are you trapped in that oak tree?"

She was full of curiosity and determined to find out all she could, but in that practiced way that the boy had, he artfully turned the conversation onto a different track, and she never did get an answer to her questions.

It rained that night, but the next night the skies were clear. The moon hung above the Mondream Wood like a fat ball of golden honey; the stars were so bright and close Sara felt she could just reach up and pluck one as though it was an apple, hanging in a tree. She had crept from her bedroom in the northwest tower and gone out into the garden, stepping secretly as a thought through the long, darkened corridors of the house until she was finally outside.

She was looking for magic.

Dreams were one thing. She knew the difference between what you found in a dream and when you were awake; between a fey red-haired boy who lived in a tree and real boys; between the dreamlike enchantments of the books she'd been reading— enchantments that lay thick as acorns under an oak tree—and the real world where magic was a card trick, or a stage magician pulling a rabbit out of a hat on the *Ed Sullivan Show*.

But the books also said that magic came awake in the night. It crept from its secret hidden places—called out by starlight and the moon—and lived until the dawn pinked the eastern skies. She always dreamed of the red-haired boy when she slept under his oak in the middle of the garden. But what if he was more than a dream? What if at night he stepped out of his tree—really and truly, flesh and blood and bone real?

There was only one way to find out.

* * *

Sara felt restless after Julie went home. She put away her guitar and then distractedly set about straightening up her room. But for every minute she spent on the task, she spent three just looking out the window at the garden.

I never dream, she thought.

Which couldn't be true. Everything she'd read about sleep research and dreaming said that she had to dream. People just needed to. Dreams were supposed to be the way your subconscious cleared up the day's clutter. So, ipso facto, everybody dreamed. She just didn't remember hers.

But I did when I was a kid, she thought. Why did I stop? How could I have forgotten the red-haired boy in the tree?

Merlin.

Dusk fell outside her window to find her sitting on the floor, arms folded on the windowsill, chin resting on her arms as she looked out over the garden. As the twilight deepened, she finally stirred. She gave up the pretense of cleaning up her room. Putting on a jacket, she went downstairs and out into the garden.

Into the Mondream Wood.

Eschewing the paths that patterned the garden, she walked across the dew-wet grass, fingering the damp leaves of the bushes and the low-hanging branches of the trees. The dew made her remember Gregor Penev—an old Bulgarian artist who'd been staying in the house when she was a lot younger. He'd been full of odd little stories and explanations for natural occurrences—much like Jamie was, which was probably why Gregor and her uncle had gotten along so well.

"*Zaplakala e gorata,*" he'd replied when she'd asked him where dew came from and what it was for. "The forest is crying. It remembers the old heroes who lived under its branches—the heroes and the magicians, all lost and gone now. Robin Hood. Indje Voivode. Myrddin."

Myrddin. That was another name for Merlin. She remembered reading somewhere that Robin Hood was actually a Christianized Merlin, the Anglo version of his name being a variant of his Saxon name of Rof Breocht Woden—the Bright Strength of Woden. But if you went back far enough, all the names and stories got tangled up in one story. The tales of the historical Robin Hood, like those of the historical Merlin of the Borders, had acquired older mythic elements common to the world as a whole by the time they were written down. The story that their legends were really telling was that of the seasonal hero-king, the May Bride's consort, who, with his cloak of leaves and his horns and all his varying forms, was the secret truth that lay in the heart of every forest.

"But those are European heroes," she remembered telling Gregor. "Why would the trees in our forest be crying for them?"

"All forests are one," Gregor had told her, his features serious for a change. "They are all echoes of the first forest that gave birth to Mystery when the world began."

She hadn't really understood him then, but she was starting to understand him now as she made her way to the fountain at the center of the garden where the old oak tree stood guarding its secrets in the heart of the Mondream Wood. There were two forests for every one you entered. There was the one you walked in, the physical echo, and then there was the one that was connected to all the other forests, with no consideration of distance, or time.

The forest primeval. Remembered through the collective memory of every tree in the same way that people remembered myth—through the collective subconscious that Jung mapped, the shared mythic resonance that lay buried in every human mind. Legend and myth, all tangled in an alphabet of trees, remembered, not always with understanding, but with wonder. With awe.

Which was why the Druids' Ogham was also a calendar of trees.

Why Merlin was often considered to be a Druid.

Why Robin was the name taken by the leaders of witch covens.

Why the Green Man had antlers—because a stag's tines are like the branches of a tree.

Why so many of the early avatars were hung from a tree. Osiris. Balder. Dionysus. Christ.

Sara stood in the heart of the Mondream Wood and looked up at the old oak tree. The moon lay behind its branches, mysteriously close. The air was filled with an electric charge, as though a storm was approaching, but there wasn't a cloud in the sky.

"Now I remember what happened that night," Sara said softly.

* * *

Sara grew to be a small woman, but at nine years old she was just a tiny waif—no bigger than a minute, as Jamie liked to say. With her diminutive size she could slip soundlessly through thickets that would allow no egress for an adult. And that was how she went.

She was a curly-haired gamine, ghosting through the hawthorn hedge that bordered the main path. Whispering across the small glade guarded by the statue of a little horned man that Jamie said was Favonius, but she privately thought of as Peter Pan, though he bore no resemblance to the pictures in her Barrie book. Tiptoeing through the wildflower garden, a regular gallimaufry of flowering plants, both common and exotic. And then she was near the fountain. She could see Merlin's oak, looming up above the rest of the garden like the lordly tree it was.

And she could hear voices.

She crept nearer, a small shadow hidden in deeper patches cast by the fat yellow moon.

"—never a matter of choice," a man's voice was saying. "The lines of our lives are laid out straight as a dodman's leys, from event to event. You chose your road."

She couldn't see the speaker, but the timbre of his voice was deep and resonating, like a deep bell. She couldn't recognize it, but she did recognize Merlin's when he replied to the stranger.

"When I chose my road, there was no road. There was only the trackless wood; the hills, lying crest to crest like low-backed waves; the glens where the harps were first imagined and later strung. Ca'canny, she told me when I came into the Wood. I thought go gentle meant go easy, not go fey; that the oak guarded the Borders, marked its boundaries. I never guessed it was a door."

"All knowledge is a door," the stranger replied. "You knew that."

"In theory," Merlin replied.

"You meddled."

"I was born to meddle. That was the part I had to play."

"But when your part was done," the stranger said, "you continued to meddle."

"It's in my nature, Father. Why else was I chosen?"

There was a long silence then. Sara had an itch on her nose, but she didn't dare move a hand to scratch it. She mulled over what she'd overheard, trying to understand.

It was all so confusing. From what they were saying it seemed that her Merlin was the Merlin in the stories. But if that was true, then why did he look like a boy her own age? How could he even still be alive? Living in a tree in Jamie's garden and talking to his father. . . .

"I'm tired," Merlin said. "And this is an old argument, Father. The winters are too short. I barely step into a dream and then it's spring again. I need a longer rest. I've earned a longer rest. The Summer Stars call to me."

"Love bound you," the stranger said.

"An oak bound me. I never knew she was a tree."

"You knew. But you preferred to ignore what you knew because you had to riddle it all. The salmon wisdom of the hazel wasn't enough. You had to partake of the fruit of every tree."

"I've learned from my error," Merlin said. "Now set me free, Father."

"I can't. Only love can unbind you."

"I can't be found; I can't be seen," Merlin said. "What they remember of me is so tangled up in Romance that no one can find the man behind the tales. Who is there to love me?"

Sara pushed her way out of the thicket where she'd been hiding and stepped into the moonlight.

"There's me," she began, but then her voice died in her throat.

There was no red-haired boy standing by the tree. Instead, she found an old man with the red-haired boy's eyes. And a stag. The stag turned its antlered head toward her and regarded her with a gaze that sent shivers scurrying up and down her spine. For a long moment its gaze held hers, then it turned, its flank flashing red in the moonlight, and the darkness swallowed it.

Sara shivered. She wrapped her arms around herself, but she couldn't escape the chill.

The stag . . .

That was impossible. The garden had always been strange, seeming so much larger than its acreage would allow, but there couldn't possibly be a deer living in it without her having seen it before. Except . . . What about a boy becoming an old man overnight? A boy who really and truly did live in a tree?

"Sara," the old man said.

It was Merlin's voice. Merlin's eyes. Her Merlin grown into an old man.

"You . . . you're old," she said.

"Older than you could imagine."

"But—"

"I came to you as you'd be most likely to welcome me."

"Oh."

"Did you mean what you said?" he asked.

Memories flooded Sara. She remembered a hundred afternoons of warm companionship. All those hours of quiet conversation and games. The peace that came from her night fears. If she said yes, then he'd go away. She'd lose her friend. And the night fears . . . Who'd be there to make the terrors go away? Only he had been able to help her. Not Jamie nor anyone else who lived in the house, though they'd all tried.

"You'll go away . . . won't you?" she said.

He nodded. An old man's nod. But the eyes were still young. Young and old, wise and silly, all at the same time. Her red-haired boy's eyes.

"I'll go away," he replied. "And you won't remember me."

"I won't forget," Sara said. "I would never forget."

"You won't have a choice," Merlin said. "Your memories of me would come with me when I go."

"They'd be . . . gone forever?"

That was worse than losing a friend. That was like the friend never having been there in the first place.

"Forever," Merlin said. "Unless . . ."

His voice trailed off, his gaze turned inward.

"Unless what?" Sara asked finally.

"I could try to send them back to you when I reach the other side of the river."

Sara blinked with confusion. "What do you mean? The other side of what river?"

"The Region of the Summer Stars lies across the water that marks the boundary between what is and what has been. It's a long journey to that place. Sometimes it takes many lifetimes."

They were both quiet then. Sara studied the man that her friend had become. The gaze he returned her was mild. There were no demands in it. There was only regret. The sorrow of parting. A fondness that asked for nothing in return.

Sara stepped closer to him, hesitated a moment longer, then hugged him.

"I do love you, Merlin," she said. "I can't say I don't when I do."

She felt his arms around her, the dry touch of his lips on her brow.

"Go gentle," he said. "But beware the calendaring of the trees."

And then he was gone.

One moment they were embracing, and the next her arms held only air. She let them fall limply to her sides. The weight of an awful sorrow bowed her head. Her throat grew thick, her chest tight. She swayed where she stood, tears streaming from her eyes.

The pain felt like it would never go away.

But the next thing she knew she was waking in her bed in the northwest tower and it was the following morning. She woke from a dreamless sleep, clear-eyed and smiling. She didn't know it, but her memories of Merlin were gone.

But so were her night fears.

* * *

The older Sara, still not a woman but old enough to understand more of the story now, fingered a damp leaf and looked up into the spreading canopy of the oak above her.

Could any of that really have happened? she wondered.

The electric charge she'd felt in the air when she'd approached the old oak was gone. That pregnant sense of something about to happen had faded. She was left with the moon, hanging lower now, the stars still bright, the garden quiet. It was all magical, to be sure, but natural magic—not supernatural.

She sighed and kicked at the autumn debris that lay thick about the base of the old tree. Browned leaves, broad and brittle. And acorns. Hundreds of acorns. Fred the gardener would be collecting them soon for his compost—at least those that the black squirrels didn't hoard away against the winter. She went down on one knee and picked up a handful of them, letting them spill out of her hand.

Something different about one of them caught her eye as it fell, and she plucked it up from the ground. It was a small brown ovoid shape, an incongruity in the crowded midst of all the capped acorns. She held it up to her eye. Even in the moonlight she could see what it was.

A hazelnut.

Salmon wisdom locked in a seed.

Had she regained memories, memories returned to her now from a place where the Summer Stars always shone, or had she just had a dream in the Mondream Wood where as a child she'd thought that the trees dreamed they were people?

Smiling, she pocketed the nut, then slowly made her way back into the house.

OTTAWA AND THE VALLEY

OTTAWA AND THE VALLEY

I've said that I love writing short stories, and I do, but the truth is, with a few exceptions, I don't really have the time to write them on spec—by which I mean writing one in the hopes that I'll sell it. The novels take up most of my time, and my schedule is tight, so when I write a story, it's usually been commissioned for a particular themed anthology.

And I like that aspect of short-story writing: knowing the general theme of the anthology and writing something to fit it. But I've always gone my own way, so when I do write one of these commissioned stories, I like to see how far I can get away from its theme, yet still make the story fit.

THIS STORY, originally commissioned by Jane Yolen and Marty Greenberg, pretty much fit the theme like a glove: teenage vampires

There's No Such Thing

"KEN PARRY," APPLES SAID.

Cassie nodded.

"Is a vampire."

Cassie nodded again.

Apples had heard that Ken needled the kids he baby-sat, but this was the first she'd heard about his claiming to be a vampire.

"But there's no such thing," she said.

"Samantha said she saw him turn into a bat one night—right in front of her house when he didn't think she was looking. He was baby-sitting her and instead of walking home when her parents got back, he *flew*."

"Flew."

Cassie nodded solemnly.

Apples tapped her hairbrush against her hand, then set it down on her dresser.

Their mother had been heavily into mythology when she got out of the university, which was how, though they had a nice normal surname like Smith, the two girls ended up saddled with their given names of Appoline and Cassandra. Apples had looked them both up at the public library one day, hoping to find something she could use to stop the incessant teasing that they got, but Appoline just meant having something to do with Apollo— the Greek god of music, poetry, archery, prophecy, and healing.

That sounded nice on paper, but came out sucky when you tried to explain it to someone. Cassandra had been a prophetess that Apollo was all hot and heavy over—and that would really be fuel for some bad-news ribbing if it ever got out.

Apples wasn't much good with music or poetry. She was lucky to get a "C" in either at school. She couldn't read the future and about the most she could do along the healing line was put on a Band-Aid. But hunting milkweed seedpods in the field behind her house as a kid, she'd learned to shoot a mean arrow. Trouble was, that didn't mean much when you were sixteen—not unless you were planning to go in for the Olympics or something, which wasn't exactly an ambition that Apples had set her sights upon.

Cassie couldn't read the future either. She was a sweet twelve-year-old with curly blond hair and a smile that just wouldn't quit. She should have had a great life laid out in front of her, except she had severe asthma so she couldn't go anywhere without her bronchodilator. Then there was her right leg which was half the size of her left and a good three inches shorter. The only way she could walk around was by wearing a leg brace that gained her sympathy, or weird stares, but wasn't exactly endearing.

Except to Apples. She'd do anything for Cassie.

But give up her first date with Rob D'Lima, considering that she'd been mooning over him for three months before he finally asked her out?

"You know there's really no such thing as vampires," she said.

Cassie only regarded her with all the graveness that a twelve-year-old can muster when they know they're right but can't prove it.

Apples sighed.

"I've seen him in the middle of the day," she said. "I thought they couldn't go out in the sunlight."

"That's just part of their legend," Cassie explained. "They've made up all kinds of things about themselves so that people will think they're safe from them. You know, like the bit with the mirror . . . and crosses and garlic. The only thing that's real is that they have to be invited into your house, and Mom and Dad have *done* that."

Apples picked up her hairbrush again.

"You're really scared, aren't you?" she said.

"Wouldn't you be?"

Apples smiled. "I guess I would. Okay. I'll stay home with you tonight."

"It won't do any good."

Apples thought Cassie was talking about her date with Rob.

"If Rob's half as nice as I think he is, he'll understand," she said. "Maybe he'll even come over and the three of us can . . ."

Her voice trailed off as Cassie started shaking her head.

"I already asked Mom," Cassie said, "and she said no way."

"You told her Ken was a vampire?"

"I had to . . ."

Apples sighed again. While Cassie hadn't been gifted with the ability to see into the future, she had been born with an overactive imagination. Their parents had long since lost patience with her stories.

"You should have come to me first," Apples said.

"You were late coming back from volleyball practice and I didn't know if you'd be back in time for me to tell you about it."

"I'm sorry."

"It's okay."

"So what can we do about this?" Apples asked.

"Could you, maybe, come home early?"

Apples smiled and tousled her sister's hair. "You bet. I'll be back as soon as the movie's over. We'll send Ken packing and then we'll pig out on popcorn and watch some music videos."

"It'll be past my bedtime."

Apples laughed. "Like that's ever stopped you."

* * *

Rob was really nice about it. After the show was over, they went back to Apples's house. Ken seemed surprised to see them, but that was about it. No fangs. No big black cape. Apples paid him from the house money her mom kept in a jar in the dry goods cupboard and closed the front door behind him.

"Just let me go check on the munchkin," Apples said as Rob settled down on the couch. "Won't take a moment. You . . . " She hesitated. "If she wants to sit up with us for a little while, you won't mind, will you?"

Rob shook his head. "That's one of the things I like about you, Apples; the way you take care of Cassie. Most kids hate their little brothers and sisters. Me, I just wish I had one."

"Well, you can share mine tonight," Apples said.

"I'll hold you to that."

Be still my heart, Apples thought as she headed upstairs to Cassie's room.

She was thinking about how it would feel to have Rob kiss her when she stepped into the room and her heartbeat jumped into double-time. Cassie was huddled on her bed, hunched over and making wheezing sounds.

Oh, jeez, Apples thought. She's having an attack and that bloody fool Ken never checked up on her.

But when she got to Cassie's side, she found that her sister was crying, not struggling for breath. Apples sat down on the bed, the bedsprings dipping under her weight. Before she could reach out a hand, Cassie had turned and buried her face against Apples's shoulder.

"It's okay, it's okay," Apples murmured, stroking Cassie's short hair.

She was going to kill Ken Parry.

"What happened?" she asked.

"He . . . he . . ."

Apples had an awful thought.

"Did he . . . touch you, Cassie?"

Cassie nodded and started to sob louder. Apples held her until her crying had subsided, then she brushed the damp hair away from Cassie's brow and had a good look at her little sister. There were questions she knew she should ask, but somehow she felt the best thing to do right now was to get Cassie over the immediate trauma. The poor kid looked miserable. Her face was all puffed, and her eyes were red. She sniveled, then blew her nose when Apples handed her a tissue.

"He said," Cassie began. She hesitated, then started over. "I . . . I woke up and he . . . he was sitting on the bed and he'd pulled my nightie up, but then . . . then you came home. . . ."

"Oh, Cassie."

"He . . . he said if I told anyone he'd come back in the night and he'd . . . he'd hurt me. . . . "

"No one's going to come and no one's going to hurt you," Apples told her. "I promise you."

"Everything all right in here?"

Apples looked up to find Rob standing in the doorway. She nodded.

"Ken just scared her, that's all," she said.

She felt inordinately pleased when she saw his hands clench into fists at his sides and anger flare up in his eyes.

"Sounds like this guy needs a lesson in—"

Apples cut him off.

"There's not much we can do—not without getting into trouble ourselves. This is the kind of thing that my parents are going to have to handle."

"But—"

Apples gave a meaningful nod to her sister—it said, not in front of Cassie, please—and was grateful to see that he caught its meaning without her having to actually say the words aloud.

He took a breath, then let it out slowly and put a smile on his face.

"You promised me some popcorn," he said. "I hope you're not going back on the deal now."

Apples gave him a grateful look. "Not a chance. How about you, Cassie? Do you feel like having some with us or are you going to make us eat it all on our own? You know me, I eat like a bird. Maybe I should put mine in a birdfeeder."

The smile she got back was small, but it was there, and by the time the popcorn was popping in the microwave and a Richard

Marx video was booming from the television set, Cassie was almost back to her old self again. All except for the hurt look in the back of her eyes that Apples was afraid might never go away.

* * *

Rob left before her parents got back.

"You're going to talk to them about this guy?" he asked when they were standing out on the stoop.

"I'll get it all worked out," Apples said. "I promise."

"But if you need some help . . . "

"You'll be the first I'll call."

The kiss was everything she'd hoped it would be—multiplied maybe a hundred times more. She felt a little breathless as she watched him go down the walk, and the tingle he'd called up from deep inside her didn't go away for hours.

She was in bed when her parents got home and didn't say anything to them except for a sleepy good night that was half muffled by her pillow. She waited until she was sure they were asleep before she got up again.

She couldn't get Ken Parry out of her mind. Not even thinking of Rob helped. Her mind just kept coming back to Ken and what he'd tried to do to Cassie.

Mr. Vampire. Right.

She had to talk to him, and talk to him now. But first she had to get his attention. With a guy like Ken, there was only one way to do that.

She went to her closet and rummaged around in it until she came up with a short black leather miniskirt and a scoop-neck blouse. She brushed her hair and tied it back, put on a slash of red lipstick, then tiptoed down the stairs and out of the house.

She put her high heels on when she was outside and click-clacked her way along the sidewalk, two blocks north, one block west, another north, until she was standing in front of Ken Parry's house.

The streetlight cast enough light for her to make out the Batman poster in the left front bedroom on the second floor. There was only one kid living here, so it had to be his room.

Stooping awkwardly in the short skirt, she picked up some small bits of gravel from the Parry driveway and tossed them up at the window. It took three tries before a very sleepy-looking Ken Parry slid up the window and peered down at her.

He woke up quickly when he saw who it was.

"What do you want?" he called down in a loud whisper.

"I thought we could make a trade," she whispered back. "I'll give you something you'll like and you leave my little sister alone."

"You're kidding."

Apples put a hand on her waist and thrust out a hip. "Do I look like I'm kidding?"

He made a soft noise in the back of his throat.

"I . . . I'll be right down."

When he opened the door, she was standing on the porch.

"Aren't you going to invite me in?" she purred.

"I . . . my parents . . ."

"Are sleeping, I'll bet."

"Uh, sure. You, uh, come on in."

He stood aside to let her pass by.

Apples gave him a considering look as she stepped into his house—just to be sure. One look at him was all it took to confirm it. Ken Parry wasn't a vampire. She should know. Her only regret as she let him lead her downstairs to the rec room was what his dumb stunt had forced her to tell Cassie.

There's no such thing as vampires.

Because it was the first time she'd ever lied to her little sister.

* * *

Ken Parry never came back to school. Rumor in the halls had it that he'd come down with a kind of anemia that the doctors simply couldn't diagnose. It left him too weak for normal teenage pursuits, so weak that he ended up staying in the hospital until his family finally moved away just before midterm exams.

Apples didn't miss him. She only needed to feed once a month, and there were always other people around, just like him, who got their kicks out of tormenting some little kid.

She didn't give Ken or any of them the Gift itself—not the way that the woman had given her the Gift in the parking lot behind the Civic Centre after a Bryan Adams concert this past summer. She never did find out why the woman chose her. All she knew was that vampires lived forever, and she didn't want any of those guys around for that long.

No, she was saving the Gift. Vampires never got sick and if there was something wrong with them when they got that special bite, then the Gift cured them. So she was waiting for Cassie to turn sixteen.

Until then she had to figure out a way to deal with her parents always remarking on how she just never seemed to get any older. And she had to decide if Rob really was someone she'd want to be with forever.

ALTHOUGH "THERE'S No Such Thing" was written almost a decade ago, I never could get the characters out of my head. I was always curious about what happened next, so when Sharyn asked me for at least one original story in this collection, I knew it had to be about Apples and Cassie.

I should also note that while there are a few little digs at a certain blond-haired TV character in the following novelet, Buffy the Vampire Slayer *is my favorite TV show, and has been since the pilot first aired. I could go on and on about the smart writing, how Joss Whedon is a genius, how they take their characters seriously but still have fun, how the continuity runs from the very first show through to the latest, and a hundred other things, but there's no point. If you get it, you love it. If you don't, you don't, and you probably never will.*

Sisters

One: Appoline

IT'S NOT LIKE ON THAT TV SHOW, YOU KNOW WHERE THE cute blond cheerleader type stakes all these vampires and they blow away into dust? For one thing, they don't disappear into dust, which would be way more convenient. Outside of life in televisionland, when you stake one, you've got this great big dead corpse to deal with, which is not fun. Beheading works, too, but that's just way too gross for me, and you've still got to find some place to stash both a head and a body.

The trick is to not turn your victim in the first place—you

know, not drain all their blood so that they rise again. When that happens, you have to clean up after yourself, because a vamp is forever, and do you really want these losers you've been feeding on hanging around until the end of time? I don't think so.

The show gets a lot of other things wrong, too, but then most of the movies and books do. Vamps don't have a problem with mirrors (unless they're ugly and don't want to look at themselves, I suppose), crosses (unless they've got issues with Christianity), or garlic (except who likes to smell it on anybody's breath?). They don't have demons riding around inside them (unless they've got some kind of satanic inner child), they can't turn into bats or rats or wolves or mist (I mean, just look at the physics involved, right?), and sunlight doesn't bother them. No spontaneous combustion— they just run the same risk of skin cancer as anybody else.

I figure if the people writing the books and making the movies actually do have any firsthand experience with vampires, they're sugar-coating the information so that people don't freak out. If you're going to accept that they exist in the first place, it's much more comforting to believe that you're safe in the daylight, or that a cross or a fistful of garlic will keep them at bay.

About the only thing they do get right is that it takes a vamp to make a vamp. You do have to die from the bite and then rise again three days later. It's as easy as that. It's also the best time to kill a vamp—they're kind of like rag dolls, all loose and muddy-brained, for the first few hours.

Oh, and you do have to invite us into your house. If it's a public place, we can go in the same as anyone else.

What's that? No, that wasn't a slip of the tongue. I'm one,

too. So while I like the TV show as much as the next person, and I know it's fiction, blond cheerleader types still make me twitch a little.

- 2 -

Appoline Smith was raking yellow maple leaves into a pile on the front lawn when the old four-door sedan came to a stop at the curb. She looked up to find the driver staring at her. She didn't recognize him. He was just some old guy in his thirties who'd been watching way too many old *Miami Vice* reruns. His look—the dark hair slicked back, silk shirt opened to show off a big gold chain, fancy shades—was so been-there it was prehistoric. The pair of dusty red-and-white velour dice hanging from the mirror did nothing to enhance his image.

"Why don't you just take a picture?" she asked him.

"Nobody likes a lippy kid," he said.

"Yeah, nobody likes a pervert either."

"I'm not some perv."

"Oh really? What do you call a guy cruising a nice neighborhood like this with his tongue hanging out whenever he sees some teenage girl?"

"I'm looking for A. Smith."

"Well, you found one."

"I mean, the initial 'A,' then 'Smith.' "

"You found that, too. So why don't you check it off on your life list and keep on driving."

The birder reference went right over his head. All things considered, she supposed most things would.

"I got something for you," he said.

He reached over to the passenger side of the car's bench seat, then turned back to her and offered her an envelope. She supposed it had been white once. Looking at the dirt and a couple of greasy fingerprints smeared on it, she made no move to take it. The guy looked at her for a long moment, then shrugged and tossed it onto the lawn.

"Don't call the cops," he said and drove away.

As if they didn't have better things to do than chase after some guy in a car making pathetic attempts to flirt with girls he happened to spy as he drove around. He was one of just too many guys she'd met, thinking he was Lothario when he was just a loser.

She waited until he'd driven down the block and turned the corner before she stepped closer to look at the envelope he'd left on the lawn.

Okay, she thought, when she saw that it actually had "A. Smith" and the name of her street written on it. So maybe it wasn't random. Maybe he was only stalking her.

She picked up the envelope, holding it distastefully between two fingers.

"Who was in the car?"

She turned to see her little sister limping down the driveway toward her, and quickly stuck the envelope in her jacket pocket.

"Just some guy," she told Cassie. "How're you doing?"

Cassie'd had a bad asthma attack that morning and had still been lying down in the rec room watching videos when Apples had come out to rake leaves.

"I'm okay," Cassie told her. "And besides, I've got my buddy," she added, holding up her bronchodilator. "Can I help?"

"Sure. But only if you promise to take it easy."

* * *

It wasn't until a couple of hours later that Apples was able to open the envelope. She took it into the bathroom and slit the seal, pulling out a grimy sheet of paper with handwriting on it that read:

> *I no yer secret. Meet me tonite at midnite at the cow castle, or they'll be trouble. I no you got a little sister. Don't call the cops. Don't tell nobody.*

Okay, Apples thought, getting angry as she reread the note. The loser in the car just went from annoying pervert to a sick freak who needed to be dealt with.

Nobody threatened her little sister.

By "cow castle" she assumed he meant the Aberdeen Pavilion at Lansdowne Park, commonly known as the Cattle Castle because the cupola on its roof gave it a castlelike appearance. And though it was obviously a trap of some sort, she'd be there all the same. She couldn't begin to guess what he wanted from her, what he hoped to accomplish. It didn't matter. By threatening Cassie, he'd just gone to the head of her "deal with this" list.

- 3 -

Okay, here's the thing. I didn't ask to get turned, but it's not like we sat down and talked out how I felt about it. By the time it's over, I've been three days dead, I rise, and here I am, vamp girl, and I don't mean sexy, though I can play that card if I have to. Anybody can do it. It just needs the right clothes and makeup, with one secret ingredient: attitude.

It's funny. I didn't have too many friends before I got turned.

I don't have so many now either, mind you, but now it's by choice. Getting turned gave me this boost of self-confidence, I guess, and that's really what people find attractive. Everybody's intrigued by someone comfortable in their own skin because most of us aren't.

The parents freaked, of course. Not because I'm a vamp—they still don't know that—but because so far as they know, I just did the big disappearing act the night I got turned. Went to a concert and came back home four days later. Trust me, that did not go over well. I was canned for a solid month, which made feeding a real pain—having to sneak out through a window between two A.M., when Dad finally goes to bed, and dawn to find what I can at that time of the night. I never much cared for booze or drugs when I was human, and that's carried over to what I am now. I still hate the taste of it in someone's blood.

Yeah, I drink blood. But it's not as gross as it sounds. And it's not as messy as it is in some of the movies.

- 4 -

The Aberdeen Pavilion was a wonderfully eccentric building in the middle of Lansdowne Park where the Central Canadian Exhibition, the oldest agricultural fair in Canada, was held every year. The pavilion was the largest of the exhibition buildings that dotted the park, an enormous barnlike structure surrounded by parking lots, with an angled roof curved like a half-moon and topped with a cupola. For a city kid like Apples, going inside during the Ex had always been a wonderful experience. The air was redolent with farm smells—cattle, sheep, horses, hogs—and she'd loved to walk along the stalls to look at the livestock, or sit with Cassie on the wooden seats in the huge arena and watch the animals vying for first-place ribbons.

Though she still took Cassie to the midway every August, she hadn't gone inside the pavilion for a couple of years now.

As she walked across a parking lot toward the Cattle Castle, Apples wondered if this was part of the freak's plan, if he knew that this was where she'd gotten turned. It had been right here, between the Cattle Castle and the Coliseum when she'd come to see a Bryan Adams concert a few years ago.

She didn't have to close her eyes to be able to visualize the woman, that first sight of her coming out from between the parked cars. Tall and svelte, with a loose walk that lay somewhere between the grace of a panther and a runway model. Golden blond hair fountained over her shoulders and down her back in a spill of ringlets, and she was dressed all in black: short velvet skirt, low-cut T-shirt, and high-heeled ankle boots. Apples remembered two conflicting sensations: this woman was so unbelievably gorgeous and no one else seemed to notice her.

"Come with me a moment," the woman said, and without a word to her friends, Apples had left them to follow the stranger into a darker part of the parking lot.

And nothing was the same for Apples, not ever again.

I no yer secret.

Maybe he did.

The area around the Cattle Castle appeared to be deserted, though there were a handful of cars in the parking lot. Apples recognized the sedan that had come by her house earlier in the day, and walked in its direction. There was no one seated in it, but Apples could smell the driver. She assumed her semi-literate pervert was lying across the seat, waiting until she'd walked by so that he could jump out and take her by surprise.

That was okay. She had a surprise of her own. But first she wanted to know how he'd gotten her name and address. With her luck, somebody had put up a "directory of known vamps" Web site on the Internet and every would-be Van Helsing and Buffy was looking for her now.

She walked by the car and pretended to be shocked when he opened the door and confronted her, a gun in hand.

I hope you've got wooden bullets for that thing, she wanted to tell him, but she kept silent.

"Get in the car," he told her, waving the gun. "Not there," he added as she started to walk around to the passenger's side. "Behind the wheel. You can drive, right?"

To some remote location, Apples supposed. Where he'd have his nasty way with her. Or kill her. Probably, he planned to do both, hopefully in that order. Though technically, any physical relationship with her had to be classified as necrophilia. Eew.

This whole business was so clichéd that she could only sigh. Still, a remote location would work for her, too.

She came back around to the driver's side and got in.

"Where to, gun boy?" she asked.

His face reddened and she watched the veins lift on his brow.

"This isn't some joke," he told her, waving the barrel of the gun in her face. "You're in way over your head now, kid."

Apples looked at him for a long beat.

"You still haven't said where to."

He frowned. "Just drive. I'll tell you where."

"Okay. You're the boss."

She started the car and put it in drive.

"Turn right after the gate," he told her.

She did as he told her, pulling out of the parking lot and turning right onto the Queen Elizabeth Driveway.

"So what's your deal?" she asked as they went under the Lansdowne Bridge at Bank Street and continued west.

"Shut up."

"Why? Are you going to shoot me? I'm driving the car, moron."

"Just shut up."

"Where'd you get my name and address?"

"I told you, just—"

"Shut up. Yeah, yeah. Except I'm not going to. So why don't you stop sounding like a skipping CD and tell me what your problem is."

"You're the problem," he said. "End of story."

"Maybe. Except where does it begin?"

They'd driven under the bridge at Bronson now and the Rideau Canal on their right became Dows Lake. She noticed that they'd started draining the water in the canal in preparation for winter.

"Take a right at the light," he said, "and then a left on Carling."

"Not unless you start talking, I won't."

"I've got two words for you: Randall Gage."

"Those aren't words, they're a name. And they don't mean anything to me."

"You killed him."

Apples made the right onto Preston Street and stopped at the red light waiting for them at Carling Avenue. She turned to look at her captor.

"I'm not saying I did," she told him, "but how would you know anyway?"

She was always careful. There were never any witnesses.

"He told me you would."

"It's still not ringing any bells," she said.

The light turned green and she made the left turn onto Carling. She could smell the first telltale hint of nervousness coming from her captor, could almost read his mind:

Why's she so calm? Why isn't she scared?

Because I'm already dead, moron.

"Well?" Apples asked.

"Randall was about five-eight, a hundred and sixty pounds. Blond, good-looking guy. He used to come into the coffee shop where you work."

A face rose up in Apples's mind, sharp and sudden. She remembered Randall Gage now, remembered him all too well, though she hadn't known his name. After the first time he'd seen her at the Second Cup where she worked, he seemed to come in every time she had a shift. "A. Smith," he'd always read from her name tag, fishing for the first name, which she never gave him. Then he'd made the mistake of grabbing her after a late shift and forcing her into the back of his van. He'd bragged to her about other girls he'd snatched, how the last one hadn't survived, so if she wanted to live, she'd better just lie back and enjoy it, but no problem there, sweetcakes, because this he guaranteed, she *was* going to enjoy it.

Rather than find out, she'd drained him.

And then not been able to get back to where she'd stashed his body when his three days were up and he rose from the dead. She'd had to track him for most of the night before she finally found him trying to hide from the dawn in somebody's garden shed, the idiot. Like the sun was going to burn him.

"You still haven't explained how you got my address," she said.

"Legwork," her captor said.

"Or what you plan to do to me."

"Same as you did to Randall. Take the Queensway on-ramp," he added as they passed Kirkwood Avenue.

Apples felt like driving the car into the nearest lamppost, but then she reminded herself that whatever remote location he was directing her to would benefit her as well.

"He raped and killed a twelve-year-old girl," she said, her voice gone hard and cold.

Her captor shook his head. "He was never connected to anything."

"He *told* me he did, you moron."

"Don't matter. You still had no right to kill him."

"I never said I did."

"He told me you were coming for him—called me up, told me your name, where you worked, what you looked like."

Apples supposed that Gage hadn't bothered to explain that he was already dead by that point.

"So what's it to you?" she asked.

"He was my brother."

Now that Apples could understand.

- 5 -

Who turned me? I never learned her name. She just said she liked the look of me—the inside look of me. She drained me, took me away, and watched over me for the three days until I rose as a vamp. Then she cut me loose.

Yeah, of course we talked before I went home to face the music. She filled me in on the rules and regs. I don't mean there's vamp police, running around handing out tickets if you do something wrong. There's just things you can do and things you can't and she straightened me out on them. Gave me the lowdown on all the mythology. Useful stuff. She never did get into why she turned me besides what I've already told you, so your guess is as good as mine.

No, I never saw her again.

- 6 -

"How did I kill him?"

"What?"

"Your brother. How am I supposed to have killed him?"

They were on the Queensway now, the multiple lane divided highway that bisected the city from east to west. Apples kept to the speed limit—100 kilometers per hour—but they were already passing Bayshore Shopping Centre and about to leave the city. The last few kilometers they'd ridden in silence. The surviving Gage sibling rested his gun on his thigh and stared out the front windshield. He turned to Apples.

"That's one of the things I need to know."

"Have you ever killed anybody?" she asked.

He shrugged. "A couple of guys. Once was in the middle of a holdup, the other time in jail. I never got connected to either one."

"How did it feel?"

"What the hell kind of a question is that?"

Apples shot him a glance. "Did it feel good? Did it feel righteous? Did you feel sad? Did it give you a hard-on?"

"How did it feel for you?"

"Like a waste."

"So you did kill Randall."

"I never said that."

"Anybody looks at you, they see this sweet little kid—what are you, sixteen?"

I was when I died, she thought. And she hadn't aged a day since. That wasn't causing problems yet, but it would soon. Still, she had to wait only one more year. That was when Cassie turned sixteen and she planned to turn her. The thing about vamps is, they don't get sick. And if you've got something wrong with you, it's gone once you're turned. Good-bye leg brace and asthma. Cassie didn't know it, but Apples planned for them to be sixteen together. Forever.

"I'm nineteen," she told Gage.

He nodded. "But everybody looks at you and just sees this sweet little kid. Nobody knows the monster hiding under your skin."

Apples shot him another look. That was about as good a way to put it as any. How much did he know? And how many people, if any, had he told?

"I guess you'd know all about monsters," she said. "Seeing

how your little brother grew up to be one and you're not exactly an angel yourself."

Anger flickered in his eyes and the gun rose to point at her.

"You shoot me now," she reminded him, "and you're killing yourself as well."

"Just shut up and drive."

"I think we've already played that song."

- 7 -

So what are my weaknesses? You mean, beyond getting staked or beheaded? Hey, how stupid do I look? Figure it out for yourself.

Just kidding.

Apparently, the way it works is that whatever meant the most to you when you were alive becomes anathema to you when you're dead. Not people, but things and ideas. So I guess if you did worship the sun, then it could fry you as a vamp. Same if you loved eating Italian, with all that garlic in the sauces. Or maybe you were way serious about church.

Here's a funny fact: pretty much any vampire turned in the past few decades can be warded off with chocolate. And if not chocolate, then some kind of junk food, not to mention cigarettes, coffee, or beer. Junkies are probably the biggest problem for normal people since you can only ward them off with needles and drugs. There's not much by way of sacred icons anymore.

- 8 -

Apples kept following her captor's directions. Eventually they exited the Queensway and drove down increasingly small backroads in the rural area west of the city. When they finally reached a bumpy track that was only two ruts on the ground with branches raking the sides of the car, he had her stop.

"Get out," he said.

She did, stretching her back muscles and looking around her with interest. She didn't get out of the city much, but ever since she'd been turned, she'd had this real yearning to just run in the woods.

Gage slid across the bench seat and joined her on her side of the car, the gun leveled at her once more.

"So you killed Randall because he told you some b.s. story about boffing some twelve-year-old."

"Not to mention killing her."

"So how was that your business?"

"Well, call me crazy, but I take offense at misogynist morons hurting kids."

"So you're just some do-gooder."

"Not to mention his intention to do the same to me."

Gage gave a slow nod. "But I still don't get how you killed him. You're just some—"

"Slip of a girl. I know."

"With a big mouth."

He frowned at her. His nervousness was a stronger scent now, some animal part of his brain already registering what the rest of him hadn't worked out yet.

"I just don't get it," he said.

"And that's where you made your mistake," she told him. "That's the question you should have asked yourself before you ever came by my house with your little party invitation and threatening my little sister."

The gun rose, muzzle pointing at her head.

"You're way out of your league, kid."

"I don't know." She grinned, showing him a pair of fangs. "See, I'm faster than you."

Her hand moved in a blur of motion, plucking the gun from his hand and flinging it a half-dozen feet away.

"I'm stronger than you."

She grabbed his hand and twisted it, bending it up around his back, exerting pressure so that he couldn't move.

"And I'm hungry."

She bit his neck and the hollowed fangs sank deep. He began to jerk as she drew the blood up from his veins, but it was no use.

It never was.

* * *

Afterward, she sat down by his body and began to talk, conversing with the corpse as though it was asking her questions. She took her time in responding. After all, they had three days to wait.

Normally she would have simply stashed the body and come back when it was time for it to rise, but considering the problems she'd already had with his brother, she didn't feel like tempting fate a second time with one of these Gage boys. She called home on her cell phone and luckily got the answering machine, which let her leave a message without having to explain too much. Her parents would still be mad when she got home, but hey, she was nineteen now, no matter how young she might look.

When she stashed the phone back in the pocket of her jacket, she went and found a good-sized branch that she could carve into a stake while she talked and waited.

- 9 -

Do I have any regrets? Sure. I can't have babies, for one thing. Well, yeah, I can still have sex. I just can't have a baby, and that sucks. I always figured when I got old—you know, like in my twenties—I'd get married and have kids.

I miss eating, too. I mean, I can eat and drink the same as you, but I can't process it, so afterward I have to go throw it up like some bulimic. It's so gross. Annalee—she works at the coffee shop with me—caught me doing it one time and it was really awkward. She's all, "Don't do this to yourself. Trust me, you're not fat. You need help to deal with it. It's nothing to be ashamed of."

"It's not what you think," I tell her. "I've just got a touch of stomach flu."

"Every time you eat you throw up," she says, and I'm thinking, what? Are you keeping tabs on me? How weird is that? But I know she means well.

I guess the other thing I'm going to miss is growing old. I'll always look sixteen, but inside I age the same as you. What happens when I'm all old and ancient? The only guys that'll be my age—you know, in their thirties and forties—interested in being with me then are going to be these pedophile freaks. And who wants to hang out with sixteen-year-old boys forever?

But I didn't choose it, and I'm not the kind to get all weepy and do myself in. I figure, if this is what I am, then I might as well make myself useful getting rid of losers like you and your brother. I guess I read too many superhero comics when I was a kid or something.

And I really want this chance to give Cassie a shot at a better life. Well, a different one, anyway. She deserves to see what it's like to walk around without her leg brace and bronchodilator.

Maybe she'll join me in this little crusade of mine, but it'll have to be her choice. Just like getting turned has to be her choice. I'll give her the skinny, the bad and the good, and she can decide. And it's not like we *have* to kill anybody. I only do it when losers like you don't leave me any choice. Most times, I just feed on someone until they get so weak they just can't hurt anybody for a long time. I check up on them from time to time—a girl gets hungry, after all—and if they've gone back to their evil ways, I turn them into these anemics again. They usually figure it out. When they don't . . . well, that's what stakes are for, right?

My weakness? I guess I can tell you that. It's anything to do with Easter. I used to be an Easter maniac—I loved every bit of it. I guess because it's like Halloween, a serious candy holiday, but without the costumes. I was never one for dressing up and scary stuff never turned me on. Good thing, the way things worked out. Imagine if the very thought of vamps and ghouls was my nemesis. I'd be long gone by now. But Easter's tough. I have to avoid the stores—which is not easy, but better than trying to avoid Christmas—and play sick on the day itself.

- 10 -

Apples saw Gage's eyes move under his lids. She didn't get up from where she was kneeling on the ground beside his shoulder, just reached over for her now-sharpened stake and lifted it. Gage's eyes opened.

"How . . . how do you live with yourself?" he asked.

Apples shivered. She'd never stopped to think that he could

actually hear everything she'd been saying. She'd only talked to pass the time. Because there was no one else she could talk to about it.

"The only other choice is where you're going," she said.

"I welcome it."

When he said that, forgotten memories returned to her. The nightmare she'd had to undergo through her own three days of change from dead human to what she was now. It was like swimming through mud, trying to escape the clinging knowledge of the worst that people were capable of doing to each other, but drowning in it at the same time. Not for three days, but for what felt like an eternity. It had been such a horrifying experience that the only way she'd managed to deal with it was by simply blocking it away.

How had she forgotten?

Better yet, how could she forget it again? The sooner the better.

"That's because you're a loser," she said.

"And you're going to do this to your sister."

"You don't know anything about me or my sister!"

She brought the stake down harder than necessary. Long after he was dead, she was still leaning over him, pressing the stake down.

Finally, she let it go and rocked back onto her ankles. She got up and dragged his body back into the car, wiped the vehicle down for any fingerprints she might have left in it. She soaked a rag in gas, stuck it in the gas tank, and lit it.

She was out of sight of the car and walking fast when the explosion came. She didn't turn to look, but only kept walking. Her mind was in that dark place Gage had called back into existence.

How could she put Cassie through that?

But how could she go on, forever, alone?

For the first time since she'd been turned, she didn't know what to do.

Two: Cassandra

APPLES HAS A SECRET AND I KNOW WHAT IT IS.

Her real name's Appoline, but everybody calls her Apples, just like they call me Cassie instead of Cassandra, except for Mom. She always calls us by our given names. But that's not the secret. It's way bigger than having some weird name.

* * *

My sister is so cool—not like I could ever be.

I was born with a congenital birth defect that left me with one leg shorter than the other so I have to wear this Frankenstein monster leg brace all the time. At least that's what the kids call it. "Here comes the bride of Frankenstein," they used to say when I came out for recess—I was always last to get outside. I'm glad Apples doesn't know, because she'd beat the crap out of them and you can't do that just 'cause people call you names.

I've also got asthma real bad, so I always have to carry my puffer around with me. Even if I didn't have the leg brace and could run, the asthma wouldn't let me. I get short of breath whenever I try to do anything too strenuous, but I'm lucky 'cause

I've only had to go to the hospital a few times when an attack got too severe.

I know you shouldn't judge people by their physical attributes, but we all do, don't we? And if you just aren't capable of simple things like walking or breathing properly, you're not even in the running so far as most people are concerned. People see any kind of a disability and they immediately think your brain's disabled as well. They talk to me slower and never really listen to what I'm saying.

Oh, I'm not feeling sorry for myself. Honest. I'm just being pragmatic. I'm always going to be this dorky kid with a bum leg who can't breathe. I could live to be eighty years old, with a whole life behind me, but inside, that's who I'll always be.

But Apples has never seen or treated me that way, not even when we have a fight, which isn't that often anyway. I know that sounds odd, because siblings are just naturally supposed to argue and fight, but we don't. We get along and share pretty much everything. Or at least we did up until the night of that Bryan Adams concert. She went with a bunch of friends and then didn't come back home until four days later. Boy, were Mom and Dad mad. I was just really worried, and then I guess I felt hurt because she wouldn't tell me where she'd been.

"It's not that I won't," she'd tell me. "It's that I can't. That chunk of time is just like this big black hole in my head."

But I know she remembers something from it. She just doesn't think I can handle whatever it was.

And that was when she changed. Not slowly, over time, like everybody does, you get older, you stop playing with Barbies, start listening to real music. But bang, all of a sudden. She was always fun, but after that four-day-long night out, she became this breezy, confident person that I still adored but felt I had to get to know all over again.

That wouldn't be a problem, but she also got all *X-Files*, too. All mysterious about simple things. Like I'll never forget her face when I announced just before dinner one day that I was now a vegetarian. I simply couldn't condone the slaughter of innocent animals just so that I could live. "You are what you eat," I told them, not understanding Apples's anguished expression until much later.

And Easter was particularly weird when it came around the following year. Used to be her favorite holiday, bar none, but that year she claimed she'd developed a phobia toward it and wouldn't have anything to do with any of it. When Dad asked why, she said with more exasperation than usual, "That's why they call it a phobia, Dad. It's an *unreasonable* fear."

Okay, maybe those aren't the best examples, but when you add everything together. Like there was this period when I thought she was bulimic, but although she was throwing up a lot after meals, she didn't have any of the other symptoms. She never seems overly concerned about her weight; she doesn't lose weight. In fact, she just seems to keep getting stronger and healthier all the time. So I couldn't figure out what and where she was eating.

She also stopped having a period. I caught her throwing out unused tampons one day around the time she was usually menstruating, so I watched out for it the next month, but she threw them out then, too, like she didn't want anyone to know that she wasn't still using them. It seemed unlikely that she was pregnant—

and as the months went by, it was obvious she wasn't—and she sure couldn't be hitting menopause.

By now you're thinking I'm this creepy kid, always spying on my sister, but it's not like that. I came across all these things by accident. The only reason I looked further into them was that I was worried. Wouldn't you have been, if it was happening to your sister? And the worst was I had no one to talk to about it. I couldn't bring it up with my parents, I sure wasn't going to talk about it to anyone outside of the family, and I couldn't begin to think of a way to ask Apples herself. I couldn't follow her around either, not with my leg brace and having to catch my breath all the time. So while I know she snuck out at night, I could never follow to see where she was going, what she was doing.

I got to thinking, maybe I should write one of those anonymous letters to an advice columnist. The only reason I thought of that is that I'm just this help-column junkie—Dear Abby, Ann Landers, the "Sex & Body" and "Hard Questions" columns in *Seventeen*. My favorite is Dan Savage's "Savage Love," which runs in *X press*, our local alternative weekly, though Mom and Dad'd probably kill me if they knew I was reading it. I mean, it's all about sex and gay stuff and I know I'm never going to have a boyfriend—who wants the Frankenstein monster on their arm?—but I still figure it's stuff I should know.

Imagine writing in to one of them with my problem. I'd try Dan first.

> Dear Dan,
>   My sister doesn't eat or menstruate anymore, but she's not losing weight, nor is she pregnant. She

has a phobia about Easter and sneaks out of the house late at night, going I don't know where.

I'm not trying to butt into her life, but I'm really worried. What do you think is wrong with her? What can I do?

Confused in Ottawa

What's wrong with her? I started to think that the answer lay in one of those cheesy old sci-fi or horror movies that they run late at night. That she'd become a pod person or a secret monster of some kind. Except not in a bad way. She's not mean to me, or anyone else that I can see. She's just . . . weird.

And then on my sixteenth birthday, I find out. It's after the big dinner and presents and everything. I'm lying on my bed, looking up at the ceiling and trying to figure out why I don't feel different—I mean, turning sixteen's supposed to be a big deal, right?—when Apples comes in and closes the door behind her. I scoot up so that I'm leaning against a pillow propped up at my headboard. She props the other pillow up and lies down beside me. We've done this a thousand times, but tonight it feels different.

"I've got something to tell you," she says, and my head fills up with worry and questions that only gets worse when she goes on to add, "I'm a vampire."

I turn to look at her.

"Oh, please."

"No, really," she says.

As she starts to explain how it all began after that concert when she did her four-day mystery jaunt, all the oddities and weirdnesses of the past few years start to make sense—or at least they make sense if I'm willing to accept the basic premise that my sister's turned into a teenage Draculetta.

"Why didn't you ever tell me before?" I ask.

"I wanted to wait until you were the same age as I was when I . . . got turned."

"But *why?*"

"Because I want to turn you."

She's sitting cross-legged on the bed now, facing me, her face so earnest.

"If you get changed," she goes on, "you can get rid of both your leg brace and your puffer."

"Really?"

I can't imagine life without them. The chance to be normal. Then I catch myself. Normal, but dead.

But Apples is nodding, a big grin stretching her lips. She holds out her right hand, pointer finger extended.

"Remember when I lost my nail in volleyball practice?" she asks. "The whole thing came right off."

I nod. It was so gross.

"Well, look," she says, still waving her finger in front of my face. "It's all healed."

"Apples," I say. "That was four years ago. Of *course* it's healed."

"I mean it healed when I changed. I had no fingernail the night I went to the concert, but there it was when I came back four days later. The . . . woman who changed me, she said the change heals anything."

"So you're just going to bite me or something and I become like you?"

She nods. "But we have to work this out just right. It takes three days before you're changed, so we'll have to figure out how and where we can do that so that no one gets suspicious. But don't worry. I'll be there for you the whole time, watching over you."

"And then we'll live forever?"

"Forever sixteen."

"What about Mom and Dad?"

"We can't tell them," she says. "How could we even begin to explain this to them?"

"You're explaining it to me."

But she shakes her head. "They wouldn't understand—how could they?"

"The same way you think I can."

"It's not the same."

"So we live forever, but Mom and Dad just get old and die?"

She gets this look on her face that tells me she never thought it out that far.

"We can't change everybody," she says after a long moment.

"Why not?"

"Because then there'd be no one left for us to . . . "

"What?" I ask when her voice trails off.

She doesn't say anything for a long moment, won't meet my gaze.

"To feed on," she says finally. I guess I pull a face, because she quickly adds, "It's not as bad as it sounds."

She's already told me a whole lot of things about the differences between real vamps and the ones in the books and movies, but drinking blood's still part of the deal, and I'm sorry, but it still sounds gross.

Apples get up from the bed. She looks—I don't know. Embarrassed. Sad. Confused.

"I guess you need some time to process all of this stuff I've been telling you," she says.

I give her a slow nod. I'd say something, but I don't know what. I feel kind of overloaded.

"Okay, then," she says, and she leaves me in my bedroom.

I slouch back down on the bed and stare at the ceiling again, thinking about everything she's told me.

My sister's a vampire. How weird is that?

Does she still have a soul?

I guess that's a bizarre question in some ways. I mean, do any of us have souls? It's like asking "Who is God?" I guess. The best answer I've heard to that is when Deepak Chopra says, "Who is asking?" It makes sense that God would be different to different people, but also different to you, depending on who you are at the time you're asking.

I guess I believe we have souls. And when we die, they go on. But what that means for Apples, I don't know. She's dead, but she's still here.

She's different now—but she's still the big sister I knew growing up. There's just *more* to her now. Maybe it's like asking "Who is God?" She's who she is depending on who I am when I'm wondering about her.

Sometimes I think it's only kids that wonder about existential stuff like this. Grown-ups always seem to be worried about money, or politics, or just stuff that has physical presence. It's like somewhere along the way they lost the ability to think about what's inside them.

Here's a story I like: One day Ramakrishna, this big-time spiritual leader back in the nineteenth century, is praying, when he suddenly has this flash that what he's doing is meaningless. He's looking for God, but already everything is God—the rituals he's using, the idols, the floor under him, the walls, *everything*. Wherever he looks, he sees God. And he's just so blown away by this, he can't find the words to express it. All he can do is dance, like, for hours. This joyful Snoopy whirling and dervishing and spinning.

I just love the image of that—some old wise man in flowing robes, just getting up and dancing.

I'd love to be able to dance. I love music. I love the way I can feel it in every pore of my body. When your body's moving to the music, it's like you're part of the music. You're not just dancing to it anymore, you're somehow helping to create it at the same time.

But the most I can do is sort of shuffle around until I get all out of breath, and I never let anyone see me trying to do it. Not even Apples.

Boy, can she dance. Every movement she makes is just so liquid and smooth. She's graceful just getting up from a chair or crossing a room. And I don't say this because of the contrast between us.

But none of this helps with what she's told me. All I can do is feel the weight of the door that she closed behind her and stare at the ceiling, my head full of a bewildering confusion.

Normally when I have something I can't work out, Apples is the one who helps me deal. But now she's the problem. . . .

* * *

Did you ever play the game of if you could only have one wish, what would you wish for? It's so hard to decide, isn't it? But I know what I would do. I would wish that all my wishes would come true.

But real life isn't like that. And too often you find that the things you think you really, really want are the last things in the world that you should get.

I've always wanted to be able to walk without my leg brace, to run and jump and dance and just be normal. And breathing. Everybody takes it for granted. Well, I wish I could. And here's my chance. Except it comes with a price, just like in all those old fairy tales I used to read as a kid.

I have to choose. Go on like I am, a defect, a loser—at least in other people's eyes. Or be like Apples, full of life and vigor, and live forever. Except to do that I've got to drink other people's blood and everybody else I care about will eventually get old and die.

What kind of a choice is that?

This is the hardest thing I've ever had to try to work out.

* * *

I get Mom to drive me to the mall the next day. I know she worries about me being out on my own, but she's good about it. She reminds me not to overexert myself and we arrange what door she'll meet me at in a couple of hours, and then I'm on my own.

I don't want to go shopping. I just want to sit someplace on my own, and there's no better place to do that than in the middle of a bunch of strangers like in the concourse of this mall.

I watch the people go by and find myself staring at their throats. I can't imagine drinking their blood. And then there's this whole business that Apples explained about how she only feeds on bad people. That just makes me feel sicker. When she told me that, all I could think about was that time at dinner when I announced I was becoming a vegetarian and the look on her face when I told them why.

You are what you eat.

I don't want the blood of some freak serial killer nourishing me. I don't even want the blood of a jaywalker in me.

After a while I make myself stop thinking. I do the people-watching thing, enjoying the way all these people are hurrying by my little island bench seat. But of course, as soon as I start to relax a little, some middle-aged freak in a trench coat has to sit down beside me, putting his lame moves on me. He walks by, once, twice, checks out the leg brace, sees I'm alone, and then he's on the bench and it's "That's such a beautiful blouse—what kind of material is it made of?" and he's reaching over and rubbing the sleeve between his fingers. . . .

If I was Apples, with this vamp strength she was telling me about, I could probably knock him on his ass before he even knew what was happening. Or I could at least run away. But all I can do is shrink away from him, feeling scared, until I see one of the mall's rent-a-cops coming.

"Officer!" I yell. They're all wanna-be-cops and love it when you act like they're real policemen.

The pervert beside me jumps up from the bench and bolts down the hall before the security guard even looks in my direction. But that's okay. I don't want a scene. I just want to be left alone.

"Was he bothering you?" the guard asks.

I see him take it in. The leg brace. Me, so obviously help-less—and damn it, it's true. And he's all solicitous and pretty nice, actually. He asks if I'm on my own and, when I tell him I'm meet-ing my mom later, offers to walk me to the door where I'm sup-posed to meet her.

I take him up on it, but I'm thinking, it doesn't have to be this way. If I let Apples change me, nobody will ever bother me again. It'd be like my own private human genome project. Only maybe I'm not supposed to be healthy. I keep thinking that maybe my asthma and bad leg are compensating for some other talent that just hasn't shown up yet.

I think of people throughout history who've overcome their handicaps to give us things that no one but they could have. Stephen Hawking. Vincent van Gogh with his depressions. Terry Fox. Teddy Roosevelt. Stevie Wonder. Helen Keller.

I'm not saying that they had to be handicapped to share their gifts with us, but if they hadn't been handicapped, maybe they would have gone on to be other people and not become the in-spirations or creative people they came to be.

And I'm not saying I'm super smart or talented, or that I'm going to grow up and change the world. But it doesn't seem right to just become something else. I won't have earned it. It's just too . . . too easy, I guess.

* * *

"There's a reason why I am the way I am," I tell Apples later.

We're sitting in the rec room, the TV turned to MuchMusic, but neither of us is really watching the Christina Aguilera video that's playing. Dad's in the kitchen, making dinner. Mom's out in the garden, planting tulip and crocus bulbs.

"You mean like it's all part of God's plan?" Apples asks.

"No. I don't know that I believe in God. But I believe everything has a purpose."

Apples shakes her head. "You can't tell me you believe your asthma and your leg are a good thing."

"It might seem like they weaken me, but they actually make me strong. Maybe not physically, but in my heart and spirit."

Apples sighs and pulls me close to her. "You always were a space case," she says into my hair. "But I guess that's part of the reason I love you as much as I do."

I pull back so that we can look at each other.

"I don't want you to change me," I say.

Apples has always been good at hiding what she's feeling, but she can't hide the disappointment from me.

"I'm sorry," I tell her.

"Don't be," she says. "You need to do what's right for you."

"I feel like I'm letting you down."

"Cassie," she says. "You could never let me down."

But she moved out of the house the next day.

Three: Appoline

LIFE SUCKS.

Or maybe I should say, death sucks, since I'm not really alive—but everybody thinks death sucks because for them it's the big end. So that doesn't work either.

Okay. How about this: undeath sucks.

Or at least mine does.

I had to move out of the house. After four years of waiting to be able to change Cassie, I just couldn't live there anymore once she turned me down. I can't believe how much I miss her. I miss the parents, too, but it's not the same. I've never been as close to them as Cassie is. But I adore her and talking on the phone and seeing her a couple of times a week just isn't enough.

Trouble is, when I do see her or talk to her, that hurts, too. Everything just seems to hurt these days.

I've been thinking a lot about Sandy Browning, my best friend in grade school. We were inseparable until we got into junior high. That's when she starting getting into these black moods. Half the time you couldn't see them coming. It was like these black clouds would drift in from nowhere and just envelop her. When I discovered she was cutting herself—her arms and stomach were criss-crossed with dozens of little scars—I couldn't deal with it and we sort of drifted apart.

There's two reasons people become cutters, she told me once, trying to explain. There's those that can't feel anything—the cutting makes them feel alive. And then there are the ones like her, who have this great weight of darkness and despair inside them. The cutting lets it out.

I couldn't really get it at the time—I couldn't imagine having that kind of a bleak shadow swelling inside me—but I understand her now. Ever since Cassie turned me down, I've got this pressure inside me that won't ease and I feel like the only way I can release it is to open a hole to let it out. But it doesn't work for me. The one time I ran a razor blade along the inside of my forearm, it hardly bled at all and the cut immediately started to seal up. Within half an hour, there wasn't a mark on my skin.

Sandy had been completely addicted to it. Her family moved away the year before I became a vamp and I don't know what ever happened to her. I wish I'd been a better friend. I wish a lot of things these days.

I wish I'd never talked to Cassie about my wanting to turn her.

Sometimes I wonder: did I want to do it for her, so that she could finally put aside the limitations of her physical ailments, or did I do it for me, so I wouldn't have to be alone?

I guess it doesn't matter.

I'm sure alone now.

I live in a tiny apartment above the Herb and Spice Natural Foods shop on Bank Street. I like the area. During the day, it's like a normal neighborhood, with shops along Bank Street—video store, comic book shop, gay bookstore, restaurants—and mostly residential buildings on the side streets. But come the night, the blocks up north around the clubs like Barrymore's become prime hunting grounds for someone like me. All the would-be toughs, the scavengers and the hunters, come out of the woodwork, hoping to prey on the people who come to check out the bands and the scene.

And I prey on them.

But even stopping them from having their wicked way doesn't really mean all that much anymore. I'm too lonely. It's not that I can't make friends. Ever since I got turned, that's the least of my problems. It's that I don't have a foundation of normalcy to return to anymore. I don't have a home and family. I just have my apartment. My job at the coffee shop. My hunting. I can't seem to get close to anyone because as soon as I do, I remember that

I'm going to be like I am forever, while they age and die. Sometimes I imagine I can see them aging, that I can see the cells dying. It's even worse when I'm back home, seeing it happen to Cassie and my parents, so it's not like I can move back there again either.

That's when I decide it's time to track down the woman who turned me.

It's harder than I think. I don't really know where to start. Because she found me outside a concert at the Civic Centre, I spend most of December and January going to the clubs and concerts, thinking it's my best chance. Zaphod Beeblebrox 2 closes down at the end of November, but Barrymore's is still just up the street from where I live, so I drop in there almost every night, sliding past the doorman like I'm not even there. I can almost be invisible if I don't want to be noticed—don't ask me how that works. That's probably why I can't find the woman, but I don't give up trying.

I frequent the Market area, checking out the Rainbow and the Mercury Lounge, the original Zaphod's and places like that. Cool places where I think she might hang out. I go to the National Arts Centre for classical recitals and the Anti–Land Mines concert in early December. To Centrepoint Theatre in Nepean. Further west to the Corel Centre. I even catch a ride up to Wakefield, to the Black Sheep Inn, for a few concerts.

This calls for more serious cash than I can get from my salary at the coffee shop and the meager tips we share there, so I take to lifting the wallets of my victims, leaving them with less cash as well as less blood. My self-esteem's taking a nosedive, what with already being depressed, making no headway on finding the woman, and having become this petty criminal as well as the occasional murderer—I ended up having to kill another guy when I discovered he was raping his little sister and I got so mad, I just drained him.

It's weird. I exude confidence—I know I do from other people's reactions to me, and it's not like I'm unaware of how well I can take care of myself. But my internal life's such a mess that sometimes I can't figure out how I make it through the day with my mind still in one piece. I feel like such a loser.

I have this to look forward to forever?

Cassie's the only one who picks up on it.

"What's the matter?" she asks when I stop by for a visit during her Christmas holidays.

"Nothing," I tell her.

"Right. That's why you're so mopey whenever I see you." She doesn't look at me for a moment. When she does look back, she has this little wrinkle between her eyes. "It's because of me, isn't it? Because I didn't want to become a . . . to be like . . . "

"Me," I say, filling in for her. "A monster."

"You're not a monster."

"So what am I? Nothing anybody else'd ever choose to be."

"You didn't choose to be it either," she says.

"No kidding. And I don't blame you. Who'd ever *want* to be like this?"

She doesn't have an answer, and neither do I.

* * *

Then one frosty January evening I'm walking home from the coffee shop and I see her sitting at a window table of the Royal Oak. I stop and look at her through the glass, struck again by how gorgeous she is, how no one else seems to be aware of it, of her. I go inside when she beckons to me. Today she's casual chic: jeans, a black cotton sweater, cowboy boots. Like me, she probably doesn't feel the cold anymore, but she has a winter coat draped over the back of her chair. There's a pint glass in front of her, half full of amber beer.

"Have a seat," she says, indicating the empty chair across from her.

I do. I don't know what to do with my hands. I don't know where to look. I want to stare at her. I want to pretend I'm cool, that this is no big deal. But it is.

"I've been looking for you," I finally say.

"Have you now."

I nod. Ignoring the hint of amusement in her eyes, I start to ask, "I need to know—"

"No, don't tell me," she says, interrupting. "Let me guess. First you tried to turn . . . oh, your best friend, or maybe a brother or a sister, and they turned you down and made you feel like a monster even though you only feed on the wicked. But somehow, even that doesn't feel right anymore. So now you want to end it all. Or at least get an explanation as to why I turned you."

I find myself nodding.

"We all go through this," she says. "But sooner or later—if we survive—we learn to leave all the old ties behind: friends, family, ideas of right and wrong. We become what we are meant to be. Predators."

I think of how I wanted to turn Cassie and start to feel a little sick. Up until this moment, her refusing to be turned had seemed such a personal blow. Now I'm just grateful that of the two of us, she, at least, had some common sense. Bad enough that one of us is a monster.

"What if I don't want to be a predator?" I ask.

The woman shrugs. "Then you die."

"I thought we couldn't die."

"For all intents and purposes," she says. "But we're not invincible. Yes, we heal fast, but it's genetic healing. We can deal with illnesses and broken bones, torn tissues and birth defects. But if a car hits us, if we take a bullet or a stake in the heart or head, if we're hurt in such a way that our accelerated healing facilities don't have the chance to help us, we can still die. We don't need Van Helsings or chipper cheerleaders in short skirts to do us in. Crossing the street at the wrong time can be just as effective."

"Why did you turn me?"

"Why not?"

All I can do is stare at her.

"Oh, don't take it so dramatically," she says. "I know you'd like a better reason than that—how I saw something special in you, how you have some destiny. But the truth is, it was for my own amusement."

"So it was just a . . . whim."

"You need to stop being so serious about everything," she tells me. "We're a different species. The old rules don't apply to us."

"So you just do whatever you want?"

She smiles, a predatory smile. "If I can get away with it."

"I'm not going to be like that."

"Of course you won't," she says. "You're different. You're special."

I shake my head. "No, I'm just stronger. I'm going to hold on to my ideals."

"Tell me that again in a hundred years," she says. "Tell me how strong you feel when anything you ever cared about, when everybody you love, is long dead and gone."

I get up to leave, to walk out on her, but she beats me to it. She stands over me, and touches my hair with her long cool fingers. For a moment I imagine I see a kind of tenderness in her eyes, but then the mockery is back.

"You'll see," she says.

I stay at the table and watch her step outside. Watch her back as she walks on up Bank Street. Watch until she's long gone and there are only strangers passing by the windows of the Royal Oak.

The thing that scares me the most is that maybe she's right.

I realize leaving home wasn't the answer. I'm still too close to the people I love. I have to go a lot farther than I have so far. I have to keep moving and not make friends. Forget I have family. If I don't have to watch the people I love age and die, then maybe I won't become as cynical and bitter as the woman who made me what I am.

But the more I think of it, the more I feel that I'd be a lot better off just dying for real.

Four: Cassandra

IN THE END, I DID IT FOR APPLES, THOUGH SHE DOESN'T know that. I don't think I can ever tell her that. She thinks I did it to be able to run and breathe and be as normal as an undead person can be. But I could see how being what she is and all alone was tearing her apart, and I started to think, Who do I love the best in the world? Who's always been there for me? Who stayed in with her weak kid sister when she could have been out having fun? Who never complained about taking me anywhere? Who always, *genuinely* enjoyed the time she spent with me?

She never said anything to me about what she was going through, but I could see the loneliness tearing at her and I couldn't let her be on her own anymore. I started to get scared that she might take off for good, or do something to herself, and how could I live with that?

Besides, maybe this *is* my destiny. Maybe with our enhanced abilities we can be some kind of dynamic duo superhero team, out rescuing the world, or at least little human pieces of the world.

The funny thing is, when I told her I wanted her to turn me, she was the one who argued against it. But I wouldn't take no and she finally gave in.

And it's not so bad. Even the bloodsucking's not so bad, though I do miss eating and drinking. I guess the worst part was those three days I was dead. You're aware, but not aware, floating in some kind of goopy muck that feels like it's made up of all the bad things people have ever done or thought.

But you get over it.

What's my fear? Fuzzy animal slippers. I used to adore them, back when I was alive. Even at sixteen years old, I was still wearing them around the house. Now I break into a cold sweat just thinking about them.

Pretty lame, huh? But I guess it's a better weakness than some you can have. Because, really, how often do you unexpectedly run into someone wearing fuzzy animal slippers?

I still have this idea that we should turn Mom and Dad, too, but I'm going to wait a while before I bring it up again. I think I understand Apples's nervousness better after she told me what she learned the last time she saw the woman who turned her. I don't think it's that she doesn't love our parents. She's just nervous that they won't make the transition well. That they'll be more like the woman than us.

"Let's give it a year or two," she said, "till we see how we do ourselves."

Mom and Dad sure weren't happy about me moving out and into Apples's apartment. I wish I could at least tell them that I'm not sick anymore, but I'm kind of stuck having a secret identity whenever we go back home for a visit. I have to carry around my puffer and pretend to use it. I have to put the leg brace on again, though we had to adjust it since my leg's all healed.

What's going to happen to us? I don't know. I just know that we'll be together. Always. And I guess, for now, that's enough.

I GREW up on fairy tales and myths and while I loved what writers such as Tolkien and Lord Dunsany did with elves and all when I first read them in my late teens, there's always remained a fond spot in my heart for the little people as seen by the Victorians and in folklore. Not to mention the delightful flower fairies from Cicely Mary Barker's books.

Here's what happened to one discovered in the Ottawa suburbs. . . .

Fairy Dust

AT FIRST MARINA THOUGHT THAT JASON HAD CAUGHT SOME sort of odd bug. He came into her backyard where she was weeding the vegetable garden and handed her an old jam jar with nail holes poked into its metal lid. She sat back on her haunches to look at his prize. The jar held a twig that went almost all the way from the bottom to its top in two branched lengths. Holding on to the twig was a thin iridescent shape, about the length of a man's index finger.

"Don't look at it straight on," Jason told her as she held it up to her eyes.

Obediently, Marina moved the jar to one side until she was looking at the bug from the corner of her eye. It remained a blur until suddenly, like the viewfinder of a camera finally snapping into focus, the iridescent shape shivered into clarity.

Marina's eyes went round and she almost dropped the jar. What she'd supposed was a bug looked for all the world like a tiny winged person—thin angular limbs, dragonfly wings folded back along its spine. A short tunic of some sort of gossamer fabric covered its torso. The eyes were closed, the tiny head leaning against the side of the twig for support. Two needle-thin antennae protruded from out of a mass of miniature corkscrew curls the color of dark red sumac fruit.

"Where . . . where did you get it?" she breathed.

"At the bottom of the garden. Isn't it *something*?"

Reluctantly, Marina took her gaze from the captured fairy to settle on Jason.

"You can't keep it."

"Why not?"

"It . . . it just wouldn't be right. It's something so magical—" so impossible, she added to herself "—that it would be wrong to keep it."

But it wasn't just the wrongness that bothered her. She was also thinking of what happened in her book of fairy tales whenever people came into contact with creatures from the Middle Kingdom: something always went terribly awry, especially when you actually meddled with the otherworld beings.

Jason looked uncomfortable. Two years junior to Marina's fourteen, he often seemed far younger to her. Her mother had told her once that girls matured much faster than boys. At times like this, it was far too obvious that she was right.

"I can't just let it go," he said.

"Jason!"

"I'll only keep it overnight," he compromised. "Okay? I'll let it go in the morning. I promise."

It still wasn't right, Marina thought, but it wasn't her fairy. Jason had caught it.

"You'd better keep that promise," she said.

But the next morning, the fairy was dead. All that remained in the bug jar was the branched twig with what looked like the husk of a long thin dead beetle still attached to it. At the bottom of the jar lay a small mound of gray-brown dust and bits of things that might have been the fairy's limbs, so bone dry they were almost translucent.

And Jason was sick.

He lay in his bed, features washed out and thin as though he were the victim of a long debilitating disease that had plagued him for months. Marina almost couldn't recognize him, he was so changed.

"Get . . . get it . . . out of here," he managed to tell her before his mother shooed Marina out.

"Until the doctor comes by, we won't know if what he has is contagious or not," Jason's mother said. "So better safe than sorry, right?"

She was trying to hide her worry, but doing a poor job of it. And no wonder, Marina thought. Jason looked awful, as though he was about to die.

"You really can't stay," Jason's mother said.

Clutching the bug jar, Marina nodded mutely and fled for home.

* * *

An hour later, she was still sitting at the picnic table in her own backyard, staring at the contents of the bug jar.

I warned him, she thought. I told him he shouldn't keep it. But he wouldn't listen. Jason rarely did. And now he was going to die of a fairy curse.

It wasn't fair. Discovering a fairy should have been a wonderful, magical moment, but Jason had reduced it to simple bug collecting. She thought she could imagine what her mother would say. She'd feel sorry for Jason, but then she'd add, "It doesn't surprise me at all. The only way people judge things anymore is by their material value—as something they can possess, important because they're the only one who has one, or as something that they can use to turn a profit."

It wasn't a whole lot different from how her father had often complained about how people took all that was wonderful and beautiful about the earth and used it up and polluted it and ruined it so that by the time children Marina's age grew up, there'd hardly be anything left of it at all. Just memories of how it had once been. If that.

Marina often got the idea from things her mother had told her about her father that he and her mother'd had a lot of the same ideas about the important things in life. Which made it even harder for Marina to understand how her mother could have divorced him.

* * *

Marina had only one real memory of her father. She was twelve years old at the time and had forgotten her house key so she couldn't let herself in. Sitting on the front steps, waiting for her mother to get home from work, she'd watched an old derelict come shambling down the street. She'd seen people like that before, but only over by the public housing project. Never in her own neighborhood. It was only when he got closer that she realized the man wasn't all that old, but his clothes were certainly threadbare. He looked as though he hadn't had a decent meal for a week.

He stopped at her walk and then came up its short length until he stood directly in front of her. He looked uncomfortable as he pulled a battered little book out of his pocket.

"I don't expect you know who I am," he said.

Marina shook her head. Surreptitiously, she glanced down the street, hoping to see her mother's car approaching. The man made her nervous. Her mother's endless admonishment—"Don't talk to strangers"—rang clearly in her head. It probably went double for an old bum like this.

"Doesn't matter," the man said. "This is for you."

He handed her the book, which she took automatically before she remembered what her mother had also said about accepting gifts from strangers. But as soon as the book was in her hand, the man stepped back from her.

"Whatever you do," he said, "don't grow up to be like me. Make sure you're always considerate—not just to those who love you, but to everyone."

And then he walked away.

Marina looked at the book. On the cover were the simple words *Fairy Tales*. She opened the book and there, in a neat script under the stamp that said "Property of the Ottawa Public Library," had been written: "For my daughter Marina, in the hope that she will never consider herself too old to dream. Your loving father, Frank."

When Marina's mother talked about the man she had kicked out of her house the week after Marina was born, her voice was always affectionate until she got to one aspect of his personality. "He wanted to live on dreams," she'd tell Marina, her frustration plain. "He had no common sense, not a practical bone in his body."

"Did you love him, Mom?"

It seemed to Marina that love should be enough—wasn't it supposed to conquer all?

Her mother would nod. "But it was the wrong kind of love. It was the love that was only fire and heat; all it left behind was hurt."

Marina remembered her father's purported lack of practicality as she looked down at the book in her hand.

It figured, she thought. The first time I ever meet my father, all he does is give me a book he stole from the library. Worse, it was a book of fairy tales. Who read this kind of stuff anyway?

Having been brought up to do the right thing, Marina took the book back to the library that weekend, her apology for what had been written in it all ready to be offered. But the librarian only smiled.

"It was very conscientious of you to bring it back," she told Marina, "but this was sold in one of our book sales."

"You *sell* books?"

"Only when no one wants to borrow them from us anymore." She flipped to the inside back cover. "You see? It hadn't been taken out in twenty years."

No wonder. Who'd want to borrow a dumb old book of fairy tales?

But she was relieved that her father hadn't stolen it. And

then, because it was all she had from him, she did read it. And was surprised to discover that she loved the stories. They weren't the simple fairy tales that she'd long ago decided she didn't much care for—the ones from the storybooks that her mother used to read to her. The language and plots of these were a lot more complicated than the ones her mother would read. They were all twisty, like a rose garden gone wild, and full of strange turns that gave her little shivers.

She loved the pictures, too. Delicate watercolor reproductions that had been tipped in, rather than printed as part of the book, so that it was as though someone had glued the appropriate pictures into a photo album after first searching them out in flea markets or boxes of old prints in an antique shop. A few were missing, but she delighted in the ones that remained.

For some reason, she never told her mother about her brief meeting with her father, or showed her the book. If asked, she might have said it was to spare her mother's feelings, but she knew that wasn't the real reason. The real reason was that it was all she had in terms of firsthand experience with her father—a brief conversation, a funny old book—and she wanted to keep it, not so much secret, as private.

* * *

Looking at the bug jar, Marina remembered the book again. Last night, her head filled with the premonitions she'd had about the wrongness of keeping the fairy jarred, she'd reread the story in it where a farmer named John Goodman captured a fairy in the woods and took her to be his wife, but she pined and pined for her freedom until one day John came home and found her gone.

All that remained of her was a little heap of old twigs and leaves and bits of moss, lying right there in the middle of the bed.

He took the changeling bits of what had been his wife, wrapped them up in his best cloak, and carried them into the forest where he buried the bundle under an old oak tree. When he was done, he stood there with his head bowed and wept until he realized he was no longer alone. A strange old man had approached him on silent feet, his limbs all bent and gnarled, his hair like the fine hairs on a tree's roots, his cloak made of moss and leaves.

John knew right away that the old man was a fairy, too.

"Can't you bring her back?" he asked.

"I could," the old man told John, "but she wouldn't be the same."

"What do you mean?"

"She wouldn't be able to laugh or cry anymore, to be angry or content, or to feel anything at all. She would simply be—like a stone or a tree." Someone had underlined the next thing the old fairy man said; Marina thought it might have been her father. "Fairy are like thoughts. If you cage them, they will only wither and die."

It was the saddest story, not just because of what had happened to the poor fairy woman, but because of how terrible John had felt when he finally realized what he'd done. His love had blinded him until it was too late. Because he felt that he had made a mockery of it, he changed his surname to Sorrow.

After rereading the story, Marina had wanted to sneak into Jason's house and let the fairy go, but she'd been afraid of Jason's parents catching her in their house. What would she have said?

So she'd waited for the morning, until she, just like John Sorrow in the story, was too late as well.

* * *

Marina arose after a while and went into her house. She got the beautiful silk scarf that her mother had given her for her last birthday and brought it out to the picnic table. As carefully as she could, she took the twig from the jar and detached the beetlelike exoskeleton from it. She laid it in the center of her scarf, then poured the dust and bits and pieces from the bottom of the jar on top of it. Bundling it all up, she took it and a spade to the bottom of Jason's garden.

There was a cedar hedge there, separating Jason's garden from a strip of grassy land owned by the power company. It cut a swath through the subdivision to let the electrical towers march in a long uninterrupted row. They looked, Marina often thought, just like giant metal stick people, connected only by their humming wires.

Marina buried her scarf under the hedge. It was hard work, spading through the dense roots of the cedars, but she felt she deserved worse than a little hard work for the part she'd played in the fairy's death. When she was finally done, she knelt in the grass beside the hedge.

"I'm so very sorry," she said. "Truly I am. And I know Jason meant no harm, so please let him get well again. If anything, I'm more to blame. He didn't know, but I did and I didn't do anything, and I think maybe that's worse."

There was no reply, but she hadn't really expected one. She

just went on, her voice sounding awkward and tight in her ears, but she knew she had to finish.

"Please don't bring her back. It would be too horrible knowing that she was alive but could have no feelings."

She hesitated a moment, then added, "If I ever see someone doing something I know is wrong again, I promise I won't . . . I won't just stand by and watch."

Then her eyes filled with tears. Her chest got tight and her throat felt too constricted. She couldn't speak anymore, but there was nothing left to say.

* * *

When Jason did get better, he didn't remember having caught the fairy. He didn't remember it at all—or at least so he said. But all the same, he put away his net and jars and never went hunting butterflies again.

Still Marina remembered, and she kept her promise. The empty bug jar, sitting beside the book titled simply *Fairy Tales* on her bookshelf, served as a reminder in case she ever forgot.

Before my wife MaryAnn and I got our own cottage (which is actually an old school bus with a kitchen attached to it, but it does look out on a beautiful lake), we brought a trailer up to her parents' cottage at Otty Lake near Perth, Ontario, and left it there. On weekends we'd go out on the lake with her dad, antiquing with her mother, or just hang out, playing tunes on the dock or going for walks.

All the places in this story are real, but we never did find a brass egg the way Marguerite did. . . .

A Wish Named Arnold

MARGUERITE KEPT A WISH IN A BRASS EGG AND ITS NAME WAS Arnold.

The egg screwed apart in the middle. Inside, wrapped in a small piece of faded velvet, was the wish. It was a small wish, about the length of a man's thumb, and was made of black clay in the rough shape of a bird. Marguerite decided straightaway that it was a crow, even if it did have a splash of white on its head. That just made it more special for her, because she'd dyed a forelock of her own dark hair a peroxide white just before the summer started, much to her parents' dismay.

She'd found the egg under a pile of junk in Miller's while tagging along with her mother and aunt on their usual weekend tour of the local antique shops. Miller's was near their cottage on Otty Lake, just down the road from Rideau Ferry, and considered to be the best antique shop in the area.

The egg and its dubious contents were only two dollars, and

maybe the egg was dinged up a little and didn't screw together quite right, and maybe the carving didn't look so much like a crow as it did a lump of black clay with what could be a beak on it, but she'd bought it all the same.

It wasn't until Arnold talked to her that she found out he was a wish.

"What do you mean you're a wish?" she'd asked, keeping her voice low so that her parents wouldn't think she'd taken to talking in her sleep. "Like a genie in a lamp?"

Something like that.

It was all quite confusing. Arnold lay in her hand, an unmoving lump that was definitely not alive even if he did look like a bird, sort of. That was a plain fact, as her father liked to say. On the other hand, someone was definitely speaking to her in a low buzzing voice that tickled pleasantly inside her head.

I wonder if I'm dreaming, she thought.

She gave her white forelock a tug, then brushed it away from her brow and bent down to give the clay bird a closer look.

"What sort of a wish can you give me?" she asked finally.

Think of something—any one thing that you want—and I'll give it to you.

"Anything?"

Within reasonable limits.

Marguerite nodded sagely. She was all too familiar with *that* expression. "Reasonable limits" was why she had only one forelock dyed instead of a whole swath of rainbow colors like her friend Tina, or a Mohawk like Sheila. If she just washed her hair and let it dry, *and* you ignored the dyed forelock, she had a most reasonable short haircut. But all it took was a little gel that she kept hidden in her purse and by the time she joined her friends down at the mall, her hair was sticking out around her head in a bristle of spikes. It was just such a pain wearing a hat when she came home, and having to wash out the gel right away.

Maybe that should be her wish. That she could go around looking just however she pleased and nobody could tell her any different. Except that seemed like a waste of a wish. She should probably ask for great heaps of money and jewels. Or maybe for a hundred more wishes.

"How come I only get one wish?" she asked.

Because that's all I am, Arnold replied. *One small wish.*

"Genies and magic fish give three. In fact *everybody* in *all* the stories usually gets three. Isn't it a tradition or something?"

Not where I come from.

"Where *do* you come from?"

There was a moment's pause, then Arnold said softly, *I'm not really sure.*

Marguerite felt a little uncomfortable at that. The voice tickling her mind sounded too sad, and she started to feel ashamed of being so greedy.

"Listen," she said. "I didn't really mean to . . . you know . . ."

That's all right, Arnold replied. *Just let me know when you've decided what your wish is.*

Marguerite got a feeling in her head then as though something had just slipped away, like a lost memory or a half-remembered thought, then she realized that Arnold had just gone back to wherever it was that he'd been before she'd opened the egg.

Thoughtfully, she wrapped him up in the faded velvet, then shut him away in the egg. She put the egg under her pillow and went to sleep.

* * *

All the next day she kept thinking about the brass egg and the clay crow inside it, about her one wish and all the wonderful things that there were to wish for. She meant to take out the egg right away, first thing in the morning, but she never quite found the time. She went fishing with her father after breakfast, and then she went into Perth to shop with her mother, and then she went swimming with Steve who lived two cottages down and liked punk music as much as she did, though maybe for different reasons. She didn't get back to her egg until bedtime that night.

"What happens to you after I've made my wish?" she asked after she'd taken Arnold out of his egg.

I go away.

Marguerite asked, "Where to?" before she really thought about what she was saying, but this time Arnold didn't get upset.

To be somebody else's wish, he said.

"And after that?"

Well, after they've made their *wish, I'll go on to the next and the next. . . .*

"It sounds kind of boring."

Oh, no. I get to meet all sorts of interesting people.

Marguerite scratched her nose. She'd gotten a mosquito bite right on the end of it and felt very much like Pinocchio, though she hadn't been telling any lies.

"Have you always been a wish?" she asked, not thinking again.

Arnold's voice grew so quiet that it was just a feathery touch in her mind. *I remember being something else . . . a long time ago. . . .*

Marguerite leaned closer, as though that would help her hear him better. But there was a sudden feeling in her as though Arnold had shaken himself out of his reverie.

Do you know what you're going to wish for yet? he asked briskly.

"Not exactly."

Well, just let me know when you're ready, he said, and then he was gone again.

Marguerite sighed and put him away. This didn't seem to be at all the way this whole wishing business should go. Instead of feeling all excited about being able to ask for any one thing—*anything!*—she felt guilty because she kept making Arnold feel bad. Mind you, she thought, he did seem to be a gloomy sort of a genie when you came right down to it.

She fell asleep wondering if he looked the same wherever he went to when he left her as he did when she held him in her hand. Somehow his ticklish raspy voice didn't quite go with the lumpy clay figure that lay inside the brass egg. She supposed she'd never know.

* * *

As the summer progressed they became quite good friends, in an odd sort of way. Marguerite took to carrying the egg around with her in a small quilted cotton bag that she slung over her shoulder. At opportune moments, she'd take Arnold out and they'd talk about all sorts of things.

Arnold, Marguerite discovered, knew a lot that she hadn't supposed a genie would know. He was current with all the latest bands, seemed to have seen all the best movies, knew stories that could make her giggle uncontrollably or shiver with chills under her blankets late at night. If she didn't press him for information about his past, he proved to be the best friend a person could want, and she found herself telling him things that she'd never think of telling anyone else.

It got to the point where Marguerite forgot he was a wish. Which was fine until the day that she left her quilted cotton bag behind in a restaurant in Smith Falls on a day's outing with her mother. She became totally panic-stricken until her mother took her back to the restaurant, but by then her bag was gone, and so was the egg, and with it Arnold.

Marguerite was inconsolable. She moped around for days and nothing that anyone could do could cheer her up. She missed Arnold passionately. Missed their long talks when she was supposed to be sleeping. Missed the weight of his egg in her shoulder bag and the companionable presence of just knowing he was there. And also, she realized, she'd missed her chance of using her wish.

She could have had anything she wanted. She could have asked for piles of money. For fame and fortune. To be a lead singer in a band like 10,000 Maniacs. To be another Molly Ringwald and star in all kinds of movies. She could have wished that Arnold would stay with her forever. Instead, jerk that she was, she'd never used the wish and now she had nothing. How could she be so stupid?

"Oh," she muttered one night in her bed. "I wish I . . . I wish . . . ."

She paused then, feeling a familiar tickle in her head.

Did you finally decide on your wish? Arnold asked.

Marguerite sat up so suddenly that she knocked over her water glass on the night table. Luckily it was empty.

"Arnold?" she asked, looking around. "Are you here?"

Well, not exactly here, *as it were, but I can hear you.*

"Where have you *been?*"

Waiting for you to make your wish.

"I've really missed you," Marguerite said. She patted her comforter with eager hands, trying to find Arnold's egg. "How did you get back here?"

I told you, Arnold said. *I'm not exactly* here.

"How come you never talked to me when I've been missing you all this time?"

I can't really initiate these things, Arnold explained. *It gets rather complicated, but even though my egg's with someone else, I can't really be their wish until I've finished being yours.*

"So we can still talk and be friends even though I've lost the egg?"

Not exactly. I can fulfill your wish, but since I'm not with you, as it were, I can't really stay unless you're ready to make your wish.

"You can't?" Marguerite wailed.

Afraid not. I don't make the rules, you know.

"I've got it," Marguerite said. And she did have it, too. If she wanted to keep Arnold with her, all she had to do was wish for him to always be her friend. Then no one could take him away from her. They'd always be together.

"I wish . . ." she began.

But that didn't seem quite right, she realized. She gave her dyed forelock a nervous tug. It wasn't right to *make* someone be your friend. But if she didn't do that, if she wished something else, then Arnold would just go off and be somebody else's wish. Oh, if only things didn't have to be complicated. Maybe she should just wish herself to the moon and be done with all her problems. She could lie there and stare at the world from a nice long distance away while she slowly asphyxiated. That would solve everything.

She felt that telltale feeling in her mind that let her know that Arnold was leaving again.

"Wait," she said. "I haven't made my wish yet."

The feeling stopped. *Then you've decided?* Arnold asked.

She hadn't, but as soon as he asked, she realized that there was only one fair wish she could make.

"I wish you were free," she said.

The feeling that was Arnold moved blurrily inside her.

You what? he asked.

"I wish you were free. I *can* wish that, can't I?"

Yes, but . . . Wouldn't you rather have something . . . well, something for yourself?

"This *is* for myself," Marguerite said. "Your being free would be the best thing I could wish for because you're my friend and I don't want you to be trapped anymore." She paused for a moment, brow wrinkling. "Or is there a rule against that?"

No rule, Arnold said softly. His ticklish voice bubbled with excitement. *No rule at all against it.*

"Then that's my wish," Marguerite said.

Inside her mind, she felt a sensation like a tiny whirlwind spinning around and around. It was like Arnold's voice and an autumn leaves smell and a kaleidoscope of dervishing lights, all wrapped up in one whirling sensation.

Free! Arnold called from the center of that whirligig. *Free free free!*

A sudden weight was in Marguerite's hand, and she saw that the brass egg had appeared there. It lay open on her palm, the faded velvet spilled out of it. It seemed so very small to hold so much happiness, but fluttering on tiny wings was the clay crow, rising up in a spin that twinned Arnold's presence in Marguerite's mind.

Her fingers closed around the brass egg as Arnold doubled, then tripled his size in an explosion of black feathers. His voice was like a chorus of bells, ringing and ringing between Marguerite's ears. Then with an exuberant caw, he stroked the air with his wings, flew out the cottage window, and was gone.

Marguerite sat quietly, staring out the window and holding the brass egg. A big grin stretched her lips. There was something so *right* about what she'd just done that she felt an overwhelming sense of happiness herself, as though she'd been the one trapped in a treadmill of wishes in a brass egg, and Arnold had been the one to free *her*.

At last she reached out and picked up from the comforter a small glossy black feather that Arnold had left behind. Wrapping it in the old velvet, she put it into the brass egg and screwed the egg shut once more.

* * *

That September a new family moved in next door with a boy her age named Arnold. Marguerite was delighted and, though her parents were surprised, she and the new boy became best friends almost immediately. She showed him the egg one day that winter and wasn't at all surprised that the feather she still kept in it was the exact same shade of black as her new friend's hair.

Arnold stroked the feather with one finger when she let him see it. He smiled at her and said, "I had a wish once. . . ."

THIS STORY takes place in much the same part of Ontario as "A Wish Named Arnold," but the setting is about a half an hour farther south. As in that previous story, none of the characters are real, but the farm that Liz visits is (it's where my sister-in-law Jane lived for many years), as is the old barn on the hill where Liz discovers that it's not only people who can make music.

As I reread this story for its inclusion here, I also realized that this might well be the first appearance of the animal people that have come to populate many of my later books such as Trader, Someplace to Be Flying, *and* Forests of the Heart.

Wooden Bones

"I REALLY DON'T NEED THIS," LIZ SAID.

She was standing in front of her uncle's house, looking around at the clutter that filled the front yard. What a mess. There was an old car with one door sagging open, stacks of pink insulation, tools and scrap wood, a battered RV trailer, sheets of Styrofoam and Black Joe, a discarded sink—all the debris of a handyman's livelihood and then some, left out to the weather.

Tom Bohay, her uncle, had a renovation business that he ran from the family farm—a hundred acres set right on the Big Rideau Lake. The lake was a hundred yards from the back of the house, which was in the middle of being renovated itself, had been for the past two years ever since the farmhouse up on the hill burned down and her uncle had decided to fix up what had been an oversized cottage, rather than rebuild. According to Liz's mom, Tom was real good at working on other peoples' places, but not so hot when it came to the home front.

Staying here was going to be like living in a junkyard. Liz felt as though she were on the set of *Sanford & Son*, except it was worse, because there wasn't any urban sprawl beyond the property. No downtown or malls or any place interesting at all. Instead it was out in the middle of nowhere. Pasture and bush and rocky hillsides. A neighbor kept cows on the hilly pasture between the road leading into the farm and the house. If you went for a walk anywhere past the yard itself, you had to watch out that you didn't step in a cow pie.

Wonderful stuff.

"I *really* don't need this," she repeated.

"Need what?" her cousin asked, coming up behind her.

Standing together, the two girls presented a picture of opposites. Annie Bohay wore her long dark hair pulled back in a ponytail. She had a roundish face, with large brown eyes that gave her the look of an owl. Her taste in clothing leaned toward baggy jeans, running shoes, and T-shirts, none of which did much for her plump figure. In contrast, Liz was bony and thin, her own jeans tight, her black leather boots narrow-toed and scuffed, her T-shirt cut off at the shoulders and emblazoned with a screaming skull's head and the words "Mötley Crüe," her blond hair short and spiky.

"Any of this," she said, waving an arm that took in the whole of the farm.

"Aw, c'mon," Annie said. "It's not so bad."

Maybe not if you don't know any better, Liz said to herself, but she kept that thought tactfully to herself. After all, she was stuck here for the summer. No point in alienating her cousin, who was probably going to be her only contact with anyone even remotely her own age for the next three months.

Yesterday Annie had taken her on a tour of the property. They'd gone around a wooded point that jutted out into the lake until they came to a sandy beach—the swimming was good off the dock near the house, but the shore was all rocky—and then up to a plateau that Annie called "the Moon." The name made sense, Liz thought when they got there. The broad hilltop was a wide flat expanse of white marble limestone, spring-fed pools and junipers, enclosed by stands of apple trees, that had a real other-worldly feel to it.

From the Moon they went down another steep slope to a cow path leading back to the house. Instead of going back home when the path joined the lane, however, Annie had taken her the other way, up the lane with the cow pastures on either side, back to the road leading in to the farm. Here there were the rusted hulks of abandoned farm machinery and the remains of outbuildings and barns that looked, to Liz's city eyes, like the skeletons of ancient behemoths, vast wooden rib cages lifting from the fields to towering heights.

The grass on either side of the lane was cropped short and dotted with cow pies and thistles standing upright like steadfast little soldiers. At the very top of the hill, where the lane met the road under a canopy of enormous trees, was an old barn that had survived the years still mostly in one piece. It had a fieldstone foundation, gray weathered wood for its timbers and planking.

Inside it was mysteriously shadowed, with a thick flooring of old hay bales on one end, wooden boards on the other. What light entered came in through places where side boards were missing—sudden shafts of sunlight that made the shadows even darker. Liz found the place fascinating and creepy, all at the same time.

From there they headed straight down to the lake and followed the shore back home, and that was it. The end of the tour.

Surprisingly, Liz had enjoyed herself, exploring and wandering about, but that first evening after supper she'd looked out the window at the dark fields—it was *so* dark in the country—and realized that this was it. In one afternoon she'd done everything there was to do. So what was she going to do for the rest of the summer?

Because she was stuck here. Abandoned just like the rusted machinery and outbuildings up on the hill.

Things had been going from bad to worse for Liz over the past couple of years. On Christmas Eve, when she was twelve, her father had walked out on her and her mother, and they hadn't heard a word from him in the two years since. At first his departure had been a relief from all the shouting and fighting that had gone on, but then her mother started drinking, bringing boyfriends home—a different one every weekend—and Liz had ended up spending more time crashing with friends, or just wandering the streets, than at home.

Then her mother got a job in a hotel out in Banff.

"It's just for the summer," she'd explained to Liz. "I know it doesn't seem fair, but if you come with me, we'll end up spending all the extra money that I was hoping to save for us this winter. You don't mind staying with Aunt Emma, do you?"

At fourteen, Liz had long since realized, you don't have any rights. And there were times you just didn't argue. Especially not after what she'd overheard her mother telling her latest boyfriend just the night before.

"What do you do with a kid like her? She's out of control and I don't know what to do with her anymore. I've got to have some life of my own. Is that so very wrong?"

Naturally the boyfriend told her she was doing the right thing and, "C'mon, baby. Let's party now."

Right.

It hurt. She wasn't going to pretend it hadn't. But at least she hadn't cried.

I sure hope life gets better, Liz thought, standing with her cousin now in the front yard. Because if it doesn't, then I'm out of it. I can't take any more.

She could feel a burning behind her eyes, but she blinked fiercely until it went away. You've just got to tough it out, she told herself as she turned to look at Annie.

"So what do you want to do?" she asked her cousin.

Annie pointed to a heap of recently split firewood. "Well, Dad asked me to get that stacked today. Do you want to help?"

Liz's heart sank, but she kept a smile on her lips. Of course. They cooked on a wood stove, heated the place with it in the winter. Only why would anybody *choose* to live like this?

"Sure," she said. "Sounds like fun." She spoke the words cheerfully enough, but the look on her face added: About as much fun as banging my head against a wall.

* * *

There was really *nothing* to do in the evenings. The TV was a twelve-inch black and white that was kept in her aunt and uncle's bedroom. To watch it, you had to sit on the bed with them—not exactly Liz's scene, though Annie didn't seem to mind. Of course, they were her parents. Liz had brought some cassettes with her, but her boombox was broken and the amp here only worked on one channel. Besides, nobody cared much for Bon Jovi or Van Halen, much less the Cult or some hard-core heavy metal.

Definitely a musical wasteland.

That night, after staring at the walls for about as long as she could take, she announced that she was going out for a walk.

"I don't think that's such a good idea," her aunt began.

"Give the girl some slack," her uncle broke in. "How's she going to get into trouble out here? You just keep to the lane," he added to Liz. "It gets darker in the country than you'll be used to, and it's easy to get lost."

"I'll be careful," Liz said, willing to promise anything just to get out of there for a few moments.

Get lost, she thought when she was standing outside. Sure. As if there weren't a million side roads whichever way you turned. But it *was* dark. As soon as she left the yard and its spotlights, the night closed in on either side of her. Moonless, with clouds shrouding the stars, there wasn't much to see at all. A pinprickle of uneasiness stole up her spine.

She looked back at the well-lit yard; it didn't seem nearly so bad now. Kind of comforting, really. She was of half a mind to just plunk herself down in the front seat of the old car with its door hanging ajar, when she cocked her head. What was that sound?

She turned slowly and a glimmer of light caught her eye on top of the hill near the road. It came from the barn, a dim yellow glow against the darkness. And the sound was coming from there as well. A fiddle playing something that sounded a little like country music, only it wasn't quite the same. There was no way a bunch of hokey guys in rhinestone outfits were playing this stuff.

Curious, her fear forgotten, Liz started up the lane, crossing over the field when she was opposite the barn. She walked carefully, eyes on the ground as she tried to spot the cow pies. The fiddling was louder now, an infectious sound.

When she reached the outer wall of the barn, her nervousness returned. Who was out here, playing music in an old barn in the middle of the night? It was a little too weird. But having come this far . . .

She stood up on her tiptoes to peer through a broken slat and blinked with surprise. Everything was different inside. An oil lamp lit row upon row of wooden carnival horses, all leaning against one another along one side of the barn. Their polished finish gleamed in the lamplight, heads cocked as though they were listening to the music. Their painted eyes seemed to turn in her direction. Sitting facing them, with his back to her, was the man playing the fiddle. He had a floppy wide-brimmed black hat from which two chestnut and pink ribbons dangled. His clothes were so patched that it was hard to tell what their original color had been.

Close as she was, with the barn magnifying and echoing the music, it sounded to Liz as though there was more than one fiddler playing. She could also hear a tap-tapping sound which, she realized as she looked more closely, came from the man's boot heels where they kept the tune's rhythm on the old barn's wooden floor.

When the tune ended, Liz wondered if she should say hello or just hang out here, listening. It was kind of neat, this—

The man turned just then and all rational thought fled. Those weren't ribbons hanging down from under his hat. They were ears. Because his face was a rabbit's—big brown eyes, twitching nose, protruding jaws. The bizarreness of what she was seeing made her head spin.

She scrambled back, a scream building up in her throat. Turning, she fled, stumbled, fell. As she tried to scrabble to her feet a big black wave came washing over her and the world just went away as though someone had thrown its switch from on to off.

When she finally blinked her eyes open, she found herself lying on the grass in front of her uncle's house, screaming. The front door burst open and her uncle and aunt were there.

"There was . . . there was . . ." Liz tried to explain, pointing back toward the hilltop barn, but there were no lights up there now. No music drifting down the hill. And how had she gotten all the way down here anyway? The last thing she remembered was turning away from that grotesque face. . . .

She let her uncle help her into the house. Annie and her aunt put her to bed. Lying there in the upstairs loft that she was sharing with Annie, she could hear her aunt and uncle arguing down below.

"I tell you she's on drugs and I won't have it," her aunt was saying. "Not in this house. I know she's your sister's daughter, Tom, but—"

"She just got scared," her uncle said. "That's all. City kid.

Probably heard a 'coon rustling around in the brush and thought it was a bear."

"She's trouble. I don't see why we have to look at that sullen face all summer long."

"Because she's family," her uncle said, his voice angry. "That's why. We don't turn away family."

Liz pushed her hands against her ears, shutting out the voices. The features of that rabbit-faced fiddler rose up to haunt her as soon as she closed her eyes. I don't do drugs, she thought. So I've got to be going crazy.

* * *

Liz was very subdued in the following days. She tried to stay on her best behavior—smiling, helping out where she could. She was scared about a lot of things. If her aunt and uncle kicked her out, they sure weren't going to put her on the bus back to Toronto and let her go her own merry way. They'd call her mother, and her mother was going to be really mad. She'd threatened often enough to turn Liz over to Children's Aid because she just couldn't handle her. Who knew where she'd end up if that happened?

And then there was the fiddler.

He haunted her. At first, thinking back, she decided that she'd just seen some flaky tramp wearing a Halloween mask. Only the features had seemed too real—she had an inexplicable certainty that they *were* real—and there'd been something too weird about the whole situation for her to believe that she'd just made it up. She kept hearing his music, seeing his face.

Up on the Moon with Annie one day, she thought she heard

the strains of his fiddle again, but when she asked Annie if *she'd* heard anything, her cousin just gave her a strange look.

"Like what?" Annie asked.

"Some kind of music—fiddle music."

Annie grinned and leaned conspiratorially closer. "He hides in the trees, a big old bear of a man, smelling like a swamp and playing his fiddle, trying to lure unwary travelers close so that he can chew on their bones."

Liz shivered. "Really?"

"Of course not!" Annie said, shaking her head. "That's just a story the old-timers spread around. People sometimes hear music out in the woods around here—or at least they think they do. It's been going on for years, but it's just the wind in the trees or blowing through a hole in a fence or a barn."

"These old-timers . . . do they ever tell stories about an old tramp with the head of a rabbit playing that fiddle?"

"Get serious."

But Liz kept hearing the music. Or they'd be down by the lake and she would spot a rabbit looking at them from out of a cedar stand—a big rabbit, its fur the same odd chestnut color of the fiddler's ears. Its eyes too human for comfort. Watching her. Considering.

She *had* to be going crazy.

Finally she just couldn't take it anymore. A week after the night she'd first seen him, she waited until everybody else had turned in, then got dressed and crept out of the house. Looking up the hill to the barn, she could see the dull glow of lantern light coming from between its broken sideboards, but there was no music. Chewing her lip, she started up the hill.

When she reached the barn she had to stand for a long moment, trying to calm the rapid drum of her heartbeat.

This is nuts, the sensible part of her said.

Yeah, she thought. I know. But I've got to see it through.

Taking a deep breath, she walked around to the side of the barn that faced the road and stepped in through the doorway.

Except for the lack of music, it was all the same as it had been the other night. The oil lamp hanging from a crossbeam, throwing off its yellow light. The rows of wooden carnival horses. The fiddler, his instrument set down on a bale of hay beside him, was still dressed in his raggedy patched clothes. His floppy hat lying beside his fiddle. He was carving a piece of wood with a long sharp knife and looked up to where she stood, not saying a word.

Trying not to look at the knife, Liz swallowed dryly. Now that she was here, she didn't know why she'd come. That wasn't a mask he was wearing. It was real. The twitch of the nose. The sly look in those eyes.

"Wh-what do you . . . want from me?" she managed finally.

The fiddler stopped carving. "What makes you think I want anything?"

"I . . . you . . . you're haunting me. Everywhere I turn, I see your face. Hear your music."

The fiddler shrugged. "That's not so strange. I live around here. Why shouldn't we meet in passing?"

"Nobody else sees you."

"Maybe they're not looking properly. You new people are like that a lot."

"New people?"

The rabbit-man grinned. "That's what we call you." The grin

faded. "We're the ones that were here first. Everything changed when you came."

"What's your name?"

"Is a name so important?"

"Sure. Or how does anybody know who you are?"

"I know who I am, and that's enough."

Oddly enough, the more they talked, the more at ease Liz began to feel. It was like being in a dream where, because of its context, you didn't question anything. The weirdest things made sense. She sat down on a broad wooden beam across from the fiddler, her feet dangling, heels tapping against the wood.

"But what do other people call you?" she asked.

"Your people or my people?"

"Whichever."

For a long moment the fiddler said nothing. He took out a tobacco pouch and rolled a cigarette, lit it. Gray-blue smoke wreathed around his head when he exhaled.

"Let me tell you a story," he said. "There was once a girl who lived with her parents in a house in a city. One day her father went away and never came back and she thought it was because of her. Her mother had a picture in her head as to what the girl should be and she never let up trying to fit the girl's odd angles into the perfect mold she had sitting there in her head, and the girl thought because she didn't fit, that was her fault too.

"But she had a will of her own, and maybe she didn't know exactly what she wanted to be, but she wanted to be able to find out on her own what it was, not have everyone else tell her what it should be. So when someone said one thing, she did another.

She wore a frown so much that she forgot how to smile. And all the time she was carrying around this baggage in her head. Useless stuff.

"The baggage was like the rot that gets into an old tree sometimes. Eventually it just ate her away and there was nothing left of her that she could call her own. On that day, the people around her put her in a box and stuck her in the ground and that's where she is to this day."

Liz stared at him. A coldness sat in her chest, making it hard to breathe.

"You . . . you're talking about me," she said. "About what I've been . . . what's going to happen to me."

The fiddler shrugged. "It's just a story."

"But I can't help it. Nobody ever gives me a chance."

"The old people—my people—we make our own chances."

"Easy for you to say. You're not fourteen with everybody running your life. I don't have any rights."

"Everybody's got rights. Take responsibility for what's yours, and let the rest slide. It's not always easy, but it's not that hard once you learn the trick of it."

"But it hurts."

The fiddler nodded. "I know."

Liz stared down at her boots, trying to understand what was going on. The fiddler carefully butted out his cigarette and put the dead butt in his pocket. Picking up his instrument, he began to play.

Liz heard things in that music. Her father's voice, her mother's voice. Her aunt, her teachers. The policeman who'd caught her shoplifting. Everybody saying she was no good until she began to believe it herself, until she wore the part and made it true.

But when she closed her eyes and really listened to the music, images flooded her mind. She saw her uncle's farm as a place where two worlds met. One world was that of the new people, her people; the other was that of those who'd been here first. The old people, the first people.

Lost things from her world found a home in the world of the old people, the music told her. And in this part of that old world their keeper was a man with the face of a rabbit who didn't have a name. He looked after the lost things. Like the carousel horses, sleeping at night, prancing through the fields by day. Liz knew she couldn't see them in the barn when she was in her own world, but they were here all the same. The old people made the lost welcome—for some it became their home; for others it was a resting place until they could go on again.

Lost things. Lost people. Like her.

It was a kind of magic—maybe real, maybe not, but that didn't matter. They were what they were, just like she had to be what she was. The best she that she could be—not the image that others had of her. Not the she weighted down with a baggage of anger and guilt.

She blinked when the music stopped. Looking up, she saw that the fiddler had laid aside his instrument once more. He had his knife out again and had gone back to carving the piece of wood he'd been working on when she first arrived.

"What kind of music is that?" she asked.

"I heard it from the first new people who came here—got my fiddle from one of them."

It had a sound like nothing Liz had ever heard before. It had a depth to it. Where heavy metal just walled away her feelings behind its headbanging thunder, this music seemed to draw those feelings out so that she could deal with them instead.

"It sounds really . . . special," she said.

The fiddler nodded. "Needs something more, though." He held up the carving and studied it in the lamplight. "Looks about right." Taking a twin to it from his pocket, he held the two curved pieces of wood between his fingers and moved his arm in a shaking motion. The pieces of wood rattled rhythmically against each other, sending up a clickity-clack that echoed comfortably in the old barn.

"Here," he said, handing them over to her and showing her how to hold them. "You give it a try."

"What are they?"

"Bones. Wooden bones. They're usually made from ribs of animals, but I like the sound of the wood, so I make them from the ribs of the old barns instead."

When Liz tried to copy his movement, one of the bones fell from her hand. She gave an embarrassed shrug. Picking up the fallen one, she started to hand them back to the fiddler, but he shook his head.

"I can't make them work," she said.

"That's because you've hardly given them a try. Take them with you. Practice. It's like everything else—takes a little work to make it go right."

Like life, Liz thought. She closed her fingers around the bones.

"All right," she said. "I will."

The fiddler smiled. "That's right. Build on the hurt. Let it temper who you become instead of wearing you down. It's not always easy, but it's—"

"Not that hard once you learn the trick of it?"

"Exactly. Time you were going."

"But—" Liz began.

Before she could finish, she felt a sense of vertigo. She shut her eyes. When she opened them again, she was standing in front of her uncle's house, blinking in the spotlights that lit up the yard, a pair of wooden bones clutched in her hand. She looked up to the old barn, dark and quiet on the top of the hill.

A dream . . . ? she asked herself. Had it all been just a dream? But she still had these. She lifted her hand, looking at the gleam of the wooden bones she was still holding.

"Will I ever see you again?" she asked.

"Look for me, and I'll be there," a voice said softly in her ear. "Listen, and you'll hear me."

She started and turned sharply, but there was no one there. Placing the bones between her fingers the way he'd shown her, she gave an experimental shake of her hand. Still nothing. But she wasn't going to give up. Not with these. Not with anything.

OTHERWORLDS:
Past and Future

OTHERWORLDS: PAST AND FUTURE

When I first began to write, I knew I wanted to write fantasy, but I thought fantasy could only take place in a secondary world setting—somewhere other than the world we all inhabit. I learned that wasn't true as I continued to stretch and grow as a writer, and eventually found myself spending all of my time writing stories set in the here and now, with the fantasy element only stopping by for a visit.

I call what I write now "mythic fiction"—a term that my friend Terri Windling and I decided to use for our work, feeling that if our stories were going to be put in a genre (as fantasy usually is), it might as well be one we choose for ourselves.

This is what we mean by mythic fiction: stories that take place in more mainstream settings that use the material of myths, folk tales, and folklore to illuminate their themes. For more about it, and a site that's simply a wonderful collection of stories, art, and dialogue, you should visit the artists' collective that Terri has created on the Internet: www.endicott-studio.com.

The Graceless Child

I am not a little girl anymore.
And I am grateful and lighter
for my lessened load.
I have shouldered it.
        —Ally Sheedy,
            from "A Man's World"

TETCHIE MET THE TATTOOED MAN THE NIGHT THE WILD dogs came down from the hills. She was waiting in among the roots of a tall old gnarlwood tree, waiting and watching as she did for an hour or two every night, nested down on the mossy ground with her pack under her head and her mottled cloak wrapped around her for warmth. The leaves of the gnarlwood had yet to turn, but winter seemed to be in the air that night.

She could see the tattooed man's breath cloud about him, white as pipe smoke in the moonlight. He stood just beyond the spread of the gnarlwood's twisted boughs, in the shadow of the lone standing stone that shared the hilltop with Tetchie's tree. He had a forbidding presence, tall and pale, with long fine hair the color of bone tied back from his high brow. Above his leather trousers he was bare-chested, the swirl of his tattoos crawling across his blanched skin like pictographic insects. Tetchie couldn't read, but she knew enough to recognize that the dark blue markings were runes.

She wondered if he'd come here to talk to her father.

Tetchie burrowed a little deeper into her moss and cloak nest at the base of the gnarlwood. She knew better than to call attention to herself. When people saw her, it was always the same. At best she was mocked, at worst beaten. So she'd learned to hide. She became part of the night, turned to the darkness, away from the sun. The sun made her skin itch and her eyes tear. It seemed to steal the strength from her body until she could only move at a tortoise crawl.

The night was kinder and protected her as her mother once had. Between the teachings of the two, she'd long since learned a mastery over how to remain unseen, but her skills failed her tonight.

The tattooed man turned slowly until his gaze was fixed on her hiding place.

"I know you're there," he said. His voice was deep and resonant; it sounded to Tetchie like stones grinding against each other, deep underhill, the way she imagined her father's voice would sound when he finally spoke to her. "Come out where I can see you, trow."

Shivering, Tetchie obeyed. She pushed aside the thin protection of her cloak and shuffled out into the moonlight on stubby legs. The tattooed man towered over her, but then so did most folk. She stood three and a half feet high, her feet bare, the soles callused to a rocky hardness. Her skin had a grayish hue and her features were broad and square, as though chiseled from rough stone. The crudely fashioned tunic she wore as a dress hung like a sack from her stocky body.

"I'm not a trow," she said, trying to sound brave.

Trows were tall, trollish creatures, not like her at all. She didn't have the height.

The tattooed man regarded her for so long that she began to fidget under his scrutiny. In the distance, from two hills over and beyond the town, she heard a plaintive howl that was soon answered by more of the same.

"You're just a child," the tattooed man finally said.

Tetchie shook her head. "I'm almost sixteen winters."

Most girls her age already had a babe or two hanging on to their legs as they went about their work.

"I meant in trow terms," the tattooed man replied.

"But I'm not—"

"A trow. I know. I heard you. But you've trow blood all the same. Who was your dame, your sire?"

What business is it of yours? Tetchie wanted to say, but something in the tattooed man's manner froze the words in her throat. Instead she pointed to the longstone that reared out of the dark earth of the hilltop behind him.

"The sun snared him," she said.

"And your mother?"

"Dead."

"At childbirth?"

Tetchie shook her head. "No, she . . . she lived long enough . . . "

To spare Tetchie from the worst when she was still a child. Hanna Lief protected her daughter from the townsfolk and lived long enough to tell her, one winter's night when the ice winds stormed through the town and rattled the loose plank walls of the shed behind the Cotts Inn where they lived, "Whatever they tell you, Tetchie, whatever lies you hear, remember this: I went to him willingly."

Tetchie rubbed at her eye with the thick knuckles of her hand.

"I was twelve when she died," she said.

"And you've lived—" the tattooed man waved a hand lazily to encompass the tree, the stone, the hills. "—here ever since?"

Tetchie nodded slowly, wondering where the tattooed man intended their conversation to lead.

"What do you eat?"

What she could gather in the hills and the woods below, what she could steal from the farms surrounding the town, what she could plunder from the midden behind the market square those rare nights that she dared to creep into the town. But she said none of this, merely shrugged.

"I see," the tattooed man said.

She could still hear the wild dogs howl. They were closer now.

* * *

Earlier that evening, a sour expression rode the face of the man who called himself Gaedrian as he watched three men approach his table in the Cotts Inn. By the time they had completed their passage through the inn's common room and reached him, he had schooled his features into a bland mask. They were merchants, he decided, and was half right. They were also, he learned when they introduced themselves, citizens of very high standing in the town of Burndale.

He studied them carelessly from under hooded eyes as they eased their respective bulks into seats at his table. Each was more overweight than the next. The largest was Burndale's mayor; not quite so corpulent was the elected head of the town guilds; the smallest was the town's sheriff, and he carried Gaedrian's weight and half again on a much shorter frame. Silk vests, stretched taut over obesity, were perfectly matched to flounced shirts and pleated trousers. Their boots were leather, tooled with intricate designs and buffed to a high polish. Jowls hung over stiff collars; a diamond stud gleamed in the sheriff's left earlobe.

"Something lives in the hills," the mayor said.

Gaedrian had forgotten the mayor's name as soon as it was spoken. He was fascinated by the smallness of the man's eyes and how closely set they were to each other. Pigs had eyes that were much the same, though the comparison, he chided himself, was insulting to the latter.

"Something dangerous," the mayor added.

The other two nodded, the sheriff adding, "A monster."

Gaedrian sighed. There was always something living in the hills; there were always monsters. Gaedrian knew better than most how to recognize them, but he rarely found them in the hills.

"And you want me to get rid of it?" he asked.

The town council looked hopeful. Gaedrian regarded them steadily for a long time without speaking.

He knew their kind too well. They liked to pretend that the world followed their rules, that the wilderness beyond the confines of their villages and towns could be tamed, laid out in as tidy an order as the shelves of goods in their shops, of books in their libraries. But they also knew that under the facade of their order, the wilderness came stealing on paws that echoed with the click of claw on cobblestone. It crept into their streets and their dreams and would take up lodging in their souls if they didn't eradicate it in time.

So they came to men such as himself, men who walked the border that lay between the world they knew and so desperately needed to maintain, and the world as it truly was beyond the cluster of their stone buildings, a world that cast long shadows of fear across their streets whenever the moon went behind a bank of clouds and their streetlamps momentarily faltered.

They always recognized him, no matter how he appeared among them. These three surreptitiously studied the backs of his hands and what they could see of the skin at the hollow of his throat where the collar of his shirt lay open. They were looking for confirmation of what their need had already told them he was.

"You have gold, of course?" he asked.

The pouch appeared as if by magic from the inside pocket of the mayor's vest. It made a satisfying clink against the wooden tabletop. Gaedrian lifted a hand to the table, but it was only to grip the handle of his ale flagon and lift it to his lips. He took a long swallow, then set the empty flagon down beside the pouch.

"I will consider your kind offer," he said.

He rose from his seat and left them at the table, the pouch still untouched. When the landlord met him at the door, he jerked a thumb back to where the three men sat, turned in their seats to watch him leave.

"I believe our good lord mayor was buying this round," he told the landlord, then stepped out into the night.

He paused when he stood outside on the street, head cocked, listening. From far off, eastward, over more than one hill, he heard the baying of wild dogs, a distant, feral sound.

He nodded to himself and his lips shaped what might pass for a smile, though there was no humor in the expression. The townsfolk he passed gave him uneasy glances as he walked out of the town, into the hills that rose and fell like the tidal swells of a heathered ocean, stretching as far to the west as a man could ride in three days.

* * *

"What . . . what are you going to do to me?" Tetchie finally asked when the tattooed man's silence grew too long for her.

His pale gaze seemed to mock her, but he spoke very respectfully, "I'm going to save your wretched soul."

Tetchie blinked in confusion. "But I . . . I don't—"

"Want it saved?"

"Understand," Tetchie said.

"Can you hear them?" the tattooed man asked, only confusing her more. "The hounds," he added.

She nodded uncertainly.

"You've but to say the word and I'll give them the strength to tear down the doors and shutters in the town below. Their teeth and claws will wreak the vengeance you crave."

Tetchie took a nervous step away from him.

"But I don't want anybody to be hurt," she said.

"After all they've done to you?"

"Mama said they don't know any better."

The tattooed man's eyes grew grim. "And so you should just . . . forgive them?"

Too much thinking made Tetchie's head hurt.

"I don't know," she said, panic edging into her voice.

The tattooed man's anger vanished as though it had never lain there burning in his eyes.

"Then what *do* you want?" he asked.

Tetchie regarded him nervously. There was something in how he asked that told her he already knew, that this was what he'd been wanting from her all along.

Her hesitation grew into a long silence. She could hear the dogs, closer than ever now, feral voices raised high and keening, almost like children crying in pain. The tattooed man's gaze bore down on her, forcing her to reply. Her hand shook as she lifted her arm to point at the longstone.

"Ah," the tattooed man said.

He smiled, but Tetchie drew no comfort from that.

"That will cost," he said.

"I . . . I have no money."

"Have I asked for money? Did I say one word about money?"

"You . . . you said it would cost. . . ."

The tattooed man nodded. "Cost, yes, but the coin is a dearer mint than gold or silver."

What could be dearer? Tetchie wondered.

"I speak of blood," the tattooed man said before she could ask. "Your blood."

His hand shot out and grasped her before she could flee.

Blood, Tetchie thought. She cursed the blood that made her move so slow.

"Don't be frightened," the tattooed man said. "I mean you no harm. It needs but a pinprick—one drop, perhaps three, and not for me. For the stone. To call him back."

His fingers loosened on her arm and she quickly moved away from him. Her gaze shifted from the stone to him, back and forth, until she felt dizzy.

"Mortal blood is the most precious blood of all," the tattooed man told her.

Tetchie nodded. Didn't she know? Without her trow blood, she'd be just like anyone else. No one would want to hurt her just because of who she was, of how she looked, of what she represented. They saw only midnight fears; all she wanted was to be liked.

"I can teach you tricks," the tattooed man went on. "I can show you how to be anything you want."

As he spoke, his features shifted until it seemed that there was a feral dog's head set upon that tattooed torso. Its fur was the same pale hue as the man's hair had been, and it still had his eyes, but it was undeniably a beast. The man was gone, leaving this strange hybrid creature in his place.

Tetchie's eyes went wide in awe. Her short, fat legs trembled until she didn't think they could hold her upright anymore.

"Anything at all," the tattooed man said, as the dog's head was replaced by his own features once more.

For a long moment, Tetchie could only stare at him. Her

blood seemed to sing as it ran through her veins. To be anything at all. To be normal . . . But then the exhilaration that filled her trickled away. It was too good to be true, so it couldn't be true.

"Why?" she asked. "Why do you want to help me?"

"I take pleasure in helping others," he replied.

He smiled. His eyes smiled. There was such a kindly air about him that Tetchie almost forgot what he'd said about the wild dogs, about sending them down into Burndale to hunt down her tormentors. But she did remember, and the memory made her uneasy.

The tattooed man seemed too much the chameleon for her to trust. He could teach her how to be anything she wanted to be. Was that why he could appear to be anything she wanted *him* to be?

"You hesitate," he said. "Why?"

Tetchie could only shrug.

"It's your chance to right the wrong played on you at your birth."

Tetchie's attention focused on the howling of the wild dogs as he spoke. To right the wrong . . .

Their teeth and claws will wreak the vengeance you crave.

But it didn't have to be that way. She meant no one ill. She just wanted to fit in, not hurt anyone. So, if the choice was hers, she could simply choose not to hurt people, couldn't she? The tattooed man couldn't *make* her hurt people.

"What . . . what do I have to do?" she asked.

The tattooed man pulled a long silver needle from where it had been stuck in the front of his trousers.

"Give me your thumb," he said.

* * *

Gaedrian scented trow as soon as he left Burndale behind him. It wasn't a strong scent, more a promise than an actuality at first, but the farther he got from the town, the more pronounced it grew. He stopped and tested the wind, but it kept shifting, making it difficult for him to pinpoint its source. Finally he stripped off his shirt, letting it fall to the ground.

He touched one of the tattoos on his chest and a pale blue light glimmered in his palm when he took his hand away. He freed the glow into the air where it turned slowly, end on shimmering end. When it had given him the source of the scent, he snapped his fingers and the light winked out.

More assured now, he set off again, destination firmly in mind. The townsfolk, he realized, had been accurate for a change. A monster did walk the hills outside Burndale tonight.

* * *

Nervously, Tetchie stepped forward. As she got closer to him, the blue markings on his chest seemed to shift and move, rearranging themselves into a new pattern that was as indecipherable to her as the old one had been. Tetchie swallowed thickly and lifted her hand, hoping it wouldn't hurt. She closed her eyes as he brought the tip of the needle to her thumb.

"There," the tattooed man said a moment later. "It's all done."

Tetchie blinked in surprise. She hadn't felt a thing. But now that the tattooed man had let go of her hand, her thumb started to ache. She looked at the three drops of blood that lay in the tattooed man's palm like tiny crimson jewels. Her knees went weak again, and this time she did fall to the ground. She felt hot and flushed, as though she were up and abroad at high noon, the sun broiling down on her, stealing her ability to move.

Slowly, slowly, she lifted her head. She wanted to see what happened when the tattooed man put her blood on the stone, but all he did was smile down at her and lick three drops with a tongue that seemed as long as a snake's, with the same kind of a fork at its tip.

"Yuh . . . nuh . . ."

Tetchie tried to speak—What have you done to me? she wanted to say—but the words turned into a muddle before they left her mouth. It was getting harder to think.

"When your mother was so kindly passing along all her advice to you," he said, "she should have warned you about not trusting strangers. Most folk have little use for your kind, it's true."

Tetchie thought her eyes were playing tricks on her, then realized that the tattooed man must be shifting his shape once more. His hair grew darker as she watched, his complexion deepened. No longer pale and wan, he seemed to bristle with sorcerous energy now.

"But then," the tattooed man went on, "they don't have the knowledge I do. I thank you for your vitality, halfling. There's nothing so potent as mortal blood stirred in a stew of faerie. A pity you won't live long enough to put the knowledge to use."

He gave her a mocking salute, fingers tipped against his brow, then away, before turning his back on her. The night swallowed him.

Tetchie fought to get to her own feet, but she just wore herself out until she could no longer even lift her head from the ground. Tears of frustration welled in her eyes. What had he done to her? She'd seen it for herself, he'd taken no more than three drops of her blood. But then why did she feel as though he'd taken it all?

She stared up at the night sky, the stars blurring in her gaze, spinning, spinning, until finally she just let them take her away.

* * *

She wasn't sure what had brought her back, but when she opened her eyes, it was to find that the tattooed man had returned. He crouched over her, concern for her swimming in his dark eyes. His skin had regained its almost colorless complexion, his hair was bone white once more. She mustered what little strength she had to work up a gob of saliva and spat in his face.

The tattooed man didn't move. She watched the saliva dribble down his cheek until it fell from the tip of his chin to the ground beside her.

"Poor child," he said. "What has he done to you?"

The voice was wrong, Tetchie realized. He'd changed his voice now. The low grumble of stones grinding against each other deep underhill had been replaced by a soft melodious tonality that was comforting on the ear.

He touched the fingers of one hand to a tattoo high on his shoulder, waking a blue glow that flickered on his fingertips. She flinched when he touched her brow with the hand, but the contact of blue fingers against her skin brought an immediate easing to the weight of her pain. When he sat back on his haunches, she found she had the strength to lift herself up from the ground.

Her gaze spun for a moment, then settled down. The new perspective helped stem the helplessness she'd been feeling.

"I wish I could do more for you," the tattooed man said.

Tetchie merely glared at him, thinking, Haven't you done enough?

The tattooed man gave her a mild look, head cocked slightly as though listening to her thoughts.

"He calls himself Nallorn on this side of the Gates," he said finally, "but you would call him Nightmare, did you meet him in the land of his origin, beyond the Gates of Sleep. He thrives on pain and torment. We have been enemies for a very long time."

Tetchie blinked in confusion. "But . . . you. . . ."

The tattooed man nodded. "I know. We look the same. We are brothers, child. I am the elder. My name is Dream; on this side of the Gates I answer to the name Gaedrian."

"He . . . your brother . . . he took something from me."

"He stole your mortal ability to dream," Gaedrian told her. "Tricked you into giving it freely so that it would retain its potency."

Tetchie shook her head. "I don't understand. Why would he come to me? I'm no one. I don't have any powers or magics that anyone could want."

"Not that you can use yourself, perhaps, but the mix of trow and mortal blood creates a potent brew. Each drop of such blood is a talisman in the hands of one who understands its properties."

"Is he stronger than you?" Tetchie asked.

"Not in the land beyond the Gates of Sleep. There I am the elder. The Realms of Dream are mine and all who sleep are under my rule when they come through the Gates." He paused, dark eyes thoughtful, before adding, "In this world, we are more evenly matched."

"Nightmares come from him?" Tetchie asked.

Gaedrian nodded. "It isn't possible for a ruler to see all the parts of his kingdom at once. Nallorn is the father of lies. He creeps into sleeping minds when my attention is distracted elsewhere and makes a horror of healing dreams."

He stood up then, towering over her.

"I must go," he said. "I must stop him before he grows too strong."

Tetchie could see the doubt in his eyes and understood then that though he knew his brother to be stronger than him, he would not admit to it, would not turn from what he saw as his duty. She tried to stand, but her strength still hadn't returned.

"Take me with you," she said. "Let me help you."

"You don't know what you ask."

"But I want to help."

Gaedrian smiled. "Bravely spoken, but this is war and no place for a child."

Tetchie searched for the perfect argument to convince him, but couldn't find it. He said nothing, but she knew as surely as if he'd spoken why he didn't want her to come. She would merely slow him down. She had no skills, only her night sight and the slowness of her limbs. Neither would be of help.

During the lull in their conversation when that understanding came to her, she heard the howling once more.

"The dogs," she said.

"There are no wild dogs," Gaedrian told her. "That is only the sound of the wind as it crosses the empty reaches of his soul." He laid a hand on her head, tousled her hair. "I'm sorry for the hurt that's come to you with this night's work. If the fates are kind to me, I will try to make amends."

Before Tetchie could respond, he strode off, westward. She tried to follow, but could barely crawl after him. By the time she reached the crest of the hill, the longstone rearing above her, she saw Gaedrian's long legs carrying him up the side of the next hill. In the distance, blue lightning played, close to the ground.

Nallorn, she thought.

He was waiting for Gaedrian. Nallorn meant to kill the dreamlord and then he would rule the land beyond the Gates of Sleep. There would be no more dreams, only nightmares. People would fear sleep, for it would no longer be a haven. Nallorn would twist its healing peace into pain and despair.

And it was all her fault. She'd been thinking only of herself. She'd wanted to talk to her father, to be normal. She hadn't known who Nallorn was at the time, but ignorance was no excuse.

"It doesn't matter what others think of you," her mother had told her once, "but what you think of yourself. Be a good person and no matter how other people will talk of you, what they say can only be a lie."

They called her a monster and feared her. She saw now that it wasn't a lie.

She turned to the longstone that had been her father before the sun had snared him and turned him to stone. Why couldn't that have happened to her before all of this began, why couldn't she have been turned to stone the first time the sun touched her? Then Nallorn could never have played on her vanity and her need, would never have tricked her. If she'd been stone . . .

Her gaze narrowed. She ran a hand along the rough surface of the standing stone, and Nallorn's voice spoke in her memory.

I speak of blood.

It needs but a pinprick—one drop, perhaps three, and not for me. For the stone. To call him back.

To call him back.

Nallorn had proved there was magic in her blood. If he hadn't lied, if . . . *Could* she call her father back? And if he did return, would he listen to her? It was night, the time when a trow was strongest. Surely when she explained, her father would use that strength to help Gaedrian?

A babble of townsfolk's voices clamored up through her memory.

A trow'll drink your blood as sure as look at you.

Saw one I did, sitting up by the boneyard, and wasn't he chewing on a thighbone he'd dug up?

The creatures have no heart.

No soul.

They'll feed on their own, if there's no other meat to be found.

No, Tetchie told herself. Those were the lies her mother had warned her against. If her mother had loved the trow, then he couldn't have been evil.

Her thumb still ached where Nallorn had pierced it with his long silver pin, but the tiny wound had closed. Tetchie bit at it until the salty taste of blood touched her tongue. Then she squeezed her thumb, smearing the few drops of blood that welled up against the rough surface of the stone.

She had no expectations, only hope. She felt immediately weak, just as she had when Nallorn had taken the three small drops of blood from her. The world began to spin for the second time that night, and she started to fall once more, only this time she fell into the stone. The hard surface seemed to have turned to the consistency of mud and it swallowed her whole.

* * *

When consciousness finally returned, Tetchie found herself lying with her face pressed against hard-packed dirt. She lifted her head, squinting in the poor light. The longstone was gone, along with the world she knew. For as far as she could see, there was only a desolate wasteland, illuminated by a sickly twilight for which she could discover no source. It was still the landscape she knew; the hills and valleys had the same contours as those that lay west of Burndale, but it was all changed. Nothing seemed to grow here anymore; nothing lived at all in this place, except for her, and she had her doubts about that as well.

If this was a dead land, a lifeless reflection of the world she knew, then might she not have died to reach it?

Oddly enough, the idea didn't upset her. It was as though, having seen so much that was strange already tonight, nothing more could surprise her.

When she turned to where the old gnarlwood had been in her world, a dead tree stump stood. It was no more than three times her height, the area about it littered with dead branches.

The main body of the tree had fallen away from where Tetchie knelt, lying down the slope.

She rose carefully to her feet, but the dizziness and weakness she'd felt earlier had both fled. In the dirt at her feet, where the longstone would have stood in her world, there was a black pictograph etched deeply into the soil. It reminded her of the tattoos that she'd seen on the chests of the dreamlord and his brother, as though it had been plucked from the skin of one of them, enlarged and cast down on the ground. Goose bumps traveled up her arms.

She remembered what Gaedrian had told her about the land he ruled, how the men and women of her world could enter it only after passing through the Gates of Sleep. She'd been so weak when she offered her blood to the longstone, her eyelids growing so heavy. . . .

Was this all just a dream, then? And if so, what was its source? Did it come from Gaedrian, or from his brother Nallorn at whose bidding nightmares were born?

She went down on one knee to look more closely at the pictograph. It was a bit like a man with a tangle of rope around his feet and lines standing out from his head as though his hair stood on end. She reached out with one cautious finger and touched the tangle of lines at the foot of the rough figure. The dirt was damp there. She rubbed her finger against her thumb. The dampness was oily to the touch.

Scarcely aware of what she was doing, she reached down again and traced the symbol, the slick oiliness letting her finger slide easily along the edged grooves in the dirt. When she came to the end, the pictograph began to glow. She stood quickly, backing away.

What had she done?

The blue glow rose into the air, holding to the shape that lay in the dirt. A faint rhythmic thrumming rose from all around her, as though the ground was shifting, but she felt no vibration underfoot. There was just the sound, low and ominous.

A branch cracked behind her, and she turned to the ruin of the gnarlwood. A tall shape stood outlined against the sky. She started to call out to it, but her throat closed up on her. And then she was aware of the circle of eyes that watched her from all sides of the hilltop, pale eyes that flickered with the reflection of the glowing pictograph that hung in the air where the longstone stood in her world. They were set low to the ground—feral eyes.

She remembered the howling of the wild dogs in her own world.

There are no wild dogs, Gaedrian had told her. *That is only the sound of the wind as it crosses the empty reaches of his soul.*

As the eyes began to draw closer, she could make out the triangular-shaped heads of the creatures they belonged to, the high-backed bodies with which they slunk forward.

Oh, why had she believed Gaedrian? She knew him no better than Nallorn. Who was to say that *either* of them was to be trusted?

One of the dogs rose up to its full height and stalked forward on stiff legs. The low growl that arose in his chest echoed the rumble of sound that her foolishness with the glowing pictograph had called up. She started to back away from the dog, but now another and a third stepped forward and there was no place to which she could retreat. She turned her gaze to the silent figure that stood in among the fallen branches of the gnarlwood.

"Puh—please," she managed. "I . . . I meant no harm."

The figure made no response, but the dogs growled at the sound of her voice. The nearest pulled its lips back in a snarl.

This was it, Tetchie thought. If she wasn't dead already in this land of the dead, then she soon would be.

But then the figure by the tree moved forward. It had a slow, shuffling step. Branches broke underfoot as it closed the distance between them.

The dogs backed away from Tetchie and began to whine uneasily.

"Be gone," the figure said.

Its voice was low and craggy, stone against stone, like that of the first tattooed man. Nallorn, the dreamlord's brother, who turned dreams into nightmares. It was a counterpoint to the deep thrumming that seemed to come from the hill under Tetchie's feet.

The dogs fled at the sound of the man's voice. Tetchie's knees knocked against each other as he moved closer still. She could see the rough chiseled shape of his features now, the shock of tangled hair, stiff as dried gorse, the wide bulk of his shoulders and torso, the corded muscle upon muscle that made up arms and legs. His eyes were sunk deep under protruding brows. He was like the first rough shaping that a sculptor might create when beginning a new work, face and musculature merely outlined rather than clearly defined as it would be when the sculpture was complete.

Except this sculpture wasn't stone, nor clay, nor marble. It was flesh and blood. And though he was no taller than a normal man, he seemed like a giant to Tetchie, towering over her as though the side of a mountain had pulled loose to walk the hills.

"Why did you call me?" he asked.

"C-call?" Tetchie replied. "But I . . . I didn't. . . ."

Her voice trailed off. She gazed on him with sudden hope and understanding.

"Father?" she asked in a small voice.

The giant regarded her in a long silence. Then slowly he bent down to one knee so that his head was level with hers.

"You," he said in a voice grown soft with wonder. "You are Hanna's daughter?"

Tetchie nodded nervously.

"*My* daughter?"

Tetchie's nervousness fled. She no longer saw a fearsome trow out of legend, but her mother's lover. The gentleness and warmth that had called her mother from Burndale to where he waited for her on the moors washed over her. He opened his arms and she went to him, sighing as he embraced her.

"My name's Tetchie," she said into his shoulder.

"Tetchie," he repeated, making a low rumbling song of her name. "I never knew I had a daughter."

"I came every night to your stone," she said, "hoping you'd return."

Her father pulled back a little and gave her a serious look.

"I can't ever go back," he said.

"But—"

He shook his head. "Dead is dead, Tetchie. I can't return."

"But this is a horrible place to have to live."

He smiled, craggy features shifting like a mountainside suddenly rearranging its terrain.

"I don't live here," he said. "I live . . . I can't explain how it is. There are no words to describe the difference."

"Is Mama there?"

"Hanna . . . died?"

Tetchie nodded. "Years ago, but I still miss her."

"I will . . . look for her," the trow said. "I will give her your love." He rose then, looming over her again. "But I must go now, Tetchie. This is unhallowed land, the perilous border that lies between life and death. Bide here too long—living or dead—and you remain here forever."

"But—"

Tetchie had wanted to ask him to take her with him to look for her mother, to tell him that living meant only pain and sorrow for her, but then she realized she was only thinking of herself again. She still wasn't sure that she trusted Gaedrian, but if he had been telling her the truth, then she had to try to help him. Her own life was a nightmare; she wouldn't wish for all people to share such a life.

"I need your help," she said, and told him then of Gaedrian and Nallorn, the war that was being fought between Dream and Nightmare that Nallorn could not be allowed to win.

Her father shook his head sadly. "I can't help you, Tetchie. It's not physically possible for me to return."

"But if Gaedrian loses . . ."

"That would be an evil thing," her father agreed.

"There must be *something* we can do."

He was silent for long moments then.

"What is it?" Tetchie asked. "What don't you want to tell me?"

"I can do nothing," her father said, "but you . . ."

Again he hesitated.

"What?" Tetchie asked. "What is it that I can do?"

"I can give you of my strength," her father said. "You'll be able to help your dreamlord then. But it will cost you. You will be more trow than ever, and remain so."

More trow? Tetchie thought. She looked at her father, felt the calm that seemed to wash in peaceful waves from his very presence. The townsfolk might think that a curse, but she no longer did.

"I'd be proud to be more like you," she said.

"You will have to give up all pretense of humanity," her father warned her. "When the sun rises, you must be barrowed under-hill or she'll make you stone."

"I already only come out at night," she said.

Her father's gaze searched hers and then he sighed.

"Yours has not been an easy life," he said.

Tetchie didn't want to talk about herself anymore.

"Tell me what to do," she said.

"You must take some of my blood," her father told her.

Blood again. Tetchie had seen and heard enough about it to last her a lifetime tonight.

"But how can you do that?" she asked. "You're just a spirit. . . ."

Her father touched her arm. "Given flesh in this half-world by your call. Have you a knife?"

When Tetchie shook her head, he lifted his thumb to his mouth and bit down on it. Dark liquid welled up at the cut as he held his hand out to her.

"It will burn," he said.

Tetchie nodded nervously. Closing her eyes, she opened her mouth. Her father brought his thumb down across her tongue. His blood tasted like fire, burning its way down her throat. She shuddered with the searing pain of it, eyes tearing so that even when she opened them, she was still blind.

She felt her father's hand on her head. He smoothed the tangle of her hair and then kissed her.

"Be well, my child," he said. "We will look for you, your mother and I, when your time to join us has come and you finally cross over."

There were a hundred things Tetchie realized that she wanted to say, but vertigo overtook her and she knew that not only was he gone but the empty world as well. She could feel grass under her, a soft breeze on her cheek. When she opened her eyes, the longstone reared up on one side of her, the gnarlwood on the other. She turned to look where she'd last seen the blue lightning flare before she'd gone into the stone.

There was no light there now.

She got to her feet, feeling invigorated rather than weak. Her night sight seemed to have sharpened; every sense was more alert. She could almost read the night simply through the pores of her skin.

The townsfolk were blind, she realized. *She* had been blind. They had all missed so much of what the world had to offer. But the townsfolk craved a narrower world, rather than a wider one, and she . . . she had a task yet to perform.

She set off to where the lightning had been flickering.

* * *

The grass was all burned away, the ground itself scorched on the hilltop that was her destination. She saw a figure lying in the dirt and hesitated, unsure as to who it was. Gaedrian or his brother? She moved cautiously forward until finally she knelt by the still figure. His eyes opened and looked upon her with a weak gaze.

"I was not strong enough," Gaedrian said, his voice still sweet and ringing, but much subdued.

"Where did he go?" Tetchie asked.

"To claim his own: the Land of Dream."

Tetchie regarded him for a long moment, then lifted her thumb to her mouth. It was time for blood again—but this would be the last time. Gaedrian tried to protest, but she pushed aside his hands and let the drops fall into his mouth: one, two, three. Gaedrian swallowed. His eyes went wide with an almost comical astonishment.

"Where . . . how . . . ?"

"I found my father," Tetchie said. "This is the heritage he left me."

Senses all more finely attuned, to be sure, but when she lifted an arm to show Gaedrian, the skin was darker, grayer than before and tough as bark. And she would never see the day again.

"You should not have—" Gaedrian began, but Tetchie cut him off.

"Is it enough?" she asked. "Can you stop him now?"

Gaedrian sat up. He rolled his shoulders, flexed his hands and arms, his legs.

"More than enough," he said. "I feel a hundred years younger."

Knowing him for what he was, Tetchie didn't think he was exaggerating. Who knew how old the dreamlord was? He would have been born with the first dream.

He cupped her face with his hands and kissed her on the brow.

"I will try to make amends for what my brother has done to you this night," he said. "The whole world owes you for the rescue of its dreams."

"I don't want any reward," Tetchie said.

"We'll talk of that when I return for you," Gaedrian said.

If you can find me, Tetchie thought, but she merely nodded in reply.

Gaedrian stood. One hand plucked at a tattoo just to one side of his breastbone and tossed the ensuing blue light into the air. It grew into a shimmering portal. Giving her one more grateful look, he stepped through. The portal closed behind him, winking out in a flare of blue sparks, like those cast by a fire when a log's tossed on.

Tetchie looked about the scorched hilltop, then set off back to Burndale. She walked its cobblestoned streets, one lone figure, dwarfed by the buildings, more kin to their walls and foundations than to those sleeping within. She thought of her mother when she reached the Cotts Inn and stood looking at the shed around back by the stables where they had lived for all of those years.

Finally, just as the dawn was pinking the horizon, she made her way back to the hill where she'd first met the tattooed men. She ran her fingers along the bark of the gnarlwood, then stepped closer to the longstone, standing on the east side of it.

It wasn't entirely true that she could never see the day again. She could see it, if only once.

Tetchie was still standing there when the sun rose and snared her, and then there were two standing stones on the hilltop keeping company to the old gnarlwood tree, one tall and one much smaller. But Tetchie herself was gone to follow her parents, a lithe spirit of a child finally, her gracelessness left behind in stone.

AS YOU'VE probably noticed by now, myths and folktales fascinate me, not only for their content, but for how they came to be. Though my stories usually juxtapose old mythic matter with the modern world, or enthusiastically embrace what Jan Harold Brunvand calls "Urban Legends"—contemporary folktales and myths—I've occasionally, as in the following story set long after a worldwide disaster, dabbled in the origins of myths as well.

I don't often work in a science fiction context—and really, this is more science fantasy, rather than being based upon any actual scientific speculation—but no writer wants to limit him- or herself to one kind of story. So, this is a rare excursion for me. The only other one that comes immediately to mind is my novel Svaha *(1989), which, come to think of it, might very well take place in the same futuristic setting as this story, albeit in a different city.*

A Tattoo on Her Heart

> *The world is too much with us.*
> —William Wordsworth
> *Myth is the natural and indispensable intermediate stage between unconscious and conscious cognition.* —Carl Jung, *Memories, Dreams, Reflections*

NIGHT FELL AND THE TRIBES HIT THE STREET.

Their yelps and howls filled the night air—a cacophony of mock beast sounds to match the beast masks that they wore. Underpinning the dissonance was the insistent rhythm of palms dancing across skin-headed drums, of hands banging sticks against each other, or against cans and sheets of metal. Mouths lipped whistles and flutes to cast out brittle handfuls of high skirling notes. Fingers plucked chords from oddly shaped guitarlike instruments, or else drew bows across tightly wound strings to wake weird yowls and moans.

The sound Catherine-wheeled between the tumbled-down tenements—a full moon madness of disconnected noise that hurt the ear and made melody nothing more than a vague memory. But then, slowly, the dissonance resolved into a kind of music. The dervishing whirls of masked figures that twisted and spun amidst the rubble became a set dance with patterned steps. Torches were cast into metal drums, the oiled paper and debris inside flaring to heights of two meters and better. The bobbing masks of the dancers appeared almost real in the sudden flickering light. Wood and metal frames, plastic and papier mâché coverings, the decorations of feather and coiled wires, shells and bottlecaps, lost their man-made origins and became mythic.

Jorey crouched in the shadows at the mouth of an alley, her homemade fetish clutched in one hot sweaty hand. Wide-eyed, she watched them.

Wolf and eagle, rat and salamander, bear and pigeon. And more. Raccoon and cricket, snake and cat, roach and sparrow. And still more.

Totems dancing in the dead streets of the city.

The tribes were calling up the past.

Not the past that had been—the truth of unemployment and hunger and overcrowded cities and fouled air and melting polar caps and limited nuclear exchange—but the past that lived in their hearts that told of how things might have been.

Of how things should have been.

A past where the shaman called up totems to lead the people out of their hell-bent demolition course to self-destruction, a past where the tribes at least had listened.

* * *

It was all make-believe, Auntie liked to say. It was all lies. But it kept them happy. And that was why the jackets allowed the tribes their revels. That was why they never came down out of their towers, weapons in hand, to put them down. Citizens didn't get hurt so long as they weren't on the streets on a revel night.

Jorey had been intrigued by the tribes from the first time she was old enough to sit perched high on a windowsill, and looked down on the dancing figures, the thin wail of their music rising up from the street to where she sat. It woke something in her. A need. A yearning. Nothing that could be put into words, but she knew instinctively that no matter what Auntie said, there was something important happening on the streets on a revel night.

"How do they know when it's going to happen?" she would ask Auntie.

There was no fixed night for a revel. Sometimes the moon was full, sometimes not. Sometimes weeks went by between them, sometimes they came two nights in a row.

Auntie only shook her head.

"You ask me," she said, "the jackets spray something in the air, that's what makes it happen. They see the hopeless anger building up until it's going to spill out of the streets and into their towers. So then, before it gets out of hand, they just lock up their citizens and let the night swallow the tribes with its craziness. It's a kind of safety valve."

"Did you never want to . . . you know, go out yourself?" Jorey asked.

Auntie gave her a withering look. "I'm poor, girl. Not crazy."

"But—"

"And I don't want to find you sneaking out some revel night. We're people. Human beings. Not animals."

* * *

Jorey slept in a locked room at nights and Auntie kept the key. But that didn't matter. Auntie had her own lies about the past and how things were. Jorey was her fourteen-year-old niece, but what was true once wasn't necessarily so anymore. Times had changed. There were no longer any schools or malls or playgrounds—not if poverty stole away your citizenship. Jorey spent most of her days on the street, and one of the first things she learned was how to pick a lock.

So now she was out here on revel night. Watching. Hoping.

She didn't have a totem, so she didn't have a mask. At least not a proper one. But she'd gone down to the clay field behind the old plastics factory and smeared white clay in her short hair, twisting and pulling out strands until they stood out straight from her head like a hedgehog's spikes. She'd dabbed it on her cheeks and temples as well—white stylized streaks like a street version of some vid singer's glamor lines.

Studying her reflection in a piece of broken glass, she realized that she actually looked like a dried-up old weed about to be blown apart by the wind. But it didn't matter. It was still a kind of mask.

And then there was her fetish.

* * *

Ricia said you needed a fetish to call your totem to you.

"Get yourself a little plastic bag," she'd told Jorey, "and fill it with bits of everything that means anything to you. You have to make it a focus—a distillation of everything that makes you *you*—so that the totem can find you when you call it to you."

Ricia was two years older than Jorey. She was a tall, striking young woman with mocha-colored skin and actually had a job—six hours a week at one of the restaurants in the towers. She watched the servitor belt, kitchen-side, guarding against the anomalies that the computer sometimes tossed out in place of a food order.

"Auntie says there's no such thing as totems," Jorey told her. "She says the revels are just something the jackets came up with so that we don't go too crazy."

Ricia only laughed. "What does she know?"

Being old didn't automatically make you wrong, Jorey thought.

"Doesn't make you right, either," Ricia said, knowing Jorey well enough to as much as read her mind.

* * *

Jorey's fetish bag was a used WaterPure tablet package. In it she'd put a tiny book wafer about riverside animals filched from the library; a hair from a horse's mane that came from the head of a doll that Auntie had given her; three real wooden buttons she'd found on the street; nail parings from the last time she'd trimmed her nails; a sliver of shimmery metal that Moakes swore was a true Shuttle Remnant and for which she'd traded two food credits and a cotton shammy; little bits of animals—a pigeon feather, the shiny delicate back of a cockroach, a dried rat's tail—not because she wanted any one of them for a totem, but because they were a part of her life; one tear, dropped onto a swatch of brightly colored cotton; the tip of an aloe leaf that Ricia had given her; and her prize possession—a cat's eye alley that Auntie said had once belonged to Jorey's father.

What would it call to her—just supposing totems were real?

Clutching the fetish, she looked out at where the tribes were still dancing in winding spiral lines between the fires, instruments sending up a wild clamor that, while it was recognizably music now, was a kind of music you'd never hear on a citizen vid. And they were singing, too. A boisterous, almost feral vocalizing that was wordless, but eloquent with meaning.

It woke a buzzing in her head—a not-quite whine that was more pleasant than not. The buzzing was immediately followed by a strange, indescribable sensation that skittered up her spine like scurrying roaches. Moakes had described tripping on wire to her once, and this, she realized, was what it must be like.

A feeling of dislocation from her body settled over her so that it was as though she was floating just above her body, apart from it, but a part of it still.

Her mind seemed to expand so that it not only encompassed her immediate surroundings, but went whispering and peeking and peering for blocks around her. Part of her viewed the group mind of the tribes as they reveled; part of her looked in on those like Auntie who hid away in their run-down buildings, minds closed against the strange reveling sorcery that rode the city air; and part of her—that part not yet connected to the revel, because she was still without a totem, she supposed—found the source of the revel.

A half-dozen jackets, hidden in a nearby building, black clothing making them almost invisible in the shadows except for the gleam and wink of the embroidered silver thread on their stylized jackets that shaped the symbol of the citizen security force of which they were members. Five of them—two women, three men—kept watch, gleaming weapons in hand. The sixth was bent over a machine on which tiny lights flickered and strobed. He adjusted dials and knobs with deft, graceful movements of his slender fingers, looking for all the world like a syntharp player standing center stage on a vid, concertoing and symphonying, an entire orchestra sampled and hidden away in the small flat black box that lay on his lap.

They all wore earplugs, though Jorey could hear no sound.

Auntie had been right, she realized, the thought coming to her in a detached, almost disinterested fashion. The revels did have their origin in the towers. But what stopped people like Auntie from hearing whatever it was that the jackets were calling up with their odd little machine?

Maybe you had to want to hear it?

Maybe you needed a totem?

But I hear it, she thought.

She *did* hear something. The revel spirit of the tribes had filled her, hadn't it, until her body strained and trembled to join the whirling figures in their winding dance. Her throat could feel the sting of their song as it escaped her lips, her hands beat a rhythmic tattoo against her thighs. . . .

She had wanted to hear it.

Could the technology of the towers be so refined that it could read peoples' minds? Or was it like Auntie had said the time Jorey asked her why the citizens let the rest of them live the way they did, eking out a hungry and poor existence in the dead streets of the city.

"They see us," Auntie had explained, "but we just don't register."

That was why Auntie and those like her didn't join the tribes in their revels. They heard whatever it was that the jackets' machines pumped into the city air on a revel night, but it just didn't register.

And that was why the tribes didn't pay any attention to the source of a revel night, to the black-jacketed man standing over his machine as it called up the dance.

Her consciousness narrowed until she was back near her body again. A masked figure stood over her—the weird features of a fly on top of a woman's body. Jorey fled back into her skin, wanting to bolt from the strange apparition, but wanting to stay at the same time. The figure reached out a hand to her, bug-head dipping low, the glass-glitter of her multifaceted eyes casting weird patterns of light into the alleyway.

"Come on, Jorey," the figure said.

She recognized Ricia's voice. She took her hand from her fetish and let the plastic bag bounce against her chest as Ricia drew her to her feet.

The dance lay inside her—its steps and its tune. A pattern that was now indelibly etched into her mind, tattooed on her heart. It didn't matter that it had its source in a small flat box manipulated by the clever fingers of some jacket. It was a part of her now, and she made it her own.

Laughing, she let Ricia lead her onto the street and there—

She just danced.

* * *

It was in the early hours of the morning that she finally collapsed where she'd been dancing, exhausted, but happy. She slept more peacefully than she'd ever slept before, feeling safe and warm, though a cold wind was frosting its way down the street. When she woke, dawn was a pale wash of yellow in the smoggy sky.

She found herself surrounded by the tribes. They were recognizably her neighbors now, masks set aside, humanity returned. As they rose from their makeshift beds, there was a sense of camaraderie in the air that was as unfamiliar as it was heady. People talked and joked among themselves as they gathered their masks and instruments and slowly made their way home.

"It's always like this," Ricia explained, as she walked Jorey back to Auntie's. "We're always so . . . close. Sometimes it lasts for days before the feeling fades. I wish it would never fade."

Jorey nodded. An indefinable exuberance still whistled and hummed in her veins.

"But then there's always the next revel," Ricia said with a

bright smile as they reached Auntie's door. She looked at Jorey, then added, "Did you find your totem?"

Jorey nodded again.

"Don't tell me," Ricia said before Jorey could speak. "Surprise me at the next revel."

Then she was off, heading down the street, dodging the refuse and rubble with a practiced stride, her mask swinging in one hand, tapping her flute against her thigh with the other.

Jorey watched her go. She fingered her fetish, smiling.

Auntie had been both right and wrong. The revels did originate in the towers, from the machines of the jackets, but it didn't turn people into animals. The city did that. The hunger and the poverty, the emptiness and uselessness of their lives . . . that was what pushed people apart until they lived in worlds where they barely registered to themselves, much less had time for their neighbors.

The revels connected people to each other again. It didn't make them animals; it reminded them of their humanity.

Jorey didn't doubt that all the jackets had in mind with the revels was to create a safety valve—just as Auntie had determined. Something to keep the poor in line so that their frustration and hunger and pain and anger wouldn't become so furious that they would rise to storm the towers. But the people had taken those nights and made them their own. Somewhere between jacket machine and tribal mind, a token—a promise—had been born, and on revel nights it blazed from candle flicker to solar flare.

It was a good thing. All it lacked was a way to keep the connection going beyond a revel night.

Had she found her totem? Ricia had asked her.

Jorey smiled and went inside to wash off the clay from her face and hair. When she'd scrubbed herself clean, she set about making her totem mask.

Under her hands, it came to life. Carved wood and plastic for its features, wire coils for hair. Painted lips.

A human face.

BORDERTOWN

BORDERTOWN

Fifty years from now, Elfland came back. It stuck a finger into a large city, creating a borderland between our world and that glittering realm with its elves and magic. As the years went by, the two worlds remained separate, co-existing only in that place where magic and reality overlap. A place called Bordertown.

* * *

That's the original premise as set up by Terri Windling, the creator and editor of the Bordertown series, with creative input from Mark Alan Arnold, and later from Delia Sherman. Once Terri had roughly sketched in the background, she let the rest of us in to play. (By us, I refer to the authors who filled the first volume of the series with their stories: Bellamy Bach, Steven R. Boyett, Ellen Kushner, and myself.) And we had some fun, because the shared world of Bordertown was different from other shared worlds. It had an edge, and a relevance to the here and now, that went beyond the image of a Mohawked elf in leathers riding through a gritty city street on a chopper.

The imagery was certainly fun—part Child ballad, part MTV—but what made Bordertown important to those of us who transcribed its stories, and to those of us who read them, was that it presented us with an opportunity to address modern concerns in a contemporary manner, while still getting to bounce riffs off each other's stories (in the best tradition of a musical jam), not to mention giving us a chance to play with the faerie of Elfland and the cu-

rious juxtapositioning of its magic against the gritty reality of Bordertown's rock'n'roll clubs, back alleys, and city streets.

Because, for all the distance in time from the present day, for all its magic which remains so shimmeringly impossible in our mundane world, Bordertown is still about the here and now. For all their trappings, the stories are about us, living in this world, as much as they are about the inhabitants of Bordertown.

THE STORY that follows originally appeared in Borderland (1986), the first of the Bordertown anthologies. Although they're all a little hard to find now, the subsequent volumes were: Life on the Border *(1991) and* The Essential Bordertown *(1998).*

There's a lot of music in this story, and that was one of the things that attracted me to Bordertown. I've played in bands for years, much longer than I've been writing for publication, and being able to make up bands and their repertoires, as well as have my characters jam with musicians from the stories written by the other authors, really added to the fun for me.

Much of the same thing happens at conventions when Mary Ann and I get together with some of the other Bordertown authors and editors and we have impromptu musical sessions.

You'll also find some slang in the story that's indigenous to Bordertown. Hopefully, most of it's obvious in context, but perhaps I should at least tell you that Bloods are pureblooded elves, rather intolerant of any one of mixed blood such as Manda.

Stick

Then to the Maypole haste away
For 'tis now our holiday.

—from "Staines Morris"
English traditional

STICK PAUSED BY HIS VINTAGE HARLEY AT THE SOUND OF A scuffle. Squinting, he looked for its source. The crumbling blocks of Soho surrounded him. Half-gutted buildings and rubble-strewn lots bordered either side of the street. There could be a hundred pairs of eyes watching him—from the ruined buildings, from the rusted hulks of long-abandoned cars—or there could be no one. There were those who claimed that ghosts haunted this part of Soho, and maybe they did, but it wasn't ghosts that Stick was hearing just now.

Some Bloods out Pack-bashing. Maybe some of the Pack out elf-bashing. But it was most likely some rats—human or elfin, it didn't matter which—who'd snagged themselves a runaway and were having a bit of what they thought was fun.

Runaways gravitated to Bordertown from the outside world, particularly to Soho, and most particularly to this quarter, where there were no landlords and no rent. Just the scavengers. And the rats. But they could be the worst of all.

Putting his bike back on its kickstand, Stick pocketed the elfin spell-box that fueled it.

Lubin growled softly from her basket strapped to the back of the bike—a quizzical sound.

"Come on," Stick told the ferret. He started across the street without looking to see if she followed.

Lubin slithered from the basket and crossed the road at Stick's heels. She was a cross between a polecat and a ferret, larger than either, with sharp pointed features and the lean build of the weasel family. When Stick paused in the doorway of the building from which the sounds of the scuffle were coming, she flowed over the toes of his boots and into its foyer, off to one side. Her hiss was the assailants' first hint that they were no longer alone.

They were three Bloods, beating up on a small unrecognizable figure that was curled up into a ball of tattered clothes at their feet. Their silver hair was dyed with streaks of orange and black; their elfin faces, when they looked up from their victim to see Stick standing in the doorway, were pale, skin stretched thin over high-boned features, silver eyes gleaming with malicious humor.

They were dressed all of a kind—three assembly-line Bloods in black leather jackets, frayed jeans, T-shirts, and motorcycle boots.

"Take a walk, hero," one of them said.

Stick reached up over his left shoulder and pulled out a sectional staff from its sheath on his back. With a sharp flick of his wrist, the three two-foot sections snapped into a solid staff, six feet long.

"I don't think so," he said.

"He don't think so," the first of the Bloods mocked.

"This here's our meat," a second said, giving their victim another kick. He reached inside his jacket, his hand reappearing with a switchblade. Grinning, he thumbed the button to spring it open.

Knives appeared in the hands of the other two—one from a wrist sheath. Stick didn't bother to talk. While they postured with their blades, he became a sudden blur of motion.

The staff spun in his hands, leaving broken wrists and airborne switchblades in its wake. A moment later, the Bloods were clutching mangled wrists to their chests. Stick wasn't even winded.

He made a short feint with the staff, and all three Bloods

jumped as though they'd been struck again. When he stepped toward their victim, they backed away.

"You're dead," one of them said flatly. "You hear me, Choc'let?"

Stick took a quick step toward them, and they fled. Shaking his head, he turned to look at where Lubin was snuffling around their prize.

It was a girl, and definitely a runaway, if the ragged clothes were anything to go by. Considering current Soho fashion, that wasn't exactly a telling point. But her being here . . . that was another story. She had fine pale features and spiked hair a mauve she was never born with.

Stick crouched down beside her, one hand grasping his staff and using it for balance. "You okay?" he asked.

Her eyelids flickered, then her silver eyes were looking into his.

"Aw, shit," Stick said.

No wonder those Bloods'd had a hard-on for her. If there was one thing they hated more than the Pack, it was a halfling. She wasn't really something he had time for either.

"Can you stand?" he asked.

A delicate hand reached out to touch his. Pale lashes fluttered ingenuously. She started to speak, but then her eyes winked shut and her head drooped against the pile of rags where she'd been cornered by the Bloods.

"Shit!" Stick muttered again. Breaking down his staff, he returned it to its sheath.

Lubin growled and he gave her a baleful look.

"Easy for you to side with her," he said as he gathered the frail halfling in his arms. "She's probably related to you as well as the Bloods."

Lubin made querulous noises in the back of her throat as she followed him back to the bike.

"Yeah, yeah, I'm taking her already."

As though relieved of a worry, the ferret made a swift ascent onto the Harley's seat and slipped into her basket. Stick reinserted his spell-box, balanced his prize on the defunct gas tank in front of him, and kicked the bike into life. He smiled. The bike's deep-throated roar always gave him a good feeling. Putting it into gear, he twisted the throttle and the bike lunged forward. The girl's body was only a vague weight cradled against his chest. The top of her head came to the level of his nose.

For some reason, he thought she smelled like apple blossoms.

* * *

She woke out of an unpleasant dream to a confused sense of dislocation. Dream shards were superimposed on unfamiliar surroundings. Grinning Blood faces, shattered like the pieces of a mirror, warred with a plainly furnished room and a long-haired woman who was sitting on the edge of the bed where she lay. She closed her eyes tightly, opened them again. This time only the room and the woman were there.

"Feeling a little rough around the edges?" the woman asked. "Try some of this."

Sitting up, she took the tea.

"Where am I? The last thing I remember . . . there was this black man. . . . "

"Stick."

"That's his name?"

The woman nodded.

"Is he . . . " Your man, she thought. "Is he around?"

"Stick's not much for company."

"Oh. I just wanted to thank him."

The woman smiled. "Stick's great for making enemies, but not too good at making friends. He sticks—" she smiled "—to himself mostly."

"But he helped me. . . . "

"I didn't say he wasn't a good man. I don't think anyone really knows what to make of him. But he's got a thing for runaways. He picks them up when they're in trouble—and usually dumps them off with me."

"I've heard his name before."

"Anyone who lives long enough in Bordertown eventually runs into him. He's like Farrel Din—he's just always been around." The woman watched her drink her tea in silence for a few moments, then asked: "Have you got a name?"

"Manda. Amanda Woodsdatter."

"Any relation to Maggie?"

"I'm her little sister."

The woman smiled. "Well, my name's Mary and this place you've been dumped is the home of the Horn Dance."

"No kidding? Those guys that ride around with the antlers on their bikes?"

"That's one way of describing us, I suppose."

"Jeez, I . . . "

Looking at Mary, Manda's first thought had been that she'd ended up in some old hippie commune. There were still a few of them scattered here and there through Bordertown and on the Borders. Mary's long blond hair—like one of the ancient folk singers Manda had seen pictures of—and her basic Whole Earth Mother wardrobe of a flowered ankle-length dress, feather earrings, and the strands of multicolored beaded necklaces around her neck didn't exactly jibe with what Manda knew of the Horn Dance.

In ragged punk clothing, festooned with patches and colored ribbons, their bikes sporting stag's antlers in front of their handlebars, the Horn Dance could be seen cruising anywhere from the banks of the Mad River to Fare-you-well Park. They were also a band, playing music along the lines of Eldritch Steel—a group that her sister had played with that had mixed traditional songs with the hard-edged sound of punk, and only lasted the one night. Unlike Eldritch Steel, though, the Horn Dance was entirely made up of humans. Which was probably the reason they were still around.

Eldritch Steel's first and only gig had been in Farrel Din's Dancing Ferret and had sparked a brawl between the Pack and the Blood that had left the place in shambles. Farrel Din, needless to say, hadn't been pleased. The band broke up, lead singer Wicker disappearing while the rest of the group had gone their separate ways.

"What are you thinking of?" Mary asked.

Manda blinked, then grinned sheepishly. "Mostly that you don't look as punky as I thought you guys were."

"I'm the exception," Mary said. "Wait'll you meet Teaser, or Oss."

"Yeah, well . . . " Manda looked around the room until she spotted her clothes on a chair by the door.

She wasn't so sure that she'd be meeting anyone. There were things to do, places to go, people to meet. Yeah. Right.

"Do you need a place to stay?" Mary asked.

"No, I'm okay."

"Look, we don't mind if you hang out for a few days. But there's a couple of things I'd like to know."

"Like?"

"You're not from the Hill, are you?"

"Why?"

"Runaways from the Hill can be a problem. Up there, they've got ways of tracking people down and we don't need any trouble with elves."

"They're not like the Bloods up on the Hill," Manda said. "But like I told you, I'm Maggie's little sister. We grew up in Soho."

Mary smiled. "And so you know your way around."

"I lost my shades—that's all. Those Bloods were out to kick ass and when they caught a glam of my eyes, that was it."

"Stick told me—three to one are never good odds."

Manda shrugged. "I'm not a fighter, you know?"

"Sure. And what about your folks—are they going to come looking?"

"I'm on my own."

"Okay. We just like to know where we stand when irritated people come knocking on the door—that's all." She stood up from the bed, then fished in her pocket, coming up with a pair of sunglasses. "I thought you might like another pair—just to save you from the hassle you had last night being repeated."

"Thanks. Listen, I'll just get dressed and be on my way. I don't want to be a pain."

"It's no problem."

"Yeah, well . . . " She hesitated, then asked, "Where can I find Stick?"

"You don't want to mess with him, Manda. He's great to have around when there's trouble, but when things are going fine he just gets antsy."

"I want to thank him, that's all."

Mary sighed. "You know the old museum up by Fare-you-well Park?"

"Sure. That's his place?"

Mary nodded.

"The *whole* thing?"

"That I couldn't tell you. I've never been there and I don't know anyone who has. Stick doesn't take to visitors."

"Well, maybe I'll wait and check him out on the street some time."

"That would be better. I've porridge still warm, if you want something to eat before you go."

The idea of porridge first thing in the morning reminded Manda of too many mornings at home. She'd never even liked porridge—that was Mom's idea of a treat. But her stomach rumbled and she found a smile.

"That'd be great."

Mary laughed. "Look, don't mind me, Manda. The Hood always says that I've got a bad case of the mothering instinct. Why do you think Stick drops off his strays with me?"

"Who's the Hood?"

"Toby Hood—our bowman."

Manda shook her head. "There's a lot about you folks I don't know."

"Well, if you shake a leg, you'll be able to find out some—we're just getting ready to ride. If you want, you can come along."

"No kidding?"

Wouldn't that be something, riding around with the Horn Dance?

"Well?" Mary asked.

"I'm up, I'm up."

She threw aside the covers as Mary left the room and got out of the bed to put on her clothes. There was a mirror by the dresser. Looking in it, she studied her face. The bruises were already fading. She didn't feel so sore either. That was one good thing about having elf blood—you healed fast.

Riding with the Horn Dance, she thought. She gave her reflection a wink, put on her new shades, and headed out the door.

* * *

"This sucks, man."

Fineagh Steel stared out the window onto Ho Street, his back to his companion. When he turned, the sunlight coming through the dirty windowpane haloed his spiked silver hair. He was a tall elf, with razor eyes and a quick sneer, wearing a torn Guttertramps T-shirt and black leather pants tucked into black boots.

Slouching on a beat-up sofa, Billy Buttons took a long swig of some homebrew, then set the brown glass bottle on the floor by his feet. Taking out a knife, he flicked it open and began to clean his nails.

"Hey, I'm talking to you," Fineagh said.

Billy eyed the current leader of the Blood, then shrugged. "I'm listening. What do you want me to say?"

Fineagh's lip curled and he turned back to look out the window once more. "Stick's got to go."

That made Billy sit up. He ran his fingers through his black and orange Mohawk, scratched at the stubble above his ears.

"Hey," he said. "It was their own fault—bashing on his turf."

"Our turf," Fineagh said sharply. "It's *our* turf. And anyone that comes into it takes their chances. If you were to listen to Stick, you'd think the whole damn city was his turf."

Maybe it is, Billy thought, but he didn't say the words aloud. There was something spooky about Stick—you just didn't want to mess with him. But Billy was in the room with Fineagh right now and he wasn't into messing with Fineagh either.

"So what do you want to do?" he asked.

Fineagh left the window and went to where his jacket lay on the floor by the door. From the inside pocket he took out a vintage Smith & Wesson .38. Billy's eyes went wide.

"Where the hell did you get that?" he asked.

"Lifted it—in Trader's Heaven."

"You got bullets?"

"What do you think?"

"Does it still work?"

Fineagh pointed it at Billy. "Bang!" he said softly.

Billy jumped as though he *had* been shot.

"Oh, yeah," Fineagh said. "It works all right. We're talking primo goods here. Every bullet guaranteed to fire."

Billy stared at the weapon with awe. The hand guard, the gleaming barrel, everything about the gun made him shiver. It was obviously in mint condition and probably stolen from some High Born's collection if it actually worked this close to the Border. Most guns didn't.

"Where are you going to take him down?" he asked. "On the street?"

Fineagh shook his head. "We're going to beard ol' Choc'let in his den, my man. Maybe when we're done we'll turn his place into a club—what do you think? We'll call it Fineagh's Palace."

"How're we going to get in? That museum's like a fortress."

"We're going to play a tune on Stick's heartstrings," Fineagh said with a tight-lipped smile. "There'll be this runaway, see, getting his poor little head bashed in, right there in front of ol' Choc'let's digs. . . . "

* * *

"Your sister's a drummer, right?" Yoho asked.

Manda nodded. "She plays skin drums."

Yoho was one of the Horn Dance's riders, a big black man with a buzz of curly dark hair and a weight lifter's body. Manda had been introduced to them all, but the names slid by too quickly for her to put a face to every one and still remember it. A few stuck out.

Oss, with his Mohawk mane like a wild horse and wide-set

eyes. Teaser, all gangly limbs, hair a bird's nest of streaked tangles, and his jester's leathers—one leg black, the other red, the order reversed on his jacket. Mary, of course. Johnny Jack, another of the riders, a white man as big as Yoho and as hairy as a bear. And the Hood, dressed all in green like some old-fashioned huntsman, a tattoo of a crossed bow and arrow on his left cheek, and his hair a ragged cornfield of stiff yellow spikes.

"What about you? Do you play an instrument?"

Manda turned to the girl who'd spoken. A moment's thought dredged up her name. Bramble. One of the band's musicians. A year or so older than Manda's sixteen, she was a tall willowy redhead with short red stubble on the top of her head; the rest of her hair hung down in dozens of beaded braids.

"I used to play guitar—an electric," Manda said, "but someone lifted my spell-box and amp. I can't afford another, so I don't play much anymore."

Bramble nodded. "It's not so much fun when the volume's gone. I know. I got ripped off a couple of years ago myself. Went crazy after a month, so I waitressed days in the Gold Crown and played nights on a borrowed acoustic until I could afford a new one."

Teaser rattled a jester's stick in Manda's face to get her attention. "So are you any good on yours?" he asked.

"Well, Maggie said we'd put a band together if I can get a new amp."

"We could use an axe player right now," Bramble said. "The pay's the shits, but I've got a spare amp I could lend you."

"But you don't even know me—you don't know if I'm any good."

"Bramble's got a feel for that kind of thing," Mary said.

"And I've got a feel that we should be riding," Yoho broke in. "So are we going, or what?" He thrust a patched and ribbon-festooned jacket at Manda. "Here. You can wear this today. Consider yourself an honorary Horn Dancer."

"But—"

"You ride with us, you need the look," Yoho replied. "Now let's *go!*"

In a motley array of colors and tatters, they all crowded outside to where the bikes stood in a neat row behind their house.

"You can come on my machine," Bramble said.

Manda smiled her thanks. "What's this all about?" she asked as they approached Bramble's bike. "What is it that you guys *do?*"

"Well, it's like this," Bramble said. "On one level we're like any other gang—the Pack, the Bloods, Dragon's Fire, you name it. We like each other. We like to hang around together. But— have you ever heard of Morris dancing?"

Manda nodded. "Sure." When Bramble gave her a considering look, she added: "I like to read—about old things and what goes on . . . anywhere, I guess. Across the Border. In the outside world."

"Well, what we are is like one of those old Morris teams— that's why we're set up the way we are—the six stags, three white and three black. Oss is the Hobby Horse. Teaser's the fool."

"And Mary?"

"She's like the mother in the wood—Maid Marion. Robin Hood's babe."

Manda smiled. "I've heard of him."

"Yeah. I guess he's been around long enough.

"Anyway, what we do is . . . " She gave a little laugh. "This is going to sound weird, or spacey, but we're like Bordertown's luck, you know? The dance we do, winding through the city's streets, the music . . . it's all something that goes back to the Stone Age—in Britain, anyway. It's really old, all tied up with fertility and luck and that kind of thing. We make our run through the city, at least every couple of days, and it makes things sparkle a bit.

"We get all kinds of good feedback—from old-timers as well as the punks. And it makes us feel good, too. Like we're doing something important. Is this making any sense?"

"I . . . guess."

"Are we riding or jawing?" Yoho called over to them.

Bramble laughed and gave him the finger. "Come on," she said to Manda. "You'll get a better idea of what I was talking about just by getting out and doing it with us."

"What would happen if you didn't make your ride?" Manda asked.

"I don't know. Maybe nothing. Maybe the sewers would back up. Maybe we'd all go crazy. Who knows? It just feels right doing it."

Manda climbed on the back of Bramble's bike. "I think I know what you mean," she said. "I always got a good feeling when I saw you guys going by. I never caught any of your gigs, but—"

"Yeah. There's a lot of bands in this city. It's hard to catch them all."

"But still," Manda said. "Ever since Mary asked me if I wanted to come along—I've felt like I've just won a big door prize."

"*Wheel of Fortune*," Bramble said.

"What?"

"It was an old game show."

"You mean like on television?"

"The entertainment of the masses—in the world outside, at least. Did you ever watch it?"

"No. Did you?"

"Yeah. A friend of mine had a machine that recorded the shows. It was great. We used to watch all kinds of weird stuff on these old tapes of his. But then someone ripped it off."

The bikes coughed into life, up and down the line, cutting off further conversation. Bramble kicked her own machine awake. The bike gave a deep-throated roar as she twisted the throttle.

"Hang on!" she cried.

Manda put her arms around the other girl's waist and then suddenly they were off. Before they got to the end of the block, she found herself grinning like the fool's head on the end of Teaser's jester's stick.

* * *

Sitting in the Dancing Ferret, the two men made a study in contrasts. Farrel Din was short and portly, smoking a pipe and wearing his inevitable patched trousers and a quilted jacket. A full-blooded elf, born across the border, he still gave the impression of a fat innkeeper from some medieval *chanson de geste*. Stick, on the other hand, was all lean lines in black jeans, boots, and a leather jacket. With his deep coffee-brown skin and long dark dreadlocks, he tended to merge with shadows.

The men had the club to themselves except for Jenny Jingle,

a small elfin pennywhistle player, who sat in a corner playing a monotonous five-note tune on her whistle while Stick's ferret danced by her feet. From time to time she gave the men a glance. She knew Stick by sight, though not to talk to. Trading off between waitressing, odd jobs, and the occasional gig in the club, she saw him often enough, but tended to spend the times that he came into the Ferret amusing Lubin, who had developed a firm interest in Breton dance tunes.

Stick wasn't one that you could cozy up to. Though he seemed to know just about everyone in Bordertown, the only people one could definitely call his friends were Farrel Din and Berlin, and she spent most of her time working with the Diggers or hanging with the old blues players like Joe Doh-dee-oh.

Farrel Din and Stick seemed to go back a long way, which was odd, Jenny'd thought more than once. Not because Farrel Din was a full-blooded elf and Stick was definitely human—and not that old a human at that, if appearances were anything to go by—but because Stick seemed to remember the times before Elfland returned to the world as though he'd been there when it had happened.

She finished the gavotte she was playing with a little flourish, and Lubin collapsed across her feet to look hopefully up at her for more. Watching them, Farrel Din smiled.

"Seems like just yesterday when we put this place together," he said.

"It's been a lot of yesterdays," Stick replied.

He nodded as Farrel Din offered to refill his glass. Amber wine, aged in Bordertown, but originating in Elfland's vineyards, filled his glass. They clinked their glasses together in a toast, drank, then leaned back in their chairs. Farrel Din fiddled with his pipe. When he had the top ash removed from its bowl, he frowned for a moment, concentrating. A moment later, the tobacco was smoldering and he stuck it in his mouth.

"There's a Blood out on the streets with a gun," he said around the stem.

Stick gave him a sharp look.

"Oh, it's the real McCoy—no doubt about that, Stick. The sucker'd even work across the Border. Mother Mandrake had it, only someone lifted it from her booth yesterday. She didn't see it happen, but she had a bunch of Bloods in that afternoon."

"Who told you this?" Stick asked.

"Got it from John Cocklejohn. He was in to see Magical Madness playing last night."

"Wonderful. Any idea who's got the gun now?"

Farrel Din shook his head. "But there's an edgy mood out on the street and I think there's going to be some real trouble."

Stick stood up and finished his wine in one long gulp.

"That's no way to treat an elvish vintage," Farrel Din told him.

"I've got to find that gun," Stick said. "I don't mind the gangs bashing each other, but this could go way beyond that."

"Maybe they'll just use it for show," Farrel Din said hopefully. "You know how kids are."

"What do you think the chances of that are?"

Farrel Din sighed. "I wouldn't take odds on it."

"Right." Stick gave a quick sharp whistle and Lubin left her dancing to join him. "Thanks for amusing the brat, Jenny," he told the whistle player, then he left, the ferret at his heels.

Jenny blinked, surprised that he'd even known her name.

At his own table, Farrel Din put down his pipe and poured himself some more wine, filling the glass to its brim.

Aw, crap, he thought. He wished he hadn't had to tell Stick about the gun. But there was no one else he could think of who could track it down as quickly, and what they didn't need now was the trouble that gun could cause. Not with tensions running as high as they were. So why did he feel like the gun was going to come to Stick anyway, whether he looked for it or not?

Farrel Din frowned, downing his glass with the same disregard for the vintage that Stick had shown earlier. Maybe he could dull the sense of prescience that had lodged in his head. Since he had left Elfland, the ability had rarely made itself known. Why did it have to come messing him up now?

He poured himself another glass.

* * *

Manda had a glorious time that day. The Horn Dancers took turns having her ride on the back of their bikes, and she wound up renewing a childhood love affair with the big deep-throated machines. She'd always wanted one. She'd even settle for a scooter if it came down to that, but given her druthers, she'd take one of these rebuilt machines—or better yet, a vintage Harley like Stick had.

Johnny Jack had given her a mask at their first stop so that she could *really* feel a part of the Dancers. It was like a fox's head, lightweight with tinted glass in the eyeholes so that her silver eyes wouldn't give her away. The mask had just been collecting dust, he assured her when she tried to give it back to him with a halfhearted protest. Whether that was true or not—and Manda was willing to lean toward the former if he was—she accepted it greedily.

Masked and with her ribboned jacket, Morris bells jingling on her calves, she happily joined in on an impromptu dance at the corner of Ho Street and Brews, hopping from one foot to the other along with the rest of them while Bramble played out a lively hornpipe on a beat-up old melodeon. Then it was back on the bikes and they were off again, a ragged line of gypsy riders leaving a sparkle as real as fairy dust behind in the eyes of those who watched them pass by.

That night the Horn Dance had a gig at the Wheeling Heart, a club on the outskirts of the Scandal District that was in a big barnlike warehouse. Manda was too shy to play, but she enjoyed standing near the stage in her new gear and watching the show. The audience was fun to watch, too, an even mix between pogo-ing punks and an older crowd doing English country dances. By the end of the second set there were punks with their leathers and spiked hair doing the country dances, and old-timers pogo-ing. The main concern seemed to be to have fun.

Manda was still feeling shy as the band started its third set, but she was itching to play. That always happened when she saw a good band. Her fingers would start shaping chords down by her leg. When Bramble came to ask if she'd join them on some of the numbers she knew, it didn't take a whole lot of urging.

"The Road to the Border," "Up Helly-O," "The Land of Apples," "Tommy's Going Down to Berks."

The tunes went by and Manda grinned behind her fox's mask, even joining in on the singing when the band launched into "Hal-an-Tow." Listening to the words, she realized that the song pretty well said what the band was all about.

> *Do not scorn to wear the horn*
> *It was the crest when you was born*
> *Your father's father wore it and*
> *Your father wore it, too.*

> *Hal-an-tow, jolly rumble-o*
> *We were up, long before the day-o*
> *To welcome in the summer*
> *To welcome in the May-o*
> *For summer is a-coming in*
> *and winter's gone away-o.*

It didn't matter what time of year it was, Manda thought, as she chorded along on the chorus. The song wasn't just about the change of the seasons, but about day following night, good times following the bad; how there was always a light waiting for you on the other side—you just had to go looking for it, instead of stewing in what had brought you down.

Bramble laid down a synthesized drone underneath a sharp rhythm of electronic drums. Yoho was playing bass. Teaser hopped around in front of the stage, waving his jester's stick, while the rest of the band crowded around a couple of microphones. The Hood sang lead. Manda smiled as he began the third verse.

Robin Hood and Little John
Have both gone to the fair-o
And we will to the merry green wood
To hunt the bonny hare-o.
Hal-an-tow, jolly rumble-o. . . .

The music had a sharp raw edge to it that never quite overpowered the basic beauty of the melody. Voices rose and twisted in startling harmonies. Manda found herself jigging on the spot as she played her borrowed guitar. There was a certain rightness about the fact that it was the same canary yellow as her own Les Paul.

God bless the merry old man
And all the poor and might'-o
God bring peace to all you here
And bring it day and night-o.

The final chorus rose in a crashing wave that threatened to lift the roof off of the club. Punkers and old-timers were mixed in whirling dervish lines that made patterns as intricate as the song's harmonies. When the final note came down with a thunderous chord on the synthesizer, there was a long moment of silence. Then the crowd clapped and shouted their approval with almost as much volume as the band's electric instruments.

"I knew you'd be hot," Bramble said as she and Manda left the stage. "Did you have fun?"

Manda nodded. She bumped into Teaser who thrust his jester's stick up to her face.

"Says Tom Fool—you're pretty cool," he sang to her, then whirled off in a flutter of ribbons and leather.

The two women made their way to the small room in the back that the club had set aside for the band to hang out in between sets. Manda slumped on a bench and tried to stop grinning. She laid her foxhead mask on the bench beside her, her silver eyes flashing.

"See, we don't have elf magic," Bramble said, plonking herself down beside Manda, "so we've got to make our own."

"What you've got's magic all right."

"Want a beer?"

"Sure. Thanks."

"I've talked to the others," Bramble said. "They were willing to go along just on my say-so, but now that they've all heard you, it's official: you want to gig with us for a while?"

Manda sat up straighter. Absently chewing on her lower lip, she had to look at Bramble to see if it was a joke.

"For true," Bramble said.

"But I'm not . . . " Human, she thought. "Like you. It could cause trouble."

"What do you mean?"

"Well, like—"

Manda never had a chance to continue. The club's owner poked his head in through the door. "Hey, have you seen Toby? There's a guy outside looking for him to—" He broke off when he saw Manda. "What're you doing in here?"

"She's with me," Bramble said.

"Uh-uh. No 'breeds in my club. You. Get out of here."

Bramble frowned and stood up. "Lay off, George. I said she's okay."

"No. You listen to me. The Blood's got their own places to hang out and I don't want them in here. This is a clean club. If I wanted to deal with the crap that the gangs hand out, I would've opened the Heart in the middle of Soho. She's out, or you're all out."

"You're acting like a bigot," Bramble told him, "not to mention an asshole."

But Manda laid a hand on her arm. "It's okay," she said. "I was just going anyway."

"Manda. We can work this—"

Manda shook her head. She should have known the day was going too well. Everything had just seemed perfect. Under the club owner's baleful eye, she stripped off the ribboned jacket and laid it on the bench beside her mask.

"I'll see you around," she told Bramble.

"At least let me get the Hood and—"

Manda shook her head again. Blinking back tears, she put on her shades and shouldered her way by the club owner.

"Manda!"

When she was out on the dance floor, Manda broke into a run. By the time Bramble had gathered a few of the band to go outside to look for her, she was long gone.

"This is crap," Bramble said. "I'm out."

"What do you mean you're out?" the Hood asked. "We've got another set to do still."

"I'm not playing for these bigots."

"Bramble, he's got a right to run the kind of club he wants."

"Sure. Just like I've got the right to tell him to stick his head where the sun don't shine. We're supposed to be putting out good vibes, right? Be the 'luck of the city' and all that other good stuff? Well, I liked that kid, Hood, and I *don't* like the idea of being around people who can't see beyond the silver in her eyes."

"But—"

"I'll pick up my gear at the house tomorrow."

"Where you going now?" Mary asked.

"To see if I can find her."

"I'll come with you," Johnny Jack said.

Bramble shook her head. "You guys go on and finish the gig, if that's what you want to do, okay? Me, I just want to think some things through."

"I've got an idea where she might have gone," Mary said.

"Where's that?"

"Stick's place."

"Oh, great. That's all we need. To get him pissed off."

"Bramble, listen to me," the Hood tried again, catching hold of her arm.

Bramble shook off his hand. "No, you listen to me. Didn't you see how that kid took to what's supposed to be going down with us? She fit right in. I have a feel for her, man. She could be something and I want to see her get that chance."

"Okay," the Hood said. "Go look for her. But don't turn your back on us. Let's at least talk things out tomorrow."

Bramble thought about that. "Okay. If I find her, I'll be by tomorrow."

"We've got a commitment to fulfill here," the Hood went

on. "For tonight at least. We don't have to come back."

"We shouldn't be in a place like this at all," Bramble muttered under her breath as she headed for her bike. "Not when it turns out they're a bunch of racist wankers."

* * *

Manda didn't think it could hurt so much. It wasn't like she'd spent her whole life with the Dance or anything. So what if it had seemed so perfect? It wasn't like she'd ever fit in anywhere. Not with the kids her own age, not with Maggie's friends, not with anyone. Some people just weren't meant to fit in. That's all it was. They got born with a frigging pair of silver eyes and everybody dumped on them, but who cared? That was just the way it goes sometimes, right?

Yeah, sure. Right. Screw the world and go your own way. That's what it came down to in the end.

Be a loner. You could survive. No problem.

A brown face surrounded by dreadlocks came into her mind. It was good enough for Stick, wasn't it? Sure. But how come it had to hurt so much? Did it hurt him? Did he ever get lonely?

She was crying so hard now, she couldn't see where she was going. Dragging her shades from her eyes, she shoved them in her pocket and wiped away the flow of tears with her sleeve.

Maybe she'd just go ask Stick how he did it. She hadn't even had a chance to thank him yet, anyway.

Still sniffling, she headed for the museum by Fare-you-well Park.

* * *

Around the same time as the Horn Dance was leaving the stage of the Wheeling Heart, Stick pulled his Harley up in front of the museum. Cutting the engine, he stretched stiff neck muscles, then put the bike on its stand.

"End of the line," he said.

Lubin left her basket to perch on the seat. Wrinkling her nose, she made a small rumbly noise in the back of her throat.

"Yeah I know. It's long past supper."

What a night, he thought.

Pocketing his spell-box, he chained the bike to the iron grating by the museum's door and went up the broad steps. Lubin flowed up the steps ahead of him. By the time he reached the door, she'd already slid through her own private entrance to wait for him inside.

"Get the stew on!" he called to her through the door as he dug around in his jacket pocket for his keys.

He was just about to fit the key into the lock when he heard it.

Oh, crap, he thought. Not again.

Turning, he tried to pinpoint the source of what he'd just heard—a young voice raised in a high cry of pain. Now who'd be stupid enough to mess around this close to his digs? It was bad enough that he'd spent the better part of the day and evening unsuccessfully trying to run down a lead on Farrel Din's rumor without this kind of shit.

The sound of the fight came from an alleyway across the street. Stick took out his staff and snapped it into one solid length as he crossed the street. Packers or Bloods, somebody was getting their head busted because he was not in a mood to be gentle with bashers tonight.

He slowed down to a noiseless glide as he approached the mouth of the alley. Hugging the wall to the right, he slipped inside. Bloods. Bashing some kid. It was hard to make out if it was a boy or a girl, a runaway or one of the Pack. He didn't stop to think about it. His staff shot out in a whirling blur, hitting the closest Blood before any of them even seemed to be aware he was there.

The one he hit went down hard. The rest scattered toward the back of the alley.

Stick smiled humorlessly. Seemed they didn't know the alley had a dead end.

He moved after them, sparing their victim a quick glance before going on. Looked like a Blood—a small one, but a Blood all the same. Now that didn't make much—

"Hey, Stick. How's it hanging?"

Stick's gaze went up. The Bloods were making a stand. Well, that was fine with him. There were seven—no, eight of them. He shifted his feet into a firmer stance, staff held out horizontally in front of him. As he began to cat-step toward them, the ones in front broke ranks. Stick had no trouble recognizing the figure that moved forward. Fineagh.

"Times hard?" Stick asked. "Haven't seen you getting your own hands dirty for a while. I thought you just let your bullyboys handle crap like this."

"Well, this is personal," Fineagh replied.

Stick gave him a tight-lipped smile. "Pleasure's mine."

"I don't think so," Fineagh said. Taking his hand from his pocket, the Blood leader pointed the stolen .38 at Stick. "Bye-bye, Choc'let."

Oh, man. He'd been set up like some dumbass kid who should know better.

He started for Fineagh, staff whistling through the air, but he just wasn't fast enough.

The gunshot boomed loud in the alleyway. The bullet hit him high in the shoulder, the force of the impact slamming him back against the brick wall. His staff dropped from numbed fingers as he tried to stay on his feet. A second bullet hit him just above the knee, searing through muscle and tendon. His leg buckled under him and he sprawled to the ground.

"You always were just *too* damn good," Fineagh said conversationally. He kicked the staff just out of reach of Stick's clawing fingers, then hunched down, eyes glittering with malicious pleasure. "Never could deal with you like we could anybody else. So you had to come down, ol' Choc'let on a stick—you see that, don't you? We got a rep to maintain." He grinned mockingly. "Nothing personal, you understand?"

Stick saved his breath, trying to muster the energy for a last go at Fineagh, but it just wasn't there. The wounds, the shock that was playing havoc with his nervous system, had drained all his strength. He kept his gaze steady on the Blood leader's eyes as Fineagh centered the .38, but that didn't stop him from seeing the elf's finger tightening on the trigger. He could see every pore of Fineagh's pale skin. The silver death's head stud in his ear. The spill of dark laughter in his eyes . . .

Though he tried not to, he still flinched when the gun went off again.

* * *

Manda hitched a ride with a friend of Maggie's that she ran into on Cutter Street, arriving at the museum just in time to see Stick enter the alleyway. She was at the far end of the street, though, and paused, not sure what to do. She could hear the fight. Stick wouldn't want her getting in the way. But when she heard the first gunshot, she took off for the alley at a run, speeding up when the sharp crack of gunfire was repeated.

Lubin reached it before her, streaking across the street from the museum to disappear into the mouth of the alley.

When Manda got there, she caught a momentary glimpse of Stick's sprawled form, the circle of Bloods around him, Fineagh with the gun. . . .

Just as Fineagh squeezed off his third shot, Manda saw the ferret launch herself at the elf's arm. Her teeth bit through to the bone, throwing off his shot. The bullet spat against the wall, showering Stick with bits of brick. The gun tumbled from Fineagh's nerveless fingers to fly in a short arc toward Manda, hitting the pavement with a spit of sparks. Hardly realizing what she was doing, she ran forward and claimed the weapon.

Fineagh screamed, trying to shake the ferret from his wrist. It wasn't until one of his companions reached for her that Lubin dropped free to crouch protectively over Stick. Fineagh aimed a kick at her.

"D-don't do it!" Manda called nervously. The gun was a heavy cold weight in her fist as she aimed it down the alley.

The Bloods turned to face her.

Fineagh's eyes narrowed. He clutched his wrist, blood dripping between his fingers, but gave no sign of the pain he had to be feeling.

"Hey, babe," he said. "Why don't you just give me that back—maybe we'll leave you in one piece."

Manda shook her head.

Fineagh shrugged. "Your funeral."

As he started toward her, Manda closed her eyes and pulled the trigger. The gun bucked in her hands, almost flying from her grip, but her fingers had tightened with surprise as the weapon jerked. That was the only thing that kept her from losing it. Her shot went wild, but the Bloods no longer seemed so eager to confront her.

"Hey, come on," one of them said to Fineagh. "Let's get out of here."

Billy Buttons stepped up to the lean elf's side. "Nabber's right. We got what we came for, Fineagh. Time to blow."

Fineagh turned to him. "You want to leave her with that piece?"

"I just want to get the hell out of here."

Biting at her lower lip, Manda listened to them argue. She didn't know what she'd do if they charged her. How many bullets did this thing have left anyway? Not that she was sure she could even hit anything, no matter how many bullets there were.

Fineagh glared at Billy, at the ferret guarding Stick, at Manda.

"Sure," he said finally. "We're gone."

Manda backed away from the mouth of the alley as the Bloods approached, standing well away from them as they stepped out onto the street.

"I won't forget," Fineagh said, pointing a finger at her. "I *never* forget."

"Come on," Billy said. "Let's get that wrist looked at."

"Screw the wrist! You hear me, babe? Fineagh Steel's got

your number. You are not going to like what I'm going to do to you next time we meet."

"You . . . you can just . . . " Manda was so scared, the words stuck in her throat.

Fineagh took a step toward her. "I ought to rip your—"

He stopped when she raised the gun. She hoped desperately that they couldn't see how badly she was shaking.

Fineagh gave her an evil smile. "Later, babe. You and me."

He turned abruptly and led the gang away.

Manda waited until they turned the corner, then ran back into the alley.

"Easy," she said soothingly to the ferret. "Good boy. Don't bite me now. I'm here to help."

Help. Right. She almost threw up when she looked at the mess the bullets had made. There was blood everywhere. Stick was so pale from shock and loss of blood that she didn't think he'd have any trouble passing himself off as a white man if he wanted to. The light in his eyes was dimming.

"F-funny . . . seeing you . . . here . . . " he mumbled.

Manda swallowed thickly. "Don't try to talk," she said.

She laid the gun down on the ground and knelt down beside him. Lubin made a suspicious noise and sniffed at her, then backed slowly away, growling softly. Manda closed her eyes and took a deep steadying breath. Leaning over him, eyes still closed, she began to hum monotonously. The sound helped keep her head clear for what she meant to do.

She sustained the drone for a few moments, then laid her left hand gently on Stick's thigh, covering the wound, her right on his shoulder. Here was one thing that silver eyes were good for. Elf blood. She stopped humming as she concentrated fully on the task at hand. The part inside her that was connected to her elfish heritage reached out and assessed the damage done to Stick's body, mended the broken bones, reconnected arteries and nerves, healed the flesh, all the while taking the pain into herself. Not until the last of his cells was healed did she sit back and take her hands away.

Stick's pain, curdling inside her, rose up and hit her like a blow. She tumbled over on her side. Her body, drained of the energy she'd used to heal Stick, tried to deal with the pain, shutting down all but the most essential life systems when it couldn't. She curled into a fetal position as a black wave knifed through her, sucking away her consciousness.

Lubin crept up to Stick, sniffing at where his wounds had been, then put her nose up against Manda's cheek. She whined, but there was no response from either of them.

* * *

Bramble pulled up in front of the museum and parked her bike beside Stick's. She put it on its kickstand, disconnected her spellbox, and walked up to the big front door. There she hammered on the broad wooden beams for what seemed like the longest time. There was no reply.

"Aw, crap," she said.

She knew Stick was here—or at least his bike was. But what were the chances he'd take Manda in even if she had come knocking on his door? Thinking of what Stick was like, Bramble realized that it wasn't bloody likely. Okay, so where else might she have gone?

Back to the Horn Dance's house? Even more unlikely.

That left only the streets.

Bramble tried the door again, then sighed. Heading back to her bike, she kicked it into life. It looked like she was in for a night of cruising the streets. But she wasn't going to leave the poor kid out there on her own—not feeling as messed up as she'd obviously been when she'd fled the Heart.

She revved the throttle a couple of times, then took off, heading for Soho's club district.

* * *

The sound of Bramble's engine as she drove off roused Stick from a dream of a warm soft place. He'd felt as though he'd been lying somewhere with a beautiful earth goddess, his whole body nestled between her generous breasts. When he opened his eyes to find himself lying in the alley, it took him a few moments to remember where he was and how he'd come to be there.

Bloods. Bashing a kid. Who'd turned out to be a Blood. All part of a trap. And he'd gone charging in like a idiot and got himself shot.

He lifted a hand to his shoulder. His jacket had a hole in it and it was sticky with blood, but there was no wound there.

He peered down and looked at his thigh. Same story. Only there he could see the scar. How the . . . ?

That was when he saw her, lying there on the pavement, the kid he'd helped last night, all curled up in a ball. Half elf—and with an elf's healing ability, it seemed. That's what it had to have been. He had a dim recollection of her facing down the Bloods.

Somehow she'd got hold of Fineagh's gun and sent the whole crew packing.

"You're really something, kid," he said.

He looked for the gun and saw it lying just beyond her. Reaching over, he hefted it thoughtfully, then pocketed it. Lubin nuzzled his hand.

"Yeah, yeah," he said, ruffling her fur. "I remember you going one-on-one with Fineagh. Got myself a regular pair of guardian angels, don't I?"

He got slowly to his feet, marveling that he was still alive. Retrieving his staff, he broke it down and replaced it in its sheath. Then he picked up the girl and headed for home.

"This is getting to be a habit," he said, talking to himself more than to her, for she was still unconscious. "Only this time I'm taking care of you myself—I figure I owe you that much."

Not to mention that Fineagh wasn't likely to forget this. Stick knew that both he and the girl were looking to be in some serious trouble and it was going to be coming down all too soon.

* * *

Stick awoke, stiff from a night on the sofa. He groaned as he sat up and swung his legs to the floor. Don't complain, he told himself. It sure beats lying dead in an alleyway with a bullet in your head.

Pulling on his jeans, he padded across the room to the doorway of his bedroom. His guest was already up and gone. Finding a shirt, he went to see if she'd left the museum or was just exploring. He found her on the ground floor, gazing with awe at a full-size skeleton display of a brontosaurus.

"Jeez," she said as he approached her. "This place is really something."

"How're you feeling?"

"Okay. A good night's sleep is all I usually need to recover from something like last night."

"Yeah," Stick said. "About last night. Thanks."

Manda grinned. "Hey, I owed you one." She looked back at the display. "Do you really have this whole place to yourself?"

From the outside, the five-story museum looked like a castle. Inside, the first four floors held natural history displays, everything from dinosaurs to contemporary wildlife—contemporary to the world outside, at least, for there were no examples of the strange elvish creatures that now inhabited the borderlands. All the natural sciences were represented. Geology, zoology, anthropology. Manda had spent the morning wandering from floor to floor, captivated by everything she saw. Her favorites, so far, were the Native American displays and the dinosaurs.

The fifth floor was where Stick lived. It had originally contained the museum's offices and research labs. Now most of the rooms stored the vast library that Stick had accumulated—books, music recordings, videotapes, and DVDs: a wealth of pre-Elfland knowledge unmatched this side of the Border. A few rooms served as his living quarters.

"Except for Lubin," Stick said, "I've pretty much got the place to myself."

"Well, now I know why you know so much about the old days," Manda said. "But it does seem kind of decadent."

"What do you mean?"

"Well, there's all this neat stuff in here. It doesn't seem right to just keep it all to yourself."

"So what do you think I should do—open it to the public?"

"Sure."

Stick shook his head. "It wouldn't work."

"I know *lots* of folks who'd die to see this stuff."

"Sure. And when they got bored? They'd probably trash the place."

Manda gave him a funny look, then thought about what was left of the various pre-Elfland galleries and the like that she'd seen.

"I guess you're right." She ran a hand along a smooth phalanx of the brontosaurus. "It seems a shame, though."

"This place had a use after Elfland came back," Stick said. "The Bloods that wanted to go into the outside world used to come here to learn a thing or two about the way things work over on the other side of the Border. So that they could fit in better— at least those that didn't want to be noticed."

"Really?"

"Um-hmm. That's why I've got power—there's a generator that runs off a big spell-box that they left behind—and a lot of technological stuff works in here where it wouldn't out on the street."

"You mean those TV sets and stereos and other equipment up on the top floor are for real?"

Stick nodded.

"Wow. I'd love to check out some of that stuff. I've only read about them before."

"Come on," Stick said. "I'll show you how they work." He bent down and held out his arm so that Lubin could slip into its crook, then led the way upstairs.

"Would you look at all this stuff!" Manda cried in the music room. She pulled records from the big bookshelf racks that lined the walls. "Jimi Hendrix. David Bowie. The Nazgul." She looked up. "Is this stuff really as good as it's supposed to be?"

"Better."

Manda's mouth formed a silent "Wow."

"Listen," Stick asked as he turned the stereo on. "Have you got a place you can stay? Someplace out of the way, I mean. Like across the border?"

"I . . ."

Well, what had she been thinking anyway, Manda asked herself. That she was just going to be able to move in here or something? Jeez, it was really time that she grew up.

Stick saw the disappointment cross her face.

"I'm not throwing you out," he said. "You seem like an okay kid and I owe you."

"That's okay. I can go. I've got lots of places to stay."

"You're taking this wrong. See, the thing is, Fineagh—you know Fineagh?"

Manda nodded. "Sure. At least I've heard of him. He's the Bloods' latest leader."

"He's also the guy you put down last night."

Manda blanched. "Oh, boy."

"Right. So the problem is, he's going to come looking for us, and this time he'll bring every frigging Blood he can lay his hands on. I've got a feeling that they're going to lay siege to this place, and it'll be going down today."

"Can . . . can they actually get in?" Manda asked. She thought of what the museum looked like from the outside—an impregnable fortress.

"Well, the place's got a certain amount of built-in security, left behind by the elves who used it, but there's no way it could stand up to a concentrated assault."

"So what are we going to do?"

Stick smiled. "Well, I want to get *you* someplace safe, for starters."

"No way."

"Listen, you don't know how bad it's going to get when—"

"I did pretty good last night, didn't I?"

"Yeah, sure. But—"

"And besides," Manda added. "I really want to hear some of this music."

"Listen, kid, you—"

"Manda."

"What?"

"My name's Manda."

"Okay. Manda."

Before he could go on, Manda laid down the stack of records she'd pulled out and walked over to where he was standing.

"I'm not a hero," she said, "but I can't just walk away from this."

"Sure you can. You just—"

"Then, why don't *you* just walk away?" Manda couldn't believe it. Here she was arguing with Stick, like were they old pals or something. This was just too weird.

"That's different," Stick told her. "I've got a responsibility."

"To what? To this place that no one ever gets to see? To the people out on the streets who let you help them, but who you never let help you?"

"You don't know what you're talking about," Stick said.

But listening to her, hearing the conviction in her voice, he found himself wondering what had ever happened to that sense of rightness he'd felt when he was her age. There was nothing he didn't have an opinion on back then—and a damn strong opinion at that—but somehow the years had drained it away. Where once his head had been filled with a pure sense of where he was going and what his place in the world was, he'd fallen into living by habits. Still doing things, but no longer sure just exactly why he was doing them.

Such as patrolling the streets like some comic book superhero . . .

He was so still, his face squinted in a frown, that Manda figured she'd gone too far.

"Listen," she said. "I didn't mean to mouth off like that. You can do whatever you want—I mean, it's your place. If you want me to get out of your way, I'll go."

Stick shook his head. "No," he said. "You're right. Doesn't matter where you go, sooner or later you're going to have to settle this thing between Fineagh and you—same as I do. It might as well be now. But I'll tell you, Manda, we don't have a hope in hell of getting out of this in one piece—not if he musters as many Bloods as I think he will."

"Do you want to split?" Manda asked.

"Can't."

She grinned. "Well then, let's listen to some rock and roll."

She held up a record jacket with a full-face photo of a handsome curly-haired man. She was attracted to the group's name as much as the photo—mostly because of the time she'd just spent downstairs in the dinosaur display. The group was called Tyrannosaurus Rex.

"Are they any good?" she asked.

"Yeah. They're great. Do you want to hear it?"

Manda nodded. She rubbed her hair nervously, making the mauve spikes stand up at attention. Way down inside, she was about as scared as she could get. What she really needed right now was something to take her mind off of what was going to be coming down all too soon. A little time was all she needed. Sure. And then she'd just face down Fineagh and his gang all by herself.

Music blasted from the speakers then, a mix of electric and acoustic instruments that pushed the immediacy of her fears to the back of her mind. After a short intro, the lead singer's curiously timbered voice sounded across the instruments, singing about a "Woodland Bop." By the time the second chorus came, she was singing along, Lubin dancing at her feet.

Stick left them to it while he went to see to some weapons. The gun they'd taken from Fineagh last night was out of bullets and his staff just wasn't going to cut it, not with what Fineagh was going to bring down on them.

* * *

Bramble spent a fruitless night, going from club to club, stopping on street corners, asking after Little Maggie Woodsdatter's younger sister Manda from everyone she met. She didn't have much luck.

Dawn was just pinking the sky when she finally ran down a

rumor that was just starting to make the rounds of the Soho streets. Hearing it, she headed straight for home.

Mary was the only one up when Bramble came into the kitchen.

"Any luck?" Mary asked.

Bramble shook her head.

Mary sighed. "About last night," she said. "You know what the Hood's like. He's really into fulfilling obligations."

"Yeah. I know. But—"

"Anyway," Mary broke in. "We won't be playing there again—not even if we wanted to."

"Why not?"

"After the gig, the Hood collected our bread, then he decked George. 'That's for the kid,' he said. Left him with a beautiful shiner."

Bramble smiled. "I wish I'd seen that."

"Oh, I'm sure he'll be more than happy to give you a complete blow-by-blow rundown if you ask." She eyed Bramble thoughtfully. "So now what are you going to do? Are you still planning to pack it in?"

"No. Just before I got here, I heard a story that's making the rounds. Something about Stick and some kid facing down Fineagh and a bunch of his Bloods. Whatever happened, the Bloods are planning a full-scale assault on Stick's place this afternoon."

"What's that?"

The sound of their conversation had woken a few other members of the band. The Hood sat down at the table with them, while Teaser and Johnny Jack fought a mock battle for the teapot. It was the Hood who'd spoken.

Bramble gave them what details that she'd been able to pick up. By the time she finished, most of the band was awake and had joined them.

"This kid with Stick," Johnny Jack asked. "You think it's Manda?"

Bramble nodded.

"It makes sense," Mary added. "She was asking about him yesterday morning."

The Hood looked around at the rest of them. "Anybody here *not* want to get involved?"

"She seemed like a nice kid," Oss volunteered.

"And she *is* an honorary member of the band still," Johnny Jack added.

Mary shook her head. "But what can *we* do?" she asked. "We're not fighters."

"Oh, I don't know about that," Yoho said. "I've been known to kick some ass."

Mary sighed. "You know what I mean. How could we possibly stand up to the numbers Fineagh can put together?"

There was a long silence. One by one heads turned to look at the Hood.

"Hell," he said after a moment. "It's simple. We just dance 'em into surrendering."

"Come on," said Bramble. "This is serious."

"I *am* being serious," the Hood replied. "The only thing is, we're going to need a wizard."

* * *

It was shaping up even worse than Stick had imagined it would.

"What are we going to do?" Manda said, joining him at the window.

Behind them, the needle lifted from an LP by Big Audio Dynamite, and the turntable automatically shut off. Neither of them noticed. All their attention was focused on the street below that fronted the museum.

Bloods rounded the corner and came down the street in a slow wave. There were easily more than a hundred of them, bedecked in jeans and leather, silver eyes glittering in the afternoon light. Their hair was a multicolored forest, ranging from elfin silver through every color of the spectrum. They were armed with knives and cudgels, broken lengths of pipe and chains, traditional elfin bows and arrows. The front ranks had sledgehammers and crowbars. They were making it obvious that, one way or another, they'd be cracking the museum open today.

The Bloods alone were bad enough. But word had spread and the various other gangs of Bordertown were showing up in force to watch the show. The Pack, in their leathers. Dragon's Fire, down from the Hill, looking soft beside the real street gangs. Scruffy headbangers and Soho rats, runaways and burn-outs.

Staring down at the crowd, Stick had visions of the bloodbath that was just a few wrong words away from exploding. He checked the load of his pump shotgun. With a quick snapping motion, he pumped a shell into place. Inside the museum, he had no doubt as to its reliability. But outside, beyond the elfin spells that kept the building and its contents in working order, he knew he'd be lucky if one shot in three fired.

Manda swallowed hard.

"Scared?" Stick asked.

She nodded.

"Me, too." When she looked at him in surprise, he added: "It might not be too late to get out the back."

"And do what?"

There was that, Stick thought. No matter where they went, they were going to have to face Fineagh sooner or later. Taking off now just meant the museum was going to get trashed and they'd still have the Blood leader on their case. Making a stand here—maybe it was just suicide. But there didn't seem to be any other option.

"Did you ever get lonely?" Manda asked. "You know, just being here by yourself all the time?"

"I went out a lot. I've got friends. Berlin. Farrel. And besides, Lubin's good company."

The ferret was crouched on the windowsill in front of them. Manda gave her soft fur a pat.

"Yeah, but you don't exactly hang out a lot when you *do* go out," she said.

"How would you know?"

"Hey, you're famous, Stick."

He sighed. "That's the kind of thing that got me into this in the first place. Always being the do-gooder." He gave her a quick look. "Okay. So maybe I get a little lonely from time to time. I guess it just comes with the territory."

"You've helped an awful lot of people—did you never find one of them you liked well enough to be your friend?"

The look of an old hurt crossed his features, gone so quick Manda wasn't sure she'd even seen it.

"It's not that simple," he told her. "See, I've got to keep some distance between myself and the street. Without it, I can't do my job properly."

Manda nodded. "After being in here with you today, I can tell you're not as scary as you make yourself out to be down there." She nodded to where the gangs were gathering. "But how'd this get to be your job?"

"Kind of fell into it, I guess. The kids didn't have anyone looking after them and the gangs just started getting too rough on them. Hell, I'm no shining knight—don't get me wrong. But someone had to look out for them. Only now . . . " He shook his head. "I don't know how it got so out of control."

Manda looked down. She could make out Fineagh, standing at the head of the Bloods. He seemed so small from this height that she felt she could just reach out and squeeze him between her fingers like she might a bug.

"I guess we should . . . get down there," she said.

Stick nodded grimly. "Maybe I can shame Fineagh into going one-on-one with me—winner take all."

"Do you think he'd just—" Manda interrupted herself before she could finish the question. "Look!" she cried.

But she didn't have to point it out to Stick.

Forcing a way through the spectators came a familiar band of bikers. It was the Horn Dance. An open-backed pickup truck followed the path the bikes made. That was the portable stage and power generator that they needed for their amps and sound system.

The bikes pulled up at the front steps, forming a semicircle around the truck. The truck stopped, its cab facing the museum doors, its bed directly in front of Fineagh.

"What are they trying to pull?" Stick muttered as the band members began to strap on instruments.

The whine of feedback and the sound of guitars and synthesizers being tuned rose up to their window.

"I think they're trying to help," Manda said.

"We'd better get down there," Stick said.

He strode off, Lubin at his heels, going so fast that Manda had to trot to keep up with him.

* * *

"Did you get it yet?" the Hood asked Farrel Din.

The wizard sat frowning behind the amplifiers in the bed of the Horn Dance's pickup. He looked at an old bumper sticker that was stuck to one of the wooden slats that made up the sides of the bed. It read, I'D RATHER BE DANCING. Well, he'd rather be anywhere, doing anything, he thought, than be here.

"Farrel?" the Hood prompted him.

"I'm thinking. I always have trouble with the simple spells. They're so easy that they just go out of my mind."

"Well, if you know some big smash-up of a one, go for it instead. We could use just about anything right about now."

Farrel Din sighed. "I never could learn the big ones," he admitted.

"We should have gotten a different wizard," Bramble told the Hood.

"Nobody else seemed to have a better idea before we went and asked Farrel."

"Sure, but—"

"Will you go away and let me think!" Farrel Din shouted at

them. "Why don't you start playing or something and as soon as I get it, I'll let you know."

"If you get it," Bramble muttered.

Farrel Din sighed, and returned to his task.

It was such a stupidly simple spell, surely even *he* could remember it. Couldn't he? It had been such a favorite—long ago, before Elfland ever left the outside world in the first place. But there hadn't been much call for it in the last few centuries and he'd never been much of a wizard anyway. Why else did he run the Ferret? He'd always been better serving up beers than serving up spells.

Up front, Johnny Jack was arguing with Fineagh. The Blood leader wasn't ready to just wipe out the Horn Dance—they were too popular for him to risk that—but he was rapidly approaching the point where he just wouldn't care anymore. He hadn't expected so many of the other gangs to show up either—but screw them as well.

The Bloods were ready to take on anyone.

"Listen, you jackass," he told Johnny Jack. "I'm giving you two minutes to get this crap out of my way, or we're just going through you. Understand?"

"Everybody tuned?" the Hood asked from the bed of the pickup.

He'd been keeping a wary eye on the Bloods and knew that they couldn't hold off much longer.

Farrel Din, he thought. Get it together and we'll play your club for a month—free of charge.

"We're rooting to toot," Teaser called to him.

"Then let's get this show on the road!" the Hood cried.

* * *

Stick and Manda stepped out of the museum's front door at the same time as the Horn Dance kicked into the opening bars of a high-powered version of the "Morris Call." The sheer volume of sound stopped them in their tracks. The Bloods looked to Fineagh for direction, but the rest of the crowd immediately began to stamp their feet.

"All right!" someone shouted.

Shouts and whistles rose up from the crowd, but were drowned by the music. Bramble kept an eye on Fineagh, then turned to see how Farrel Din was doing, all the while playing her button accordion. The portly wizard was hunched over, muttering to himself.

Great plan, Hood, Bramble thought. She turned back to face the crowd. Most of the punkers and runaways were dancing— their usual combination of shuffled country dance steps and pogoing. The Rats eyed the Bloods, ready to rumble. Everyone else seemed to be trying to figure out if they'd come to a free concert or a street fight, with the crowd from the Hill hanging back as usual—wanting to be a part of things, but nervous about a free-for-all.

Stick started down the steps, Manda and Lubin trailing a few paces behind. Fineagh's eyes narrowed as he took in Stick's shotgun. The Horn Dance broke into a medley of "Barley Break" and "The Hare's Maggot."

"Come on!" the Hood shouted at Farrel Din.

"Easy for you to say," the wizard replied. He counted on his fingers, shaking his head. "No. That's shit into gold. Maybe . . . ?"

He squeezed his eyes shut, trying to think, while the music thundered on.

Stick moved along the side of the truck, the shotgun held down by his side. With his finger in the trigger guard, he only needed to swing it up to fire.

Bramble tried to catch Manda's eye. If Stick and Fineagh started in on each other it wouldn't make any difference if Farrel found the spell or not. But Manda's gaze was locked on the tall Blood leader who awaited their approach. The Bloods began to press closer to Fineagh. Those armed with bows notched arrows.

Stick stopped when he was a few paces away from Fineagh.

"Kill the music," Fineagh said, nodding at the band.

"Not my party," Stick told him.

Fineagh turned to his followers, but before a command could leave his lips, Farrel Din sat up in the back of the truck.

"Got it!" he cried.

He jumped up and ran over to Bramble, tripped over a power cord, and fell against the willowy redhead. The two went down in a tumble. Bramble was carrying the tune. When she fell, her accordion made a discordant wheezing sound. The band faltered at the loss of the melody line.

Farrel Din grinned into Bramble's face. "Play 'Off She Goes,'" he said as they disentangled themselves.

"But—"

"Trust me. Just play it."

Bramble nodded to the Hood. The band stopped trying to find the tune they'd lost as she broke into the jig. She played the first few bars on her own, the others quickly joining in when they recognized the tune. While they played, Farrel Din stood directly in front of Bramble, eyes closed in concentration. Hopping from one foot to the other, he waved his fingers around her accordion in a curious motion, all the while singing something in the old elfin tongue.

The effect was almost instantaneous.

Anyone not already moving to the music immediately began to dance, whether they wanted to or not. Rats and Bloods shuffled in time to the lilting rhythm. Those in the crowd who were already dancing moved into high gear, happily swinging partners and generally having a grand old time. In the back, the crowd from the Hill looked embarrassed as they flung themselves about, but like everyone else, they were unable to stop themselves.

The Bloods fought the glamor, but the spell, combined with the music, gave them no choice. They lifted one foot, then the other, keeping time with the beat, frowns on their faces. Only Fineagh, through the sheer stubbornness of his will, stood still.

Fineagh and Stick.

Jigging on the spot, Manda couldn't believe that they weren't affected. Even Lubin was dancing—though the ferret loved to dance at any excuse so perhaps that didn't count. But then Manda saw that even the two men's feet were tapping slightly.

"This doesn't stop anything, Choc'let," Fineagh said. Fires flickered in his eyes.

Stick shrugged. "It doesn't have to be like this—you could just walk away."

"Can't."

"You mean you won't."

The hate in the elf's silver eyes became a quicksilvering smolder. Stick knew they were both moments away from falling prey to the glamor in the music.

"Give it up," he said.

Even if he said yes, Manda wondered, how could they trust him?

But the Blood leader had no intention of giving up. One minute his hand was empty, in the next a throwing knife had dropped into it from a wrist sheath. The blade left his hand, flying straight and true for Stick.

Stick brought up the shotgun and knocked the knife from the air. Leveling the gun, he pulled the trigger. The shell was a dud.

A second knife appeared in Fineagh's hand at the same time as Stick pumped a new shell into place. The boom of the shotgun was lost in the thundering music, but Fineagh's chest exploded as the load hit him. He was lifted into the air and thrown back a half-dozen feet, dead before he hit the ground.

The band's music stopped as suddenly as though someone had pulled the plug. Hundreds of eyes stared at the blood-splattered remains of the tall elf. The sound of Stick's pumping a new shell into place was loud in the abrupt silence. He leveled the shotgun at the ranks of Bloods.

"Anybody else want a piece?" he asked. "Now's the time to make your play."

Nobody moved.

Their leader was dead, and gone with him was the mania that had brought them all to this point. The Bloods were suddenly aware of just how dangerously outnumbered they were.

"Hell, no," Billy Buttons said finally. "We're cool."

Turning, he shouldered his way through the Bloods. Long

tense moments passed, but slowly the Bloods followed him, leaving Fineagh's corpse where it lay.

"That . . . that's it?" Manda asked softly.

Stick looked at her, then at the Horn Dance and the crowds still gathered.

"It's not enough?" he asked.

Manda swallowed. "Sure. I mean . . . "

Stick nodded. "I know."

With that, he turned and retraced his way back up the museum's steps, the shotgun hanging loosely in his hand.

Lubin ran ahead, disappearing inside before him. Stick paused at the door to look back.

"Come visit," he said. "Anytime."

Then he too was gone.

The door closed with a loud thunk.

Manda stared at it, but all she could see was the pain she'd discovered in Stick's eyes. Damn him! Didn't he realize that it didn't have to be like this? He had friends. The Horn Dance had turned out to help him. Farrel Din had. She was here. Tears welled up in her own eyes, and she wasn't sure if they were from feeling hurt, or for him.

She started to move for the door, but Bramble appeared at her side. She caught Manda's arm.

"But I want . . . I should . . . "

"Not a good time," Bramble said.

"But . . . "

Bramble pulled a couple of notes from her button accordion, then softly sang.

There was an old woman
    tossed up in a blanket
ninety-nine miles, beyond the moon.
And under one arm
    she carried a basket
and under t' other she carried a broom.
Old woman, old woman, old woman, cried I
O whither, O whither, O whither, so high?
I'm going to sweep cobwebs
    beyond the sky
but I'll be back again, by and by.

She ended with a flourish on the accordion and gave Manda a lopsided smile.

"I don't understand," Manda said.

"Clean your own house, and let him clean his. You heard what he said. He *did* ask you to come visit him . . . anytime."

"Sure, but—"

"But now's not 'by and by,'" Bramble said. "Come on. Give the Horn Dance a chance. We've got a captive audience—what with Farrel's spell. We could use your licks, kiddo."

Manda looked up at the museum's fifth floor. Was there a movement at the window?

But then she realized that Bramble was right. While Manda wasn't sure what she wanted from Stick, it had to come at its own pace. She'd give him a bit of a grace period, but if he didn't wise up soon, then he'd find her camped out on his front steps.

"Hey!" Yoho called from the back of the truck.

Manda looked up at him and saw he was holding out Bramble's canary yellow Les Paul. She followed Bramble up onto the back of the truck and took the instrument with a smile of thanks.

Someone had already removed Fineagh Steel's body. Bramble led the band in a rousing version of the "Staines Morris." Teaser and Mary moved amongst the crowd, showing the steps. Manda was about to start playing when Johnny Jack caught her by the arm.

"I think you're forgetting something," he said.

He held out her foxhead and mask and the ribbon-festooned jacket.

Manda propped the Les Paul up against its amp and put them on. Then she slung the guitar on and joined the tune with a flashy spill of notes. Bramble gave her a grin.

Leaning into the tune's chords, Manda looked out at the sea of bobbing faces. The Rats had left soon after the Bloods. The crowd that remained didn't need Farrel Din's glamor to join in. And neither did she, Manda thought, jigging on the spot with Johnny Jack. The music was good and the people were good. Maybe it was about time that she stopped backing away from things and took the plunge. If she couldn't do it herself, how could she ever expect to set an example for Stick?

She glanced up at the fifth floor again, and this time, while she didn't see Stick, she could see Lubin dancing on the windowsill. Smiling, she turned her attention back to the music.

I DON'T *think books are the place to lecture anyone, but just allow me a few words here. You've probably noticed by now that many of my characters have less than happy childhoods.*

Some of us are born lucky, born into families that love and care for us, and some of us aren't. It seems to me that the lucky ones, and those who manage to survive their private terror times, owe it to the less fortunate to do what we can to help them, even if it's only keeping a dialogue open about what goes on behind too many locked doors. We need to be there for them, to give them comfort and respect, and to listen to their stories. And if they can't tell their own stories, then we need to tell their stories for them.

The world will only become a better place if we all work to make it better. And while that isn't possible as things stand—we can't make *people be different—we can at least live by example ourselves, making a difference in the small part of the world that lies around us.*

This story originally appeared in The Essential Bordertown *(1998).*

May This Be Your Last Sorrow

IT WAS JOE DOH-DEE-OH WHO TOLD HER ABOUT THE gargoyle that perches on a cornice of the Mock Avenue Bell Tower, how if the clock in its belfry ever chimed the correct time, the gargoyle would be freed from his body of stone.

"I'm sure," she'd replied.

She waited for the teasing look to come into Joe's eyes, but all he did was shrug, as though to say, "Well, if you don't want to believe me . . . "

* * *

I'm nobody really; any glitter I've got's just fallout from people I know. Borrowed limelight. But that's okay. I never wanted to be anybody special in the first place. I like being part of the faceless audience—the people that attend the theaters and concerts, that sit in the dark and appreciate the skill of the performers. I read the books without any urge to write one myself. I'm the one who goes to the galleries, not by invitation on opening night, but later, when the anonymous people come to steal a glimpse of what made the artists' spirits sing so fiercely that they just had to find a way to give it physical dimension.

You'll find me in the back of a club, sitting by myself and enjoying the band, instead of trying to talk over the music to describe my own next project. I'm the one you see walking through a museum with the big goofy smile on my face because everything's just so amazing. I'm not full of ideas about what I'm going to do; I'm appreciating all the wonderful things that have already been done.

I think there's too much emphasis put on having to be Someone, on making something out of nothing. It's not a road that everybody can follow. It's not a road that anybody should have to want to follow.

I'm not making up excuses for having no talent, really I'm not. I don't know whether I've got any or not; all I know is I'm short on the inclination.

You know the old argument about whether talent comes from your genes or your environment? Well, I give lie to both.

See, my mom's Deeva. You never heard of her? She was the "Elf Acid House *chanteuse*," as her recording company liked to put it. That was because, when the Change came, she was the first to take the visuals from across the Border and use them in her music and videos.

There was a time when all she had to do was just think about putting out a new recording and it'd go triple platinum. She was the first of the post-Madonna dance artists who did everything— wrote, sang, produced, played all the instruments with nothing sampled, not even the drum track. She directed and choreographed her own videos, too. At the peak of her career she was a one-woman industry, all by herself. Amazing, really, when you think about it.

And my dad? He was Ned Bradley. Uh-huh. *That* Ned Bradley, the one who played Luke on *Timestop for Chance*. It's funny. I thought music'd make a way bigger impression in a place like this than a TV series would, but I guess I understand. I've gotta admit the show was pretty cool. I mean, he started shooting *Timestop* way before I was born, so it's like, really old stuff. The first show aired twenty years ago, right? But I could still relate to all those kids. It'd be so weird if reincarnation really worked and you could remember it the way they could. I think that's what made it so popular. It didn't matter what historical era they used for the background on any particular year, the continuity was so fascinating and the cast worked so well together that they just made each episode sing.

Anyway, so there's, like, more talent in my house when I'm growing up then anyone could know what to do with. Not just my parents, but all their friends, too. I guess the biggest disappointment to my parents was that I didn't show much of an aptitude for anything.

My mom must have tried to teach me to play a half-dozen instruments. She'd get real mad and tell me I wasn't applying myself; she wouldn't listen when I told her I loved music—just to listen to, not to make. That's something so alien to her that she must've just tuned it out. I mean, she still can't listen to a new recording—doesn't matter what style of music it is—without her fingers twitching and her wanting to head down to the studio to lay down a few tracks herself.

My dad's another story. I'm not unattractive, but I'm not as pretty as Deeva is, either—who really is? My mom sure isn't. She's just Anna Westway until she does that amazing makeup and puts on her Deeva wig, you know? I like her better as Anna Westway, but who's going to listen to me? Anyway, my dad tried to get me into commercials and bit parts in shows that his friends were producing—stuff like that—but it never took. I wasn't Deeva. I have no camera presence. Zip. Nada. Which my dad just *couldn't* believe.

You see when my dad's doing his thing—doesn't matter whether it's on the big screen or a dinky little TV set—he just commands your attention. I think the thing that really proves his talent was how he managed to never overshadow whoever was in a scene with him. With as riveting a screen presence as he had that wasn't exactly an easy thing to pull off.

Anyway, needless to say, I was a big disappointment to them both. They tried to get me interested in anything creative—writing, painting, sculpting—but none of it took. It was kind of embarrassing for them, I guess, but what could I do? I'm just me; I can't be anybody else. I wouldn't know how.

My parents kind of gave up on me by the time I turned thirteen. They didn't turn mean or anything, they just sort of forgot that I existed, I think. Mom was working on a comeback; my dad got a part in *Traffic*—yeah, he plays the holograph man. Great part, isn't it?

That was about the worst year of my life. It wasn't just the way things were at home. I was having the shittiest time in school, too. You know what I think is really weird? It's how everyone thinks that rich people can't have real problems. It's like, if you've got all that money, you can't possibly be hurting emotionally.

When I first started high school, people thought I was pretty cool, considering who my parents were, but that wore off real fast when I wouldn't, like, get them free tickets to some concert, or introduce them to that kid in Dad's new show, Tommy Marot—you know, Mr. Heartthrob? I like to be quiet, but they just figured I was stuck up—with nothing to be stuck up about.

So that's why I ran away. There was nothing for me at home, nothing for me at school, nothing for me anywhere except here. I don't think my parents even know I'm gone. I used to check the papers, during the first few weeks, but there was never anything about Deeva and Ned Bradley's kid having turned up missing. No mention at all. I guess they were kind of relieved to be rid of me, that's what I think.

Why'd I pick this place? I dunno. Not because it's so cool. I mean, I still get a kick out of seeing elves and everything, but that's not really why I came. I think it was because I heard that this was a place where people left you alone.

And I love it here, I really do. It was tough at first, but I'm staying with the Diggers now and they're really nice—especially Berlin. And Joe, even if he does tease me sometimes. So long as I pull my weight, I'll always have a place to crash and something to eat.

Nobody bugs me; nobody's trying to make me be something I'm not. If I don't want to talk, they don't get in my face about it. They just let me go my own way.

What I like the best is the clubs and galleries, though. It's like all the best talent from the outside world and across the Border's been distilled into this magic potion. You take a sip, and it just takes you away. Who needs drugs in a place like this? I get high on the music and the art; that's the real magic, I think. Something about being this close to the Border hones this edge onto any-thing that's created in its shadow.

And I like the way nobody's pushy; they just leave you alone. That's the way it should be. People should just let you have your own space.

So I know I did the right thing. Really. I just wish I didn't feel so . . . lonely sometimes, you know?

I think you're the only one who really understands.

* * *

The stone gargoyle on top of the Mock Avenue Bell Tower watched the small figure climb down from the belfry. He enjoyed her visits, even if they always left a melancholy pang deep in his stone chest.

When she got to the bottom rung of the ladder, she disappeared from sight. He shifted his gaze over the edge of the cornice, waiting until she stepped out the tower door far below. Her slim shoulders were bowed under her tattered jacket, her unruly tangles of hair hanging in her face to hide the tears that had been welling up in her eyes before she left the belfry.

He watched as she dried her eyes on the sleeve of her jacket, straightened her shoulders, and then marched off down the street.

If he could speak, he would advise her to approach another human the way she did him. But he couldn't speak. And if he could, he doubted she would listen anyway. But he would still try.

She needed a friend. Anyone could see that, if they only took the time to look beyond her bravado.

The belfry clock chimed twelve although it was only the middle of the afternoon.

Was there ever such a bittersweet, forlorn sound? the gargoyle wondered as he had far too often in the two hundred years he had kept watch over the city from the bell tower.

What might have been a sigh shivered his stone skin.

I think you're the only one who really understands, she'd said.

He did understand. He understood all too well.

NEWFORD:
In and Out of the City

NEWFORD: IN AND OUT OF THE CITY

I *used to set all my books and stories in Ottawa, or in the area around Ottawa. There was a simple reason for this: I could research the background by walking around the city, or driving through the countryside nearby. There's nothing like first-hand experience to make your subject matter feel alive. And when it feels alive to you as a writer, there's a good chance it will do the same for your readers.*

I did get the urge to write stories in other locales. For my novel The Little Country *(1991), MaryAnn and I saved up and took a three-week trip to Cornwall, England, so that I could research the background for it.*

But occasionally I wanted to write stories set in a larger urban setting than Ottawa could provide. I'd visited such places (Toronto, London, New York City, L.A., Chicago, Vancouver, etc.), but didn't think I had spent enough time in any of them to be able to capture the right feel of the place.

Then one day an editor named Paul F. Olson asked me to write a story for Post Mortem *(1989), an anthology he was editing with David B. Silva, and that urge came over me again. This time I gave in to it, deciding to set the story in a made-up city, incorporating bits and pieces of various large cities I had been in, but not having to worry about which way the one-way streets run, or if that coffee shop is really on* that *corner.*

The story was "Timeskip," and it's the first official Newford story, although the city didn't have a name at the time, and a few

Newford stalwarts had been introduced in an earlier novelet, "Uncle Dobbin's Parrot Fair."

The next time I was asked to contribute to an anthology, I used the same setting, and three or four stories later, I realized I should come up with a name for the city, work out a bit of the pattern of its streets, and that sort of thing.

It's now twelve years and more since that first Newford story, and these days I feel I know this city better than any place I've actually lived or visited, because I spend so much time there. Happily, many readers feel the same way, and continue to journey with me through its streets, catching up on the gossip of the old friends who wander around in the background of the stories.

Where is Newford? It's in North America. A little more east than west. A little more south than north. But where is it really? It's in that place we go when we daydream of otherworlds that are only a little bit different from our own.

THIS NEXT story doesn't take place in the city, or even close by. I include it in the Newford cycle because one of the characters eventually moves to Newford and my editor, Sharyn, agreed that it should stay here.

One Chance

IT WAS THE SUMMER THEY SHARED THEIR UNHAPPINESS.

Susanna sped down Main Street, standing up on the pedals to get her bike going, the front panels of her khaki army jacket flapping against her arms. The jacket was a couple of sizes too big for her. She had to roll the sleeves up and the waistband hung down around her thighs.

It had belonged to her grandfather, and when she'd found it in the attic up at the top of his old house at the beginning of summer, he had given it to her with a sad smile. It was the same smile he'd worn when he fixed up Teddy Baker's old one-speed bike for her. The kind of smile that said, If we weren't so poor . . . The kind of look her parents got sometimes, only they didn't smile.

She knew she looked stupid wearing it, riding her balloon-tire bike. She could see it in the eyes of the people she passed. She heard it from the other kids. "Suzy Four-eyes, get a coat your own size." And Tommy Cothorn asking her if she was an old lady because she rode an old lady's bike and she sure was too ugly to be a girl.

But she didn't feel stupid wearing it. She felt free in that old jacket, riding her bike. She was an army scout, down behind enemy lines. Whizzing down Main Street, swinging left on Powers without using the brakes, not slowing down at all, just leaning into the corner, so close to the Coca-Cola truck parked there that she could swear she'd brushed the side of the truck with her arm.

She was trying very hard to hold back tears. The bike helped. Air rushing against her face. The rubber hum of its big fat tires on the pavement. The jacket brought her close to her grandfather. It was the same jacket he'd worn when he went overseas. No matter how often it was washed, for her it always smelled like him. Like dry apples and leaves burning in autumn. But her back still hurt from where she'd fallen against the bench in the park when Tommy's brother Bobby pushed her down. And then everybody had laughed as she sat there, trying not to cry, trying to find her glasses, just wanting to get away.

At the corner of Blaylock Avenue and Powers, she steered left into the alleyway beside old man Koontz's junk shop, skimmed between two garbage cans like a circus trick rider, and then she was bumping over the uneven ground of the empty lot behind the grocery store.

Billy was already there.

As she brought her bike to a halt, he turned to look at her, fingers tight around the paperback copy of *Witch Week* that she'd lent him. Her own unhappiness fled when she saw the big smudged bruise on Billy's face. His right eye was so swollen it was almost closed. Laying her bike down, she walked over to where he was sitting. She leaned back against the rear wall of the grocery store as he was doing and looked out across the lot.

It was hard to be eleven and hold so much unhappiness in such small bodies.

Susanna took off her glasses. The rivets on the left hinge

were loose, but they couldn't be tightened anymore. A piece of black tape held the hinge to the temple. She cleaned the lenses on the hem of her jacket, then put the glasses back on. The bridge was a little tight because she was outgrowing them. Her mother had promised her a new pair next year.

"He got real mad last night," Billy said.

He didn't lie to her like he did to everyone else. He didn't say he fell going down the stairs, or he'd walked into a door, or anything like that. His dad went out drinking after work, and sometimes he came home happy, but sometimes he came home and you couldn't say anything to him. One wrong word and his big fist would come as if out of nowhere and send Billy flying halfway across the room. Sometimes it didn't even have to take a wrong word.

"I was just sitting on the couch, reading your book," Billy said, "and he hit me. He didn't say anything, he just hit me. And when I tried to get up, he hit me again. And then he pushed me off the couch and he lay down and he passed out."

There were no tears lying in wait behind Billy's eyes. His voice was flat and even and he just kept on staring out across the lot. But then he turned to look at Susanna.

"If I stay there any longer, he's gonna kill me, or I . . . I'm . . . "

His voice trailed off.

"Bobby Cothorn caught me in the park," Susanna said.

She knew what had happened to her wasn't even vaguely on the same level as what happened to Billy, but it was a way of sharing the pain. Sharing their unhappiness.

"I'm going away," Billy said.

Susanna didn't say anything for a long moment.

"You can't," she said finally.

"I've *got* to, Suze," he said. "I can't take it anymore. Not the kids picking on me, not my dad hitting me. School's starting in two weeks. We can hide in places like this in the summer, we can get away from the other kids so they won't hurt us, but what are we gonna do when school starts? We won't be able to hide from them then. And I can't hide from my dad—not unless I go away."

"But you're just a kid," Susanna said, being practical. "Where will you go? How will you live? The cops'll just track you down and bring you back home and then you'll *really* be in trouble."

"I'm going someplace they can't ever find me."

Susanna shook her head. There wasn't anywhere an eleven-year-old could go that they couldn't be found. For an afternoon, sure. But not forever.

"Can't be done," she said.

"What about Judy Lidstone?" he replied.

Susanna shivered. Judy Lidstone had lived just a few blocks from her on Snyder Avenue. She'd disappeared in the spring.

"She didn't run away," Susanna said. "Some psycho got her. They just . . . they just never—"

"Found her body?"

"Yeah."

"Well, I know different."

"Bull."

Billy shook his head and leaned conspiratorially closer. "She went *away*," he said, and there was something in the way he said "away" that stopped Susanna cold. She shivered again, but it was a different kind of a chill that touched her now. Born not so much of fear as of wonder. At the unknown.

"Where did she go?" she asked.

"I don't know the name of the place, but I know how to get there: By magic."

The shivery feeling left Susanna. "Oh, get real," she said. She looked away from him and began to poke about in a hole in her jeans with a dirt-smudged finger.

"You've got to have a key to get to that place," Billy said as though she hadn't spoken. "You've got to have the right key and you've got to believe it's going to work. *Really* believe. And then, if the key works—*when* it works—you go away."

"Where to?"

"To a better place. Someplace where your dad doesn't beat on you and kids don't make fun of you. Where you don't have to ever hide again."

"Who told you this?" Susanna asked.

"Judy did—before she left."

Susanna's shiver returned. Billy looked so serious, so believing, that she couldn't help but wonder, What if it *is* true?

"But you've got to go when the door opens to that other place—right then. You don't get another chance."

"Judy told you?" Susanna said.

Billy nodded.

"And you never told anybody?"

"Who'm I going to tell?" Billy asked. "Who's going to believe me?"

"How come you never told me?"

"I'm telling you now," Billy said.

Susanna took off her glasses and began to clean them again,

lingering over the job. To go away. To go to a place where no one dumped on you. If it was possible . . .

"Remember Judy just disappeared from her room?" Billy said. "In the middle of the night? Well, how's some psycho going to get into her house without waking her parents? No. She told me about the key before she went, and she told me where she'd leave it. I thought it was just a load of bull, but then she *did* disappear, so I figured it had to be true. I went into her backyard and the key was lying there in back behind her dad's toolshed—just like she said it would be."

"What does it look like?"

Billy laid her book on the ground between them and pulled a brass object from his pocket—a figurine of a wolf, so tarnished it almost looked like bronze. He gave it a rub on the knee of his jeans, then passed it over to Susanna. It didn't look like any kind of a key she had ever seen before.

"How does it work?" she asked.

"He's like the guy who guards the door," Billy said, stroking the figurine. "You've got to hold this real tight and call him. And you've got to believe he'll come. . . ."

Susanna nodded slowly, almost to herself. "When . . . when are you going?" she asked.

"Now, Suze. Right now. Are you coming?"

"I . . ."

Susanna thought of Bobby Cothorn and his pals catching her in the park, pushing her back and forth between them. "You better hope you grow into a beautiful bod," someone had said, "because with a face like yours, you'll need all the help you can get."

With a face like hers. Mouth too big, teeth crooked. Ears sticking out. She didn't need a mirror to tell her she was ugly. All she had to do was to look in somebody's eyes. Anybody's.

"I'll come," she said.

Billy grinned, his swollen eye giving his face a strange cast. "All *right*," he said.

"So what do we do?" Susanna added.

Billy scrambled to his feet. "We call him," he said, tapping his chest. "In here. And we have to really *believe* he's going to come."

Somewhat doubtfully, Susanna got to her feet as well. "Just like that?"

"It's got something to do with how badly we need to get away," Billy said. "At least that's what Judy said. All I know is that we only get the one chance."

He turned away and stared at the middle of the lot, brow furrowed with concentration. Susanna looked at him for a moment, then let her gaze follow his.

There was something too simple about this, she thought. Didn't magic have to be more complicated? This was something anybody could do. Except, she answered herself, you had to have the wolf figurine first. You had to have the key.

If anybody else had told her about this, she'd have thought, Yeah. Sure. And you better be good 'cause Santa is watching you. But this was Billy. Billy didn't go in for that kind of stuff except in books. He knew the difference between what was real and what wasn't. And he was tough. Too small to stand up to the bigger kids when they wanted to dump on someone, but tough enough to take it when it was dished out. He didn't run home and cry.

No, Susanna thought. Because what was waiting at home for him was ten times worse than what he'd get in the schoolyard.

So a wolf. She was game to call him. She felt sort of goofy doing it, but if the wolf could do a Peter Pan and take them away. . . .

She felt Billy trembling beside her and flicked her eyes open, not even able to remember when she'd shut them. She looked at Billy, realizing that she'd *felt* him tremble, except he was still standing a few feet away. It was as though the air had moved between their bodies, set into motion by the shiver of his skin to tickle hers. She could see him shake now, hands tight at his sides, trembling.

A funny look had come over his face. A happy look. She wondered if she'd ever seen him look this happy before—just dreamy, relaxed happy. She was about to call his name, when she heard a faint thrumming in the air. Then she realized that Billy wasn't just concentrating on calling the wolf—he was seeing something, out there in the middle of the lot.

Slowly she turned to see what it was. She thought she'd die.

There, in the middle of the lot, standing in amongst the weeds and broken bottles and refuse, was the biggest dog she'd ever seen. No. Not a dog. It had to be a wolf. *The* wolf. Its grizzled hackles were bushy like a lion's mane. Its chest was deep, its head broad. And its eyes . . . they were the color of a Siberian husky's, but this was no husky. This was something wild. Feral. With its crystal blue eyes that were like bright sunlight coming through an icicle.

Billy turned to her with shining eyes. "Oh, Suze . . . " His voice was a whispering breath.

Susanna nodded. It had come. She started to grin, but something was happening with the wolf. It was . . . changing. Standing on its hind legs now, nose lifted high, and its body began to shift and change until what stood out there in the empty lot was some hybrid creature, part man, part wolf.

Oh, jeez, Susanna thought. It's the wolfman from the late-night *Creature Feature* movies.

She took a nervous step back. Maybe she hadn't really believed, but Billy sure had and something—

(had to be a trick)

—had come. There it stood, something that shouldn't have been possible. But it wasn't scary—not like in the movies. Its eyes . . . they were distant, cool and warm all at the same time. You could get lost in those eyes. They promised relief from every pain. They could heal anything. Except the world didn't work that way, did it? There weren't any easy ways out—were there?

(had to be a trick)

Any minute now, the Cothorn brothers and some of their pals were going to come out from behind the fence on the other side of the lot, laughing and pointing at them. The wolfman was going to deflate because it—

(had to be a trick)

—was just a balloon. Or a cardboard cutout. A trick.

Except the wolfman really moved, and behind it now, opening like one of those futuristic doors in a science fiction movie that worked like a camera shutter, was an oval window into another world. Through that gap in the air they could see green fields unrolling under a blue sky, the colors so bright they hurt the eye. It—

(had to be a trick)

—was a mirage or a hallucination. Because there weren't wolfmen and if there were, they'd be in a zoo or a laboratory somewhere. And there was no such thing as magic, except for special effects in movies, and that was all tricks. And there weren't other worlds that you could just step into through a hole in the air. Except—

Billy took her arm. "Come on, Suze," he said, and he began to lead her toward the wolfman with its crystal eyes filled with promise. And now she could smell the world beyond it—a clean rich scent that was all good smells—autumn leaves burning, roses in summer, lilac blossoms in spring—all mixed together. The air that came wafting out of that hole in the air, from that other-world, was so pure and clean, you could almost see the difference between it and the tired old air of the lot.

They were going to step right in through that hole, Susanna thought. The wolfman was already turning, stepping gracefully over the lip, one hairy foot in that impossibly green grass, the other still in the dull end-of-summer weeds of the lot. It turned to look back, to make sure they were following.

They reached the hole in the air and Susanna pulled free of Billy's grip.

"Suze?" he said, confused. He looked from her, to the land through the gateway. Was the gateway getting smaller already?

"Don't you see?" Susanna said. "It—"

(has to be a trick)

"—can't be real."

Billy backed away from her. "No," he said, shaking his head.

The bruise on his face was like a dark accusation. "Don't say that, Suze."

She knew what he saw—years of hiding from school bullies, of beatings from his father. At least she had her family. But she saw . . . What did she see? That she was as scared of this as she was of everything else? Of leaving her house, because the other kids would dump on her? Of walking down the school halls to sniggers and laughter?

She wanted to believe that it was real. Billy stepped over the lip of the gateway. Behind him the wolfman watched her, a sad look in his blue eyes. Like the look in her grandfather's eyes when he'd given her his old jacket. Like the look in her parents' eyes when they'd tried to explain why she had to do without new glasses, or braces to straighten her crooked teeth, or all the other things they couldn't afford.

She wanted to believe, but she couldn't shake the fear that it was a trick. That she would step toward it, try to cross over, and then the laughter would start. All that endless laughter that was worse than being pushed or getting hit.

There came a humming in the air and she could see the sides of the gateway shimmering as they closed.

All I know is we only get the one chance, she heard Billy say in her mind.

She reached forward, she took a step closer, then hesitated again. This wasn't right. Maybe it wasn't a trick. Maybe the wolfman and that land through the gateway really *were* real. But it wasn't right. Maybe for Billy it was, but not for her. You didn't run away from your problems. That was what her parents said. And Grandad, too.

When she thought of her parents, and of the hurt that would be in her grandfather's eyes . . .

That wasn't the way you treated those you loved. She was scared to go, sure, but more than that she knew it would be wrong for her to run away.

So she let them go, Billy and the wolfman, running through those green fields. Just before the gate closed she saw that they were both wolves now, one big and one small, gamboling like puppies. Then the gateway was gone and she was standing all alone in the middle of the lot with a ringing in her ears. She moved through the spot where the gateway had been, but there was nothing there now. No gateway. No otherworld. But no Billy either.

She bent down and picked up the brass figurine. For one moment it seemed to shift in her hand, from wolf to man to wolf again. It was still warm from Billy's grip. It hadn't been a trick after all.

"B-billy?" she called.

The tears she'd kept at bay earlier this afternoon came welling up behind her eyes in a flood.

One chance, she thought she heard Billy say, but his voice was distant and very far away, like an echo. From an otherworld. *That's all.*

Loneliness settled in her and made her chest hurt. The emptiness of the weedy lot seemed to mock her decision, but she knew she'd done the right thing. The right thing. Why did doing the right thing have to hurt so much sometimes?

Bowing her head, she dropped the figurine into the dirt for someone else to find—someone who could use it, like she couldn't. No. Like she wouldn't. She turned away and shuffled slowly toward her bike. Pulling it up from the ground, she started to wheel it away, then turned for one last look.

"Say hello to . . . to Judy for me, Billy," she called softly.

And then she was standing up on the pedals, pumping away, tears shining in her eyes and dribbling down her cheeks and onto her jacket. The bike bumped across the field, and the alleyway swallowed her whole.

So THINGS got a little better for Susanna and her family. Her dad got a new job in Newford, and she survived her childhood troubles, but she wasn't really any happier than she'd been in the small midwestern town where she'd grown up.

Alone

IT SEEMED TO SUSANNA THAT SHE WAS ALWAYS FEELING miserable.

She pedaled her new mountain bike down Shady Lane, an incongruous name for the street if there ever was one. It was wide, lined on either side by bungalows and neatly trimmed lawns. The only trees were a few years old. No shade. No lane.

But then what could you expect from a place called Woodforest Gardens? The double arboreal adjective just seemed to mock the fact that if there ever had been a proper forest in the area, the developers of this latest patch of suburbia, newly tacked onto the suburban quilt that made up the northern outskirts of the city, had long since bulldozed it over.

She knew she should be happy. Her dad's new job might have uprooted them from the Midwest, but they had a nice house now, she had a new bike and a bedroom filled with furniture that she'd been able to pick out herself, her parents weren't bickering at all anymore, and they'd even been able to afford the braces that the dentist back home had said she'd needed years ago.

It wasn't even that she missed Johnstown; she'd been miserable there, too. But it had been a familiar misery. There she'd known who to avoid so that she wouldn't get teased—she could just imagine what Bobby Cothorn would have to say about the mouthful of steel that gleamed every time she forgot about the braces and opened her mouth to smile or talk.

("Susanna, would you please stop mumbling," was her mother's newest litany.)

In Johnstown she'd known all the best places to go to be alone so that no one could get on her case. Here the only good spot she'd found was a fifteen-minute bike ride to the far northern border of the development, where the fields began. It had all been farmland once; now it was overgrown bush.

The pavement under her bike's wheels petered out into a dead end, but a path led on through the field. Her mountain bike took to the rough trail with an alacrity that proved, for a change, that not all advertising was a lie. She'd been thinking of giving the bike a name, but at fourteen, she'd half-convinced herself doing so wouldn't be very mature.

It took her almost another ten minutes of traveling through fields thick with browning weeds and goldenrod to get to the spot she'd discovered about three weeks after they'd moved here. She leaned her bike up against an old oak tree. Its leaves overhead were just beginning to redden.

Now this was a tree, she thought, that belonged in a place called Woodforest Gardens. It had to be a hundred years old and was so undeniably *here* that it couldn't be ignored—not like all the tasteful designer greenery that only added to the development's sense of being a movie set instead of a place where real people lived.

She pushed her way through the brush until the ground suddenly dropped away underfoot and she stood on the very rim of the ravine. The drop on her side was seventy feet straight down, bare rock with a jumble of boulders at the bottom.

This had become a forbidden place. A week and a half ago one of the kids in her new school had fallen over the edge and died. Even without any friends at school, Susanna had heard the rumor that he hadn't fallen. He'd jumped.

The thought of it made her shiver. It was hard for a lot of kids her age to know what death meant, but not for her. A month before they left Johnstown, right in the middle of all the preparations of moving, her grandfather had died. He'd lived with them for as long as Susanna could remember and he'd been her best friend.

Missing him was a dull ache that just wouldn't go away. She still found herself, three months after he'd died, thinking at least a couple of times a day when she saw something neat, Wait'll I tell Grandad, and then remembering. . . .

She kicked a stone over the edge of the ravine and watched it fall.

Had the kid really jumped?

A twig snapped behind her and she started, losing her balance. She was falling forward, hands grabbing at the air, when someone caught hold of her jacket and hauled her back to safe ground. She turned, heartbeat accelerating, only to find herself face-to-face with Buddy Lapaglia.

She wasn't sure if she was relieved or not at being rescued.

There wasn't a wrong side of the tracks in Woodforest Gardens, but if there had been, Buddy would have lived there. He dressed like James Dean in the famous movie stills from *Rebel without a Cause*—white T-shirt, jeans, leather jacket and boots, hair slicked back—but his face had harder lines and his eyes were a cold gray. Dean was a romantic icon; Buddy was just plain scary.

He attended Mawson High where Susanna went, though he was rarely actually in class. In the various hierarchies of the schoolyard, he was the leader of the motorcycle brigade—bikers who eschewed Japanese makes for Harley Davidsons and Nortons. Where other kids would graduate and go on to university, these guys gave her the impression that the only thing they would graduate into was a serious biker gang like the Devil's Dragon.

Susanna had never been this close to any one of them before. When Buddy let go of her jacket, she almost stepped back over the edge of the ravine again, simply to put some space between them. Remembering that awful drop at the last moment, her pulse still hammering, she edged sideways. Buddy merely looked at her, then shook a cigarette out of a battered pack and lit up.

"You shouldn't smoke," Susanna found herself saying. "Don't you know it's bad for your health?"

Oh, God, she thought. What had made her say that?

"So's falling off cliffs," Buddy said.

That moment when she knew she was going to fall and nothing could save her returned to Susanna in a rush. Her mouth opened and closed soundlessly until she realized she must look like a fish.

"Uh, thanks," she said.

Buddy's eyebrows rose in a question.

"For, you know . . . pulling me back."

Buddy shrugged. He looked away from her, down into the ravine.

"Pete didn't fall," he said finally. "And he didn't jump."

Susanna blinked in confusion, then realized that he was talking about Peter Reid, the boy who'd died. They'd been friends, she remembered hearing at school, Buddy and Peter Reid. But if Peter hadn't fallen and he hadn't jumped, then that left only one other way he could have died.

"What are you saying?" she asked.

Buddy took another drag from his cigarette then dropped it on the leaves at their feet.

"Work it out for yourself," he said.

He turned and walked away through the trees. Susanna ground his smoldering cigarette butt under the toe of her shoe, then hurried after him, her fear swallowed by curiosity. Before she could reach the edge of the field, she heard him kick-start his motorcycle. She reached her own bicycle just in time to see him roar off down the narrow footpath on his Harley, the weeds and goldenrod slapping his elbows and knees as he sped through them.

She looked at where the motorcycle had been parked. She hadn't noticed it at all when she'd arrived. He'd been nearby, doing what? Watching her, she supposed, and that gave her the creeps. But before that, before she'd ever ridden up, what had he been doing here? From the tone of his voice, he hadn't been mourning Peter Reid's death. No, he'd sounded angry.

Susanna understood that feeling all too well. She'd raged when Grandad died. Raged and cried and . . .

She took off her glasses and rubbed her sleeve up against her eyes. The sound of Buddy's Harley had dwindled to a distant echo now. She looked back to where the ravine lay invisible beyond the trees.

If Peter Reid hadn't fallen and he hadn't jumped, that meant he had to have been pushed. But who had pushed him? And what did Buddy know about it?

* * *

She gathered up all her courage at school the following Monday. Waiting until he was by himself for a moment, she approached him, hands damp on her school books. He gave her a once-over, looked as though he was going to dismiss her as not worth his time, but finally nodded. It was neither a welcoming nor unfriendly gesture, but Susanna took it as an opening.

"Were you there?" she asked. "When he—Peter—when he died?"

Buddy's eyes narrowed to cold slits. "Where'd you get that idea?"

Susanna backed up a step. "Just, uh, from what you were saying on Saturday. How else could you know what happened to him?"

"What do you care?"

"I . . . I like to read mysteries," Susanna said finally. "I like to figure things out."

Buddy gave her another long, considering look.

"Why don't you ask Keith Thomson who was at the ravine that day," he said finally. "Maybe Pete was messing with his girlfriend."

Susanna shook her head. Keith Thomson and Judy Corbin were among Mawson High's aristocracy. He was the head boy and quarterback for the football team; she was the head of the debating club and a cheerleader. Susanna didn't know either of them personally, but she couldn't see Judy going with one of

Buddy's friends, nor could she believe that a Mawson High student could actually kill someone.

"We're all just kids," she said.

"And Pete's just dead," Buddy replied.

* * *

Susanna found herself watching Keith Thomson whenever she could, trying to see if there really could be a killer hidden behind the facade of a high school student. She went to football practices, sitting in the stands while the coach put the team through its moves. She tried to sit near his table in the lunchroom, hung around near the water fountain by his locker. It just didn't fit.

Finally she turned to Laurie Spoole, who was the closest she'd come to making a real friend since the school year had started. Laurie had attended Mawson right from public school so that even if she didn't know everybody personally, she at least knew the gossip.

"What do you know about Keith Thomson?" she asked.

Laurie laughed. "He's not going to ask you to the dance, if that's what you're thinking. Just take a good look at Judy Corbin and you don't even have to wonder why. She's gorgeous."

"I know that. I was just wondering what he's like."

"In two words: the perfect hunk. I can't think of anybody who doesn't like him, except maybe for some of the guys in the greaser crowd that hang around with your friend Buddy Lapaglia."

"He's not my friend."

Laurie shrugged. "Well, when I saw you talking to him in the parking lot a couple of days ago I just assumed . . ."

Susanna almost told Laurie what she and Buddy had been

talking about, but she quickly reconsidered. Laurie was nice enough, but she liked to talk. Susanna wasn't so sure it would be fair to let what Buddy had told her be grist for the school's rumor mill. Not when she was certain that it couldn't be true. But at the same time, the whole mystery of it was like a scab that she couldn't stop picking at.

"I was only asking him about his bike," she said. "A friend of mine back home always wanted to get one just like it."

Laurie shook her head. "You'd better stay away from Buddy." She leaned closer. "I hear that if you want to get high, you can get anything you want from him—any kind of drug at all. All you need is to have the money. A guy like that's just plain dangerous."

"Not like Keith Thomson," Susanna said, making a question of it.

"Not like Keith at all," Laurie agreed. "Except, well, if you're a guy, I wouldn't go making any moves on his girlfriend."

"He gets jealous?"

"He gets crazy. I remember when your friend Buddy—"

"He's not my friend," Susanna said automatically.

"—broke up with Angela Gatton at the beginning of the summer. He tried to put the make on Judy then while Keith and his family went out to Cape Cod for two weeks like they do every summer. I heard that Keith almost killed Buddy when he found out. It took two guys to pull him off."

She hadn't wanted to hear this, Susanna realized, but it was too late now. She looked across the crowded lunchroom to where Keith Thomson held court and suddenly felt queasy. She wanted to ask if Peter Reid had ever tried to come on to Keith's girlfriend as well, but her throat was too dry for her to form the words.

Happily, Laurie moved on to a new topic of conversation.

* * *

It wasn't easy to talk about Peter Reid around the high school; his death had affected everyone. Although he'd been Buddy's best friend, he wasn't completely a part of Buddy's greaser crowd. He'd made the football team this year; he'd written for the school paper last year. Susanna had gone through some of those old issues, reading his articles. They were opinion pieces, funny but they made a point at the same time.

The picture in the previous year's school yearbook that she borrowed from Laurie showed a dark-haired boy with strong features, a cowlick hanging over his brow, and deep thoughtful eyes. He'd had a story published in that same yearbook, about a boy losing his grandfather, that cut too close to home for Susanna. It made her cry.

She found herself wishing she'd known him. And she was more determined than ever to find out what had really happened to him.

The pieces of his life—at least how his classmates remembered him—became more complete as the weeks went by. Susanna was discreet about bringing him up, but she found ways. She grew more outgoing, through necessity. And one day, oddly enough, she realized that she was more accepted at this school than she'd ever been at home, glasses, braces, and all. Her search for the truth about Peter Reid's death had become a bit of an obsession, but it was helping her as well.

Finally, when she could still find no connection between

Peter and Keith, she brought the subject up with Laurie again.

"How come Keith never got on Peter Reid's case when he made a play for Judy?" she asked.

Laurie gave her a blank look for a long moment, then shook her head.

"You've gotten it mixed up," she said. "It wasn't Keith's girl-friend that Peter was with, it was Buddy's. That's why Buddy and Angela broke up."

"But you said that was at the beginning of last summer," Susanna said.

"It was. The way I heard it, Buddy knew she'd been seeing somebody, but he couldn't find out who. They kept arguing about it until she broke up with him. It wasn't until just before school started this year that he found out it had been Peter."

A sick feeling grew in Susanna's stomach.

"And what . . . what happened?" she asked.

"Nothing," Laurie said. "It was all history by then, I suppose. Buddy just laughed it off." Laurie gave her a considering look, and then added: "How come you're always asking about Peter?"

Susanna fought her nausea. She gave what she hoped was a casual shrug.

"I don't know," she said. "Nobody I went to school with ever died before, I guess. I just find myself curious about him."

Laurie shook her head. "You're weird, Susanna. That's al-most depraved."

"I suppose."

"And definitely not healthy."

Not to mention that it would probably be all over school by tomorrow, Susanna thought, although maybe she wasn't being fair. Still, how close were they? It wasn't as though she and Laurie were best friends. And then when you found out what best friends could do to each other, that someone could betray their best friend the way Peter had done by going out with Angela behind Buddy's back, and when Buddy could go out to the ravine with his best friend and . . . and . . .

She shivered.

She didn't want it to be true—even more than she hadn't wanted it to be true with Keith, because with Keith it would at least have been passion, but with Buddy, it seemed so planned. . . .

* * *

That night she couldn't sleep. She wished Grandad was in the room next to hers, the way he'd been back home in Johnstown— back in their real home. She needed someone to talk to, someone who would listen to her and take her seriously, even though she was only fourteen. Because she didn't know what to do. She knew she had to do something, but she just didn't know what.

Finally she got out of bed. She put on jeans and a sweater, tied up the laces of her hightops, and shrugged on her jacket. Keeping to the side of the hall that ran past her parent's bedroom so the floor wouldn't creak, she slipped out of the house.

It was cold outside. The development seemed transformed at this time of night. It was so silent and still that it felt more than ever like a movie set. She eased her bicycle out the side door of the garage and wheeled it to the street. Then she got on and pedaled for all she was worth, down the street, up another, the wind blowing frosty on her face, turning her cheeks red and making her eyes tear behind her glasses.

She stopped finally outside a house that looked no different from her own—only a little older. She wondered which room was Buddy's, wondered how she could get his attention without waking his parents, wondered why in God's name she was here in the middle of the night.

She could hear Laurie's voice in her head. *A guy like that's just plain dangerous.*

More dangerous than you could know, Laurie. Way more dangerous.

This was stupid. She wasn't some hard-boiled P.I., closing in on a killer with a gun in her hand the way it happened in the books she read. She was just a kid. Doing a stupid thing.

But she couldn't not do it. No one would listen to her, that was a given. Not her parents, not her teachers, not the police. She needed proof—all those same mystery books had drummed that into her head long ago—but proof was something she didn't have. She just *knew*, that was all. She'd put it all together, from what Buddy had told her, from what she'd learned about Peter Reid at school, from talking to Laurie.

She caught her kickstand with the toe of her shoe and tugged it into place so that her bike could stand on its own. Wiping her damp palms on her jeans, she took a deep steadying breath and started toward the house. Before she got more than a couple of steps, a voice came from the dark street behind her, stopping her in her tracks.

"What the hell are you doing here?"

She turned slowly, pulse drumming. The Lapaglia house was in between streetlights, so the figure that stood on the shadowed street in front of her was featureless. But she'd recognized Buddy's voice.

"I know what happened at the ravine," she said.

He made no response—didn't speak, didn't move. It was as though all the stillness of the night had settled into him.

"What I don't understand is why you wanted me to know," she added.

Still no response. Susanna remembered someone at school telling her that a lot of the greasers carried switchblades and that they weren't afraid to use them. She swallowed dryly.

"Buddy," she began.

"I didn't kill him," he said finally. "Angela did."

He stepped forward, his features coming into focus as he drew closer. Susanna wanted to bolt, but she was rooted to the spot, not so much by fear, but by a sense of responsibility toward Peter. It was funny, really. She'd never met Peter Reid when he was alive, but her efforts on his behalf had ended up making it so easy for her to fit in at the new school that she felt she owed him. She'd been so busy thinking about Peter that she hadn't had time to feel self-conscious or shy or stupid the way she usually did.

"Angela killed him?" she asked, her voice quiet.

Buddy nodded. "If she'd never . . . never slept with him . . . "

There was so much pain in his voice that Susanna found herself unaccountably wanting to comfort him, murderer or not. Instead she said, "But I heard you just laughed it off when you found out."

The toughness returned to his voice. "What was I supposed to do? It was old history by then. But I couldn't stop thinking about them, laughing at me all that time. You know what he said to me when I found out? 'Hey, I'm sorry, man. It just happened.' Jesus."

He reached into his pocket and Susanna tried to think of what she'd do if it was a knife he pulled out. All he did was take out his cigarettes and light one up. She couldn't help but notice his hands shaking.

"They were the two people I cared about most," Buddy went on. "They were the only people I ever cared about." He paused, then added, "Did you ever lose somebody you really cared about?"

Susanna thought of her grandfather and nodded.

But I didn't kill him, she thought.

"What happened at the ravine?" she asked.

"We used to go there all the time and party—me and Pete and Angie and whoever Pete brought along. It was a place where we had a lot of good times. Pete called me up that day and asked me to meet him there, said he wanted to talk. Things hadn't been the same since I found out, you know, but I was hoping maybe we could work it out, so I said sure, I'd meet him there.

"Well, he starts in again about how sorry he was about what happened, but that something had just clicked between the two of them. They broke it up, because they knew it was wrong, but they couldn't stop thinking about each other. They stayed apart the whole rest of the summer, but since it was out in the open now, and I'd just laughed about it when I found out it had been him, he wanted to tell me that he was going to start seeing Angie again. But first, before they made it public, he wanted to clear it with me."

Buddy shook his head as though he still couldn't believe it. "He wanted me to say it'd be okay. No hard feelings and all that."

He fell silent and finished his smoke. When he had the last drag, he flicked it away. It hit the street in a shower of sparks.

"And did you?" Susanna asked.

He looked at her for a long moment, then shook his head. "I couldn't believe what I was hearing. It was, like, it had been bad enough, knowing that they'd had to have been laughing at me all summer, and I'd tried to be cool when I found out, you know, but this . . . this . . .

"I shouted something at him, and he told me to take it easy, and then I just gave him a shove and he was over the edge. He screamed all the way down. He . . . Jesus, I hear him screaming still. Every night, I hear him."

Susanna cleared her throat softly. "It . . . it doesn't sound like you meant to push him. . . . "

He cut her off. "You know what I thought when he first went over the edge? I felt like laughing. I felt like yelling, 'This is what it feels like, sucker, when you mess with Buddy Lapaglia,' but then he hit the ground and I . . . he . . . I've never heard anything like that sound before and I hope to hell I never will again."

Susanna wasn't sure how she knew, but one minute he was standing there and in the next he would have just dropped to his knees if she hadn't caught hold of his arm and steered him over to the lawn. He sank down on the grass, head between his legs, hands in his hair.

"I miss him," he said. "Jesus, I miss him. . . . "

Susanna sat down beside him.

"What happens now?" she asked.

She no longer had to ask why he'd wanted her to find out what had happened. She knew now that he simply hadn't been able to keep the enormity of what had happened that afternoon to himself. No one could, not and still consider themselves human.

"I don't know what to do," he told her.

"There's only one thing you can do: you've got to tell the truth."

"But so far as the cops know, Pete just fell off that cliff. Or jumped. They're not looking for anybody, case closed."

"But you know," Susanna said.

He nodded slowly.

"And what about Peter—do you really want to have people thinking that maybe he did jump? What he did with Angela was pretty rotten, but you weren't much better yourself, going after Keith's girlfriend."

He nodded again, still drawn into himself.

"Peter didn't deserve to die," Susanna said. "And he doesn't deserve to be remembered as a loser."

When he turned to her, there were tears in his eyes. For the first time, Susanna realized that for all his toughness, Buddy was still just a kid, not that much older than she was herself.

She stayed there, sitting beside him, for a while longer, then finally got up. The night felt big around her, the stars beyond the streetlights were impossibly distant. She moved in front of where he sat and looked down at him.

"You know what you've got to do," she said when his gaze rose to meet hers.

He nodded.

"I'm scared," he said.

Susanna thought of being alone back in Johnstown, of how much her grandfather had meant to her, how important it had been knowing that at least one person cared, one person understood. She reached a hand down to him.

"I'll go with you," she said.

Buddy hesitated for a long moment, then he reached for her hand.

MAISIE FLOOD is a favorite character of mine, for all that the two stories in this collection are the only ones that feature her as a lead. She also appears in "The Pochade Box" in The Ivory and the Horn *(1995), and has a cameo in* The Onion Girl *(2001). Actually, most of the regular Newford characters appear in* The Onion Girl *at one point or another.*

What I like about Maisie is her resilience and her strong sense of ethics. She invariably does the right thing, even when it hurts.

But for the Grace Go I

You can only predict things
after they've happened.
                                                    —Eugene Ionesco

I INHERITED TOMMY THE SAME WAY I DID THE DOGS. FOUND him wandering lost and alone, so I took him home. I've always taken in strays—maybe because a long time ago I used to hope that someone'd take me in. I grew out of that idea pretty fast.

Tommy's kind of like a pet, I guess, except he can talk. He doesn't make a whole lot of sense, but then I don't find what most people have to say makes much sense. At least Tommy's honest. What you see is what you get. No games, no hidden agendas. He's only Tommy, a big guy who wouldn't hurt you even if you took a stick to him. Likes to smile, likes to laugh—a regular guy. He's just a few bricks short of a load, is all. Hell, sometimes I figure all he's got is bricks sitting back in there behind his eyes.

I know what you're thinking. A guy like him should be in an institution, and I suppose you're right, except they pronounced him cured at the Zeb when they needed his bed for somebody whose family had money to pay for the space he was taking up and they're not exactly falling over themselves to get him back.

We live right in the middle of that part of Newford that some people call the Tombs and some call Squatland. It's the dead part of the city—a jungle of empty lots filled with trash and abandoned cars, gutted buildings and rubble. I've seen it described in the papers as a blight, a disgrace, a breeding ground for criminals and racial strife, though we've got every color you can think of living in here and we get along pretty well together, mostly because we just leave each other alone. And we're not so much criminals as losers.

Sitting in their fancy apartments and houses, with running water and electricity and no worry about where the next meal's coming from, the good citizens of Newford have got a lot of names and ways to describe this place and us, but those of us who actually live here just call it home. I think of it as one of those outlaw roosts like they used to have in the Old West—some little ramshackle town, way back in the badlands, where only the outlaws lived. Of course those guys like L'Amour and Short who wrote about places like that probably just made them up. I find that a lot of people have this thing about making crap romantic, the way they like to blur outlaws and heroes, the good with the bad.

I know that feeling all too well, but I broke the only pair of rose-colored glasses I had the chance to own a long time ago. Sometimes I pretend I'm here because I want to be, because it's the only place I can be free, because I'm judged by who I am and what I can do, not by how screwed up my family is and how dirt poor looked pretty good from the position we were in.

I'm not saying this part of town's pretty. I'm not even saying I like living here. We're all just putting in time, trying to make do. Every time I hear about some kid OD'ing, somebody getting knifed, somebody taking that long step off a building or wrapping their belt around their neck, I figure that's just one more of us who finally got out. It's a war zone in here, and just like in Vietnam, they either carry you out in a box, or you leave under your own steam carrying a piece of the place with you—a kind of cold shadow that sits inside your soul and has you waking up in a cold sweat some nights, or feeling closed in and crazy in your new workplace, home, social life, whatever, for no good reason except that it's the Tombs calling to you, telling you that maybe you don't deserve what you've got now, reminding you of all those people you left behind who didn't get the break you did.

I don't know why we bother. Let's be honest. I don't know why I bother. I just don't know any better, I guess. Or maybe I'm just too damn stubborn to give up.

Angel—you know, the do-gooder who runs that program out of her Grasso Street office to get kids like me off the streets? She tells me I've got a nihilistic attitude. Once she explained what that meant, all I could do was laugh.

"Look at where I'm coming from," I told her. "What do you expect?"

"I can help you."

I just shook my head. "You want a piece of me, that's all, but I've got nothing left to give."

That's only partly true. See, I've got responsibilities, just like a regular citizen. I've got the dogs. And I've got Tommy. I was joking about calling him my pet. That's just what the bikers who're squatting down the street from us call him. I think of us all—me, the dogs, and Tommy—as family. Or about as close to family as any of us are ever going to get. I can't leave, because what would they do without me? And who'd take the whole pack of us, which is the only way I'd go?

Tommy's got this thing about magazines, though he can't read a word. Me, I love to read. I've got thousands of books. I get them all from the dump bins in back of bookstores—you know, where they tear off the covers to get their money back for the ones they don't sell and just throw the book away? Never made any sense to me, but you won't catch me complaining.

I'm not that particular about what I read. I just like the stories. Danielle Steel or Dostoyevsky, Somerset Maugham or Stephen King—doesn't make much difference. Just so long as I can get away in the words.

But Tommy likes his magazines, and he likes them with his name on the cover—you know, the subscription sticker? There's two words he can read: Thomas and Flood. I know his first name's Tommy, because he knows that much and that's what he told me. I made up the last name. The building we live in is on Flood Street.

He likes *People* and *Us* and *Entertainment Weekly* and *Life* and stuff like that. Lots of pictures, not too many words. He gets me to cut out the pictures of the people and animals and ads and stuff he likes and then he plays with them like they were paper dolls. That's how he gets away, I guess. Whatever works.

Anyway, I've got a post office box down on Grasso Street near Angel's office and that's where I have the subscriptions sent. I go down once a week to pick them up—usually on Thursday afternoons. It's all a little more than I can afford—makes me work a little harder at my garbage picking, you know?—but what am I going to do? Cut him off from his only pleasure? People think I'm hard—when they don't just think I'm crazy—and maybe I am, but I'm not mean.

The thing about having a post office box is that you get some pretty interesting junk mail—well at least Tommy finds it interesting. I used to throw it out, but he came down with me to the box one time and got all weirded out when he saw me throwing it out, so I bring most of it back now. He calls them his surprises. First thing he asks when I get back is "Were there any surprises?"

* * *

I went in the Thursday this all started and gave the clerk my usual glare, hoping that one day he'll finally get the message, but he never does. He was the one who sicced Angel on me in the first place. Thought nineteen was too young to be a bag lady, pretty girl like me. Thought he could help.

I didn't bother to explain that I'd chosen to live this way. I've been living on my own since I was twelve. I don't sell my bod and I don't do drugs. My clothes may be worn down and patched, but they're clean. I wash every day, which is more than I can say for some of the real citizens I pass by on the street. You can smell their B.O. half a block away. I look pretty regular except on garbage day when Tommy and I hit the streets with our shopping carts, the dogs all strung out around us like our own special honor guard.

There's nothing wrong with garbage picking. Where do you think all those fancy antique shops get most of their high-priced merchandise?

I do okay, without either Angel's help or his. He was probably just hard up for a girlfriend.

"How's it going, Maisie?" he asked when I came in, all friendly, like we're pals. I guess he got my name from the form I filled out when I rented the box.

I ignored him, like I always do, and gathered the week's pile up. It was a fairly thick stack—lots of surprises for Tommy. I took it all outside where Rexy was waiting for me. He's the smallest of the dogs, just a small little mutt with wiry brown hair and a real insecurity problem. He's the only one who comes everywhere with me, because he just falls apart if I leave him at home.

I gave Rexy a quick pat, then sat on the curb, sorting through Tommy's surprises. If the junk mail doesn't have pictures, I toss it. I only want to carry so much of this crap back with me.

It was while I was going through the stack that this envelope fell out. I just sat and stared at it for the longest time. It looked like one of those ornate invitations they're always making a fuss over in the romance novels I read: almost square, the paper really thick and cream-colored, ornate lettering on the outside that was real high-class calligraphy, it was so pretty. But that wasn't what had me staring at it, unwilling to pick it up.

The lettering spelled out my name. Not the one I use, but my real name. Margaret. Maisie's just a diminutive of it that I read about in this book about Scotland. That was all that was there, just "Margaret," no surname. I never use one except for when the cops decide to roust the squatters in the Tombs, like they do from time to time—I think it's like some kind of training exercise for them—and then I use Flood, same as I gave Tommy.

I shot a glance back in through the glass doors because I figured it had to be from the postal clerk—who else knew me?—but he wasn't even looking at me. I sat and stared at it a little longer, but then I finally picked it up. I took out my penknife and slit the envelope open, and carefully pulled out this card. All it said on it was "Allow the dark-robed access tonight and they will kill you."

I didn't have a clue what it meant, but it gave me a royal case of the creeps. If it wasn't a joke—which I figured it had to be—then who were these dark-robed and why would they want to kill me?

Every big city like this is really two worlds. You could say it's divided up between the haves and the have-nots, but it's not that simple. It's more like some people are citizens of the day and others of the night. Someone like me belongs to the night. Not because I'm bad, but because I'm invisible. People don't know I exist. They don't know and they don't care, except for Angel and the postal clerk, I guess.

But now someone did.

Unless it was a joke. I tried to laugh it off, but it just didn't work. I looked at the envelope again, checking it out for a return address, and that's when I realized something I should have noticed straightaway. The envelope didn't have my box number on it, it didn't have anything at all except for my name. So how the hell did it end up in my box? There was only one way.

I left Rexy guarding Tommy's mail—just to keep him occupied—and went back inside. When the clerk finished with the customer ahead of me, he gave me a big smile, but I laid the envelope down on the counter between us and didn't smile back.

Actually, he's a pretty good-looking guy. He's got one of those flat-top haircuts—shaved sides, kinky black hair standing straight up on top. His skin's the color of coffee, and he's got dark eyes with the longest lashes I ever saw on a guy. I could like him just fine, but the trouble is he's a regular citizen. It'd just never work out.

"How'd this get in my box?" I asked him. "All it's got is my name on it, no box number, no address, nothing."

He looked down at the envelope. "You found it in your box?"

I nodded.

"I didn't put it in there and I'm the one who sorts all the mail for the boxes."

"I still found it in there."

He picked it up and turned it over in his hands.

"This is really weird," he said.

"You into occult shit?" I asked him.

I was thinking of dark robes. The only people I ever saw wear them were priests or people dabbling in the occult.

He blinked with surprise. "What do you mean?"

"Nothing."

I grabbed the envelope and headed back to where Rexy was waiting for me.

"Maisie!" the clerk called after me, but I just ignored him.

Great, I thought as I collected the mail Rexy'd been guarding for me. First Joe postal clerk's got a good Samaritan complex over me—probably fueled by his dick—now he's going downright weird. I wondered if he knew where I lived. I wondered if he knew about the dogs. I wondered about magicians in dark robes and whether he thought he had some kind of magic that was going to deal with the dogs and make me go all gooshy for him—just before he killed me.

The more I thought about it, the more screwed up I got. I wasn't so much scared as confused. And angry. How was I supposed to keep coming back to get Tommy's mail, knowing he was there? What would he put in the box next? A dead rat? It wasn't like I could complain to anybody. People like me, we don't have any rights.

Finally I just started for home, but I paused as I passed the door to Angel's office.

Angel's a little cool with me these days. She still says she wants to help me, but she doesn't quite trust me anymore. It's not really her fault.

She had me in her office one time—I finally went, just to get her off my back—and we sat there for a while, looking at each other, drinking this crappy coffee from the machine that someone donated to her a few years ago. I wouldn't have picked it up on a dare if I'd come across it on my rounds.

"What do you want from me?" I finally asked her.

"I'm just trying to understand you."

"There's nothing to understand. What you see is what I am. No more, no less."

"But why do you live the way you do?"

Understand, I admire what Angel does. She's helped a lot of kids that were in a really bad way, and that's a good thing. Some people need help because they can't help themselves.

She's an attractive woman with a heart-shaped face, the kind of eyes that always look really warm and caring and long dark hair that seems to go on forever down her back. I always figured something really bad must have happened to her as a kid for her to do what she does. It's not like she makes much of a living. I think the only thing she really and honestly cares about is helping people through this sponsorship program she's developed where straights put up money and time to help the down-and-outers get a second chance.

I don't need that kind of help. I'm never going to be much more than what I am, but that's okay. It beats what I had before I hit the streets.

I've told Angel all of this a dozen times, but she sat there behind her desk, looking at me with those sad eyes of hers, and I knew she wanted a piece of me, so I gave her one. I figured maybe she'd leave me alone then.

"I was in high school," I told her, "and there was this girl who wanted to get back at one of the teachers—a really nice guy named Mr. Hammond. He taught English. So she made up this story about how he'd molested her and the shit really hit the van. He got suspended while the cops and the school board looked into the matter and all the time this girl's laughing her head off behind everybody's back, but looking real sad and screwed up whenever the cops and the social workers are talking to her.

"But I knew he didn't do it. I knew where she was, the night she said it happened, and it wasn't with Mr. Hammond. Now I wasn't exactly the best-liked kid in that school, and I knew what this girl's gang was going to do to me, but I went ahead and told the truth anyway.

"Things worked out pretty much the way I expected. I got

the cold shoulder from everybody, but at least Mr. Hammond got his name cleared and his job back.

"One afternoon he asks me to see him after school and I figure it's to thank me for what I've done, so I go to his classroom. The building's pretty well empty and the scuff of my shoes in the hallway is the only sound I hear as I go to see him. I get to the math room and he takes me back into his office. Then he locks the door and he rapes me. Not just once, but over and over again. And you know what he says to me while he's doing it?

"'Nobody's going to believe a thing you say,' he says. 'You try to talk about this and they're just going to laugh in your face.'"

I looked over at Angel and there were tears swimming in her eyes.

"And you know what?" I said. "I knew he was right. I was the one that cleared his name. There was *nobody* going to believe me, and I didn't even try."

"Oh, Jesus," Angel said. "You poor kid."

"Don't take it so hard," I told her. "It's past history. Besides, it never really happened. I just made it up because I figured it was the kind of thing you wanted to hear."

I'll give her this: she took it well. Didn't yell at me, didn't pitch me out onto the street. But you can see why maybe I'm not on her list of favorite people these days. On the other hand, she doesn't hold a grudge—I know that, too.

I felt like a hypocrite going in to see her with this problem, but I didn't have anyone else to turn to. It's not like Tommy or the dogs could give me any advice. I hesitated for the longest moment in the doorway, but then she looked up and saw me standing there, so I went ahead in.

I took off my hat—it's this fedora that I actually bought new because it was just too cool to pass up. I wear it all the time, my light brown hair hanging down from it, long and straight, though not as long as Angel's. I like the way it looks with my jeans and sneakers and this cotton shirt I found at a rummage sale that only needed a tear fixed on one of its shirttails.

I know what you're thinking, but hey, I never said I wasn't vain. I may be a squatter, but I like to look my best. It gets me into places where they don't let in bums.

Anyway I took off my hat and slouched in the chair on this side of Angel's desk.

"Which one's that?" she asked, pointing to Rexy who was sitting outside by the door like the good little dog he is.

"Rexy."

"He can come in if you'd like."

I shook my head. "No. I'm not staying long. I just had this thing I wanted to ask you about. It's . . ."

I didn't know where to begin, but finally I just started in with finding the envelope. It got easier as I went along. That's one thing you got to hand to Angel—there's nobody can listen like she does. You take up *all* of her attention when you're talking to her. You never get the feeling she's thinking of something else, or of what she's going to say back to you, or anything like that.

Angel didn't speak for a long time after I was done. When I stopped talking, she looked past me, out at the traffic going by on Grasso Street.

"Maisie," she said finally. "Have you ever heard the story of the boy who cried wolf?"

"Sure, but what's that got to do with—oh, I get it." I took out the envelope and slid it across the desk to her. "I didn't have to come in here," I added.

And I was wishing I hadn't, but Angel seemed to give herself a kind of mental shake. She opened the envelope and read the message, then her gaze came back to me.

"No," she said. "I'm glad you did. Do you want me to have a talk with Franklin?"

"Who's that?"

"The fellow behind the counter at the post office. I don't mind doing it, although I have to admit that it doesn't sound like the kind of thing he'd do."

So that was his name. Franklin. Franklin the creep.

I shrugged. "What good would that do? Even if he did do it—" and the odds looked good so far as I was concerned "—he's not going to admit to it."

"Maybe we can talk to his supervisor." She looked at her watch. "I think it's too late to do it today, but I can try first thing tomorrow morning."

Great. In the meantime, I could be dead.

Angel must have guessed what I was thinking, because she added, "Do you need a place to stay for tonight? Some place where you'll feel safe?"

I thought of Tommy and the dogs and shook my head.

"No, I'll be okay," I said as I collected my envelope and stuck it back in with Tommy's mail. "Thanks for, you know, listening and everything."

I waited for her to roll into some spiel about how she could do more, could get me off the street, that kind of thing, but it was like she was tuned right into my wavelength because she didn't say a word about any of that. She just knew, I guess, that I'd never come back if every time I talked to her that was all I could look forward to.

"Come see me tomorrow," was all she said as I got to my feet. "And Maisie?"

I paused in the doorway where Rexy was ready to start bouncing off my legs as if he hadn't seen me in weeks.

"Be careful," Angel added.

"I will."

* * *

I took a long route back to the squat, watching my back the whole time, but I never saw anybody that looked like he was following me, and not a single person in a dark robe. I almost laughed at myself by the time I got back. There were Tommy and the dogs, all sprawled out on the steps of our building until Rexy yelped and then the whole pack of them were racing down the street toward me.

Okay, big as he was, Tommy still couldn't hurt a flea even if his life depended on it and the dogs were all small and old and pretty well used up, but Franklin would still have to be crazy to think he could mess with us. He didn't *know* my family. You get a guy as big as Tommy and all those dogs . . . well, they just looked dangerous. What did I have to worry about?

The dogs were all over me then with Tommy right behind them. He grinned from ear to ear as I handed him his mail.

"Surprises!" he cried happily, in that weird high voice of his. "Maisie bring surprises!"

We went inside to our place up on the second floor. It's got this big open space that we use in the summer when we want the air to have a chance to move around. There are books everywhere. Tommy's got his own corner with his magazines and all the little cutout people and stuff that he plays with. There's a couple of mismatched kitchen chairs and a card table. A kind of old cabinet that some hobos helped me move up the one flight from the street holds our food and the Coleman stove I use for cooking.

We sleep on the mattresses over in another corner, the whole pack together, except for Chuckie. He's this old lab that likes to guard the doorway. I usually think he's crazy for doing so, but I wouldn't mind tonight. Chuckie can look real fierce when he wants to. There are a couple of chests by the bed area. I keep our clothes in one and dry kibbles for the dogs in another. They're pretty good scavengers, but I like to see that they're eating the right kind of food. I wouldn't want anything to happen to them. One thing I can't afford is vet bills.

First off I fed the dogs, then I made supper for Tommy and me—lentil soup with day-old buns I'd picked up behind a bakery in Crowsea. We'd been eating the soup for a few days, but we had to use it up because, with the spring finally here, it was getting too warm for food to keep. In the winter we've got smaller quarters down the hall, complete with a cast-iron stove that I salvaged from this place they were wrecking over in Foxville. Tommy and I pretty near killed ourselves hauling it back. One of the bikers helped us bring it upstairs.

We fell into our usual Thursday night ritual once we'd finished supper. After hauling down tomorrow's water from the tank I'd set up on the roof to catch rainwater, I lit the oil lamp, then Tommy and I sat down at the table and went through his new magazines and ads. Every time he'd point out something that he liked in a picture, I'd cut it out for him. I do a pretty tidy job, if I say so myself. Getting to be an old hand at it. By the time we finished, he had a big stack of new cutout people and stuff for his games that he just had to go try out right away. I went and got the book I'd started this morning and brought it back to the table, but I couldn't read.

I could hear Tommy talking to his new little friends. The dogs shifting and moving about the way they do. Down the street a Harley kicked over and I listened to it go through the Tombs until it faded in the distance. Then there was only the sound of the wind outside the window.

I'd been able to keep that stupid envelope with its message out of my head just by staying busy, but now it was all I could think about. I looked out the window. It was barely eight, but it was dark already. The real long days of summer were still to come.

So is Franklin out there? I asked myself. Is he watching the building, scoping things out, getting ready to make his move? Maybe dressed up in some black robe, him and a bunch of his pals?

I didn't really believe it. I didn't know him, but like Angel had said, it didn't seem like him and I could believe it. He might bug me, being all friendly and wanting to play Pygmalion to my Eliza Doolittle, but I didn't think he had a mean streak in him.

So where *did* the damn message come from? What was it supposed to mean? And, here was the scary part: if it wasn't a joke, and if Franklin wasn't responsible for it, then who was?

I kept turning that around and around in my mind until my head felt like it was spinning. Everybody started picking up on my mood. The dogs became all anxious and when I walked near them got to whining and shrinking away like I was going to hit them. Tommy got the shakes and his little people started tearing and then he was crying and the dogs started in howling and I just wanted to get the hell out of there.

But I didn't. It took me a couple of hours to calm Tommy down and finally get him to fall asleep. I told him the story he likes the best, the one where this count from some place far away shows up and tells us that we're really his kids and he takes us away, dogs and all, to our real home where we all live happily ever after. Sometimes I use his little cutouts to tell the story, but I didn't do that tonight. I didn't want to remind him of how a bunch'd gotten torn.

By the time Tommy was sleeping, the dogs had calmed down again and were sleeping too. I couldn't. I sat up all night worrying about that damned message, about what would happen to Tommy and the dogs if I did get killed, about all kinds of crap that I usually don't let myself think about.

Come the morning, I felt like I'd crawled up out of a sewer. You know what it's like when you pull an all-nighter? Your eyes have this burning behind them, you'd kill for a shower, and everything seems a little on edge? I saw about getting breakfast for everyone, let the dogs out for a run, then I told Tommy I had to go back downtown.

"You don't go out today," I told him. "You understand? You don't go out and you don't let anybody in. You and the dogs play inside today, okay? Can you do that for Maisie?"

"Sure," Tommy said, like I was the one with bricks for brains. "No problem, Maisie."

God I love him.

I gave him a big hug and a kiss, patted each of the dogs, then headed back down to Grasso Street with Rexy. I was about half a block from Angel's office when the headlines of a newspaper outside a drugstore caught my eye. I stopped dead in my tracks and just stared at it. The words swam in my sight, headlines blurring with the subheadings. I picked up the paper and unfolded it so that I could see the whole front page, then I started reading from the top.

GRIERSON SLAIN BY SATANISTS

Director of the City's New AIDS Clinic
Found Dead in Ferryside Graveyard
Amid Occult Paraphernalia

POLICE BAFFLED

MAYOR SAYS, "THIS IS AN OUTRAGE."

"Hey, this isn't a library, kid."

Rexy growled and I looked up to find the drugstore owner standing over me. I dug in my pocket until it coughed up a quarter, then handed it over to him. I took the paper over to the curb and sat down.

It was the picture that got to me. It looked like one of the buildings in the Tombs in which kids had been playing at ritual magic a few years ago. All the same kinds of candles and inverted pentacles and weird graffiti. Nobody squatted in that building anymore, though the kids hadn't been back for over a year. There was still something wrong about the place, like the miasma of whatever the hell it was that they'd been doing was still there, hanging on.

It was a place to give you the creeps. But this picture had something worse. It had a body, covered up by a blanket, right in the middle of it. The tombstones around it were all scorched and in pieces, like someone had set off a bomb. The police couldn't explain what had happened, except they did say it hadn't been a bomb, because no one nearby had heard a thing.

Pinpricks of dread went crawling up my spine as I reread the first paragraph. The victim, Grierson. Her first name was Margaret.

I folded the paper and got up, heading for the post office. Franklin was alone behind the counter when I got inside.

"The woman who died last night," I said before he had a chance to even say hello. "Margaret Grierson. The director of the AIDS Clinic. Did she have a box here?"

Franklin nodded. "It's terrible, isn't it? One of my friends says the whole clinic's going to fall apart without her there to run it. God, I hope it doesn't change anything. I know a half-dozen people that are going to it."

I gave him a considering look. A half-dozen friends? He had this real sad look in his eyes, like . . . Jesus, I thought. Was Franklin gay? Had he really been just making nice and not trying to jump my bones?

I reached across the counter and put my hand on his arm.

"They won't let this screw it up," I told him. "The clinic's too important."

The look of surprise in his face had me backing out the door fast. What the hell was I doing?

"Maisie!" he cried.

I guess I felt like a bit of a shit for having misjudged him, but all the same, I couldn't stick around. I followed my usual rule of thumb when things get heavy or weird: I fled.

I just started wandering aimlessly, thinking about what I'd learned. That message hadn't been for me, it had been for Grierson. Margaret, yeah, but Margaret Grierson, not Flood. Not me. Somehow it had gotten in the wrong box. I don't know who put it there, or how he knew what was going to happen last night before it happened, but whoever he was, he'd screwed up royally.

Better it had been me, I thought. Better a loser from the Tombs than someone like Grierson who was really doing something worthwhile.

When I thought that, I realized something that I guess I'd always known, but I just didn't ever let myself think about. You get called a loser often enough and you start to believe it. I know I did. But it didn't have to be true.

I guess I had what they call an epiphany in some of the older books I've read. Everything came together and made sense—except for what I was doing with myself.

I unfolded the paper again. There was a picture of Grierson near the bottom—one of those shots they keep on file for important people and run whenever they haven't got anything else. It was cropped down from one that had been taken when she cut the ribbon at the new clinic a few months back. I remembered seeing it when they ran coverage of the ceremony.

"This isn't going to mean a whole lot to you," I told her picture, "but I'm sorry about what happened to you. Maybe it should've been me, but it wasn't. There's not much I can do about that. But I can do something about the rest of my life."

I left the paper on a bench near a bus stop and walked back to Grasso Street to Angel's office. I sat down in the chair across from her desk, holding Rexy on my lap to give me courage, and I told her about Tommy and the dogs, about how they needed me and that was why I'd never wanted to take her up on her offers to help.

She shook her head sadly when I was done. She was looking a little weepy again—like she had when I told her that story before—but I was feeling a little weepy myself this time.

"Why didn't you tell me?" she asked.

I shrugged. "I guess I thought you'd take them away from me."

I surprised myself. I hadn't lied, or made a joke. Instead I'd told her the truth. It wasn't much, but it was a start.

"Oh, Maisie," she said. "We can work something out."

She came around the desk and I let her hold me. It's funny. I didn't mean to cry, but I did. And so did she. It felt good, having someone else be strong for a change. I haven't had someone be there for me since my grandma died in 1971, the year I turned eight. I hung in for a long time, all things considered, but the day that Mr. Hammond asked me to come see him after school was the day I finally gave up my nice little regulated slot as a citizen of the day and became a part of the night world instead.

I knew it wasn't going to be easy, trying to fit into the day world—I'd probably never fit in completely, and I don't think I'd want to. I also knew that I was going to have a lot of crap to go through and to put up with in the days to come, and maybe I'd regret the decision I'd made today, but right now it felt good to be back.

NEWFORD'S *A bit of a nexus for the weird and the strange, the scary and the wonderful, and draws like-minded individuals to it. The Kelledys, whom you meet in this next story, first appeared in a number of high fantasy stories I've written over the years. I don't know how they got to Newford from that otherworld where I first met them. One day I started a story called "The Drowned Man's Reel" (Dreams Underfoot, 1993), and there they were.*

At some point I should really find out, but I'll leave that puzzle for another day.

Ghosts of Wind and Shadow

There may be great and undreamed of possibilities awaiting mankind; but because of our line of descent there are also queer limitations.

—Clarence Day, from
This Simian World

TUESDAY AND THURSDAY AFTERNOONS, FROM TWO TO FOUR, Meran Kelledy gave flute lessons at the Old Firehall on Lee Street, which served as Lower Crowsea's community center. A small room in the basement was set aside for her at those times. The rest of the week it served as an office for the editor of *The Crowsea Times*, the monthly community newspaper.

The room always had a bit of a damp smell about it. The walls were bare except for two old posters: one sponsored a community rummage sale, now long past; the other was an advertisement for a Jilly Coppercorn one-woman show at the Green Man Gallery featuring a reproduction of the firehall that had been taken from the artist's *In Lower Crowsea* series of street scenes. It, too, was long out of date.

Much of the room was taken up by a sturdy oak desk. A computer sat on its broad surface, always surrounded by a clutter of manuscripts waiting to be put on diskette, spot art, advertisements, sheets of Letraset, glue sticks, pens, pencils, scratch pads, and the like. Its printer was relegated to an apple crate on the floor. A large corkboard in easy reach of the desk held a bewildering array of pinned-up slips of paper with almost indecipherable notes and appointments jotted on them. Post-its laureled the frame of the corkboard and the sides of the computer like festive yellow decorations. A battered metal filing cabinet held back issues of the newspaper. On top of it was a vase with dried flowers—not so much an arrangement as a forgotten bouquet. One week of the month, the entire desk was covered with the current issue in progress in its various stages of layout.

It was not a room that appeared conducive to music, despite the presence of two small music stands taken from their storage spot behind the filing cabinet and set out in the open space between the desk and door along with a pair of straight-backed wooden chairs, salvaged twice a week from a closet down the hall. But music has its own enchantment, and the first few notes of an old tune are all that it requires to transform any site into a place of magic, even if that location is no more than a windowless office cubicle in the Old Firehall's basement.

Meran taught an old style of flute playing. Her instrument of choice was that enduring cousin of the silver transverse orchestral flute: a simpler wooden instrument, side-blown as well, though it lacked a lip plate to help direct the airstream; keyless, with only six holes. It was popularly referred to as an Irish flute, since it was used for the playing of traditional Irish and Scottish dance music and the plaintive slow airs native to those same countries, but it had relatives in most countries of the world as well as in baroque orchestras.

In one form or another, it was one of the first implements created by ancient people to give voice to the mysteries that words cannot encompass but that they had a need to express. Only the drum was older.

With her last student of the day just out the door, Meran began the ritual of cleaning her instrument in preparation for packing it away and going home herself. She separated the flute into its three parts, swabbing dry the inside of each piece with a piece of soft cotton attached to a flute-rod. As she was putting the instrument away in its case, she realized that there was a woman standing in the doorway, a hesitant presence, reluctant to disturb the ritual until Meran was ready to notice her.

"Mrs. Batterberry," Meran said. "I'm sorry. I didn't realize you were there."

The mother of her last student was in her late thirties, a striking, well-dressed woman whose attractiveness was undermined by an obvious lack of self-esteem.

"I hope I'm not intruding . . . ?"

"Not at all; I'm just packing up. Please have a seat."

Meran indicated the second chair, which Mrs. Batterberry's daughter had so recently vacated. The woman walked gingerly into the room and perched on the edge of the chair, handbag clutched in both hands. She looked for all the world like a bird that was ready at any moment to erupt into flight and be gone.

"How can I help you, Mrs. Batterberry?" Meran asked.

"Please, call me Anna."

"Anna it is."

Meran waited expectantly.

"I . . . it's about Lesli," Mrs. Batterberry finally began.

Meran nodded encouragingly. "She's doing very well. I think she has a real gift."

"Here perhaps, but . . . well, look at this."

Drawing a handful of folded papers from her handbag, she passed them over to Meran. There were about five sheets of neat, closely written lines of what appeared to be a school essay. Meran recognized the handwriting as Lesli's. She read the teacher's remarks, written in red ink at the top of the first page—"Well written and imaginative, but the next time, please stick to the assigned topic"—then quickly scanned through the pages. The last two paragraphs bore rereading:

"The old gods and their magics did not dwindle away into murky memories of brownies and little fairies more at home in a Disney cartoon; rather, they changed. The coming of Christ and Christians actually freed them. They were no longer bound to people's expectations but could now become anything that they could imagine themselves to be.

"They are still here, walking among us. We just don't recognize them anymore."

Meran looked up from the paper. "It's quite evocative."

"The essay was supposed to be on one of the ethnic minorities of Newford," Mrs. Batterberry said.

"Then, to a believer in Faerie," Meran said with a smile, "Lesli's essay would seem most apropos."

"I'm sorry," Mrs. Batterberry said, "but I can't find any humor in this situation. This—" she indicated the essay "—it just makes me uncomfortable."

"No, I'm the one who's sorry," Meran said. "I didn't mean to make light of your worries, but I'm also afraid that I don't understand them."

Mrs. Batterberry looked more uncomfortable than ever. "It . . . it just seems so obvious. She must be involved with the occult, or drugs. Perhaps both."

"Just because of this essay?" Meran asked. She only just managed to keep the incredulity from her voice.

"Fairies and magic are all she ever talks about—or did talk about, I should say. We don't seem to have much luck communicating anymore."

Mrs. Batterberry fell silent then. Meran looked down at the essay, reading more of it as she waited for Lesli's mother to go on. After a few moments, she looked up to find Mrs. Batterberry regarding her hopefully.

Meran cleared her throat. "I'm not exactly sure why it is that you've come to me," she said finally.

"I was hoping you'd talk to her—to Lesli. She adores you. I'm sure she'd listen to you."

"And tell her what?"

"That this sort of thinking—" Mrs. Batterberry waved a hand in the general direction of the essay that Meran was holding "—is wrong."

"I'm not sure that I can—"

Before Meran could complete her sentence with "do that," Mrs. Batterberry reached over and gripped her hand.

"Please," the woman said. "I don't know where else to turn. She's going to be sixteen in a few days. Legally, she can live on her own then and I'm afraid she's just going to leave home if we can't get this settled. I won't have drugs or . . . or occult things in my house. But I . . ." Her eyes were suddenly swimming with unshed tears. "I don't want to lose her. . . ."

She drew back. From her handbag, she fished out a handkerchief which she used to dab at her eyes.

Meran sighed. "All right," she said. "Lesli has another lesson with me on Thursday—a makeup one for having missed one last week. I'll talk to her then, but I can't promise you anything."

Mrs. Batterberry looked embarrassed, but relieved. "I'm sure you'll be able to help."

Meran had no such assurances, but Lesli's mother was already on her feet and heading for the door, forestalling any attempt Meran might have tried to muster to back out of the situation. Mrs. Batterberry paused in the doorway and looked back.

"Thank you so much," she said, and then she was gone.

Meran stared sourly at the space Mrs. Batterberry had occupied.

"Well, isn't this just wonderful," she said.

* * *

From Lesli's diary, entry dated October 12:

> *I saw another one today! It wasn't at all the same as the one
> I spied on the Common last week. That one was more like a
> wizened little monkey, dressed up like an Arthur Rackham*

leprechaun. If I'd told anybody about him, they'd say that it was just a dressed-up monkey, but we know better, don't we?

This is just so wonderful. I've always known they were there, of course. All around. But they were just hints, things I'd see out of the corner of my eye, snatches of music or conversation that I'd hear in a park or the backyard, when no one else was around. But ever since Midsummer's Eve, I've actually been able to see them.

I feel like a birder, noting each new separate species I spot down here on your pages, but was there ever a bird-watcher that could claim to have seen the marvels I have? It's like, all of a sudden, I've finally learned how to see.

This one was at the Old Firehall of all places. I was having my weekly lesson with Meran—I get two this week because she was out of town last week. Anyway, we were playing my new tune—the one with the arpeggio bit in the second part that I'm supposed to be practicing but can't quite get the hang of. It's easy when Meran's playing along with me, but when I try to do it on my own, my fingers get all fumbly and I keep muddling up the middle D.

I seem to have gotten sidetracked. Where was I? Oh yes. We were playing "Touch Me If You Dare" and it really sounded nice with both of us playing. Meran just seemed to pull my playing along with hers until it got lost in her music and you couldn't tell which instrument was which, or even how many there were playing.

It was one of those perfect moments. I felt like I was in a trance or something. I had my eyes closed, but then I felt the air getting all thick. There was this weird sort of pres-

sure on my skin, as though gravity had just doubled or some-thing. I kept on playing, but I opened my eyes and that's when I saw her—hovering up behind Meran's shoulders.

She was the neatest thing I've ever seen—just the tini-est little faerie, ever so pretty, with gossamer wings that moved so quickly to keep her aloft that they were just a blur. They moved like a hummingbird's wings. She looked just like the faeries on a pair of earrings I got a few years ago at a stall in the Market—sort of a Mucha design and all deli-cate and airy. But she wasn't two dimensional or just one color.

Her wings were like a rainbow blaze. Her hair was like honey, her skin a soft-burnished gold. She was wearing— now don't blush, Diary—nothing at all on top and just a gauzy skirt that seemed to be made of little leaves that kept changing color, now sort of pink, now mauve, now bluish.

I was so surprised that I almost dropped my flute. I didn't—wouldn't that give Mom something to yell at me for if I broke it!—but I did muddle the tune. As soon as the mu-sic faltered—just like that, as though the only thing that was keeping her in this world was that tune—she disap-peared.

I didn't pay a whole lot of attention to what Meran was saying for the rest of the lesson, but I don't think she noticed. I couldn't get the faerie out of my mind. I still can't. I wish Mom had been there to see her, or stupid old Mr. Allen. They couldn't say it was just my imagination then!

Of course they probably wouldn't have been able to see her anyway. That's the thing with magic. You've got to know it's still here, all around us, or it just stays invisible for you.

After my lesson, Mom went in to talk to Meran and made me wait in the car. She wouldn't say what they'd talked about, but she seemed to be in a way better mood than usual when she got back. God, I wish she wouldn't get so uptight.

* * *

"So," Cerin said finally, setting aside his book. Meran had been moping about the house for the whole of the hour since she'd gotten home from the Firehall. "Do you want to talk about it?"

"You'll just say I told you so."

"Told you so how?"

Meran sighed. "Oh, you know. How did you put it? 'The problem with teaching children is that you have to put up with their parents.' It was something like that."

Cerin joined her in the window seat where she'd been staring out at the garden. He looked out at the giant old oaks that surrounded the house and said nothing for a long moment. In the fading afternoon light, he could see little brown men scurrying about in the leaves like so many monkeys.

"But the kids are worth it," he said finally.

"I don't see you teaching children."

"There's just not many parents that can afford a harp for their prodigies."

"But still . . ."

"Still," he agreed. "You're perfectly right. I don't like dealing with their parents; never did. When I see children put into little boxes, their enthusiasms stifled . . . Everything gets regimented

into what's proper and what's not, into recitals and passing exam-
inations instead of just playing—" He began to mimic a hoity-
toity voice. "I don't care if you want to play in a rock band, you'll
learn what I tell you to learn. . . ."

His voice trailed off. In the back of his eyes, a dark light
gleamed—not quite anger, more frustration.

"It makes you want to give them a good whack," Meran said.

"Exactly. So did you?"

Meran shook her head. "It wasn't like that, but it was almost
as bad. No, maybe it was worse."

She told her husband about what Lesli's mother had asked of
her, handing over the English essay when she was done so that
he could read it for himself.

"This is quite good, isn't it?" he said when he reached the
end.

Meran nodded. "But how can I tell Lesli that none of it's true
when I know it is?"

"You can't."

Cerin laid the essay down on the windowsill and looked out
at the oaks again. The twilight had crept up on the garden while
they were talking. All the trees wore thick mantles of shadow
now—poor recompense for the glorious cloaks of leaves that the
season had stolen from them over the past few weeks. At the base
of one fat trunk, the little monkey men were roasting skewers of
mushrooms and acorns over a small, almost smokeless fire.

"What about Anna Batterberry herself?" he asked. "Does she
remember anything?"

Meran shook her head. "I don't think she even realizes that
we've met before, that she changed but we never did. She's like

most people; if it doesn't make sense, she'd rather convince herself that it simply never happened."

Cerin turned from the window to regard his wife.

"Perhaps the solution would be to remind her, then," he said.

"I don't think that's such a good idea. It'd probably do more harm than good. She's just not the right sort of person. . . ."

Meran sighed again.

"But she could have been," Cerin said.

"Oh yes," Meran said, remembering. "She could have been. But it's too late for her now."

Cerin shook his head. "It's never too late."

* * *

From Lesli's diary, addendum to the entry dated October 12:

> *I hate living in this house! I just hate it! How could she do this to me? It's bad enough that she never lets me so much as breathe without standing there behind me to determine that I'm not making a vulgar display of myself in the process, but this really isn't fair.*
>
> *I suppose you're wondering what I'm talking about. Well, remember that essay I did on ethnic minorities for Mr. Allen? Mom got her hands on it and it's convinced her that I've turned into a Satan-worshipping drug fiend. The worst thing is that she gave it to Meran and now Meran's supposed to "have a talk with me to set me straight" on Thursday.*
>
> *I just hate this. She had no right to do that. And how am I supposed to go to my lesson now? It's so embarrassing. Not to mention disappointing. I thought Meran would un-*

derstand. I never thought she'd take Mom's side—not on something like this.

Meran's always seemed so special. It's not just that she wears all those funky clothes and doesn't talk down to me and looks just like one of those Pre-Raphaelite women, except that she's got those really neat green streaks in her hair. She's just a great person. She makes playing music seem so effortlessly magical and she's got all these really great stories about the origins of the tunes. When she talks about things like where "The Gold Ring" came from, it's like she really believes it was the faeries that gave that piper the tune in exchange for the lost ring he returned to them. The way she tells it, it's like she was there when it happened.

I feel like I've always known her. From the first time I saw her, I felt like I was meeting an old friend. Sometimes I think that she's magic herself—a kind of oak-tree faerie princess who's just spending a few years living in the Fields We Know before she goes back home to the magic place where she really lives.

Why would someone like that involve themselves in my mother's crusade against Faerie?

I guess I was just being naive. She's probably no different from Mom or Mr. Allen and everybody else who doesn't believe. Well, I'm not going to any more stupid flute lessons, that's for sure.

I hate living here. Anything'd be better.

Oh, why couldn't I just have been stolen by the faeries when I was a baby? Then I'd be there and there'd just be some changeling living here in my place. Mom could turn it into a good little robot instead. Because that's all she wants. She doesn't want a daughter who can think on her own, but a boring, closed-minded junior model of herself. She should have gotten a dog instead of having a kid. Dogs are easy to train and they like being led around on a leash.

I wish Granny Nell was still alive. She would never, ever have tried to tell me that I had to grow up and stop imagining things. Everything seemed magic when she was around. It was like she was magic—just like Meran. Sometimes when Meran's playing her flute, I almost feel as though Granny Nell's sitting there with us, just listening to the music with that sad wise smile of hers.

I know I was only five when she died, but lots of the time she seems more real to me than any of my relatives that are still alive.

If she was still alive, I could be living with her right now and everything'd be really great.

Jeez, I miss her.

* * *

Anna Batterberry was in an anxious state when she pulled up in front of the Kelledy house on McKennitt Street. She checked the street number that hung beside the wrought-iron gate where the walkway met the sidewalk and compared it against the address she'd hurriedly scribbled down on a scrap of paper before leaving home. When she was sure that they were the same, she slipped out of the car and approached the gate.

Walking up to the house, the sound of her heels was loud on the walkway's flagstones. She frowned at the thick carpet of fallen oak leaves that covered the lawn. The Kelledys had better hurry in cleaning them up, she thought. The city work crews would only be collecting leaves for one more week and they had to be neatly bagged and sitting at the curb for them to do so. It was a shame that such a pretty estate wasn't treated better.

When she reached the porch, she spent a disorienting moment trying to find a doorbell, then realized that there was only the small brass door knocker in the middle of the door. It was shaped like a Cornish piskie.

The sight of it gave her a queer feeling. Where had she seen that before? In one of Lesli's books, she supposed.

Lesli.

At the thought of her daughter, she quickly reached for the knocker, but the door swung open before she could use it. Lesli's flute teacher stood in the open doorway and regarded her with a puzzled look.

"Mrs. Batterberry," Meran said, her voice betraying her surprise. "Whatever are you—"

"It's Lesli," Anna said, interrupting. "She's . . . she . . ."

Her voice trailed off as what she could see of the house's interior behind Meran registered. A strange dissonance built up in her mind at the sight of the long hallway, paneled in dark wood, the thick Oriental carpet on the hardwood floor, the old photographs and prints that hung from the walls. It was when she focused on the burnished metal umbrella stand, which was, itself, in the shape of a partially opened umbrella, and the sidetable, on which stood a cast-iron, grinning gargoyle bereft of its roof gutter home, that the curious sense of familiarity she felt delved deep into the secret recesses of her mind and connected with a swell of long-forgotten memories.

She put out a hand against the doorjamb to steady herself as the flood rose up inside her. She saw her mother-in-law standing in that hallway with a kind of glow around her head. She was older than she'd been when Anna had married Peter, years older, her body wreathed in a golden Botticelli nimbus, that beatific smile on her lips, Meran Kelledy standing beside her, the two of them sharing some private joke, and all around them presences seemed to slip and slide across one's vision.

No, she told herself. None of that was real. Not the golden glow, nor the flickering twig-thin figures that teased the mind from the corner of the eye.

But she'd thought she'd seen them. Once. More than once. Many times. Whenever she was with Helen Batterberry . . .

Walking in her mother-in-law's garden and hearing music, turning the corner of the house to see a trio of what she first took to be children, then realized were midgets, playing fiddle and flute and drum, the figures slipping away as they approached, winking out of existence, the music fading but its echoes lingering on. In the mind. In memory. In dreams.

"Faerie," her mother-in-law explained to her, matter-of-factly.

Lesli as a toddler, playing with her invisible friends that could actually be *seen* when Helen Batterberry was in the room.

No. None of that was possible.

That was when she and Peter were going through a rough period in their marriage. Those sights, those strange ethereal beings, music played on absent instruments, they were all part and parcel of what she later realized had been a nervous breakdown. Her analyst had agreed.

But they'd seemed so real.

In the hospital room where her mother-in-law lay dying, her bed a clutter of strange creatures, tiny wizened men, small perfect women, all of them flickering in and out of sight, the wonder of their presences, the music of their voices, Lesli sitting wide-eyed by the bed as the courts of Faerie came to bid farewell to an old friend.

"Say you're going to live forever," Lesli had said to her grandmother.

"I will," the old woman replied. "But you have to remember me. You have to promise never to close your awareness to the Otherworld around you. If you do that, I'll never be far."

All nonsense.

But there in the hospital room, with the scratchy sound of the IVAC pump, the clean white walls, the incessant beep of the heart monitor, the antiseptic sting in the air, Anna could only shake her head.

"None . . . none of this is real . . ." she said.

Her mother-in-law turned her head to look at her, an infinite sadness in her dark eyes.

"Maybe not for you," she said sadly, "but for those who will see, it will always be there."

And later, with Lesli at home, when just she and Peter were there, she remembered Meran coming into that hospital room, Meran and her husband, neither of them having aged since the first time Anna had seen them at her mother-in-law's house, years, oh, years ago now. The four of them were there when Helen Batterberry died. She and Peter had bent their heads over the body at the moment of death, but the other two, the unaging musicians who claimed Faerie more silently, but as surely and subtly as ever Helen Batterberry had, stood at the window and watched the twilight grow across the hospital lawn as though they could see the old woman's spirit walking off into the night.

They didn't come to the funeral.

They—

She tried to push the memories aside, just as she had when the events had first occurred, but the flood was too strong. And worse, she knew they were true memories. Not the clouded rantings of a stressful mind suffering a mild breakdown.

Meran was speaking to her, but Anna couldn't hear what she was saying. She heard a vague, disturbing music that seemed to come from the ground underfoot. Small figures seemed to caper and dance in the corner of her eye, humming and buzzing like summer bees. Vertigo gripped her and she could feel herself falling. She realized that Meran was stepping forward to catch her, but by then the darkness had grown too seductive and she simply let herself fall into its welcoming depths.

* * *

From Lesli's diary, entry dated October 13:

> I've well and truly done it. I got up this morning and instead of my school books, I packed my flute and some clothes and you, of course, in my knapsack; and then I just left. I couldn't live there anymore. I just couldn't.
>
> Nobody's going to miss me. Daddy's never home anyway and Mom won't be looking for me—she'll be looking for her idea of me and that person doesn't exist. The city's so big that they'll never find me.

I was kind of worried about where I was going to stay tonight, especially with the sky getting more and more overcast all day long, but I met this really neat girl in Fitzhenry Park this morning. Her name's Susan and even though she's just a year older than me, she lives with this guy in an apartment in Chinatown. She's gone to ask him if I can stay with them for a couple of days. His name's Paul. Susan says he's in his late twenties, but he doesn't act at all like an old guy. He's really neat and treats her like she's an adult, not a kid. She's his girlfriend!

I'm sitting in the park waiting for her to come back as I write this. I hope she doesn't take too long because there's some weird-looking people around here. This one guy sitting over by the War Memorial keeps giving me the eye like he's going to hit on me or something. He really gives me the creeps. He's got this kind of dark aura that flickers around him so I know he's bad news.

I know it's only been one morning since I left home, but I already feel different. It's like I was dragging around this huge weight and all of a sudden it's gone. I feel light as a feather. Of course, we all know what that weight was: neuro-mother.

Once I get settled in at Susan and Paul's, I'm going to go look for a job. Susan says Paul can get me some fake ID so that I can work in a club or something and make some real money. That's what Susan does. She said that there's been times when she's made fifty bucks in tips in just one night!

I've never met anyone like her before. It's hard to be-

lieve she's almost my age. When I compare the girls at school to her, they just seem like a bunch of kids. Susan dresses so cool, like she just stepped out of an MTV video. She's got short funky black hair, a leather jacket, and jeans so tight I don't know how she gets into them. Her T-shirt's got this really cool picture of a Brian Froud faerie on it that I'd never seen before.

When I asked her if she believes in Faerie, she just gave me this big grin and said, "I'll tell you, Lesli, I'll believe in anything that makes me feel good."

I think I'm going to like living with her.

* * *

When Anna Batterberry regained consciousness, it was to find herself inside that disturbingly familiar house. She lay on a soft, overstuffed sofa, surrounded by the crouching presences of far more pieces of comfortable-looking furniture than the room was really meant to hold. The room simply had a too-full look about it, aided and abetted by a bewildering array of knickknacks that ranged from dozens of tiny porcelain miniatures on the mantle, each depicting some anthropomorphized woodland creature playing a harp or a fiddle or a flute, to a life-sized fabric maché sculpture of a grizzly bear in top hat and tails that reared up in one corner of the room.

Every square inch of wall space appeared to be taken up with posters, framed photographs, prints, and paintings. Old-fashioned curtains—the print was large dusky roses on a black background—stood guard on either side of a window seat. Underfoot was a thick carpet that had been woven into a sem-blance of the heavily leafed yard outside.

The more she looked around herself, the more familiar it all looked. And the more her mind filled with memories that she'd spent so many years denying.

The sound of a footstep had her sitting up and half-turning to look behind the sofa at who—or maybe even, what—was approaching. It was only Meran. The movement brought back the vertigo and she lay down once more. Meran sat down on an ottoman that had been pulled up beside the sofa and laid a deliciously cool damp cloth against Anna's brow.

"You gave me a bit of a start," Meran said, "collapsing on my porch like that."

Anna had lost her ability to be polite. Forsaking small talk, she went straight for the heart of the matter.

"I've been here before," she said.

Meran nodded.

"With my mother-in-law—Helen Batterberry."

"Nell," Meran agreed. "She was a good friend."

"But why haven't *I* remembered that I'd met you before until today?"

Meran shrugged. "These things happen."

"No," Anna said. "People forget things, yes, but not like this. I didn't just meet you in passing, I knew you for years—from my last year in college when Peter first began dating me. You were at his parents' house the first time he took me home. I remember thinking how odd that you and Helen were such good friends, considering how much younger you were than her."

"Should age make a difference?" Meran asked.

"No. It's just . . . you haven't changed at all. You're still the same age."

"I know," Meran said.

"But . . ." Anna's bewilderment accentuated her nervous bird temperament. "How can that be possible?"

"You said something about Lesli when you first arrived," Meran said, changing the subject.

That was probably the only thing that could have drawn Anna away from the quagmire puzzle of agelessness and hidden music and twitchy shapes moving just beyond the grasp of her vision.

"She's run away from home," Anna said. "I went into her room to get something and found that she'd left all her schoolbooks just sitting on her desk. Then when I called the school, they told me that she'd never arrived. They were about to call me to ask if she was ill. Lesli never misses school, you know."

Meran nodded. She hadn't, but it fit with the image of the relationship between Lesli and her mother that was growing in her mind.

"Have you called the police?" she asked.

"As soon as I got off the phone. They told me it was a little early to start worrying—can you imagine that? The detective I spoke to said that he'd put out her description so that his officers would keep an eye out for her, but basically he told me that she must just be skipping school. Lesli would *never* do that."

"What does your husband say?"

"Peter doesn't know yet. He's on a business trip out east and I won't be able to talk to him until he calls me tonight. I don't even know what hotel he'll be staying in until he calls." Anna reached out with a bird-thin hand and gripped Meran's arm. "What am I going to do?"

"We could go looking for her ourselves."

Anna nodded eagerly at the suggestion, but then the futility of that course of action hit home.

"The city's so big," she said. "It's too big. How would we ever find her?"

"There is another way," Cerin said.

Anna started at the new voice. Meran removed the damp cloth from Anna's brow and moved back from the sofa so that Anna could sit up once more. She looked at the tall figure standing in the doorway, recognizing him as Meran's husband. She didn't remember him seeming quite so intimidating before.

"What . . . what way is that?" Anna said.

"You could ask for help from Faerie," Cerin told her.

* * *

"So—you're gonna be one of Paulie's girls?"

Lesli looked up from writing in her diary to find that the creepy guy by the War Memorial had sauntered over to stand beside her bench. Up close, he seemed even tougher than he had from a distance. His hair was slicked back on top, long at the back. He had three earrings in his left earlobe, one in the right. Dirty jeans were tucked into tall black cowboy boots. His white shirt was half open under his jean jacket. There was an oily look in his eyes that made her shiver.

She quickly shut the diary, keeping her place with a finger, and looked around hopefully to see if Susan was on her way back, but there was no sign of her new friend. Taking a deep breath, she gave him what she hoped was a look of appropriate streetwise bravado.

"I . . . I don't know what you're talking about," she said.

"I saw you talking to Susie," he said, sitting down beside her on the bench. "She's Paulie's recruiter."

Lesli started to get a bad feeling right about then. It wasn't just that this guy was so awful, but that she might have made a terrible misjudgment when it came to Susan.

"I think I should go," she said.

She started to get up, but he grabbed her arm. Off balance, she fell back onto the bench.

"Hey, look," he said. "I'm doing you a favor. Paulie's got ten or twelve girls in his string and he works them like they're dogs. You look like a nice kid. Do you really want to spend the next ten years peddling your ass for some homeboy who's gonna have you hooked on junk before the week's out?"

"I—"

"See, I run a clean shop. No drugs, nice clothes for the girls, nice apartment that you're gonna share with just one other girl, not a half dozen the way Paulie runs his biz. My girls turn maybe two, three tricks a night and that's it. Paulie'll have you on the street nine, ten hours a pop, easy."

His voice was calm, easygoing, but Lesli had never been so scared before in her life.

"Please," she said. "You're making a mistake. I really have to go."

She tried to rise again, but he kept a hand on her shoulder so that she couldn't get up. His voice, so mild before, went hard.

"You go anywhere, babe, you're going with me," he said. "There are no other options. End of conversation."

He stood up and hauled her to her feet. His hand held her in a bruising grip. Her diary fell from her grip, and he let her pick it up and stuff it into her knapsack, but then he pulled her roughly away from the bench.

"You're hurting me!" she cried.

He leaned close to her, his mouth only inches from her ear.

"Keep that up," he warned her, "and you're really gonna find out what pain's all about. Now make nice. You're working for me now."

"I . . ."

"Repeat after me, sweet stuff: I'm Cutter's girl."

Tears welled in Lesli's eyes. She looked around the park, but nobody was paying any attention to what was happening to her. Cutter gave her a painful shake that made her teeth rattle.

"C'mon," he told her. "Say it."

He glared at her with the promise of worse to come in his eyes if she didn't start doing what he said. His grip tightened on her shoulder, fingers digging into the soft flesh of her upper arm.

"Say it!"

"I . . . I'm Cutter's . . . girl."

"See? That wasn't so hard."

He gave her another shove to start her moving again. She wanted desperately to break free of his hand and just run, but as he marched her across the park, she discovered that she was too scared to do anything but let him lead her away.

She'd never felt so helpless or alone in all her life. It made her feel ashamed.

* * *

"Please don't joke about this," Anna said in response to Cerin's suggestion that they turn to Faerie for help in finding Lesli.

"Yes," Meran agreed, though she wasn't speaking of jokes. "This isn't the time."

Cerin shook his head. "This seems a particularly appropriate time to me." He turned to Anna. "I don't like to involve myself in private quarrels, but since it's you that's come to us, I feel I have the right to ask you this: Why is it, do you think, that Lesli ran away in the first place?"

"What are you insinuating? That I'm not a good mother?"

"Hardly. I no longer know you well enough to make that sort of a judgment. Besides, it's not really any of my business, is it?"

"Cerin, please," Meran said.

A headache was starting up between Anna's temples.

"I don't understand," Anna said. "What is it that you're saying?"

"Meran and I loved Nell Batterberry," Cerin said. "I don't doubt that you held some affection for her as well, but I do know that you thought her a bit of a daft old woman. She told me once that after her husband—after Philip—died, you tried to convince Peter that she should be put in a home. Not in a home for the elderly, but for the, shall we say, gently mad?"

"But she—"

"Was full of stories that made no sense to you," Cerin said. "She heard and saw what others couldn't, though she had the gift that would allow such people to see into the invisible world of Faerie when they were in her presence. You saw into that world once, Anna. I don't think you ever forgave her for showing it to you."

"It . . . it wasn't real."

Cerin shrugged. "That's not really important at this moment.

What's important is that, if I understand the situation correctly, you've been living in the fear that Lesli would grow up just as fey as her grandmother. And if this is so, your denying her belief in Faerie lies at the root of the troubles that the two of you share."

Anna looked to Meran for support, but Meran knew her husband too well and kept her own counsel. Having begun, Cerin wouldn't stop until he said everything he meant to.

"Why are you doing this to me?" Anna asked. "My daughter's run away. All of . . . all of this . . ." She waved a hand that was perhaps meant to take in just the conversation, perhaps the whole room. "It's not real. Little people and fairies and all the things my mother-in-law reveled in discussing just aren't real. She could make them *seem* real, I'll grant you that, but they could never exist."

"In your world," Cerin said.

"In the real world."

"They're not one and the same," Cerin told her.

Anna began to rise from the sofa. "I don't have to listen to any of this," she said. "My daughter's run away and I thought you might be able to help me. I didn't come here to be mocked."

"The only reason I've said anything at all," Cerin told her, "is for Lesli's sake. Meran talks about her all the time. She sounds like a wonderful, gifted child."

"She is."

"I hate the thought of her being forced into a box that doesn't fit her. Of having her wings cut off, her sight blinded, her hearing muted, her voice stilled."

"I'm not doing any such thing!" Anna cried.

"You just don't realize what you're doing," Cerin replied.

His voice was mild, but dark lights in the back of his eyes were flashing.

Meran realized it was time to intervene. She stepped between the two. Putting her back to her husband, she turned to face Anna.

"We'll find Lesli," she said.

"How? With *magic*?"

"It doesn't matter how. Just trust that we will. What you have to think of is of what you were telling me yesterday: her birthday's coming up in just a few days. Once she turns sixteen, so long as she can prove that she's capable of supporting herself, she can legally leave home and nothing you might do or say then can stop her."

"It's you, isn't it?" Anna cried. "You're the one who's been filling up her head with all these horrible fairy tales. I should never have let her take those lessons."

Her voice rose ever higher in pitch as she lunged forward, arms flailing. Meran slipped to one side, then reached out one quick hand. She pinched a nerve in Anna's neck and the woman suddenly went limp. Cerin caught her before she could fall and carried her back to the sofa.

"Now do you see what I mean about parents?" he said as he laid Anna down.

Meran gave him a mock-serious cuff on the back of his head.

"Go find Lesli," she said.

"But—"

"Or would you rather stay with Anna and continue your silly attempt at converting her when she wakes up again?"

"I'm on my way," Cerin told her and was out the door before she could change her mind.

* * *

Thunder cracked almost directly overhead as Cutter dragged Lesli into a brownstone just off Palm Street. The building stood in the heart of what was known as Newford's Combat Zone, a few square blocks of nightclubs, strip joints, and bars. It was a tough part of town with hookers on every corner, bikers cruising the streets on chopped-down Harleys, bums sleeping in doorways, winos sitting on the curbs, drinking cheap booze from bottles vaguely hidden in paper bags.

Cutter had an apartment on the top floor of the brownstone, three stories up from the street. If he hadn't told her that he lived here, Lesli would have thought that he'd taken her into an abandoned building. There was no furniture except a vinyl-topped table and two chairs in the dirty kitchen. A few mangy pillows were piled up against the wall in what she assumed was the living room.

He led her down to the room at the end of the long hall that ran the length of the apartment and pushed her inside. She lost her balance and went sprawling onto the mattress that lay in the middle of the floor. It smelled of mildew and, vaguely, of old urine. She scrambled away from it and crouched up against the far wall, clutching her knapsack against her chest.

"Now, you just relax, sweet stuff," Cutter told her. "Take things easy. I'm going out for a little while to find you a nice guy to ease you into the trade. I'd do it myself, but there's guys that want to be first with a kid as young and pretty as you are and I sure could use the bread they're willing to pay for the privilege."

Lesli was prepared to beg him to let her go, but her throat was so tight she couldn't make a sound.

"Don't go away now," Cutter told her.

He chuckled at his own wit, then closed the door and locked it. Lesli didn't think she'd ever heard anything so final as the sound of that lock catching. She listened to Cutter's footsteps as they crossed the apartment, the sound of the front door closing, his footsteps receding on the stairs.

As soon as she was sure he was far enough away, she got up and ran to the door, trying it, just in case, but it really was locked and far too solid for her to have any hope of breaking through its panels. Of course there was no phone. She crossed the room to the window and forced it open. The window looked out on the side of another building, with an alleyway below. There was no fire escape outside the window, and she was far too high up to think of trying to get down to the alley.

Thunder rumbled again, not quite overhead now, and it started to rain. She leaned by the window, resting her head on its sill. Tears sprang up in her eyes again.

"Please," she sniffed. "Please, somebody help me. . . ."

The rain coming in the window mingled with the tears that streaked her cheek.

* * *

Cerin began his search at the Batterberry house, which was in Ferryside, across the Stanton Street Bridge on the west side of the Kickaha river. As Anna Batterberry had remarked, the city was large. To find one teenage girl, hiding somewhere in the confounding labyrinth of its thousands of crisscrossing streets and avenues, was a daunting task, but Cerin was depending on help.

To anyone watching him, he must have appeared to be slightly mad. He wandered back and forth across the streets of Ferryside, stopping under trees to look up into their bare branches, hunkering down at the mouths of alleys or alongside hedges, apparently talking to himself. In truth, he was looking for the city's gossips.

Magpies and crows, sparrows and pigeons saw everything, but listening to their litanies of the day's events was like looking something up in an encyclopedia that was merely a confusing heap of loose pages, gathered together in a basket. All the information you wanted was there, but finding it would take more hours than there were in a day.

Cats were little better. They liked to keep most of what they knew to themselves, so what they did offer him was usually cryptic and sometimes even pointedly unhelpful. Cerin couldn't blame them; they were by nature secretive and, like much of Faerie, capricious.

The most ready to give him a hand were those little sprites commonly known as the flower faeries. They were the little winged spirits of the various trees and bushes, flowers and weeds, that grew tidily in parks and gardens, rioting only in the odd empty lot or wild place, such as the riverbanks that ran down under the Stanton Street Bridge to meet the water. Years ago, Cicely Mary Barker had cataloged any number of them in a loving series of books; more recently the Boston artist Terri Windling had taken up the task, specializing in the urban relations of those Barker had already noted.

It was late in the year for the little folk. Most of them were already tucked away in Faerie, sleeping through the winter, or else too busy with their harvests and other seasonal preoccupations to have paid any attention at all to what went on beyond the task at hand. But a few had seen the young girl who could sometimes see them. Meran's cousins were the most helpful. Their small pointed faces would regard Cerin gravely from under acorn caps as they pointed this way down one street, or that way down another.

It took time. The sky grew darker, and then still darker as the clouds thickened with an approaching storm, but slowly and surely, Cerin traced Lesli's passage over the Stanton Street Bridge all the way across town to Fitzhenry Park. It was just as he reached the bench where she'd been sitting that it began to rain.

There, from two of the wizened little monkeylike bodachs that lived in the park, he got the tale of how she'd been accosted and taken away.

"She didn't want to go, sir," said the one, adjusting the brim of his little cap against the rain.

All faerie knew Cerin, but it wasn't just for his bardic harping that they paid him the respect that they did. He was the husband of the oak king's daughter, she who could match them trick for trick and then some, and they'd long since learned to treat her, and those under her protection, with a wary deference.

"No sir, she didn't," added the other, "but he led her off all the same."

Cerin hunkered down beside the bench so that he wasn't towering over them.

"Where did he take her?" he asked.

The first bodach pointed to where two men were standing

by the War Memorial, shoulders hunched against the rain, heads bent together as they spoke. One wore a thin raincoat over a suit; the other was dressed in denim jacket, jeans, and cowboy boots. They appeared to be discussing a business transaction.

"You could ask him for yourself," the bodach said. "He's the one all in blue."

Cerin's gaze went to the pair and a hard look came over his features. If Meran had been there, she might have laid a hand on his arm, or spoken a calming word, to bank the dangerous fire that grew in behind his eyes. But she was at home, too far away for her quieting influence to be felt.

The bodachs scampered away as Cerin rose to his feet. By the War Memorial, the two men seemed to come to an agreement and left the park together. Cerin fell in behind them, the rain that slicked the pavement underfoot muffling his footsteps. His fingers twitched at his side, as though striking a harp's strings.

From the branches of the tree where they'd taken sanctuary, the bodachs thought they could hear the sound of a harp, its music echoing softly against the rhythm of the rain.

* * *

Anna came to once more just as Meran was returning from the kitchen with a pot of herb tea and a pair of mugs. Meran set the mugs and pot down on the table by the sofa and sat down beside Lesli's mother.

"How are you feeling?" she asked as she adjusted the cool cloth she'd laid upon Anna's brow earlier.

Anna's gaze flicked from left to right, over Meran's shoulder and down to the floor, as though tracking invisible presences.

Meran tried to shoo away the inquisitive faerie, but it was a useless gesture. In this house, with Anna's presence to fuel their
quenchless curiosity, it was like trying to catch the wind.

"I've made us some tea," Meran said. "It'll make you feel
better."

Anna appeared docile now, her earlier anger fled as though it
had never existed. Outside, rain pattered gently against the window panes. The face of a nosy hob was pressed against one lower
pane, its breath clouding the glass, its large eyes glimmering with
their own inner light.

"Can . . . can you make them go away?" Anna asked.

Meran shook her head. "But I can make you forget again."

"Forget." Anna's voice grew dreamy. "Is that what you did
before? You made me forget?"

"No. You did that on your own. You didn't want to remember, so you simply forgot."

"And you . . . you didn't do a thing?"

"We do have a certain . . . aura," Meran admitted, "which ac-
celerates the process. It's not even something we consciously
work at. It just seems to happen when we're around those who'd
rather not remember what they see."

"So I'll forget, but they'll all still be there?"

Meran nodded.

"I just won't be able to see them?"

"It'll be like it was before," Meran said.

"I . . . I don't think I like that. . . ."

Her voice slurred. Meran leaned forward with a worried expression. Anna seemed to regard her through blurring vision.

"I think I'm going . . . away . . . now . . ." she said.

Her eyelids fluttered, then her head lolled to one side and she lay still. Meran called Anna's name and gave her a little shake, but there was no response. She put two fingers to Anna's throat and found her pulse. It was regular and strong, but try though she did, Meran couldn't rouse the woman.

Rising from the sofa, she went into the kitchen to phone for an ambulance. As she was dialing the number, she heard Cerin's harp begin to play by itself up in his study on the second floor.

* * *

Lesli's tears lasted until she thought she saw something moving in the rain on the other side of the window. It was a flicker of movement and color, just above the outside windowsill, as though a pigeon had come in for a wet landing, but it had moved with far more grace and deftness than any pigeon she'd ever seen. And that memory of color was all wrong, too. It hadn't been the blue/white/gray of a pigeon; it had been more like a butterfly—

doubtful, she thought, in the rain and this time of year

—or a hummingbird—

even more doubtful

—but then she remembered what the music had woken at her last flute lesson. She rubbed at her eyes with her sleeve to remove the blur of her tears and looked more closely into the rain. Face-on, she couldn't see anything, but as soon as she turned her head, there it was again; she could see it out of the corner of her eye, a dancing dervish of color and movement that flickered out of her line of sight as soon as she concentrated on it.

After a few moments, she turned from the window. She gave the door a considering look and listened hard, but there was still no sound of Cutter's return.

Maybe, she thought, maybe magic can rescue me. . . .

She dug out her flute from her knapsack and quickly put the pieces together. Turning back to the window, she sat on her haunches and tried to start up a tune, but to no avail. She was still too nervous, her chest felt too tight, and she couldn't get the air to come up properly from her diaphragm.

She brought the flute down from her lip and laid it across her knees. Trying not to think of the locked door, of why it was locked and who would be coming through it, she steadied her breathing.

In, slowly now, hold it, let it out, slowly. And again.

She pretended she was with Meran, just the two of them in the basement of the Old Firehall. There. She could almost hear the tune that Meran was playing, except it sounded more like the bell-like tones of a harp than the breathy timbre of a wooden flute. But still, it was there for her to follow, a path marked out on a road map of music.

Lifting the flute back up to her lip, she blew again, a narrow channel of air going down into the mouth hole at an angle, all her fingers down, the low D note ringing in the empty room, a deep rich sound, resonant and full. She played it again, then caught the music she heard, that particular path laid out on the road map of all tunes that are or yet could be, and followed where it led.

It was easier to do than she would have thought possible, easier than at all those lessons with Meran. The music she followed seemed to allow her instrument to almost play itself. And as the tune woke from her flute, she fixed her gaze on the rain falling just outside the window where a flicker of color appeared, a spin of movement.

Please, she thought. Oh please. . .

And then it was there, hummingbird wings vibrating in the rain, sending incandescent sprays of water arcing away from their movement; the tiny naked upper torso, the lower wrapped in tiny leaves and vines; the dark hair gathered wetly against her miniature cheeks and neck; the eyes, tiny and timeless, watching her as she watched back and all the while, the music played.

Help me, she thought to that little hovering figure. Won't you please—

She had been oblivious to anything but the music and the tiny faerie outside in the rain. She hadn't heard the footsteps on the stairs, nor heard them crossing the apartment. But she heard the door open.

The tune faltered, the faerie flickered out of sight as though it had never been there. She brought the flute down from her lip and turned, her heart drumming wildly in her chest, but she refused to be scared. That's all guys like Cutter wanted. They wanted to see you scared of them. They wanted to be in control. But no more.

I'm not going to go without a fight, she thought. I'll break my flute over his stupid head. I'll . . .

The stranger standing in the doorway brought her train of thought to a scurrying halt. And then she realized that the harping she'd heard, the tune that had led her flute to join it, had grown in volume, rather than diminished.

"Who . . . who are you?" she asked.

Her hands had begun to perspire, making her flute slippery and hard to hold. The stranger had longer hair than Cutter. It was drawn back in a braid that hung down one side of his head and dangled halfway down his chest. He had a full beard and wore clothes that, though they were simple jeans, shirt, and jacket, seemed to have a timeless cut to them, as though they could have been worn at any point in history and not seemed out of place. Meran dressed like that as well, she realized.

But it was his eyes that held her—not their startling brightness, but the fire that seemed to flicker in their depths, a rhythmic movement that seemed to keep time to the harping she heard.

"Have you come to . . . rescue me?" she found herself asking before the stranger had time to reply to her first question.

"I'd think," he said, "with a spirit so brave as yours, that you'd simply rescue yourself."

Lesli shook her head. "I'm not really brave at all."

"Braver than you know, fluting here while a darkness stalked you through the storm. My name's Cerin Kelledy; I'm Meran's husband and I've come to take you home."

He waited for her to disassemble her flute and stow it away, then offered her a hand up from the floor. As she stood up, he took the knapsack and slung it over his shoulder and led her toward the door. The sound of the harping was very faint now, Lesli realized.

When they walked by the hall, she stopped in the doorway leading to the living room and looked at the two men that were huddled against the far wall, their eyes wild with terror. One was Cutter; the other a businessman in suit and raincoat whom she'd never seen before. She hesitated, fingers tightening on Cerin's hand, as she turned to see what was frightening them so much.

There was nothing at all in the spot that their frightened gazes were fixed upon.

"What . . . what's the matter with them?" she asked her companion. "What are they looking at?"

"Night fears," Cerin replied. "Somehow the darkness that lies in their hearts has given those fears substance and made them real."

The way he said "somehow" let Lesli know that he'd been responsible for what the two men were undergoing.

"Are they going to die?" she asked.

She didn't think she was the first girl to fall prey to Cutter so she wasn't exactly feeling sorry for him at that point.

Cerin shook his head. "But they will always have the *sight*. Unless they change their ways, it will show them only the dark side of Faerie."

Lesli shivered.

"There are no happy endings," Cerin told her. "There are no real endings ever—happy or otherwise. We all have our own stories which are just a part of the one Story that binds both this world and Faerie. Sometimes we step into each other's stories— perhaps just for a few minutes, perhaps for years—and then we step out of them again. But all the while, the Story just goes on."

That day, his explanation only served to confuse her.

* * *

From Lesli's diary, entry dated November 24:

> *Nothing turned out the way I thought it would.*
>
> *Something happened to Mom. Everybody tells me it's not my fault, but it happened when I ran away, so I can't help*

but feel that I'm to blame. Daddy says she had a nervous breakdown and that's why she's in the sanitarium. It happened to her before and it had been coming again for a long time. But that's not the way Mom tells it.

I go by to see her every day after school. Sometimes she's pretty spaced from the drugs they give her to keep her calm, but on one of her good days, she told me about Granny Nell and the Kelledys and Faerie. She says the world's just like I said it was in that essay I did for English. Faerie's real and it didn't go away; it just got freed from people's preconceptions of it and now it's just whatever it wants to be.

And that's what scares her.

She also thinks the Kelledys are some kind of earth spirits.

"I can't forget this time," she told me.

"But if you know," I asked her, "if you believe, then why are you in this place? Maybe I should be in here, too."

And you know what she told me? "I don't want to believe in any of it; it just makes me feel sick. But at the same time, I can't stop knowing it's all out there: every kind of magic being and nightmare. They're all real."

I remember thinking of Cutter and that other guy in his apartment and what Cerin said about them. Did that make my Mom a bad person? I couldn't believe that.

"But they're not supposed to be real," Mom said. "That's what's got me feeling so crazy. In a sane world, in the world that was the way I'd grown up believing it to be, that wouldn't be real. The Kelledys could fix it so that I'd forget again, but then I'd be back to going through life al-

ways feeling like there was something important that I couldn't remember. And that just leaves you with another kind of craziness—an ache that you can't explain and it doesn't ever go away. It's better this way, and my medicine keeps me from feeling too crazy."

She looked away then, out the window of her room. I looked, too, and saw the little monkey-man that was crossing the lawn of the sanitarium, pulling a pig behind him. The pig had a load of gear on its back like it was a pack horse.

"Could you . . . could you ask the nurse to bring my medicine," Mom said.

I tried to tell her that all she had to do was accept it, but she wouldn't listen. She just kept asking for the nurse, so finally I went and got one.

I still think it's my fault.

* * *

I live with the Kelledys now. Daddy was going to send me away to a boarding school, because he felt that he couldn't be home enough to take care of me. I never really thought about it before, but when he said that, I realized that he didn't know me at all.

Meran offered to let me live at their place. I moved in on my birthday.

There's a book in their library—ha! There's like ten million books in there. But the one I'm thinking of is by a local writer, this guy named Christy Riddell.

In it, he talks about Faerie, how everybody just thinks of them as ghosts of wind and shadow.

"*Faerie music is the wind,*" *he says,* "*and their move-ment is the play of shadow cast by moonlight, or starlight, or no light at all. Faerie lives like a ghost beside us, but only the city remembers. But then the city never forgets any-thing.*"

I don't know if the Kelledys are part of that ghostliness. What I do know is that, seeing how they live for each other, how they care so much about each other, I find myself feel-ing more hopeful about things. My parents and I didn't so much not get along as lack interest in each other. It got to the point where I figured that's how everybody was in the world, because I never knew any different.

So I'm trying harder with Mom. I don't talk about things she doesn't want to hear, but I don't stop believing in them either. Like Cerin said, we're just two threads of the Story. Sometimes we come together for a while and some-times we're apart. And no matter how much one or the other of us might want it to be different, both our stories are true.

But I can't stop wishing for a happy ending.

*So Maisie Flood, whom we first met in "But for the Grace Go I,"
tried hard to fit her round peg into the square hole. But sometimes
trying isn't enough, especially when you feel like you have to shoulder
the whole load on your own. Sometimes you need a little outside help.*

*One of the people she goes to is a fortune-telling street person
named Bones who shows up in a number of books, predominately*
Trader *(1997) and* The Onion Girl *(2000). But he and his sweet-
heart, Cassie, first showed up in* The Dreaming Place *(1990),
which Firebird plans to reprint in the next year or so.*

Waifs and Strays

*Do I have to dig,
Do I have to prod;
Reach into your chest
And pull your feelings out?*
—Happy Rhodes, from
"Words Weren't Made for Cowards"

- 1 -

THERE'S A BIG MOON GLOWING IN THE SKY, A SWOLLEN
circle of silvery-gold light that looks as though it's sitting right
on top of the old Clark Building, balancing there on the north-
east corner where the twisted remains of a smokestack rise up
from the roof like a long, tottery flagpole, colors lowered for
the night, or maybe like a tin giant's arm making some kind of

semaphore signal that only other tin giants can understand. I sure don't.

But that doesn't stop me from admiring the silhouette of the smokestack against that fat moon as I walk through the rubble-strewn streets of the Tombs. I feel like a stranger and I think, That moon's a stranger, too. It doesn't seem real; it's more like the painted backdrop from some forties soundstage, except there's no way anybody ever gave paint and plywood this kind of depth. We're both strangers. That moon looks like it might be out of place anywhere, but I belonged here once.

Not anymore, though. I'm not even supposed to be here. I've got responsibilities now. I've got duties to fulfill. I should be Getting Things Done like the good little taxpaying citizen I'm trying to be, but instead I'm slumming, standing in front of my old squat, and I couldn't tell you why I've come. No, that's not quite right. I know, I guess; I just can't put it into words.

"You've got to see the full moon in a country sky sometime," Jackie told me the other day when she got back from her girl-friend's cottage. "It just takes over the sky."

I look up at it again and don't feel that this moon's at all di-minished by being here. Maybe because in many respects this part of the city's just like a wilderness—about as close to the country as you can get in a place that's all concrete and steel. Some people might say you'd get that feeling more in a place like Fitzhenry Park, or on the lakefront where it follows the shore-line beyond the Pier, westward, out past the concession stands and hotels, but I don't think it's quite the same. Places like that are where you can only pretend it's wild; they look right, but they were tamed a long time ago. The Tombs, though, is like a piece of the city gone feral, the wild reclaiming its own—not asking, just taking.

In this kind of moonlight, you can feel the wilderness hiding in back of the shadows, lips pulled in an uncurbed, savage grin.

I think about that as I step a little closer to my old squat, and it doesn't spook me at all. I find the idea kind of liberating. I look at the building and all I see is a big dark, tired shape hulking in the moonlight. I like the idea that it's got a secret locked away behind its mundane facade, that's there's more to it than something that's been used up and then just tossed away.

Abandoned things make me feel sad. For as long as I can remember I've made up histories for them, cloaked them in stories, seen them as frog princes waiting for that magic kiss, princesses being tested with a pea, little engines that could if they were only given half a chance.

But I'm pragmatic, too. Stories in my head are all well and fine, but they don't do much good for a dog that some guy's tossed out of a car when he's speeding through the Tombs and the poor little thing breaks a leg when it hits the pavement so it can't even fend for itself—just saying the feral dogs that run in these streets give it half a chance. When I can—if I get to it in time—I'm the kind of person who'll take it in.

People have tried to take me in, but it never quite works out right. Bad genes, I guess. Bad attitude. It's not the kind of thing I ever worried about much till the past few weeks.

I don't know how long I'm standing on the street, not even seeing the building anymore. I'm just here, a small shape in the moonlight, a stray dream that got lost from the safe part of the city and found itself wandering in this nightland that eats small dreams, feeds on hopes. A devouring landscape that fed on itself first and now preys on anything that wanders into its domain.

I never let it have me, but these days I wonder why I bothered. Living in the Tombs isn't much of a life, but what do you do when you don't fit in anywhere else?

I start to turn away, finally. The moon's up above the Clark Building now, hanging like a fat round flag on the smokestack, and the shadows it casts are longer. I don't want to go, but I can't stay. Everything that's important to me isn't part of the Tombs anymore.

The voice stops me. It's a woman's voice, calling softly from the shadows of my old squat.

"Hey, Maisie," she says.

I feel like I should know her, this woman sitting in the shadows, but the sense of familiarity I get from those two words keeps sliding away whenever I reach for it.

"Hey, yourself," I say.

She moves out into the moonlight, but she's still just a shape. There's no definition, nothing I can pin the sliding memories onto. I get an impression of layers of clothing that make a skinny frame seem bulky, a toque pulled down over hair that might be any color or length. She's dressed for winter, though the night's warm, and she's got a pair of shopping bags in each hand.

I've known a lot of street people like that. Hottest day of the summer and they still have to wear everything they own, all at once. Sometimes it's to protect themselves from space rays; sometimes it's just so that no one'll steal the little they've got to call their own.

"Been a long time," she says, and then I place her.

It's partly the way she moves, partly the voice, partly just the shape of her, though in this light she doesn't look any different from a hundred other bag ladies.

The trouble is, she can't possibly wear the name I call up to fit her because the woman it used to belong to has been dead for four years. I know this, logically, intellectually, but I can't help trying it on for size all the same.

"Shirl?" I say. "Is that you?"

Shirley Jones, who everybody on the street knew as Granny Buttons because she carried hundreds of them around in the many pockets of her dresses and coats.

The woman on the street in front of me bobs her head, sticks her hands in the pockets of the raincoat she's wearing over all those layers of clothing, and I hear the familiar rattle of plastic against wood against bone, a soft *clickety-clickety-click* that I never thought I'd hear again.

"Jesus, Shirley—"

"I know, child," she says. "What am I doing here when I'm supposed to be dead?"

I'm still not spooked. It's like I'm in a dream and none of this is real, or at least it's only as real as the dream wants it to be. I'm just happy to see her. Granny Buttons was the person who first taught me that "family" didn't have to be an ugly word.

She's close enough that I can see some of her features now. She doesn't look any different than she did when she died. She's got the same twinkle in her brown eyes, part charm and part crazy. Her coffee-colored skin's as wrinkled as a piece of brown wrapping paper that you've had in your back pocket for a few days. I see it isn't a toque she's wearing but that same almost conical velour cap she always wore, her hair hanging out from below in hundreds of unwashed, uncombed dreadlocks festooned with tiny buttons of every shape and description. She still smells the same as well—a combination of a rosehip sachet and licorice.

I want to hug her, but I'm afraid if I touch her she'll just drift apart like smoke.

"I've missed you," I say.

"I know, child."

"But how . . . how can you *be* here?"

"It's like a riddle," she says. "Remember our treasure hunts?"

I nod my head. How can I forget? That's where I first learned about the freebies you can find behind the bookstores, where I was initiated into what Shirley liked to call "the rehab biz."

"If you cherish something enough," she told me, "it doesn't matter how old or worn or useless it's become; your caring for it immediately raises its value in somebody else's eyes. It's just like rehab—a body's got to believe in their own worth before anybody can start fixing them, but most people need someone to believe in them before they can start believing in themselves.

"You know, I've seen people pay five hundred dollars for something I took out of their trash just the week before, *only* because they saw it sitting on the shelf of some fancy antique shop. They don't even remember that it once was theirs.

" 'Course the dealer only paid me fifty bucks for it, but who's complaining? Two hours before I came knocking on his back door, it was sitting at the end of the curb in a garbage can."

Garbage days we went on our treasure hunts. Shirley probably knew more about collection days than the city crews did themselves: when each borough had its pick up, what the best areas were depending on the time of the year, when you had to make your rounds in certain areas to beat the flea-market dealers on their own night runs. We had dozens of routes, from Foxville down into Crowsea, across the river to Ferryside and the Beaches, from Chinatown over to the East End.

We'd head out with our shopping carts, sensei bag lady and her apprentice, on a kind of Grail quest. But what we found was never as important as the Zen of our being out there in the first place. Each other's company. The conversation. The night's journey as we zigzagged from one block to another, checking out this alleyway, that bin, those Dumpsters.

We were like urban coyotes prowling the city's streets. At that time of night, nobody bothered us, not the cops, not muggers, not street toughs. We became invisible knights tilting against the remnants of other people's lives.

After Shirley died, it took me over a month to go out on my own and it was never quite the same again. Not bad, just not the same.

"I remember," I tell her.

"Well, it's something like that," she says, "only it's not entirely happenstance."

I shake my head, confused. "What are you trying to tell me, Shirley?"

"Nothing you don't already know."

In back of me, something knocks a bottle off a heap of

trash—I don't know what it is. A cat, maybe. A dog. A rat. I can't help myself. I have to have a look. When I turn back to Shirley—you probably saw this coming—she's gone.

- 2 -

Pride goes before the fall, I read somewhere, and I guess whoever thought up that little homily had her finger on the pulse of how it all works.

There was a time when I wouldn't have had far to fall; by most people's standards, at seventeen, I was already on the bottom rung of the ladder, and all the rungs going up were broken as far as I'd ever be able to reach.

I never thought much about pride back in those days, though I guess I had my share. Maybe I was just white trash to whoever passed me on the street, but I kept myself cleaner than a lot of those paying taxes and what I had then sure beat the hellhole I grew up in.

I hit the road when I was twelve and never looked back because up until then family was just another word for pain. Physical pain, and worse, the kind that just leaves your heart feeling like some dead thing caught inside your chest. You know what pigeons look like once the traffic's been running over them for a couple of weeks and there's not much left except for a flat bundle of dried feathers that hasn't even got flies buzzing around it anymore?

That's like what I had in my chest until I ran away.

I was one of the lucky ones. I survived. I didn't get done in by drugs or selling my body. Shirley took me in under her wing before the lean men with the flashy suits and too much jewelry could get their hands on me. Don't know why she helped me—maybe when she saw me she was remembering the day she was just a kid stepping off a bus in some big city herself. Maybe, just looking at me, she could tell I'd make a good apprentice.

And then, after five years, I got luckier still—with a little help from the Grasso Street Angel and my own determination.

And that pride.

I was so proud of myself for doing the right thing: I got the family off the street. I was straightening out my life. I rejoined society—not that society seemed to care all that much, but I wasn't doing it for them anyway. I was doing it for Tommy and the dogs, for myself, and so that one day maybe I could be in a position to help somebody else, the way that Angel does out of her little storefront office on Grasso, the way that Shirley helped me.

I should've known better.

We've got a real place to live in—a tenement on Flood Street just before it heads on into the Tombs, instead of a squat. I have a job as a messenger for the QMS—the Quicksilver Messenger Service, run by a bunch of old hippies who get the job done but live in a tie-dyed past. Evenings, four times a week, I go to night school to get my high school diploma.

But I just didn't see it as being better than what we'd had before. Paying for rent and utilities, food, and for someone to come in to look after Tommy sucked away every cent I made. Maybe I could've handled that, but all my time was gone too. I never really saw Tommy anymore, except on the weekends, and even then I'd have to be studying half the time. I had it a little easier than a lot of the other people in my class because I always read a lot. It was my way of escaping, even before I came here to live on the streets.

Before I ran away I was a regular at the local library—it was both a source of books and refuge from what was happening at home. Once I got here, Shirley told me about how the bookstores'd strip the covers off paperbacks and just throw the rest of the book away, so I always made sure I stopped by the alleys in back of their stores on garbage days.

I hadn't read a book in months. The dogs were pining—little Rexy was taking it the worst. He's just a cat-sized wiry-haired mutt with a major insecurity problem. I think someone used to beat on him, which made me feel close to him, because I knew what that was all about. Used to be Rexy was like my shadow; nervous, sure, but so long as I was around, he was okay. These days, he's just a wreck because he can't come on my bike when I'm working and they won't let me bring him into the school.

The way things stand, Tommy's depressed, the other dogs are depressed, Rexy's almost suicidal, and I'm not in any great shape myself. Always tired, impatient, unhappy.

So I really needed to meet a ghost in the Tombs right about now. It's doing wonders for my sense of sanity—or rather lack thereof—because I know I wasn't dreaming that night, or at least I wasn't asleep.

· 3 ·

Everybody's worried about me when I finally get home—Rexy, the dogs, Tommy, my landlady Aunt Hilary who looks after Tommy—and I appreciate it, but I don't talk about where I've been or what I've seen. What's the point? I'm kind of embarrassed about anybody knowing that I'm feeling nostalgic for the old squat and I'm not quite sure I believe I saw who I think I saw there anyway, so what's to tell?

I make nice with Aunt Hilary, calm down the dogs, put Tommy to bed, then I've got homework to do for tomorrow night's class and work in the morning, so by the time I finally get to bed myself, Shirley's maybe-ghost is pretty well out of my mind. I'm so tired that I'm out like a light as soon as my head hits the pillow.

Where do they get these expressions we all use, anyway? Why out like a light and not on like one? Why do we hit the pillow when we go to sleep? Logs don't have a waking/sleeping cycle, so how can we sleep like one?

Sometimes I think about what this stuff must sound like when it gets literally translated into some other language. Yeah, I know. It's not exactly Advanced Philosophy 101 or anything, but it sure beats thinking about ghosts, which is what I'm trying not to think about as I walk home from the subway that night after my classes. I'm doing a pretty good job, too, until I get to my landlady's front steps.

Aunt Hilary is like the classic tenement landlady. She's a widow, a small but robust gray-haired woman with more energy than half the messengers at QMS. She's got lace hanging in her windows, potted geraniums on the steps going down to the pavement, an old black-and-white tabby named Frank that she walks on a leash. Rexy and Tommy are the only ones in my family that Frank'll tolerate.

Anyway, I come walking down the street, literally dragging my feet I'm so tired, and there's Frank sitting by one of the geranium pots giving me the evil eye—which is not so unusual—while sitting one step up is Shirley—which up until last night I would have thought was damned well impossible. Tonight I don't even question her presence.

"How's it going, Shirl?" I say as I collapse beside her on the steps.

Frank arches his back when I go by him, but deigns to give my shoulder bag a sniff before he realizes it's only got my school books in it. The look he gives me as he settles down again is less than respectful.

Shirley's leaning back against a higher step. She's got her hands in her pockets, *clickety-clickety-click,* her hat pushed back from her forehead. Her rosehip and licorice scent has to work a little harder against the cloying odor of the geraniums, but it's still there.

"Ever wonder why there's a moon?" she asks me, her voice all dreamy and distant.

I follow her gaze to where the fat round globe is ballooning in the sky above the buildings on the opposite side of the street. It looks different here than it did in the Tombs—safer, maybe—but then everything does. It's the second night that it's full and I find myself wondering if ghosts are like werewolves, called up by the moon's light, only nobody's quite clued to it yet. Or at least Hollywood and the authors of cheap horror novels haven't.

I decide not to share this with Shirley. I knew her pretty well, but who knows what's going to offend a ghost? She doesn't wait for me to answer anyway.

"It's to remind us of Mystery," she says, "and that makes it both a Gift and a Curse."

She's talking like Pooh in the Milne books, her inflection setting capital letters at the beginning of certain words. I've never been able to figure out how she does that. I've never been able to figure out how she knows so much about books, because I never even saw her read a newspaper all the time we were together.

"How so?" I ask.

"Grab an eyeful," she says. "Did you ever see anything so mysteriously beautiful? Just looking at it, really considering it, has got to fill the most jaded spirit with awe."

I think about how ghosts have that trick down pretty good, too, but all I say is, "And what about the curse?"

"We all know it's just an oversized rock hanging there in the sky. We've sent men to walk around on it, left trash on its surface, photographed it, and mapped it. We know what it weighs, its size, its gravitational influence. We've sucked all the Mystery out of it, but it still maintains its hold on our imaginations.

"No matter how much we try to deny it, that's where poetry and madness were born."

I still don't get the curse part of it, but Shirley's already turned away from this line of thought. I can almost see her ghostly mind unfolding a chart inside her head and plotting a new course for our conversation. She looks at me.

"What's more important?" she asks. "To be happy or to bring happiness to others?"

"I kind of like to think they go hand in hand," I tell her. "That you can't really have one without the other."

"Then what have you forgotten?"

This is another side of Shirley I remember well. She gets into this one hand clapping mode, asking you simple stuff that gets more and more complicated the longer you think about it, but if you keep worrying at it, the way Rexy'll take on an old slipper, it gets back to being simple again. To get there, though, you have to work through a forest of words and images that can be far too Zen-deep and confusing—especially when you're tired and your brain's in neutral the way mine is tonight.

"Is this part of the riddle you were talking about last night?" I ask.

She sort of smiles—lines crinkle around her eyes, fingers work the pocketed buttons, *clickety-clickety-click*. There's a feeling in the air like there was last night just before she vanished, but this time I'm not looking away. I hear a car turn onto this block, its headlights washing briefly over us, a bright light flickers, then it's dark again, with one solid flash of real deep dark just before my eyes adjust to the change in illumination.

Of course she's gone once I can see properly again and there's only me and Frank sitting on the steps. I forget for a moment about where our relationship stands and reach out to give him a pat. I'm just trying to touch base with reality, I realize as I'm doing it, but that doesn't matter to him. He doesn't quite hiss as he gets up and jumps down to the sidewalk.

I watch him swagger off down the street, watch the empty pavement for a while longer, then finally I get up myself and go inside.

- 4 -

There's a wariness in Angel's features when I step into her Grasso Street office. It's a familiar look. I asked her about it once and she was both precise and polite with her explanation: "Well, Maisie.

Things just seem to get complicated whenever you're around."

It's nothing I plan.

Her office is a one-room walk-in storefront off Grasso Street, shabby in a genteel sort of a way. She has a rack of filing cabinets along one wall, an old beat-up sofa with a matching chair by the bay window, a government surplus desk—one of those massive oak affairs with about ten million scratches and dents—a swivel chair behind the desk, and a couple of matching oak straightbacks sitting to one side. I remember thinking they looked like a pair I'd sold a few years ago to old man Kemps down the street, and it turns out that's where she picked them up.

A little table beside the filing cabinets holds a hot plate, a kettle, a bunch of mismatched mugs, a teapot, and the various makings for coffee, hot chocolate, and tea. The walls have cheerful posters—one from a travel agency that shows this wild New Orleans street scene where there's a carnival going on, one from a Jilly Coppercorn show—cutesy little flower fairies fluttering around in a junkyard.

I like the one of Bart Simpson best. I've never seen the show, but I don't think you have to to know what he's all about.

The nicest thing about the office is the front porch and steps that go down from it to the pavement. It's a great place from which to watch the traffic go by, vehicular and pedestrian, or to just hang out. No, that's not true. The nicest thing is Angel herself.

Her real name's Angelina Marceau, but everyone calls her Angel, partly on account of her name, I guess, but mostly because of the salvage work she does with street kids. The thing is, she looks like an angel. She tries to hide it with baggy pants and plain

T-shirts and about as little makeup as you can get away with wearing and still not be considered a Baptist, but she's gorgeous. Heart-shaped face, hair to kill for—a long, dark waterfall that just seems to go forever down her back—and soft warm eyes that let you know straightaway that here's someone who genuinely cares about you. Not as a statistic to add to her list of rescued souls, but as an individual. A real person.

Unless she's giving you the suspicious once-over she's giving me as I come in. It's a look you have to earn, because normally she'll bend over backward to give you the benefit of the doubt.

I have to admit, there was a time when I'd push her, just to test the limits of her patience. It's not something I was particularly prone to, but we used to have a history of her trying to help me and me insisting I didn't need any help. We worked through all of that, eventually, but I keep finding myself in circumstances that make her feel as though I'm still testing the limits.

Like the time I punched out the booking agent at the Harbor Ritz, my first day on the job at QMS that Angel had gotten me.

I'm not the heartstopper that Angel is, but I do okay in the looks department. My best feature, I figure, is my hair. It's not as long as Angel's, but it's as thick. Jackie, the dispatch girl at QMS, says it reminds her of the way they all wore their hair in the sixties—did I mention that these folks are living in a time warp? I've never bothered to tell them that the sixties have been and gone, it's only the styles are making yet another comeback.

Anyway, my hair's a nice shade of light golden brown and hangs halfway down my back. I do okay in the figure department, too, though I lean more toward Winona Ryder, say, than Kim Basinger. Still, I've had guys hit on me occasionally, especially these days since I don't put out the impression that I'm some assistant bag-lady-in-training anymore.

The Harbor Ritz booking agent doesn't know any of this. He just sees a messenger girl delivering some documents and figures he'll give me a thrill. I guess he's either hard up, or figures anyone without his equipment between their legs is just dying to have him paw them, because that's what he does when I try to get him to sign for his envelope. He ushers me into his office and then closes the door, leans back against it, and pulls me toward him.

What was I supposed to do? I just cocked back a fist and broke his nose.

Needless to say, he raised a stink, it's his word against mine, etcetera, etcetera. Except the folks at QMS turn out to be real supportive and Angel comes down on this guy like he's some used condom she's found stuck to the bottom of her shoe when she's walking through the Combat Zone. I keep my job and don't get arrested for assault like the guy's threatening to do, but it's a messy situation, right?

The look Angel's wearing says, "I hope this isn't more of the same, but just seeing you kicks in this bad feeling. . . . "

It's not more of the same, I want to tell her, but that's about as far as my reasoning can take it. What's bothering me isn't exactly something I can just put my finger on. Do I tell her about Shirley, do I tell her about the malaise I've got eating away at me, or what?

I'd been tempted to bring the whole family with me—I spend so little time with them as it is—but settled on Rexy, mostly because he's easier to control. It's hard to think when you're trying to keep your eye on six dogs and Tommy, too.

Today I could be alone in a padded cell and I'd still find it hard to think.

I take a seat on the sofa and after a moment Angel comes around from behind her desk and settles on the other end. Rexy's being real good. He licks her hand when she reaches out to pat him, then curls up on my lap and pretends to go to sleep. I know he's faking it because his ears twitch in a way they don't when he's really conked out.

Angel and I do some prelims—small talk, which is always relaxed and easy around her, but eventually we get to the nitty-gritty of why I'm here.

"I've got this problem," I say, thinking of Shirley, but I know it's not her. I kind of like having her around again, dead or not.

"At work?" Angel tries when I'm not more forthcoming.

"Not exactly."

Angel's looking a little puzzled, but curious, too.

"Your grades are good," she says.

"It's not got anything to do with grades," I tell her. Well, it does, but only because the high school diploma's part and parcel of the whole problem.

"Then what *does* it have to with?" Angel wants to know.

It's a reasonable request—more so because I'm the one who's come to her, taking up her time. I know what I want to say, but I don't know how to phrase it.

My new life's like a dress I might have wished for in a store window, saved for, finally bought, only to find out that while it's the right size, it still doesn't quite fit right. It's the wrong color. The sleeves are too long, or maybe too short. The skirt's too tight.

It's not something Angel would understand. Intellectually, maybe, but not how I feel about it. Angel's one of those people who sees everyone having a purpose in life, you've just got to figure out what it is. I don't even know where to begin figuring out that kind of stuff.

"Nothing really," I say after a few moments.

I get up suddenly, startling Rexy, who jumps to the floor and then gives me this put-upon expression of his that he should take out a patent on.

"I've got to go," I tell Angel.

"Maisie," she starts, rising herself, but I'm already heading for the door.

I pretend I don't hear her. I pretend she's not following me to the street and calling after me as I head down the block at a quick walk that you might as well call running.

I'm not in good shape, I realize. Angel's the only person I know that I could have talked with about something like this, but I couldn't do it. I couldn't even start.

All I felt like doing was crying and that would really have freaked her because I never cry.

Not where people can see.

- 5 -

"So what are you really doing here?" I ask.

We're sitting on a bench in the subway station at Williamson and Stanton, Shirley and I, with little Rexy sleeping on the toes of my running shoes. We're at the far end of the platform. It's maybe ten o'clock and there's hardly anybody else down here with us. I see a couple of yuppies, probably coming back from an early show. A black guy in a three-piece suit checking out papers in his briefcase. Two kids slouched against a wall, watching a companion do tricks with her skateboard that bring her perilously close to the edge of the platform. My heart's in my throat watching her, but her friends just look bored.

I wonder what they see when they look down this way. A bag lady and me, with my dog dozing on my feet, or just me and Rexy on our own?

Shirley's gaze is on the subway system grid that's on the opposite side of the tracks, but I doubt she's really seeing it. She always needed glasses but never got herself a pair, even when she could afford them.

"When I first got to the city," she says, "I always thought that one day I'd go back home and show everybody what an important person I had become. I wanted to prove that just because everyone from my parents to my teachers treated me like I was no good, didn't mean I really was no good.

"But I never went back."

Ghosts always want to set something right, I remember from countless books and stories. Revenge, mistakes, that kind of thing. Sometimes just to say good-bye. They're here because of unfinished business.

This is the first time I ever realized that Shirley'd had any.

I mean, I wasn't stupid, even when I was twelve and she first took me in under her wing. Even then I knew that normal people didn't live on the streets wearing their entire wardrobe on their backs. But I never really thought about why she was there. She always seemed like a part of the street, so full of smarts and a special kind of wisdom, that it simply never occurred to me that she'd been running away from something, too. That she'd had dreams and aspirations once, but all they came to was a homeless wandering to which the only end was a mishap like falling down the stairs in some run-down squat and breaking your neck.

That's what your life'll be like, I tell myself, if you don't follow through on what Angel's trying to do for you.

Maybe. But I'd respected Shirley, for all her quirks, for all that I knew she wasn't what anybody else would call a winner. I'd just always thought that whatever she lacked, she had inner peace to make up for it.

I slouch lower on the bench, legs crossed at the ankles, the back of my head leaning against the top of the bench. I'm wearing my fedora, and the movement pushes it forward so that the brim hangs low over my eyes.

"Is that why you're back?" I ask Shirley. "Because you still had things left to do here?"

She shrugs, an eloquent Shirley-gesture, for all the layers of clothes she's wearing.

"I don't really feel I ever went anywhere or came back," she says.

"But you died," I say.

"I guess so."

I try a different tack. "So what's it like?"

She smiles. "I don't really know. When I'm here, I don't feel any different from when I was dead. When I'm not here, I'm . . . I don't know where I am. A kind of limbo, I suppose. A place where nothing moves, nothing changes, months are minutes."

I don't say anything.

"I guess it's like the bus I never took back home," she adds after a moment. "I missed out on wherever it was I was supposed to go, and I don't know how to go on, where to catch the next bus, or if they're even running anymore. For me at least. They don't leave a schedule lying around for people like me who arrive too late.

"Story of my life, I guess."

I start to feel so bad for her that I almost wish she'd go back to throwing cryptic little riddles at me the way she'd done the first couple of times we'd met.

"Is there anything I can do?" I say, but the subway roars into the station at the same time as I speak, swallowing my words with its thunder.

I'm about to repeat what I said but when I turn to look at Shirley, she's not there anymore. I only just make it through the doors of the car, Rexy under my arm, before they hiss closed behind me and the train goes roaring off again into the darkness.

The story of her life, I think. I wonder, What's the story of mine?

- 6 -

I should tell you about Tommy.

He's a big guy, maybe six feet tall and running close to a hundred and eighty pounds. And he's strong. He's got brown hair, a dirtier shade than mine, though I try to keep it looking clean, and guileless eyes. He couldn't keep a secret if he knew one.

The thing is, he's simple. A ten-year-old in an adult's body. I'm not sure how old he is, but the last time I took him in for a checkup at the clinic, the doctor told me he was in his early thirties, which makes him almost half again my age.

When I say simple, I don't mean stupid, though I'll admit Tommy's not all that bright by the way society reckons intelligence. I like to think of him as more basic than the rest of us. He's open with his feelings, likes to smile, likes to laugh. He's the happiest person I know, which is half the reason I love him the way I do. He may be mentally impaired, but sometimes I figure the world would be a better place if we all maintained some of that sweet innocence that makes him so endearing.

I inherited Tommy the same way I did the rest of my family: I found him on the streets, abandoned. I worried some at first about keeping him with me, but when I started asking around about institutions, I realized he'd have something with me and the dogs that he couldn't get anywhere else: a family. All a guy like Tommy needs is someone willing to put the time into loving him. You don't get that in places like the Zeb, which is where he lived until they discharged him so that someone with more pressing problems, read money, could have his bed.

One of the things I hate about the way my life's going now is that I hardly ever see him anymore. Our landlady knows him better than I do these days, and that's depressing.

The day after I talk to Shirley in the subway, I get off early from work. There's a million things I should be doing—like the week's grocery shopping and research for a history essay at the library—but I decide the hell with it. It's a beautiful day, so I'm going to pack up a picnic lunch and take the family to the park.

I find Tommy and Aunt Hilary in the backyard. She's working on her garden, which for a postage-sized tenement lot is a work of art, a miniature farm and English garden all rolled into about twenty square feet of sunflowers, rosebushes, corn, peas, every kind of squash, tomatoes, and flower beds aflame with color and scent. Tommy's playing with the paper people that I cut out of magazines and then stick onto cardboard backings for him. The dogs are sprawled all over the place, except for Rexy, who's dogging Aunt Hilary's heels. You don't understand how apt an expression like that is until you see Rexy do his I-always-have-to-be-two-inches-away-from-you thing.

Tommy looks up when he hears the dogs starting to yap, and suddenly I'm inundated with my family, everybody trying to get a piece of hello from me at the same time. But the best thing is seeing that kind of sad expression that Tommy's wearing too much these days broaden into the sweetest, happiest smile you can imagine. I don't figure I've ever done anything to deserve all this unadulterated love, but I accept it—on credit, I guess. It makes me try harder to be good to them, to be worthy of that love.

I've got the trick down pat by now, ruffling the fur of six dogs and giving Tommy a hug without ever letting anybody feel left out. Aunt Hilary's straightening up from her garden, hands at the small of her back as she stretches the kinks from her muscles. She's smiling, too.

"We had a visitor," she tells me when the pandemonium settles down into simple chaos.

Tommy's leading me over to the big wooden tray on a patch of grass to show me what his paper people have been up to while I was gone this morning, and the dogs sort of mooch along beside us in an undulating wave.

"Anybody I know?" I ask Aunt Hilary.

"I suppose you must," my landlady says, "but she didn't leave a name. She just said she wanted to drop by to see how your family was making out—especially your son."

I blink with surprise at that. "You mean Tommy?"

"Who else?"

Well, I guess he is like my kid, I think.

"What did she look like?" I ask, half anticipating the answer.

"A bit like a homeless person, if you want to know the truth," Aunt Hilary says. "She must have been wearing three or four dresses under her overcoat."

"Was she black?"

"Yes, how did you—"

"Hair in dreadlocks with lots of buttons attached to them?"

Aunt Hilary nods. "And she kept fiddling with something in her pockets that made a rattly sort of a sound."

"That's Shirley," I say.

"So you do know her."

"She's an old friend."

Aunt Hilary starts to say something else, but I lose the thread of her conversation because all I'm thinking is, I'm not crazy. Other people *can* see her. I was being pretty cool whenever Shirley showed up, but I have to admit to worrying that her presence was just the first stage of a nervous breakdown.

Suddenly I realize that I'm missing everything my landlady's telling me about Shirley's visit.

"I'm sorry," I tell her. "What did you say?"

Aunt Hilary smiles. She's used to my spacing out from time to time.

"Your friend didn't stay long," she says. "She just told Tommy what a handsome young man he was and patted each of the dogs with utter concentration, as though she wanted to re-member them, and then she left. I asked her to stay for some lunch, or at least a cup of tea, because she looked so—well, hun-gry, I suppose. But she just shook her head and said, 'That's very kind of you, but I don't indulge anymore.' "

Aunt Hilary frowns. "At least I think that's what she said. It doesn't really make a lot of sense, when you consider it."

"That's just Shirley," I tell her.

I can tell Aunt Hilary wants to talk some more about it, but I turn the conversation to my plan for an outing to the park, invit-ing her along. She hasn't got the time, she says—is probably looking forward to a few hours by herself is what I hear, and I don't blame her—but she gets right into helping me get a knap-sack of goodies organized.

We have a great day. Nothing's changed. I've still got to deal with my malaise, I've still got the ghost of a dead friend hanging around, but for a few hours I manage to put it all aside and it's like old times again.

I haven't seen Tommy this happy since I can't remember when, and that makes me feel both glad and depressed.

There's got to be a better way to live.

· 7 ·

I decide it's time to get some expert advice, so the next day I call in sick at work and head off down to Fitzhenry Park instead.

Everybody who spends most of their time on the streets isn't necessarily a bum. Newford's got more than its share of genuinely homeless people—the ones who don't have any choice: winos, losers, the hopeless and the helpless, runaways, and far too many ordinary people who've lost their jobs, their homes, their future through no fault of their own. But it's also got a whole subculture, if you will, of street musicians, performance artists, sidewalk vendors, and the like.

Some are like me: they started out as runaways and then evolved into something like when I was making cash from trash. Others have a room in a boardinghouse or some old hotel and work the streets because that's where their inclination lies. There's not a whole lot of ways to make a living playing fiddle tunes or telling fortunes in other outlets and the overhead is very affordable.

Fitzhenry Park is where a lot of that kind of action lies. It's close to the Combat Zone, so you get a fair amount of hookers and even less reputable types drifting down when they're, let's say, off-shift. But it's also close to the Barrio, so the seedy element is balanced out with mothers walking in pairs and pushing strollers, old women gossiping in tight clusters, old men playing dominoes and checkers on the benches. Plus you get the lunch crowds from the downtown core that faces the west side of the park.

The other hot spot is down by the Pier, on the lakefront, but that's geared more to the tourists, and the cops are tight-assed about permits and the like. If you're going to get arrested for busking or hawking goods from a sidewalk cart or just plain panhandling, that's the place it'll happen.

The kind of person I was looking for now would work the park crowds, and I found him without hardly even trying. He was just setting up for the day.

Bones is a Native American—a full-blooded Kickaha with

dark coppery skin, broad features, and a braid hanging down his back that's almost as long as Angel's hair. He got his name from the way he tells fortunes. He'll toss a handful of tiny bones onto a piece of deerskin and read auguries from the pattern they make. He doesn't really dress for the part, eschewing buckskins and beads for scuffed old workboots, faded blue jeans, and a white T-shirt with the arms torn off, but it doesn't seem to hurt business.

I don't really hold much with any of this mumbo-jumbo stuff—not Bones's gig, nor what his girlfriend Cassie does with Tarot cards, or Paperjack's Chinese fortune-telling devices. But while I don't believe that any of them can foretell the future, I still have to admit there's something different about some of the people who work this schtick.

Take Bones.

The man has crazy eyes. Not crazy, you-better-lock-him-up kind of eyes, but crazy because maybe he sees something we can't. Like there really is some other world lying draped across ours and he can see right into it. Maybe he's even been there. Lots of times I figure he's just clowning around, but sometimes that dark gaze of his locks onto you and then you see this seriousness lying behind the laughter and it's like the Tombs all over again—a piece of the wilderness biding on a city street, a dislocating sensation like not only is anything possible, but it probably is true.

Besides, who am I to make judgments these days? I'm being haunted by a ghost.

"How do, Maisie?" he says when I wheel my mountain bike up to the edge of the fountain where he's sitting.

I prop the bike up on its kickstand, hang my helmet from one of the handlebars, and sit down beside him. He's fiddling with his bones, letting them tumble from one hand to the other. They make a sound like Shirley's buttons, only more muted. I find myself wondering what kind of an animal they came from. Mice? Birds? I look up from his hands and see the clown is sitting in his eyes, laughing. Maybe with me, maybe at me—I can never tell.

"Haven't see you around much these days," he adds.

"I'm going to school," I tell him.

"Yeah?"

"And I've got a job."

He looks at me for this long heartbeat and I get that glimpse of otherness that puts a weird shifting sensation in the pit of my stomach.

"So are you happy?" he asks.

That's something no one ever asks when I tell them what I'm doing now. I pick at a piece of lint that's stuck to the cuff of my shorts.

"Not really," I tell him.

"Want to see what Nanabozho's got in store for you?" he asks, holding up his bones.

I don't know who Nanabozho is, but I get the idea.

"No," I say. "I want to ask you about ghosts."

He doesn't even blink an eye. Just grins.

"What about them?"

"Well, what are they?" I ask.

"Souls that got lost," he tells me, still smiling, but serious now, too.

I feel weird talking about this. It's a sunny day, the park's full of people, joggers, skateboarders, women with baby carriages, a girl on the bench just a few steps away who probably looks sexy at night under a streetlight, the way she's all tarted up, but now she just looks used. Nothing out of the ordinary, and here we are, talking about ghosts.

"What do you mean?" I ask. "How do they get lost?"

"There's a Path of Souls, all laid out for us to follow when we die," he tells me. "But some spirits can't see it, so they wander the earth instead. Others can't accept the fact that they're dead yet, and they hang around too."

"A path."

He nods.

"Like something you walk along."

"Inasmuch as a spirit walks," Bones says.

"My ghost says she missed a bus," I tell him.

"Maybe it's different for white people."

"She's black."

He sits there, not looking at me, bones trailing from one hand to the other, making their tiny rattling sound.

"What do you really want to know?" he asks me.

"How do I help her?"

"Why don't you try asking her?"

"I did, but all she gives me back are riddles."

"Maybe you're just not listening properly," he says.

I think back on the conversations I've had with Shirley since I first saw her in the Tombs a few nights ago, but I can't seem to focus on them. I remember being with her, I remember the feeling of what we talked about, but the actual content is muddy now. It seems to shift away as soon as I try to think about it.

"I've really seen her," I tell Bones. "I was there when she

died—almost four years ago—but she's back. And other people have seen her, too."

"I know you have," he says.

I don't even know why I was trying to convince him—it's not like he'd be a person who needed convincing—but what he says stops me.

"What do you mean?" I ask. It's my question for the day.

"It's in your eyes," he says. "The Otherworld has touched you. Think of it as a blessing."

"I don't know if I like the idea," I tell him. "I mean, I miss Shirley, and I actually feel kind of good about her being back, even if she is just a ghost, but it doesn't seem right somehow."

"Often," he says, "what we take from the spirit world is only a reflection of what lies inside ourselves."

There's that look in his eyes, a feral seriousness, like it's important, not so much that I understand, or even believe what he's saying, but *that* he's saying it.

"What . . . ?" I start, but then I figure it out. Part of it anyway.

When I first came to the city, I was pretty messed up, but then Shirley was there to help me. I'm messed up again, so . . .

"So I'm just projecting her ghost?" I ask. "I need her help, so I've made myself a ghost of her?"

"I didn't say that."

"No, but—"

"Ghosts have their own agendas," he tells me. "Maybe you both have something to give to each other."

We sit for a while, neither of us speaking. I play with the whistle that hangs from a cord around my neck—all the messengers have them to blow at cars that're trying to cut us off. Finally,

I get up and take my bike off its kickstand. I look at Bones and that feral quality is still lying there in his grin. His eyes seem to be all pupil, dark, dark. I'm about to say thanks, but the words lock up in my throat. Instead I just nod, put on my helmet, and go away to think about what he's told me.

- 8 -

Tommy's got this new story that he tells me after we've cleaned up the dinner dishes. We sit together at the kitchen table and he has his little paper people act it out for me. It's about this Chinese man who falls down the crack in the pavement outside Aunt Hilary's house and finds himself in this magic land where everybody's a beautiful model or movie star and they all want to marry the Chinese guy except he misses his family too much, so he just tells them he can't marry any of them—not even the woman who won the Oscar for her part in *Misery*, who, for some reason, Tommy's really crazy about.

I've got the old black lab Chuckie lying on my feet, Rexy snuggled up in my lap. Mutt and Jeff are tangled up in a heap on the sofa so that it's hard to tell which part of them's which. They're a cross between a German shepherd and who knows what; I found Jeff first and gave the other old guy his name because the two were immediately inseparable. Jimmie's part dachshund, part collie—I know, go figure—and his long, furry body is stretched out in front of the door like he's a dust puppy. Patty's mostly poodle, but there's some kind of placid mix in there as well because she's not at all high-strung. Right now she's sitting in the bay window, checking the traffic and pretending to be a cat.

The sad thing, Tommy tells me, is that the Chinese man

knows that he'll never be able to get back home but he's going to stay faithful to his family anyway.

"Where'd you get that story?" I ask Tommy.

He just shrugs, then he says, "I really miss you, Maisie."

How can I keep leaving him?

I feel like a real shit. I know it's not my fault, I know I'm trying to do my best for all of us, for our future, but Tommy's mind doesn't work very well considering the long term and my explanations don't really register. It's just me going out all the time, and not taking him or the dogs with me.

There's a knock on the door. Jimmie gets laboriously to his feet and moves aside as Aunt Hilary comes in. She gives her wristwatch an obvious look.

"You're going to be late for school," she says, not really nagging, she just knows me too well.

I feel like saying "Fuck school," but I put Rexy down, shift Chuckie from my feet, and stand up. Six dogs and Tommy all give me a hopeful look, like we're going out for a walk, faces all dropping when I pick up my knapsack, heavy with schoolbooks.

I give Tommy a hug and kiss then make the good-bye rounds of the dogs. They're like Tommy; long term means nothing to them. All they know is I'm going out and they can't come. Rexy takes a few hopeful steps in the direction of the door, but Aunt Hilary scoops him up.

"Now, now, Rexy," she tells him. "You know Margaret's got to go to school and she can't take you."

Margaret. She's the one who goes to school and works at QMS and deserts her family five days and four nights a week. She's the traitor.

I'm Maisie, but I'm Margaret, too.

I say good-bye, trying not to look anyone in the eye, and head for the subway. My eyes are pretty well dry by the time I get there. I pause on the platform. When the southbound train comes, I don't get off at the stop for my school, but ride it all the way downtown. I walk the six blocks to the bus depot.

I get a piece of gum stuck to the bottom of my sneaker while I'm waiting in line at the ticket counter. I'm still trying to get it off with an old piece of tissue I find in my pocket—not the most useful tool for the job—when the guy behind the counter says, "Next," in this really tired voice.

Who's he got waiting at home for him? I wonder as I move toward the counter, sort of shuffling the foot with the gum stuck on it so it doesn't trap me to another spot.

"How much for a ticket?" I ask him.

"Depends where you're going."

He's got thinning hair lying flat against his head, parted way over on the left side. Just a skinny little guy in a faded shirt and pants that are too baggy for him, trying to do his job. He's got a tick in one eye, and I keep thinking that he's giving me a wink.

"Right," I say.

My mind's out of sync. Of course he needs the destination. I let my thoughts head back into the past, looking for the name of the place I want, trying to avoid the bad times that are hiding there in my memories, just waiting to jump me, but it's impossible to do.

That's another thing about street people, whether they put the street behind them or not: the past holds pain. The present may not be all that great, but it's usually better than what went before. That goes for me, for Shirley, for pretty well everybody I know. You try to live here and now, like the people who go through Twelve Step, taking it day by day.

Mostly, you try not to think at all.

"Rockcastle," I tell the guy behind the counter.

He does something mysterious with his computer before he looks up.

"Return or one way?"

"One way."

More fiddling with the computer before he tells me the price. I pay him and a couple of minutes later I'm hop-stepping my way out of the depot with a one-way ticket to Rockcastle in my pocket. I sit on a bench outside and scrape off the gum with a Popsicle stick I find on the sidewalk, and then I'm ready.

I don't go to my class; I don't go home either. Instead I take the subway up to Gracie Street. When I come up the steps from the station I stand on the pavement for a long time before I finally cross over and walk into the Tombs.

- 9 -

The moon seems smaller tonight. It's not just that it's had a few slivers shaved off one side because it's waning; it's like it got tamed somehow.

I can't say the same for the Tombs. I see kids sniffing glue, shooting up, some just sprawled with their backs against a pile of rubble, legs splayed out in front of them, eyes staring into nothing. I pass a few 'bos cooking god knows what over a fire they've got rigged up in an old jerry can. A bag lady comes lurching out between the sagging doors of an old office building and starts to yell at me. Her voice follows me as I pick a way through the litter and abandoned cars.

The bikers down the street are having a party. The buckling pavement in front of their building has got about thirty-five chopped-down street hogs parked in front of it. The place is lit up with Coleman lights, and I can hear the music and laughter from where I'm sitting in the bay window of my old squat in the Clark Building.

They don't bother me; I never exactly hung out with them or anything, but they used to consider me a kind of mascot after Shirley died, and let the word get out that I was under their protection. It's not the kind of thing that means a lot everywhere, but it helped me more than once.

No one's taken over the old squat yet, but after five months it's already got the same dead feel to it that hits you anywhere in the Tombs. It's not exactly dirty, but it's dusty and the wind's been blowing crap in off the street. There's a smell in the air; though it's not quite musty, it's getting there.

But I'm not really thinking about any of that. I'm just passing time. Sitting here, waiting for a piece of the past to catch up to me.

I used to sit here all the time once I'd put Tommy to bed, looking out the window when I wasn't reading, Rexy snuggled close, the other dogs sprawled around the room, a comforting presence of soft snores and twitching bodies as they chased dream-rabbits in their sleep.

There's no comfort here now.

I look back out the window and see a figure coming up the street, but it's not who I was expecting. It's Angel, with Chuckie on a leash, his black shadow shape stepping out front, leading the way. As I watch them approach, some guy moves from out of the shadows that've collected around the building across the street and Chuckie, worn out and old though he is, lunges at him. The guy makes a fast fade.

I listen to them come into the building, Chuckie's claws clicking on the scratched marble, the leather soles of Angel's shoes making a scuffly sound as she comes up the stairs. I turn around when they come into the squat.

"I thought I'd find you here," Angel says.

"I didn't know you were looking."

I don't mean to sound put off, but I can't keep the punkiness out of my voice.

"I'm not checking up on you, Maisie. I was just worried."

"Well, here I am."

She undoes the lead from Chuckie's collar and he comes across the room and sticks his face up against my knees. The feel of his fur under my hand is comforting.

"You really shouldn't be out here," I tell Angel. "It's not safe."

"But it's okay for you?"

I shrug. "This was my home."

She crosses the room as well. The windowsill's big enough to hold us both. She scoots up and then sits across from me, arms wrapped around her legs.

"After you came by the office, I went by your work to see you, then to your apartment, then to the school."

I shrug again.

"Do you want to talk about it?" she asks.

"What's to say?"

"Whatever's in your heart. I'm here to listen. Or I can just go away, if that's what you prefer, but I don't really want to do that."

"I . . ."

The words start locking up inside me again. I take a deep breath and start over.

"I'm not really happy, I guess," I tell her.

She doesn't say anything, just nods encouragingly.

"It's . . . I never really told you why I came to see you about school and the job and everything. You probably just thought that you'd finally won me over, right?"

Angel shakes her head. "It was never a matter of winning or losing. I'm just there for the people who need me."

"Yeah, well, what happened was—do you remember when Margaret Grierson died?"

Angel nods.

"We shared the same postal station," I tell her, "and the day before she was killed, I got a message in my box warning me to be careful, that someone was out to do a serious number on me. I spent the night in a panic and I was so relieved when the morning finally came and nothing had happened, because what'd happen to Tommy and the dogs if anything ever happened to me, you know?"

"What does that have to do with Margaret Grierson?" Angel asks.

"The note I got was addressed to 'Margaret'—just that, nothing else. I thought it was for me, but I guess whoever sent it got his boxes mixed up and it ended up in mine instead of hers."

"But I still don't see what—"

I can't believe she doesn't get it.

"Margaret Grierson was an important person," I say. "She was heading up that AIDS clinic, she was doing things for people. She was making a difference."

"Yes, but—"

"I'm nobody," I say. "It should've been me that died. But it wasn't, so I thought, well, I better do something with myself, with my life, you know? I better make my having survived meaningful. But I can't cut it.

"I've got the straight job, the straight residence, I'm going back to school and it's like it's all happening to someone else. The things that are important to me—Tommy and the dogs—it's like they're not even a part of my life anymore."

I remember something Shirley's ghost asked me, and add, "Maybe it's selfish, but I figure charity should start at home, you know? I can't do much for other people if I'm feeling miserable myself."

"You should've come to me," Angel says.

I shake my head. "And tell you what? It sounds so whiny. I mean, there are people starving not two blocks from where we're sitting, and I should be worried about being happy or not? The important stuff's covered—I'm providing for my family, putting a roof over their heads, and making sure they have enough to eat—that should be enough, right? But it doesn't feel that way. It feels like the most important things are missing.

"I used to have time to spend with Tommy and the dogs; now I have to steal a minute here, another there. . . ."

My voice trails off. I think of how sad they all looked when I left the apartment tonight, like I was deserting them, not just for the evening but forever. I can't bear that feeling, but how do you explain yourself to those who can't possible understand?

"We could've worked something out," Angel says. "We still can."

"Like what?"

Angel smiles. "I don't know. We'll just have to think it through better than we have so far. You'll have to try to open up a bit more, tell me what you're *really* feeling, not just what you think I want to hear."

"It's that obvious, huh?"

"Let's just say I have a built-in bullshit detector."

We don't say anything for a while then. I think about what she's said, wondering if something could be worked out. I don't want special dispensation because I'm some kind of charity case—I've *always* earned my own way—but I know there've got to be some changes or the little I've got is going to fall apart.

I can't get the image out of mind—Tommy with his sad eyes as I'm going out the door—and I know I've got to make the effort. Find a way to keep what was good about the past and still make a decent future for us.

I put my hand in my pocket and feel the bus ticket I bought earlier.

I have to open up a bit more? I think, looking at Angel. What would her bullshit detector do if I told her about Shirley?

Angel stretches out her legs, then lowers them to the floor.

"Come on," she says, offering me her hand. "Let's go talk about this some more."

I look around the squat and compare it to Aunt Hilary's

apartment. There's no comparison. What made this place special, we took with us.

"Okay," I tell Angel.

I take her hand and we leave the building. I know it's not going to be easy, but then nothing ever is. I'm not afraid to work my butt off; I just don't want to lose sight of what's really important.

When we're outside, I look back up to the window where we were sitting. I wonder about Shirley, how's she's going to work out whatever it is that she's got to do to regain her own sense of peace. I hope she finds it. I don't even mind if she comes to see me again, but I don't think that'll be part of the package.

I left the bus ticket for her, on the windowsill.

- 10 -

I don't know if we've worked everything out, but I think we're making a good start. Angel's fixed it so that I've dropped a few courses, which just means that it'll take me longer to get my diploma. I'm only working a couple of days a week at QMS—the Saturday shift that nobody likes and a rotating day during the week.

The best thing is I'm back following my trade again, trash for cash. Aunt Hilary lets me store stuff in her garage because she doesn't have a car anyway. A couple of nights a week, Tommy and I head out with our carts, the dogs on our heels, and we work the bins. We're spending a lot more time together and everybody's happier.

I haven't seen Shirley again. If it hadn't been for Aunt Hilary telling me about her coming by the house, I'd just think I made the whole thing up.

I remember what Bones told me about ghosts having their own agendas and how maybe we both had something to give each other. Seeing Shirley was the catalyst for me. I hope I helped her some, too. I remember her telling me once that she came from Rockcastle. I think wherever she was finally heading, Rockcastle was still on the way.

There isn't a solution to every problem, but at the very least, you've got to try.

I went back to the squat the day after I was there with Angel, and the bus ticket was gone. Logic tells me that someone found it and cashed it in for a quick fix or a bottle of cheap wine. I'm pretty sure I just imagined the lingering scent of rosehip and licorice, and the button I found on the floor was probably from one of Tommy's shirts, left behind when we moved.

But I'd like to think that it was Shirley who picked the ticket up, that this time she got to the depot on time.

THIS IS *the most recent of the reprinted stories in this book, origi-nally commissioned by Terri Windling and Ellen Datlow for an an-thology of Green Man stories called* The Green Man. *I think of it as the middle of what I call "the Lily stories." It's preceded by a chil-dren's picture book called* A Circle of Cats *(which will be published by the same company as this book you're now holding, in summer of 2003), and followed by a short novel,* Seven Wild Sisters *(2002).*

I started this series of stories as part of a collaboration with my good friend the artist Charles Vess, who illustrated the picture book and novel, and did the cover and some interior spot art for The Green Man. *We spent many an hour discussing the characters, what we were hoping to do with the stories, and of course the set-ting, which, although we've placed it just outside of my Newford, is actually based on that part of the Appalachian Mountains that sits outside the front door of Charles's house in Virginia.*

We wanted something to showcase Charles's art. But we also wanted something to bring alive the stories, mood, history, and feel of Charles's beloved mountains—an area of the world that I've fallen in love with as well.

I often have artists in my stories, mostly because I'm fascinated with the process of creating something visual out of nothing, and spend what little spare time I have messing around with paints and inks and pencils. My level of expertise is at about the same level as Lily's in this story: I can see what I want in my head, but somehow it never quite translates properly by the time I'm putting my marks down on paper or canvas. But I love to do it, which I think should be the main criterion for any artistic endeavor one takes on. That way, practicing is something you look forward to, rather that a chore.

One of these days I plan to do a fourth Lily story, and then, who knows, there might actually be a collection one day called The Lily Stories. *The title for this story, by the way, is borrowed from a song by the Incredible String Band, and this version is slightly longer than the one that appeared in Terri and Ellen's anthology.*

Somewhere in My Mind There Is a Painting Box

SUCH A THING TO FIND, SO DEEP IN THE FOREST: A PAINTER'S box nested in ferns and a tangle of sprucey-pine roots, almost buried by the leaves and pine needles drifted up against the trunk of the tree. Later, Lily would learn that it was called a pochade box, but for now she sat bouncing lightly on her ankles admiring her find.

It was impossible to say how long the box had been hidden here. The wood panels weren't rotting, but the hasps were rusted shut and it took her a while to get them open. She lifted the lid and then, and then . . .

Treasure.

Stored in the lid, held apart from each other by slots, were three 8 x 10 wooden panels, each with a painting on it. For all their quick and loose rendering, she had no trouble recognizing the subjects. There was something familiar about them, too, beyond the subject matter that she easily recognized.

The first was of the staircase waterfall where the creek took a sudden tumble before continuing on again at a more level pace. She had to fill in detail from her own memory and imagination, but she knew it was that place.

The second was of a long-deserted homestead up a side valley of the hollow, the tin roof sagging, the rotting walls falling inward. It was nothing like Aunt's cabin on its sunny slopes, surrounded by wild roses, old beehives, and an apple orchard that she and Aunt were slowly reclaiming from the wild. This was a place that would only get sun from midmorning through the early afternoon, a dark and damp hollow where the dew never had a chance to burn off completely.

The last one could have been painted anywhere in this forest but she imagined it had been done down by the creek, looking up a slope into a view of yellow birches, beech, and sprucey-pines growing dense and thick as the stars overhead, with a burst of light coming through a break in the canopy.

Lily studied each painting, then carefully set them aside on the ground beside her. There was the hint of another picture on the inside lid itself, but she couldn't make out what it was supposed to be. Perhaps it was just the artist testing his colors. Looking at it made her feel funny, as though the ground under her had gotten spongy, and she started to sway. She blinked. When she turned her attention to the rest of the box, and the feeling went away.

The palette was covered in dried paint that, like the inside lid, almost had the look of a painting itself, and lifted from the box to reveal a compartment underneath. In the bottom of the box were tubes of oil paint, brushes and a palette knife, a small bottle of turpentine, and a rag stained with all the colors the artist had been using.

Lily turned the palette over and there she found what she'd been looking for. An identifying mark. She ran a finger over the letters that spelled out an impossible name.

Milo Johnson.

Treasure.

* * *

"Milo Johnson," Aunt repeated, trying to understand Lily's excitement. At seventeen, Lily could still get as wound up about a new thing as she had when she was a child. "Should I know that name?"

Lily gave her a "you never pay attention, do you?" look and went to get a book from her bookshelf. She didn't have many, but those she did have had been read over and over again. The one she brought back to the kitchen table was called *The Newford Naturalists: Redefining the Landscape*. Opening it to the first artist profiled, she underlined his name with her finger.

Aunt read silently along with her, mouthing the words, then studied the black-and-white photo of Johnson that accompanied the profile.

"I remember seeing him a time or two," she said. "Tramping through the woods with an old canvas knapsack on his back. But that was a long time ago."

"It would have to have been."

Aunt read a little more, then looked up.

"So he's famous then," she asked.

"Very. He went painting all through these hills and he's got pictures in galleries all over the world."

"Imagine that. And you reckon this is his box?"

Lily nodded.

"Well, we'd better see about returning it to him."

"We can't," Lily told her. "He's dead. Or at least they say he's dead. He and Frank Spain went out into the hills on a painting expedition and were never heard from again."

She flipped toward the back of the book until she came to the smaller section devoted to Spain's work. Johnson had been the giant among the Newford Naturalists, his bold, dynamic style instantly recognizable, even to those who might not know him by name, while Spain had been one of a group of younger artists that Johnson and his fellow Naturalists had been mentoring. He wasn't as well known as Johnson or the others, but he'd already been showing the potential to become a leader in his own right before he and Johnson had taken that last fateful trip.

It was all in the book that Lily had practically memorized by now, she'd read it so often.

Ever since Harlene Welch had given it to her a few years ago, Lily had wanted to grow up to be like the Naturalists—especially Johnson. Not to paint exactly the way they did, necessarily, but to have her own individual vision the way that they did. To be able to take the world of her beloved hills and forest and portray it in such a way that others would see it through her eyes, that they would see it in a new way and so understand her love for it, and would want to protect it the way that she did.

Aunt considered her endless forays into the woods with pencil and paper in hand a tall step up from her earlier childhood ambition, which was simply to find the fairies she was convinced lived in the woods around them. Lily had pursued them with the same singular focus that she now devoted to her drawings of trees and stones, hillsides and hollows, and the birds and animals that made their homes in the forest.

"That was twenty years ago," Lily said, "and their bodies weren't ever recovered."

Twenty years ago. Imagine. The box had been lying lost in the woods for all that time. She must have passed by it on a hundred occasions, never noticing it until today when pure chance had it poke a corner up out of its burrow of leaves just as she was coming by.

"Never thought of painting pictures as being something dangerous," Aunt said.

"Anything can be dangerous," Lily replied. "That's what Beau says."

Aunt nodded. She reached across the table to turn the box toward her.

"So you plan on keeping it?" she asked.

"I guess."

"He must have kin. Don't you think it should go to them?"

Lily shook her head. "He was an orphan—just like me. The only people we could give it to would be in the museum and they'd just stick it away in some drawer somewheres."

"Even the pictures?"

"Well, probably not them. But the painting box for sure. . . . "

Lily hungered to try the paints and brushes she'd found in the box. There was never enough money for her to think of being able to buy either. They lived on whatever they could grow or gather from the woods around them, augmented by the small checks that Aunt's ex-husband sent every other month or so. So Lily made her brushes with wild grasses, or by crimping locks of her own hair with bits of tin and pliers, attaching them to the end of hardwood sticks. For color she used anything that came to hand—old coffee grounds and tea bags, berries, fine red mud, the hulls of nuts, and onion skins. Some, like the berries, she used as she found them. Others she'd boil up to get their color. But their faint washes lent only a ghost of color to her drawings. These paints she'd found would be like going from the gloom of dusk into the bright light of day.

"Well," Aunt said. "You found it, so I guess you get to decide what you do with it."

"I guess."

Finder's keepers, after all. But she couldn't help feeling that she was being greedy. That this find of hers—especially the paintings—belonged to everyone, not just some gangly backwoods girl who happened to come upon them while out on a ramble.

"I'll have to think on it," she added.

Aunt nodded, then got up to put on the kettle.

* * *

The next morning Lily went about her chores. She fed the chickens, sparing a few handfuls of feed for the sparrows and other birds that were waiting expectantly in the trees nearby. She milked the cow and poured some milk into a saucer for the cats that came out of the woods when she was done, purring and winding in between her legs until she set the saucer down. By the time she'd finished weeding the garden and filling the woodbox, it was midmorning.

She packed herself a lunch and stowed it in her shoulder satchel along with some carpenter's pencils and a pad of sketching paper made from cutting up brown grocery bags and tying them together on one side to make a book.

"Off again, are you?" Aunt asked.

"I'll be home for dinner."

"You're not going to bring that box with you?"

She was tempted. The tubes of paint were rusted shut, but she'd squeezed the thin metal of their bodies and found that the paint inside was still pliable. The brushes were good, too. Milo Johnson, as might be expected of a master painter, knew to take care of his tools. But much as she wanted to, her using them didn't seem right. Not yet, anyways.

"Not today," she told Aunt.

As she left the house she looked up to see a pair of dogs coming tearing up the slope toward her. They were the Shaffers' dogs, Max and Kiki, the one dark brown, the other white with black markings, the pair of them bundles of short-haired energy. The Shaffers lived beside the Welches, who owned the farm at the end of the trail that ran from the county road to Aunt's cabin—an hour's walk through the woods as you followed the creek. Their dogs were a friendly pair, good at not chasing cows or game, and showed up every few days to accompany Lily on her rambles.

The dogs danced around her now as she set off through the orchard. When she got to the Apple Tree Man's tree—that's what Aunt called the oldest tree of the orchard—she pulled out a biscuit she'd saved from breakfast and set it down at its roots. It was a habit she'd had since she was a little girl—like feeding the birds and the cats while doing her morning chores. Aunt used to tease her about it, telling her what a good provider she was for the mice and raccoons.

"Shoo," she said as Kiki went for the biscuit. "That's not for you. You'll have to wait for lunch to get yours."

They went up to the top of the hill and into the woods, the dogs chasing each other in circles while Lily kept stopping to investigate some interesting seedpod or cluster of weeds. They had lunch a couple of miles farther on, sitting on a stone outcrop that overlooked the Big Sinkhole, a two- or three-acre depression with the entrance to a cave at the bottom. The entrance went straight down for about four feet, then opened into a large cave. Lily had climbed down into it the first time she'd come here and found old bits of rotting furniture and barrels and such scattered around the dank interior. Stories abounded as to who'd been living there in the old days—from mountain men and runaway slaves to moonshiners hiding from the revenue men—but no one knew the real history of the place.

Most of the mountains around Aunt's cabin were riddled with caves of all shapes and sizes. There were entrances everywhere, though most only went a few yards in before they ended. But some said you could walk from one end of the Kickaha Hills to the other, all underground, if you knew the way. There was even a cave entrance not far from the cabin. Aunt had built shelves inside this smaller cave and they kept their root vegetables and seed potatoes for next year's planting on the wooden planks, keeping them safe from the animals with a little door made of wood and tin. It was better than having to bury them in the ground to keep them away from the frost the way some had to do.

Lunch finished, Lily slid down from the rock. She didn't feel like caving today, nor drawing. Instead she kept thinking about the painting box, how odd it had been to find it after its having been lost for so many years, so she led the dogs back to that part of the woods to see what else she might find. A shiver went up her spine. What if she found their bones?

The dogs grew more playful as she neared the spot where she'd come upon the box. They nipped at her sleeves or crouched ahead of her, butts and tails in the air, growling so fiercely they made her laugh. Finally Max bumped her leg with his head just as she was in midstep. She lost her balance and fell into a pile of leaves, her satchel tumbling to the ground, spilling drawings.

She sat up. A smile kept twitching at the corner of her mouth, but she managed to give them a pretty fierce glare.

"Two against one?" she said. "Well, come on, you bullies. I'm ready for you."

She jumped on Kiki and wrestled her to the ground, the dog squirming with delight in her grip. Max joined the tussle and soon the three of them were rolling about in the leaves like the puppies the dogs no longer were and Lily had never been. They were having such fun that at first none of them heard the shouting. When they did, they stopped their roughhousing to find a man standing nearby, holding a stick in his upraised hand.

"Get away from her!" he cried, waving the stick.

Lily sat up, so many leaves tangled in her hair and caught in her sweater that she had more on her than did some of the autumned trees around them. She put a hand on the collar of either dog, but, curiously, neither seemed inclined to bark or chase the stranger off. They stayed by her side, staring at him.

Lily studied him for a long moment, too, as quiet as the dogs.

He wasn't a big man, but he seemed solid. Dressed in a fraying broadcloth suit with a white shirt underneath and worn leather boots on his feet. His hair was roughly trimmed and he looked as if he hadn't shaved for a few days. But he had a good face— strong features, laugh lines around his eyes and the corners of his mouth. She didn't think he was much older than her.

"It's all right," she told the man. "We were just funning."

There was something familiar about him, but she couldn't place it immediately.

"Of course," he said, dropping the stick. "How stupid can I be? What animal in this forest would harm its Lady?" He went down on his knees. "Forgive my impertinence."

This was too odd for words. From the strange behavior of the dogs to the man's even stranger behavior. She couldn't speak. Then something changed in the man's eyes. There'd been a lost look in them a moment ago, but also hope. Now there was only resignation.

"You're just a girl," he said.

Lily found her voice at that indignity.

"I'm seventeen," she told him. "In these parts, there's some would think I'm already an old maid."

He shook his head. "Your pardon. I meant no insult."

Lily relaxed a little. "That's all right."

He reached over to where her drawings had spilled from her satchel and put them back in, looking at each one for a moment before he did.

"These are good," he said. "Better than good."

For those few moments while he looked through her drawings, while he looked at them carefully, one by one, before re-placing them in her satchel, he seemed different once more. Not so lost. Not so sad.

"Thank you," she said.

She waited a moment, thinking it might be rude of her to follow a compliment with a question that might be considered prying. She waited until the last drawing was back in her satchel and he sat there holding the leather bag on his lap, his gaze gone she didn't know where.

"What are you doing here in the woods?" she finally asked.

It took a moment before his gaze returned to her. He closed the satchel and laid it on the grass between them.

"I took you for someone else," he said, which wasn't an answer at all. "It was the wild tangle of your red hair—the leaves in it and on your sweater. But you're too young and your skin's not a coppery brown."

"And this explains what?" she asked.

"I thought you were Her," he said.

Lily could hear the emphasis he put on the word, but it still didn't clear up her confusion.

"I don't know what you're talking about," she said.

She started to pluck the leaves out of her hair and brush them from her sweater. The dogs lay down, one on either side of her, still curiously subdued.

"I thought you were the Lady of the Wood," he explained. "She who stepped out of a tree and welcomed us when we came out of the cave between the worlds. She wears a cloak of leaves and has moonlight in Her eyes."

A strange feeling came over Lily when he said "stepped out

of a tree." She found herself remembering a fever dream she'd once had—five years ago when she'd been snakebit. It had been so odd. She'd dreamed that she'd been changed into a kitten to save her from the snakebite, dreamed that she'd met Aunt's Apple Tree Man and another wood spirit called the Father of Cats. She'd even seen the fairies she'd tried to find for so long: foxfired shapes, bobbing in the meadow like fireflies.

It had all seemed so real.

Aunt hadn't said a thing as Lily had babbled on about her adventures. She'd only held her close, held her so tight it was hard to breathe for a moment. Tired from her long day, Lily had gone to bed as soon as they returned to their cabin and not woken for two days, when she found Beau Welch sitting in a wooden chair by her bed. His features broke into a grin when he saw her open her eyes.

"Em," he said over his shoulder. "She's back."

And then Aunt joined him, Beau's wife, Harlene, beside her.

"You gave us a right scare, you did," Aunt said, stroking Lily's brow with her fingers. "But I guess the Lord heard my prayers and He didn't take you away from me."

"There was a snake . . . " Lily began.

Harlene nodded. "You got bit bad. But you fought off that poison like a soldier. There's nothing wrong with you that a little rest won't cure."

"It was magic," Lily tried to tell them. "I got to see the fairies."

Beau chuckled. "I don't doubt you did. Folks see every sort of thing in a fever."

Lily was too tired to try to convince them that what she'd seen was real.

She'd gone to the Apple Tree Man's tree in the orchard when Aunt finally allowed she was fit enough to get out of bed.

"Thank you, thank you," she'd told him.

But he didn't step out of his tree to talk to her. She didn't see the Father of Cats again either. Or the fairies. And though she tried to hold the whole of it fast in her mind, it all began to fade the way that dreams do.

That was when she finally put aside the fancies of childhood and took up drawing—a different kind of fancy, she supposed, but at least you could hold the paper in your hands and look at what you'd drawn. The drawings didn't fade away. They were always there when you went back to look at them.

She blinked away the memories and focused on the stranger again. He'd gotten off his knees and was sitting cross-legged on the ground, a half-dozen feet from where she and the dogs were.

"What did you mean when you said 'us'?" she asked.

Now it was his turn to look confused.

"You said this lady showed 'us' some cave."

He nodded. "I was out painting with Milo when—"

As soon as he mentioned that name, the earlier sense of familiarity collided with her memory of a photo in her book on the Newford Naturalists.

"You're Frank Spain!" Lily cried.

He nodded in agreement.

"But that can't be," she said. "You don't look any older than you do in the picture in my book."

"What book?"

"The one about Milo Johnson and the rest of the Newford Naturalists that's back at the cabin."

"There's a book about us?"

"You're famous," Lily told him with a grin. "The book says you and Mr. Johnson disappeared twenty years ago while you were out painting in these very hills."

Frank shook his head, the shock plain in his features.

"Twenty . . . years?" he said slowly. "How's that even possible? We've only been gone for a few days. . . . "

"What happened to you?" Lily asked.

"I don't really know," he said. "We'd come here after a winter of being cooped up in the studio, longing to paint in the landscape itself. We meant to stay until the black flies drove us back to the city but then. . . ." He shook his head. "Then we found the cave and met the Lady. . . ."

He seemed so lost and confused that Lily took him home.

* * *

Aunt greeted his arrival and introduction with a raised eyebrow. Lily knew what she was thinking. First a painting box, now a painter. What would be next?

But Aunt had never turned anyone away from her cabin before and she wasn't about to start now. She had Lily show Frank where he could draw some water from the well and clean up, then set a third plate for supper. It wasn't until later when they were sitting out on the porch drinking tea and watching the night fall that Frank told them his story. He spoke of how he and Milo had found the cave that led them through darkness into another world. How they'd met the Lady there, with Her cloak of leaves and Her coppery skin, Her dark, dark eyes, and Her fox-red hair.

"So there is an underground way through these mountains," Aunt said. "I always reckoned there was some truth to that story."

Frank shook his head. "The cave didn't take us to the other side of the mountains. It took us out of this world and into another."

Aunt smiled. "Next thing you're going to tell me is you've been to Fairyland."

"Look at him," Lily said. She went inside and got her book, opening it to the photograph of Frank Spain. "He doesn't look any older than he did when this picture was taken."

Aunt nodded. "Some people do age well."

"Not this well," Lily said.

Aunt turned to Frank. "So what is it that you're asking us to believe?"

"I'm not asking anything," he said. "I don't believe it myself."

Lily sighed and took the book over to him. She showed him the copyright date, put her finger on the paragraph that described how he and Milo Johnson had gone missing some fifteen years earlier.

"The book's five years old," she said. "But I think we've got a newspaper that's no more than a month old. I could show you the date on it."

But Frank was already shaking his head. He'd gone pale reading the paragraph about the mystery of his and his mentor's disappearance. He lifted his gaze to meet Aunt's.

"I guess maybe we were in Fairyland," he said, his voice gone soft.

Aunt looked from Lily's face to that of her guest.

"How's that possible?" she said.

"I truly don't know," he told her.

He turned the pages of the book, stopping to read the section on himself. Lily knew what he was reading. His father had died in a mining accident when he was still a boy, but his mother had been alive when he'd disappeared. She'd died five years later.

"My parents are gone, too," she told him.

He nodded, his eyes shiny.

Lily shot Aunt a look, but Aunt sat in her chair, staring out into the gathering dusk, an unreadable expression in her features. Lily supposed it was one thing to appreciate a fairy tale but quite another to find yourself smack dab in the middle of one.

Lily was taking it the best of any of them. Maybe it was because of that snakebite fever dream she'd once had. In the past five years she still woke from dreams in which she'd been a kitten.

"Why did you come back?" she asked Frank.

"I didn't know I was coming back," he said. "That world . . . " He flipped a few pages back to show them reproductions of Johnson's paintings. "That's what this other world's like. You don't have to imagine everything being more of itself than it seems to be here like Milo's done in these paintings. Over there it's really like that. You can't imagine the colors, the intensity, the rich wash that fills your heart as much as it does your eyes. We haven't painted at all since we got over there. We didn't need to." He laughed. "I know Milo abandoned his paints before we crossed over, and to tell you the truth, I don't even know where mine are."

"I found Mr. Johnson's box," Lily said. "Yesterday—not far from where you came upon me and the dogs."

He nodded, but she didn't think he'd heard her.

"I was walking," he said. "Looking for the Lady. We hadn't seen Her for a day or so and I wanted to talk to Her again. To ask Her about that place. I remember I came to this grove of sycamore and beech where we'd seen Her a time or two. I stepped in between the trees, out of the sun and into the shade. The next thing I knew I was walking in these hills and I was back here where everything seems . . . paler. Subdued."

He looked at them.

"I've got to go back," he said. "There's no place for me here. Ma's gone and everybody I knew'll be dead like her or too changed for me to know them anymore." He tapped the book. "Just like me, according to what it says here."

"You don't want to go rushing into anything," Aunt said. "Surely you've got other kin, and they'll be wanting to see you."

"There's no one. Me and Ma, we were the last of the Spains that I know."

Aunt nodded in a way that Lily recognized. It was her way of making you think she agreed with you, but she was really just waiting for common sense to take hold of you so that you didn't go off half-cocked and get yourself in some kind of trouble you didn't need to get into.

"You'll want to rest up," she said. "You can sleep in the barn. Lily will show you where. Come morning, everything'll make a lot more sense."

He just looked at her. "How do you make sense out of something like this?"

"You trust me on this," she said. "A good night's sleep does a body wonders."

So he followed her advice—most people did when Aunt had decided what was best for them.

He let Lily take him down to the barn where they made a bed

for him in the straw. She wondered if he'd try to kiss her, and how she'd feel if he did, but she never got the chance to find out.

"Thank you," he said, and then he lay down on the blankets. He was already asleep by the time she was closing the door.

And in the morning he was gone.

* * *

That night Lily had one of what she thought of as her storybook dreams. She wasn't a kitten this time. Instead she was sitting under the Apple Tree Man's tree and he stepped out of the trunk of his tree just like she remembered him doing in that fever dream when the twelve-year-old girl she'd been was bitten by a snake. He looked the same, too, a raggedy man, gnarled and twisty, like the boughs of his tree.

"You," she only said and looked away.

"That's a fine welcome for an old friend."

"You're not my friend. Friends aren't magical men who live in a tree and then make you feel like you're crazy because they never show up in your life again."

"And yet I helped you when you were a kitten."

"In the fever dream when I *thought* I was a kitten."

He came around and sat on his haunches in front of her, all long gangly limbs and tattered clothes and bird's nest hair. His face was wrinkled like the dried fruit from his tree.

He sighed. "It was better for you to only remember it as a dream."

"So it wasn't a dream?" she asked, unable to keep the eagerness from her voice. "You're real? You and the Father of Cats and the fairies in the field?"

"Someplace we're real."

She looked at him for a long moment, then nodded, disappointment taking the place of her momentary happiness.

"This is just a dream, too, isn't it?" she said.

"This is. What happened before wasn't."

She poked at the dirt with her finger, looking away from him again.

"Why would it be better for me to remember it as a dream?" she asked.

"Our worlds aren't meant to mix—not anymore. They've grown too far apart. When you spend too much time in ours, you become like your painter foundling, forever restless and unhappy in the world where you belong. Instead of living your life, you lose yourself in dreams and fancies."

"Maybe for some, dreams and fancies are better than what they have here."

"Maybe," he said, but she knew he didn't agree. "Is that true for you?"

"No," she had to admit. "But I still don't understand why I was allowed that one night and then no more."

She looked at him. His dark eyes were warm and kind, but there was a mystery in them, too. Something secret and daunting that she wasn't sure she could ever understand. That perhaps she shouldn't want to understand.

"Your world is no less a place of marvels and wonders," he said after a long moment. "That's something humans too often forget and why what you do is so important."

She laughed. "What *I* do? Whatever do I do that could be so important?"

"Perhaps it's not what you do now so much as what you will do if you continue with your drawing and painting."

She shook her head. "I'm not really that good."

"Do you truly believe that?"

She remembered what Frank Spain had said after looking at her drawings.

These are good. Better than good.

She remembered how the drawings had, if only for a moment, taken him away from the sadness that lay so heavy in his heart.

"But I'm only drawing the woods," she said. "I'm drawing what I see, not fairies and fancies."

The Apple Tree Man nodded. "Sometimes people need fairies and fancies to wake them up to what they already have. They look so hard for the little face in the thistle, the wrinkled man who lives in a tree. But then they start to focus on the thistle itself, the feathery purples of its bloom, the sharp points of its thorns. They reach out and touch the rough bark of the tree, drink in the green of its leaves, taste of its fruit. And they're transformed. They're *in* their own world, fully and completely, sometimes for the first time since they were a child, and they're finally appreciating what it has to offer them.

"That one moment can stop them from ever falling asleep again. Just as the one glimpse such as you had can wake a lifetime of imagination. It can fuel a thousand stories and paintings. But how you use your imagination, what stories you decide to tell, will come from inside you, not from a momentary glitter of fairy wings."

"But it wakes an ache, too," Lily said.

He nodded. "That never goes away. I know. But if you were to come into our world, it still wouldn't go away. And then you'd also ache for the world you left behind. Better to leave things as they are, Lillian. Better the small ache that carries in it a seed of wonder, than the larger ache that can never be satisfied."

"So why did you come to me tonight? Why are you telling me all of this?"

"To ask you not to look for that cave," he said. "To not go in. If you do, you'll carry the yearning of what you find inside yourself forever."

* * *

What the Apple Tree Man had told her all seemed to make perfect sense in last night's dream. But when she woke to find Frank gone, what made sense then didn't seem to be nearly enough now. Knowing she'd once experienced a real glimpse into a storybook world, she only found herself wanting more.

"Well, it seems like a lot of trouble to go through," Aunt said when Lily came back from the barn with the news that their guest was gone. "To cadge a meal and a roof over your head for the night, I mean."

"I don't think he was lying."

Aunt shrugged.

"But he looked *just* like the picture in my book."

"There was a resemblance," Aunt said. "But really. The story he told—it's too hard to believe."

"Then how do you explain it?"

Aunt thought for a moment, then shook her head.

"Can't say that I can," she admitted.

"I think he's gone to look for the cave. He wants to go back."

"And I suppose you want to go looking for him."

Lily nodded.

"Are you sweet on him?" Aunt asked.

"I don't think I am."

"Can't say as I'd blame you. He was a good-looking man."

"I'm just worried about him," Lily said. "He's all lost and alone and out of his own time."

"And say you find him. Say you find the cave. What then?"

The Apple Tree Man's warning and Aunt's obvious concern struggled against her own desire to find the cave, to see the magical land that lay beyond it.

"I'd have the chance to say good-bye," she said.

There. She hadn't exactly lied. She hadn't said everything she could have, but she hadn't lied.

Aunt studied her for a long moment.

"You just be careful," she said. "See to the cow and chickens, but the garden can wait till you get back."

Lily grinned. She gave Aunt a quick kiss, then packed herself a lunch. She was almost out the door when she turned back and took Milo Johnson's painting box out from under her bed.

"Going to try those paints?" Aunt asked.

"I think so."

* * *

And she did, but it wasn't nearly the success she'd hoped it would be.

The morning started fine, but then walking in these woods of hers was a sure cure for any ailment, especially when it was in your heart or head. The dogs hadn't come to join her today, but that was all right seeing how oddly they'd acted around Frank yesterday. She wondered what they knew, what had they sensed about him?

She made her way down to that part of the wood where she'd first found the box, and then later Frank, but he was nowhere about. Either he'd found his way back into fairyland, or he was just ignoring her voice. Finally she gave up and spent a while looking for this cave of his, but there were too many in this part of the forest and none of them looked—no, none of them *felt* right.

After lunch, she sat down and opened the painting box.

The drawing she did on the back of one of Johnson's three paintings turned out well, though it was odd using her pencil on a wood panel. But she'd gotten the image she wanted: the sweeping boughs of an old beech tree, smooth-barked and tall, the thick crush of underbrush around it, the forest behind. It was the colors that proved to be a problem. The paints wouldn't do what she wanted. It was hard enough to get each tube open they were stuck so tight, but once she had a squirt of the various colors on the palette it all went downhill from there.

The colors were wonderfully bright—pure pigments that had their own inner glow. At least they did until she started messing with them, and then everything turned to mud. When she tried to mix them she got either outlandish hues or colors so dull they all might as well have been the same. The harder she tried, the worse it got.

Sighing, she finally wiped off the palette and the panel she'd been working on, then cleaned the brushes, dipping them in the little jar of turpentine, working the paint out of the hairs with a

rag. She studied Johnson's paintings as she worked, trying to figure out how he'd gotten the colors he had. This was his box, after all. These were the same colors he'd used to paint these three
amazing paintings. Everything she needed was just lying there in
the box, waiting to be used. So why was she so hopeless?

It was because painting was no different than looking for
fairies, she supposed. No different than trying to find that cave
entrance into some magic elsewhere. Some people just weren't
any good at that sort of thing.

They were both magic, after all. Art as well as fairies. Magic.
What else could you call how Johnson was able to bring the forest to life with no more than a few colors on a flat surface?

She could practice, of course. And she would. She hadn't
been any good when she'd first started drawing either. But she
wasn't sure that she'd ever feel as . . . inspired as Johnson must
have felt.

She studied the inside lid of the box. Even this abstract pattern where he'd probably only been testing his color mixes had
so much vibrancy and passion.

The odd feeling she'd gotten the first time she'd looked inside the lid yesterday returned again, but this time she didn't look
away. Instead, she leaned closer.

What was it about this pattern of colors?

She found herself thinking about her Newford Naturalists
book, about something Milo Johnson was supposed to have said.
"It's not just a matter of painting *en plein air* as the Impressionists
taught us," the author quoted Johnson. "It's just as important to
simply *be* in the wilds. Many times the only painting box I take is
in my head. You don't have to be an artist to bring something

back from your wilderness experiences. My best paintings don't hang in galleries. They hang somewhere in between my ears—an endless private showing that I can only attempt to share with others through a more physical medium."

That must be why he'd abandoned this painting box she'd found. He'd gone into fairyland only bringing the one in his head. Frank had said as much last night. Unless . . .

She smiled as the fancy came to her.

Unless the box she'd found was the one he carried in his head, made real by some magic of the world into which he and Frank had strayed.

The pattern on the lid of the box seemed to move at that moment, and she thought she heard something—an almost music. It was like listening to ravens in the woods when their rough, deep-throated croaks and cries all but seemed like human language. It wasn't, of course, but still, you felt *so* close to understanding it.

She lifted her head to look around. It wasn't ravens she heard. It wasn't anything she knew, but it still seemed familiar. Faint, but insistent. Almost like wind chimes or distant bells, but not quite. Almost like birdsong, trills and warbling melodies, but not quite. Almost like an old fiddle tune, played on a pipe or a flute, the rhythm a little ragged, or simply a little out of time like the curious jumps and extra beats in a Kickaha tune. But not quite.

Closing the painting box, she stood. She slung her satchel from her shoulder, picked up the box and turned in a slow circle, trying to find the source of what she heard. It was stronger to the west, away from the creek and deeper into the forest. A ravine cut off to the left and she followed it, pushing her way through the thick shrub layer of rhododendrons and mountain laurel. Hemlocks and tuliptrees rose up the slopes on either side with a thick understory of redbud, magnolia, and dogwood.

The almost-music continued to pull her along—distant, near, distant, near, like a radio signal that couldn't quite hang on to a station. It was only when she broke through into a small clearing, a wall of granite rising above her, that she saw the mouth of the cave.

She knew immediately that this had to be the cave Frank had been looking for, the one into which he and Milo Johnson had stepped and so disappeared from the world for twenty years. The almost-music was clearer than ever here, but it was the bas-relief worked into the stone above the entrance that made her sure. Here was Frank's Lady, a rough carving of a woman's face. Her hair was thick with leaves and more leaves came spilling out of her mouth, bearding her chin.

Aunt's general warnings, as well as the Apple Tree Man's more specific ones, returned to her as she moved closer. She lifted a hand to trace the contours of the carving. As soon as she touched it, the almost-music stopped.

She dropped her hand, starting back as though she'd put a finger on a hot stove. She looked around herself with quick, nervous glances. Now that the almost-music was gone, she found herself standing in an eerie pocket of silence. The sounds of the forest were muted, as the music had been earlier. She could still hear the insects and birdsong, but they seemed to come from far away.

She turned back to the cave, uneasy now. In the back of her mind she could hear the Apple Tree Man's voice.

Don't go in.

I won't. Not all the way.

But now that she was here, how could she not at least have a look?

She went as far as the entrance, ducking her head because the top of the hole was only as high as her shoulder. It was dark inside, too dark to see in the beginning. But slowly her eyes adjusted to the dimmer lighting.

The first things she really saw were the paintings.

They were like her own initial attempts at drawing—crude stick figures and shapes that she'd drawn on scraps of paper and the walls of the barn with the charred ends of sticks. Except where hers had been simple because she could do no better, these, she realized as she studied them more closely, were more like stylized abbreviations. Where her drawings had been tentative, these held power. The paint or chalk had been applied with bold, knowing strokes. Nothing wasted. Complex images distilled to their primal essences.

An antlered man. A turtle. A bear with a sun on its chest, radiating squiggles of light. A leaping stag. A bird of some sort with enormous wings. A woman, cloaked in leaves. Trees of every shape and size. Lightning bolts. A toad. A spiral with the face of the woman on the entrance outside in its center. A fox with an enormous striped tail. A hare with drooping ears and small deer horns.

And more. So many more. Some easily recognizable, others only geometric shapes that seemed to hold whole books of stories in their few lines.

Her gaze traveled over the walls, studying the paintings with growing wonder and admiration. The cave was one of the larger ones she'd found—easily three or four times the size of Aunt's cabin. There were paintings everywhere, many too hard to make out because they were lost in deeper shadows. She wished she had a corn shuck or lantern to throw more light than what came from the opening behind her. She longed to move closer, but still didn't dare abandon the safety of the entranceway.

She might have left it like that, drunk her fill of the paintings and then gone home, if her gaze hadn't fallen upon a figure sitting hunched in a corner of the cave, holding what looked like a small bark whistle. She'd made the same kind herself from the straight smooth branches of a chestnut or a sourwood tree—Beau had shown her how. You rubbed the bark until it came loose, then cut the naked stick to make stoppers for either end of the bark cylinder, the one by the mouthpiece having a slice taken off the front. When the stoppers were put in you could play a tune if you were musically inclined. She hadn't been bad, but she'd never been able to whistle nearly so well as what she'd been hearing Frank play earlier.

But the whistle was quiet now. Frank sat so still, enveloped in the shadows, that she might never have noticed him except as she had, by chance.

"Frank?" she said.

He lifted his head to look at her.

"It's gone," he said. "I can't call it back."

"The other world?"

He nodded.

"That was you making that . . . music?"

"It was me doing something," he said. "I don't know that I'd go so far as to call it music."

Lily hesitated a long moment, then finally stepped through the entrance, into the cave itself. She flinched as she crossed the threshold, but nothing happened. There were no flaring lights or sudden sounds. No door opened into another world, sucking her in.

She set the painting box down and sat on her ankles in front of Frank.

"I didn't know you were a musician," she said.

"I'm not."

He held up his reed whistle—obviously something he'd made himself.

"But I used to play as a boy," he said. "And there was always music there, on the other side. I thought I could wake something. Call me to it, or it to me."

Lily raised her eyes to the paintings on the wall.

"How did you cross over the first time?" she asked.

He shook his head. "I don't know. That was Milo's doing. I was only tagging along."

"Did he . . . did he make a painting?"

Frank's gaze settled on hers.

"What do you mean?" he asked.

She pointed to the walls. "Look around you. This is *the* cave, isn't it?"

He nodded.

"What do you think these paintings are for?" she asked. When he still didn't seem to get it, she added, "Perhaps it's the paintings that open a door between the worlds. Maybe this Lady of yours likes pictures more than She does music."

Frank scrambled to his feet and studied the walls as though he was seeing the paintings for the first time. Lily was slower to rise.

"If I had paint, I could try it," he said.

"There's the painting box I found," Lily told him. "It's still full of paints."

He grinned. Grabbing her arms, he gave her a kiss, right on her lips, full of passion and fire, then bent down to open the box.

"I remember this box," he said as he rummaged through the paint tubes. "We were out painting, scouting a good location— though for Milo, any location was a good one. Anyway, there we were, out in these woods, when suddenly Milo stuffs this box of his into a tangle of tree roots and starts walking. I called after him, but he never said a word, never even turned around to see if I was coming.

"So I followed, hurrying along behind him until we finally came to this cave. And then . . . then . . . "

He looked up at Lily. "I'm not sure what happened. One moment we were walking into the cave and the next we had crossed over into that other place."

"So Milo didn't paint on the wall."

"I just don't remember. But he might not have had to. Milo could create whole paintings in his head without ever putting brush to canvas. And he could describe that painting to you, stroke for stroke—even years later."

"I read about that in the book."

"Hmm."

Frank had returned his attention to the paints.

"It'll have to be a specific image," he said, talking as much to himself as to Lily. "Something simple that still manages to encompass everything a person is or feels."

"An icon," Lily said, remembering the word from another of her books.

He nodded in agreement as he continued to sort through the tubes of paint, finally choosing a color: a burnt umber, rich and dark.

"And then?" Lily asked, remembering what the Apple Tree Man had told her in her dream. "Just saying you find the right image. You paint it on the wall and some kind of door opens up. Then what do you do?"

He looked up at her, puzzled.

"I'll step through it," he said. "I'll go back to the other side."

"But why?" Lily asked. "Why's over there so much better than the way the world is here?"

"I . . ."

"When you cross over to there," Lily said, echoing the Apple Tree Man's words to her, "you give up all the things you could be here."

"We do that every time we make any change in our lives," Frank said. "It's like moving from one town to another, though this is a little more drastic, I suppose." He considered it for a moment, then added, "It's not so much better over there as different. I've never fit in here the way I do over there. And now I don't have anything left for me here except for this burn inside—a yearning for the Lady and that land of Hers that lies somewhere on the other side of these fields we know."

"I've had that feeling," Lily said, thinking of her endless search for fairies as a child.

"You can't begin to imagine what it's like over there," Frank went on. "Everything glows with its own inner light."

He paused and regarded her for a long moment.

"You could come," he said finally. "You could come with me and see for yourself. Then you'd understand."

Lily shook her head. "No, I couldn't. I couldn't walk out on Aunt, not like this, without a word. Not after she took me in when no one else would. She wasn't even real family, though she's family now." She waited a beat, remembering the strength of his arms, the hard kiss he'd given her, then added. "You could stay."

Now it was his turn to shake his head.

"I can't."

Lily nodded. She understood. It wasn't like she didn't have the desire to go herself.

She watched him unscrew the paint tube and squeeze a long worm of dark brown pigment into his palm. He turned to a clear spot on the wall, dipped a finger into the paint, and raised his hand. But then he hesitated.

"You can do it," Lily told him.

Maybe she couldn't go. Maybe she wanted him to stay. But she knew enough not to try to hold him back if he had to go. It was no different than making friends with a wild creature. You could catch them and tie them up and make them stay with you, but their heart would never be yours. Their wild heart, the thing you loved about them, it would wither and die. So why would you want to do such a thing?

"I can," Frank agreed, his voice soft. He gave her a smile.

"That's part of the magic, isn't it? You have to believe that it will work."

Lily had no idea if that was true or not, but she gave him an encouraging nod all the same.

He hummed something under his breath as he lifted his hand again. Lily recognized it as the almost-music she'd heard before, but now she could make out the tune. She didn't know its name, but the pick-up band at the grange dances played it from time to time. She thought it might have the word "fairy" in it.

Frank's finger moved decisively, smearing paint on the rock. It took Lily a moment to see that he was painting a stylized oak leaf. He finished the last line and took his finger away, stepped back.

Neither knew what to expect, if anything. As the moments dragged by, Frank stopped humming. He cleaned his hands against the legs of his trousers, smearing paint onto the cloth. His shoulders began to slump and he turned to her.

"Look," Lily said before he could speak.

She pointed to the wall. The center of the oak leaf he'd painted had started to glow with a warm, green-gold light. They watched the light spread across the wall of the cave, moving out from the central point like ripples from a stone tossed into a still pool of water. Other colors appeared, blues and reds and deeper greens. The colors shimmered, like they were painted on cloth touched by some unseen wind, and then the wall was gone and they were looking through an opening in the rock. Through a door into another world.

There was a forest over there, not much different than the one they'd left behind except that, as Frank had said, every tree, every leaf, every branch and blade of grass, pulsed with its own inner light. It was so bright it almost hurt the eyes, and not simply because they'd been standing in this dim cave for so long.

Everything had a light and a song, and it was almost too much to bear. But at the same time, Lily felt the draw of that world like a tightening in her heart. It wasn't so much a wanting, as a need.

"Come with me," Frank said again.

She had never wanted to do something more in her life. It was not just going to that magical place, it was the idea of being there with this man with his wonderfully creative mind and talent. This man who'd given her her first real kiss.

But slowly she shook her head.

"Have you ever stood on a mountaintop," she asked, "and watched the sun set in a bed of feathery clouds? Have you ever watched the monarchs settled on a field of milkweed or listened to the spring chorus after the long winter's done?"

Frank nodded.

"This world has magic, too," Lily said.

"But not enough for me," Frank said. "Not after having been over there."

"I know."

She stepped up to him and gave him a kiss. He held her for a moment, returning the kiss, then they stepped back from each other.

"Go," Lily said, giving him a little push. "Go before I change my mind."

She saw he understood that, for her, going would be as much a mistake as staying would be for him. He nodded and turned, walked out into that other world.

Lily stood watching him go. She watched him step in among the trees. She heard him call out and heard another man's voice reply. She watched as the doorway became a swirl of colors once more. Just before the light faded, it seemed to take the shape of a woman's face—the same woman whose features had been carved into the stone outside the cave, leaves in her hair, leaves spilling from her mouth. Then it was all gone. The cave was dim once more and she was alone.

Lily knelt down by Milo Johnson's paint box and closed the lid, fastened the snaps. Holding it by its handle, she stood up and walked slowly out of the cave.

* * *

"Are you there?" she asked later, standing by the Apple Tree Man's tree. "Can you hear me?"

She took a biscuit from her pocket—the one she hadn't left earlier in the day because she'd still been angry for his appearing in her dream last night when he'd been absent from her life for five years. When he'd let her think that her night of magic had been nothing more than a fever dream brought on by a snake-bite.

She put the biscuit down among his roots.

"I just wanted you to know that you were probably right," she said. "About my going over to that other place, I mean. Not about how I can't have magic here."

She sat down on the grass and laid the paint box down beside her, her satchel on top of it. Plucking a leaf from the ground, she began to shred it.

"I know, I know," she said. "There's plenty of everyday magic all around me. And I do appreciate it. But I don't know what's so wrong about having a magical friend as well."

There was no reply. No gnarled Apple Tree Man stepping out of his tree. No voice as she'd heard in her dream last night. She hadn't really been expecting anything.

"I'm going to ask Aunt if I can have an acre or so for my own garden," she said. "I'll try growing cane there and sell the molasses at the harvest fair. Maybe put in some berries and make preserves and pies, too. I'll need some real money to buy more paints."

She smiled and looked up into the tree's boughs.

"So you see, I can take advice. Maybe you should give it a try."

She stood up and dusted off her knees, picked up the painting box and her satchel.

"I'll bring you another biscuit tomorrow morning," she said.

Then she started down the hill to Aunt's cabin.

"Thank you," a soft, familiar voice said.

She turned. There was no one there, but the biscuit was gone.

She grinned. "Well, that's a start," she said, and continued on home.